D1179162

LAST TALONS OF THE EAGLE

LAST TALONS
OF THE
EAGLE

Secret Nazi Technology Which
Could Have Changed the Course
of World War II

Gary Hyland and Anton Gill

HEADLINE

First published in 1998
by HEADLINE BOOK PUBLISHING

10 9 8 7 6 5 4 3 2 1

British Library Cataloguing in Publication Data

Hyland, Gary
Last talons of the eagle: secret Nazi technology which could
have changed the course of World War II
1. Airplanes, Military – Germany – Design and construction
2. World War, 1939–1945 – Aerial operations, German
I. Title II. Gill, Anton
623.6'6'0943'09044

ISBN 0 7472 2156 1

Typeset by Avon Dataset Ltd, Bidford-on-Avon, Warwickshire

Printed and bound in Great Britain by
Mackays of Chatham PLC, Chatham, Kent

HEADLINE BOOK PUBLISHING
A division of Hodder Headline PLC
338 Euston Road
London NW1 3BH

Headline would like to thank Aerospace Publishing Ltd for providing all the
photographs except: **Section 1**: Associated Press ('Wespe' project being studied by
the group); The Hulton Getty Picture Collection Ltd (Goring and Major General Ernst
Udet); Salamander Picture Library (Gotha Go 229 V2) **Section 2**: Salamander Picture
Library (Heinkel He 280 V1) and (Henschel Hs132 V1).
Colour artworks by Bob Corley.

To all those who helped.
You know who you are.

CONTENTS

INTRODUCTION

My interest in Germany's military aircraft of the Second World War stems from walking in a snowy forest and daydreaming about the scene in *Where Eagles Dare* when the German helicopter lands at the Schloss Adler. After thinking about the question of its historical accuracy, I began to research the area of German wartime aerospace technology. As I went on, uncovering more and more material, thoughts for a book gradually filtered through.

Last Talons of the Eagle deals with all the main Luftwaffe projects of the war years; some never left the drawing board, some were developed as prototypes but never saw active service, while others went into full production. I've tried to describe all these aircraft and bring their history to life. From the origins of Germany's first jet engines through to the world's first jet aircraft to take off under its own power (the He 178), I move on to look at the He 280, the main rival to the fabled Me 262 jet fighter – the world's first jet fighter to see active service. The He 280 has remained in its shadow ever since its cancellation by the Luftwaffe; it deserves a mention now.

Not many people realise that the scene in *Where Eagles Dare* could have happened and was not just the product of Alistair MacLean's imagination. Germany was developing true helicopters from the mid-1930s. Following a triumphant display in 1938, when the famed aviatrix Hanna Reitsch flew a machine inside a Berlin sports hall, their development only accelerated. This book looks at all the major helicopter types in detail and relates their stories, culminating in the first crossing of the English Channel by a captured Fa 223 machine and its Luftwaffe crew in 1945. Had these various types actually gone into mass production, as Germany had planned, the history of the war might have been very different, such was the advance that Nazi Germany had in the field when compared with the Allies. As it was, though, they didn't go into mass production, or were developed too late.

Another field in which German technology was proving itself superior to that of the Allies at the time was in the design and construction of bespoke transport aircraft – those designed solely to carry cargo loads. The largest variant to see service was the often-overlooked Me 321/3 'Gigant', whose prodigious load capacity wouldn't shame a modern transport aircraft of today, such as Lockheed's C-130 Hercules, but a slow top speed condemned it to use away from the battlefields. And when the largest and heaviest aircraft built by the Luftwaffe during the war turns out to be a flying boat, of which only a single example was built before the war ended, this too warrants investigation. The BV 238 was sunk at its moorings by marauding Allied fighters, but it could have posed a threat to Allied shipping in its role as a maritime patrol craft had it ever seen service.

Perhaps one of the most striking principles of design for an aircraft today is that of the 'flying wing' – the recently unveiled B-2 Stealth Bomber operated by the US Air Force being one such example. Yet over fifty years ago the Horten brothers were involved in pretty much the same field, their efforts culminating in the Go 229 – the world's first flying wing jet fighter. If the Hortens' craft looks amazing now, imagine the reaction of onlookers when first seeing it back in the 1940s. Even the most sceptical observer might have been forgiven for believing that the war could yet be turned in Germany's favour at such a late stage. After looking at all the craft developed by the brothers throughout their military and civil careers, one wonders if there aren't other aircraft flying today that may have drawn inspiration from their efforts.

In the children's fantasy *Doctor Dolittle* we see an animal called a Pushme-Pullyou, yet in wartime Germany an equally strange beast was being fettled to head off the ever-advancing waves of Allied fighters and bombers – the Do 335. With an engine and propeller at either end, this is the fastest conventionally powered fighter ever built and would certainly have given the enemy a run for its money had time not snuffed out the project after only a small number of the craft had been built. And what can be said of the BV 141? This was an asymmetric aircraft in which a single engine was mounted within what resembles at first glance the normal fuselage; yet alongside the fuselage, sprouting from the wing, is a separate cockpit 'pod' in which sat the crew. As an innovative spotter aircraft this could have provided the Luftwaffe with an unrivalled reconnaissance platform, but internal politics as well as gremlins within the prototypes effectively ended its chances of production.

And politics within the Luftwaffe rise to the fore again in the story of the He 162 Volksjäger – the 'people's fighter' – which went into full production a mere three months after the first sketches were drawn. Can you imagine what a modern aero manufacturer might accomplish today in the same amount of time? With the resources available at that time, Heinkel's achievements in getting the project advanced so speedily are examined closely, as is its end as the Luftwaffe, stranded through critical fuel shortages, awaited the looming collapse of the war.

But projects such as the Volksjäger seem conventional when compared with projects such as the Bachem Ba 349 'Natter'. A rocket-propelled, vertically launched interceptor, the Natter was designed to fire a bevy of rockets into the closely serried ranks of Allied bombers seen almost daily over Germany in the closing months of the war. A few were made and flown on tests, but the Natter never saw action. Much the same was the fate of the 'improved' Me 263 version of the Messerschmitt Me 163 'Komet': problems such as spontaneously exploding fuel tanks and a tendency to kill more pilots in landing accidents than might be shot down by enemy planes led to a hasty revision of the original design – once again, too late for production. But if this smacks of desperation on the part of the Luftwaffe, consider the work of the maverick designer (and the aerodynamicist behind the 'Komet') Alexander Lippisch.

Towards the end of the war Lippisch was involved actively in developing a fighter aircraft powered by a ramjet motor that ran on *coal*. His team even went so far as to produce an unpowered glider version before the war's end, to test the aerodynamics. The Americans eventually secured this solitary example and moved it to the USA amid much secrecy. Another designer – Sänger – had proposed something even more outrageous: he wanted to build a launch rail over three kilometres long from which a space-plane he had designed could take off. Intended to operate at the very reaches of earth's atmosphere, the craft could have made a mockery of conventional long-distance travel as it then was. With hindsight gained from building high-speed craft such as Concorde, we can see the folly in the work but can only marvel at the sheer audacity of the design and concept. Certainly nothing comparable was emerging from British or American design studios at the same time. And as for the almost mythical 'Foo Fighters', much discussion since the war has still not yielded any concrete evidence regarding their existence. Their place in the overall story is assured, though, as another facet of the gradual collapse and desperation of the Nazi state.

After examining some of the projects that were captured by the Soviet Union in its relentless drive into eastern Germany, I was left with many unanswered questions and sought to track down a few answers. Via a circuitous route, I even ended up having afternoon tea with the Soviet Air Attaché to London in a search for the truth behind many rumours and assumptions behind the projects that were developed subsequently by Stalin behind the then-new Iron Curtain during the early years of the Cold War. Clarification was received from a few sources following this and is presented here, perhaps in full for the first time in the West.

Finally, after examining the German industrial position throughout the period and its ability to produce the materials for the country to wage the war, both in terms of output and fuel production, we look at perhaps the one subject never fully developed in the European theatre of war–suicide planes and their pilots. Japanese Kamikaze pilots, the men who committed suicide for their emperor in the latter stages of the war by flying their planes into ships and other targets, are well known. But the fact that a similar movement was actively being planned and promoted in Germany at the same time may come as a shocking surprise. The various types of aircraft that were developed for the purpose are examined, as is what makes someone promote such a drastic and final course of action for a leader with a tradition stretching back only twelve years – as opposed to the centuries in Japan when committing suicide for the emperor was considered an honourable death.

Writing this book with Anton has been a long journey of personal discovery and one, I'm glad to say, which has been totally fulfilling and absorbing. I hope it's a story you'll find equally interesting.

Gary Hyland
April 1998

Chapter One

JET GENESIS

The Versailles Legacy

Germany's capitulation at the end of the First World War was swiftly followed by the Treaty of Versailles, signed on 28 June 1919, which was intended to draw Germany's teeth for good. As far as military restrictions were concerned, the government of the new Weimar Republic could keep an army of only a hundred thousand men, the navy was reduced to six small battleships and only thirty other craft, with no submarines, and the air force, in which such fighter aces as Manfred, Baron von Richthofen – leader of the famous 'Flying Circus' – had served with as much bravado as distinction, was abolished completely.

Over 20,000 aircraft and 27,000 aero engines were surrendered to the Allies to be scrapped, and to an onlooker it might have seemed that Germany's air force, broken and demoralised, no longer posed any kind of threat. However, a determination remained within the corridors of power to maintain an aerial presence of some kind. The scaled-down defence ministry, the Reichswehrministerium, managed to equip the security police force (the Sicherheitspolizei) with seven air squadrons as a means of keeping the skills of the recently demobbed pilots sharp. In 1921 the Allies closed the loophole that had enabled the Germans to do this, but one of the pilots, Erhard Milch, who had been a squadron commander during the war, was later to play a major role in the resurgence of the Luftwaffe, and for that reason it is worth a brief digression to consider his career.

After leaving his police air unit, Milch went into civil aviation, rising to become director in 1928 of one of the emerging new airlines, Lufthansa, at the age of thirty-six. He joined the Nazi Party in 1929 but kept his membership secret so as not to jeopardise his position. A ruthlessly efficient businessman, Milch was not above bribing influential members of the government in order to win State subsidies for his company, and he managed to put several smaller competitors out of business in the process. Some of these people, who had also joined the National Socialists, subsequently tried to unseat Milch, who became Reichsmarschall Hermann Göring's right-hand man when the Nazis seized power. In 1933 it was alleged that Milch's father was a Jew – a charge that Milch was able to confute, though in the process a family scandal was uncovered as it emerged that Milch's natural father was in fact his apparent father's brother.

Milch, stockily built and as straightforward and no-nonsense in his manner as in his tastes, grew quickly to prominence, especially as Göring became more preoccupied with the perks of his job than with the job itself, though in the course of time the Reichsmarschall did take note of the growing power of his underling. Göring himself, a year younger than Milch, had been a distinguished fighter pilot in the First World War, and although his interests lay increasingly in drugs, hedonism and collecting fine art, he retained a commitment to the air force in which he had served, which he had seen destroyed, and which he had helped rebuild.

Early in 1939 Milch was appointed Inspector-General of the air force in addition to the post he already held as Secretary of State for Air; but when the Air Chief of Staff, Wever, died unexpectedly, Göring seized the opportunity to carry out a reshuffle which had the effect of reducing Milch's power – Wever's job went to the slightly older senior officer Albert Kesselring, and another former ace, Ernst Udet, took over the important Technical Bureau. After the outbreak of war, although Kesselring's attacks on France were successful, he met his match when confronting the RAF. In November 1940 Hitler's thoughts turned increasingly to the invasion of Russia. Göring, who regarded the so-called Operation Barbarossa as foolhardy, registered his disapproval by retiring to Rominten in East Prussia, where he stayed until January 1941, handing over control of the Luftwaffe to Milch in the interim; and after Udet's death in 1942, Milch became Head of Air Armament.

By now, Hitler regarded him as a bright star in the Nazi constellation, and despite the failure of an attempt to relieve the Sixth Army at Stalingrad in 1943, he remained in place and did much to improve aircraft production levels. Göring, however, finally grew to envy and hate him, and managed to have him dismissed in June 1944; but Milch was far from finished. He became deputy to Albert Speer in his Ministry for Armament and War Production.

Following Germany's unconditional surrender in May 1945, Milch was sentenced at Nuremberg to fifteen years. He served ten years, and found himself in 1955 a free man but unemployed. Lufthansa didn't take him back and he ended up as an adviser to Fiat and Thyssen. He died in 1972.

Although Germany failed in its attempt to retain an unofficial air force through its security police department, top-secret efforts were being made in other areas to preserve the capacity for air power. In 1920 the head of the Army General Staff was the fifty-four-year-old Generaloberst Hans von Seeckt. Seeckt was a right-wing conservative who perceived Poland's very existence as 'incompatible with the conditions of Germany's existence'. He also knew that Russia would be even happier than Germany to see Poland disappear, and realised that the newly formed USSR could be a convenient ally – at least until certain goals had been achieved. Seeckt was deeply committed to the reconstruction of a German Reich and set up within his office a secret bureau of military aviation, the Truppenamt (Luftschutz), or TA(L), in which 180 hand-picked flying officers could remain concealed. The aim of the TA(L) was to plan and build the foundations for a new air force, but its business had to be conducted under conditions of the utmost secrecy, since at the time Allied inspectors were free to roam Germany in search of any signs of covert rearmament. The first head of the TA(L) was Kapitän Helmut Wilberg, who had orders to work closely with the head of the Air Technical Bureau, Kapitän Kurt Student, whose bureau had been founded under the auspices of the Heereswaffenamt, the Army Technical Office. Student was an able officer who rose to the rank of general and commanded the paratroop regiments, masterminding the invasion of Crete in 1941.

Although the two bureaux initially acted as administrative and information-gathering facilities, with the Technical Bureau later also operating as a front for the illicit development of aircraft technologies, their other important function was to remind the army-dominated officer corps of the existence and potential of the new military service. It's worth remembering that the navy had lost much of its kudos during the revolutionary period following the First World War, when sailors had embraced the Communist cause and rebelled against their officers. The air force, with its possibilities for recruiting young men on whom any political impression had yet to be made, also had the capacity for being staffed with a new generation of officers whose thinking could be shaped to the right.

Along with the Luftwaffe, the entire German aero industry had suffered as a result of the Treaty of Versailles. The deep economic troughs of the 1920s and 1930s, which had a worldwide effect, caused further economic damage to all sectors of industry; but aeroplane manufacture was hit especially hard. After all, during the First World War it had enjoyed the benefits of producing over 44,000 aircraft, and many famous names, such as Rumpler and Albatross, were to disappear or merge, cut off in their prime as a result of the collapse. However, in 1922 the Allied signatories to Versailles allowed a limited resumption of civil aircraft production in Germany. The restrictions were severe, and sought to ensure that any plane built with a view to conversion to military use would quickly become obsolete. The industry responded, outwardly at least, by focusing on providing aircraft for mail runs and passenger traffic, and Zeppelin continued to build airships. The industry also constructed sporting gliders for both the home market and export, and in this area particularly there was a great deal of experimentation with aerodynamics.

The experience in postwar aeroplane development paid rapid dividends. By 1927 German airlines were flying greater distances and carrying more passengers than the airlines of any other country, the dominant player being the State-sponsored national carrier, Deutsches Lufthansa. The burgeoning industry didn't rest on its laurels, and inevitably designers began to ignore the prescriptions of the 1922 agreement by starting secretly to design aircraft to military specifications. It was in any case proving ever more difficult to maintain the letter of the Treaty of Versailles overall, with only the French (with some justification) holding out against further relaxations. As far as aircraft were concerned, provided they were exported in component form for assembly in the purchasing country or otherwise abroad, the 1922 agreement was not breached even if such aircraft were designed for military use. With tacit Allied approval, the Dornier Company had even entered into a contract to supply military aircraft to Chile.

Matters were to come to a head at the beginning of 1923 with the occupation by French and Belgian forces of the Ruhr in an attempt to force Germany to continue its war reparations payments, which were massive and thought increasingly by many both inside and outside Germany to be too punitive. Germany was in the grip of hyper-inflation in 1923, when the mark fell from 10,000 to the dollar in January to 160 million to the dollar in September – and it got worse: on 14 November the mark stood at 4,200 *billion* to the dollar. Only a currency reform saved the country, which was also threatened by civil war as left- and right-wing elements polarised, from sliding into total chaos. France believed that the inflation had in some way been engineered to avoid reparations payments, but luckily France's hardline prime minister, Raymond Poincaré, fell from office and the embattled German chancellor, Gustav Stresemann, was able to negotiate with the more moderate French foreign minister, Aristide Briand.

As far as the aeronautical business was concerned, matters were resolved at last by the Paris Aviation Treaty of 1926. This amendment to Versailles acknowledged the futility of trying to restrict the development of German military aeroplanes and openly permitted the export of military aircraft. Thereafter the Technical Bureau began to implement long-term redevelopment plans for a German air force, though these remained secret.

The government knew that the day would come when Germany would once again have an air force of its own, but in the meantime it had to ensure that the air industry, which was suffering from the effects of the Depression, remained in the control of German manufacturers. It implemented a policy of active intervention both within the industry as a whole and within Lufthansa. There was a setback when the Communist representatives within the re-elected Reichstag of 1928 objected to such subsidies, but the State Secretary of the Ministry of Transport, Ernst Brandenburg, who was in charge of the covert rearmament

11

programme, suggested to Erhard Milch, who was at Lufthansa by then, that he bribe other Reichstag MPs to push the subsidies through. This simple course of action was effective.

A Soviet Secret

As part of the secret rearmament programme, the Weimar administration was aware of the importance of maintaining a training programme for air crews, but this was difficult, if not impossible, to hide within the emasculated armed forces, and so the administration entered into talks with the USSR, with a view to leasing several sites and proving grounds which would be easy to conceal within the vastness of Russia. These talks followed the signing of a treaty between the USSR and Germany at Rapallo near Genoa on 16 April 1922. Ostensibly this merely renewed lapsed trade agreements, but its underlying purpose was to pave the way for a secret collaboration in armaments development masterminded by General von Seeckt. Effectively the Germans would offer credit and technical expertise in return for the unfettered use of remote, hidden bases at which it could train its pilots, unseen and unhindered by the West. All German activities in Russia were in direct violation of the Treaty of Versailles; had they become known, France might never have relinquished its occupation of the Ruhr, and the Allies in general would have been far less liberal in granting concessions to Germany as soon after Versailles as the early 1920s.

Among the first fruits of this new alliance were a Junkers aircraft-assembly plant at Fili near Moscow in 1924, three Krupp artillery-shell factories, and even a mustard-gas plant at Samara. The deal allowed the Reichswehr – the German armed forces – to claim a proportion of all production, so that, fewer than five years after Versailles, Germany was already breaking the treaty's main clauses and was in a position to stockpile both shells and poison gas.

Three secret training bases were also built to cover aspects of new military technologies first employed in the conflict of 1914–18: a tank-warfare centre was established at Kazan, a gas-warfare site at Saratov, and a centre for flight training.

Kurt Student, as head of the Technical Bureau, was responsible for the establishment of the last of these. He selected as his site the remote

Lipetsk airfield on the River Voronezh in southern Russia, evidently finding it the most suitable for his country's needs at the time. On his own arrival at Lipetsk in 1924, Student had the facilities there extended, and the first intake of pilots graduated the following summer. One of the main points of the German–Russian agreement was that, in exchange for the Soviets' guarding the bases against outside interference, data from the experiments being undertaken would be shared. And thus it was that as the first tentative forays into the assault technique that came to be known as Blitzkrieg – lightning-strike warfare – were studied at Lipetsk, the Soviets had the opportunity to view them simultaneously. So impressed were they by what they saw that the new technique was also adopted by the USSR – a policy that at least enabled them to understand the method of attack being used on them by their erstwhile guests seventeen years later in 1941.

The first aeroplanes to arrive at Lipetsk were fifty Dutch-built Fokker biplanes, originally bought in secret by the Weimar administration and intended for use in Germany's defence of the Ruhr against France – had that confrontation led to conflict. In any case the planes had arrived too late for that crisis, and they had been mothballed soon after their delivery. Initial service at Lipetsk quickly highlighted the antiquated design of the Fokkers and so, as always under conditions of the strictest secrecy, the German aeronautical firm of Heinkel was commissioned to build a number of two-seater combat trainers to replace them. These craft were powered by British Napier Lion engines, which were available on the open market and already in use in German civil aeroplanes. The trainers' role was to help evaluate how air power could be used in close support of ground units, and to further studies of the evolving use of observer-gunners in two-seater aircraft; the observer-gunner was considered at the time to be the best means of defence against attack.

During its eight-year existence, Lipetsk was to turn out only 120 pilots and 100 observers. This was hardly an inspiring number of graduates, but harsh weather conditions allowed only thirteen flying weeks a year – which makes one wonder why, after all, Student had selected the site in the first place. To maximise the facilities, pilots would arrive having already taken introductory civilian flying courses in Germany. The intention was to polish their skills at Lipetsk, and for them to learn the military applications of those skills; but limitations on any kind of quasi-military training in Germany before arrival, and limitations in the number of pilots well enough versed in military flying to give instruction, naturally meant that the output of graduates would be small.

The immense security surrounding all the joint-venture sites ensured that the potential for any kind of international scandal resulting from their discovery was averted, and the German public never knew the function, or even the existence, of certain offices within the Weimar administration. All the personnel sent to Russia were of the highest calibre and entirely trustworthy. As an additional security measure they were issued with Soviet passports and aliases for the duration of their stay, and their relatives were kept in the dark about their activities. The training sites had no official contact with the German Embassy in Moscow but reported instead to the Soviet General Staff, as did the large number of Russian personnel working on the bases. Following the relaxations resulting from the Paris Aviation Treaty, and the subsequent removal of Allied inspectors from Germany, military aircraft accessories were shipped to Lipetsk from 1928 onwards, and within a very short time gunsights, navigation equipment and new bomb-release racks were being tested in large numbers, along with a series of brand-new aircraft, including the Heinkel He 45 and He 46, the Junkers K47 and the Dornier Do 11. Meanwhile, another organisation, the German Aviation Research Institute, had established a secret laboratory at Yagi, near Moscow. It isn't known whether or not Soviet researchers and engineers, as well as workers, were employed at this site, but it is fair to assume that some exchange of ideas did occur, since similarities of design can be detected in the planes of what were to be the two opposing air forces. For example, some of the Soviet fighters operating during the Spanish Civil War of the 1930s reflected the influence of German technology – though ironically the Luftwaffe aircraft involved in the early part of that conflict lacked competitive equipment.

But the Russian honeymoon would soon be over. A combination of deteriorating relations between the two countries and a more open and cost-effective approach to training in Germany led to the bases in Russia being abandoned finally during autumn 1933.

A Resurgence in Gliding

With the Treaty of Versailles putting an end to the German air force after the end of the First World War, the vast majority of Germany's pilots returned to civilian life. Many of them, however, maintained an active interest in flying, and this led to an explosion in the number of gliding and private flying clubs throughout the country. The membership of the officially sanctioned Deutscher Luftsport-Verband (the German Aero Club) had reached 50,000 by 1928, and German pilots found themselves at the forefront of sport-gliding throughout the 1920s and 1930s. Hanna Reitsch, who was to become Germany's first female Flugkapitän in 1937 at the age of twenty-five, broke many gliding records during the 1930s and went on to become one of Hitler's principal test-pilots, testing among other craft the rocket-powered Me 163, the Me 328 and the Fi 103 Reichenberg flying bomb. Reitsch survived the war and died in 1979. She was still breaking gliding records as late as 1970.

After the National Socialist Party seized power early in 1933, the popularity of gliding continued, alongside a popular interest in powered flight at club level which was actively encouraged by the State. Throughout the 1930s Germany held airspeed records in several categories, and German aviators travelled the world, taking part in competitions, and on various propaganda tours. Their work helped boost aircraft exports and reduce Germany's continuing balance-of-payments deficit, always bad because the country was so reliant on costly imports of the raw materials that were essential to the rearmament programme.

The Birth of the Reichsluftministerium and the Luftwaffe

In 1929 Hermann Göring had suggested to the Luftsport-Verband that they should 'provide the means of recruiting an air force'. After coming to power, the Nazis immediately began planning the creation of the Luftwaffe, creating the Reichsluftministerium – the Air Ministry, known as the RLM – in the early spring of 1933, with Göring in charge and Milch, as we have seen, as his deputy. The plan involved the building-up of an undercover air force drawing on the resources of private gliding and powered-flying clubs, eventually gearing up to more open and rapid development from 1935 onwards. Milch himself had proposed in

June 1933 that initially the new air force should have over 600 aircraft by the end of 1935, including two fighter wings – known as 'Gruppen' – of 36 aircraft each. This would act as a so-called 'risk air force', capable of burning the fingers of any neighbouring country foolhardy enough to attack Germany in an attempt to prevent its rearmament. Göring's theory was that such a force, relying on numbers rather than quality at this stage, would constitute an adequate threat to Allied air forces, which at the time were still scaling down their own strength – at the end of the First World War, some British politicians argued that the RAF should be disbanded and that what air force there was should be merged with the army, as it originally had been.

Several reasons lay behind Göring's and Milch's policy. The most obvious was that Hitler's popularity could increase only if he could demonstrate to the country that he was prepared to denounce Versailles and defy the Allies. Hitler saw both the treaty and the Allies' actions as having always worked against Germany's interests, and in several speeches he drew attention to the way *his* Reich had 'been forced on to her knees by the Allies', and that 'it was now time [for Germany] to get up and take its place in the world once more'. Reminding ordinary Germans of the widely perceived injustices of Versailles before actually setting about flouting its restrictions was to prove a masterstroke of tactics in Hitler's rise to power and in getting backing for an increased rearmament programme once he had become Chancellor. In November 1933 Göring secured a budget of 20 million Reichsmarks (RM), channelled through the RLM, in order to create Milch's 'risk air force'.

The need to keep to a tight budget soon became apparent. Virtually no aeroplane then in service was fit for operational duties abroad, and much of Göring's RM 20 million was obviously going to be needed for essential development and the procurement of labour. Luckily, Hitler was strongly behind the foundation of a new air force and saw its officers as a young Nazi elite, imbued with its own *esprit de corps* in order to ensure operational harmony. He believed this to be essential in establishing the Luftwaffe, especially as it would start with such poor equipment; and if the other services grumbled that they were getting a raw deal, that would be too bad. So it was that an 'expense no object' attitude prevailed for three years or so – about the time they thought it would take to lay the foundations of a cohesive force and replace the old, obsolete aircraft with new ones. On 1 January 1934 Milch published a plan that called for the secret production of more than 1,800 combat aircraft and 1,700 trainers – a vast number, but considered essential for a viable 'risk air force'.

The large quota of training aircraft was an indication of how bad things were. Up until now, the majority of Luftsport-Verband members had been training on gliders – hence the need for almost as many two-seat trainers within the secret production programme as fighting planes. But as a whole the programme was a success: it stimulated Germany's still-fragile aero industry and taught it much-needed lessons in the field of mass-production – lessons that the industry was quick to learn and respond to. In 1933 aircraft manufacturing employed fewer than 4,000 people, and a firm like Junkers could produce only 18 Ju 52 transport aeroplanes a year. By 1937 over 230,000 people were working on airframes and engines, and in the same year Junkers produced over 300 Ju 52s.

The first long-term aircraft-purchase programme was announced on 1 July 1934; it sought to resolve the problem of aircraft demand in the face of tight budgets. The programme called for the acquisition of over 17,000 aircraft of all types by 31 March 1938, and such was the importance placed on this plan by Hitler himself that, after having had the principal Luftwaffe chiefs thoroughly brief him on its contents, he approved personally the massive budget of RM 10.5 billion. It is worth pointing out that of the aircraft constructed under this scheme, only 6,671 would be combat types; the rest would be transports and trainers. Nevertheless, for the still-secret Luftwaffe, such numbers would be essential for its smooth and rapid establishment.

As pilot-training took hold in Germany, and as the country became more confident in its own autonomy, the German–Soviet Rapallo agreement became, as mentioned, increasingly fragile. New airfields were springing up throughout Germany, under such innocuous names as 'Reich Autobahn Air Transport Centre'. The bases in Russia were replaced at home by new Fliegerwaffen – military flying – schools, which were geared to offer instruction in navigation and aerial combat. For the first time since the First World War instruction in military aviation was being given more or less openly, as Luftsport-Verband

17

pilots began training with the new aircraft. New pilots received 250 hours' instruction spread over 2 years – a great luxury, as training was to dwindle to 22 hours' instruction during the war owing to the shortage of fuel. Night flights had been introduced to the air mail services, and the pilots flying them were gaining useful experience in yet another skill. The air mail service was run in conjunction with the Reich Railway Service and used Heinkel He 111 aeroplanes – which were disguised medium bomber prototypes.

Many of the instructors were men who had trained at Lipetsk and, as mentioned, it is ironic that they and their pupils would before too long use the skills they had learned there when flying against Russia in the course of Operation Barbarossa – the doomed invasion of the USSR.

Fighter-training was also being carried out in Italy. Among the first trainees there was Adolf Galland, who became one of the best-known and most lethal aces of the Second World War, as well as one of the Reich's senior fighter pilots. Although his independent spirit did not endear him to his Nazi masters, he rose to the rank of Generalleutnant and led a squadron of Me 262 jet fighters at the very end of the war. Galland's dashing good looks also turned him into a pin-up for millions of German girls. He survived the war and went on to play a part in the West German air force as part of the NATO Alliance.

A Return of Confidence

On 1 March 1935 Hitler announced a full-scale rearmament programme, from tanks to artillery, from submarines to aeroplanes. The new air force, the Reichsluftwaffe, would be commanded by Göring, in addition to his role as Air Minister. The Nazi Party propagandists had a field day with these initiatives and were soon proclaiming confidently that the new Luftwaffe would 'put a steel roof over Germany' and 'blot out the sun' by the sheer number of its aircraft. The new sense of bullishness in relations with Germany's increasingly nervous neighbours had led Milch, only a year into his schedule, to alter production plans in favour of an increased output of combat aircraft. By the end of 1935, with military production now no longer secret and running at the rate of 300 planes a month, the Air Ministry was inviting manufacturers to compete for tenders.

The first competition, for a fighter, was won in 1936 by Messerschmitt with his ground-breaking Bf 109 project. Any thought of trying to enforce the Treaty of Versailles now was cast aside by the Allies, as they sought to contain the emerging military might of Germany, first by diplomatic means and later by appeasement. Great Britain was still happy to see Germany producing warships as late as 1935, but Germany had left the Disarmament Conference and the League of Nations in October 1933, and was beginning to be considered the loose cannon of Europe.

The initial strength of the Luftwaffe – three fighter squadrons and five bomber squadrons – was totally inadequate for its role as a military force to be reckoned with; but the motley collection of Heinkel He 51 biplane fighters, He 46 reconnaissance aircraft, new Junkers Ju 52 transports/bombers and various trainers had been built in secret, and represented only a start. Now that Germany had thrown off any attempt at secrecy, those aircraft manufacturers that had survived the recession through government subsidy looked forward to a growing order book. They were not to be disappointed: as the acquisition programme gathered pace, so both numbers of personnel and production output increased.

Meanwhile the Nazi propaganda machine was promoting in the popular imagination the old ideas of government rather than the liberal democracy which had dominated the Weimar Republic years. The virtues of militarism and conservatism were resurrected, and new military units were named after heroes of the First World War. The Luftwaffe was no exception to this, of course, and the first naming ceremony for the new force took place in March 1935, when Hitler and Göring presided over an elaborate ceremony to name Jagdgeschwader Richthofen after the famous ace whose distinctive red Fokker triplane had wrought havoc among the British until he was shot down in 1918. From then on, in tandem with the introduction of the anti-Semitic Nuremberg Laws, a succession of carefully stage-managed and spectacular rallies of the Party at Nuremberg sought to re-create German self-esteem and self-confidence throughout the armed forces and the population as whole. In fact these actions created a confused arrogance and a ferocious nationalism; but such ugly traits suited Hitler far better than any others, in the futherance of his aggressive aims. As the Nazi

Party continued along the path that would ultimately lead to war, so the Luftwaffe, under Milch and Göring, went from strength to strength.

The process was a slow one at first, and such was the shortfall in the numbers of the first Gruppen, or fighter wings, that in the beginning Göring ordered each aircraft to be repainted with different serial numbers after each mission to give the impression to onlookers and any foreign spies that a veritable flying armada had been assembled. However, the gearing-up of production lines gradually obviated the need for such deceptions.

Many new commercial designs emerging from the aeronautical draughtsmen's studios in the mid-1930s had dual capabilities – such as bombing and reconnaissance, or transport and bombing – built in from the start. This measure saved considerable development costs as well as conversion time. One example of the type was the Heinkel He 111 mail plane, which was to be transformed in wartime into a medium bomber and would form part of the force that attacked London during the Blitz. Naturally it was no coincidence that twin-engined bombers could be adapted quickly from medium-sized civil designs; and Göring, having been influenced by research at Lipetsk, favoured this size of bomber. He believed from the outset that the Luftwaffe should adopt a fluid, responsive model of combat in support of lightning ground attacks, since he envisaged the Reich's future conflicts as being short and intense. He thus allowed the planes of the German bomber fleet to be smaller and more manoevurable than those eventually developed by the Allies. Both Sir Hugh Trenchard of the RAF and USAAF General Billy Mitchell had phases of heavy attrition bombing in mind, and the long-range heavy bombers brought in by the Allies were to be used with lethal effect in Germany.

With the obvious results of the Allied doctrine viewed at first hand, the Luftwaffe decided, belatedly, to develop heavy bombers, though it didn't receive its first examples until well into the war, as German eyes turned to more distant targets than those that could be covered by its medium-range fleet. By this time, their arrival into service was too late to have serious impact. But cost had been another consideration. Germany had been crippled by reparations payments, the cost of importing essential raw materials, hyper-inflation, world recession and huge unemployment during the interwar years. In the early 1930s unemployment in Britain stood at three million, but in Germany the figure was double that. Hitler sought to solve the problem by creating employment through the massive rearmament programme and his autobahn-building scheme, but the money had to come from somewhere and the country was hopelessly overdrawn. As an opportunist and a gambler, Hitler was banking on cutting this particular Gordian knot by taking over the countries from which the raw materials came, and the countries to which Germany owed money.

As far as the Luftwaffe's funding was concerned, the medium bomber represented a production-cost saving. After all, it was reasoned, a large heavy bomber could consume twice as much material as two medium bombers, so why not build the smaller and more agile machines, and leave the enemy to build his heavy, lumbering machines – which could be preyed on easily by the faster, cheaper and more numerous Luftwaffe aircraft?

A more serious obstacle to the Luftwaffe's rearmament than the lack of heavy bombers was a failure on the part of German aero-engine manufacturers to compete directly with their foreign counterparts. This was an obstacle that could not be overcome overnight. At a meeting it convened for the major power-plant makers in 1934, the Air Ministry called for development time to be reduced from between five and six years to only two. Limited for so many years to producing low-powered engines for staid civil machines, the task of suddenly manufacturing powerful and reliable aeroplane motors for the military seemed beyond most companies, though miraculously in the event the first power plants did appear on schedule, including the first revolutionary jet engines. But even as development proceeded, the industry was forced to continue to build older designs, which rapidly became obsolete, alongside the new ones, for reasons of economic convenience.

The drawbacks of such a policy would soon be recognised.

Trials in Spain

The first real test for the new air force came with Germany's involvement on the side of Franco's fascist rebellion against the Republican government of Spain in the Civil War of 1936–9. The small initial force of twenty Ju52 'Iron Annie' transport aircraft and six

Heinkel He 51 fighters left for Spain in August 1936, but the force simply was not large enough to give Franco much of an advantage. However, after the Nazi propaganda machine had stirred the hearts of the German people with tales of derring-do against the *Bolsheviks* a number of Luftwaffe volunteers were recruited into the hurriedly organised Condor Legion. The volunteers sailed for Spain in November 1936 disguised as a Party-sponsored 'Strength through Joy' cruise. The Air Ministry supplied a further two hundred aircraft – more transports and fighters, and some bombers. As a means of testing the mettle of the new Luftwaffe, the exercise couldn't have been more opportune. As a foretaste of Germany's policy of bombing cities and civilian populations, Guernica in northern Spain was entirely destroyed on 27 April 1937.

From a strictly martial point of view, the first year of the legion's operations was to show up serious deficiencies in its tactics and equipment. At first, no one knew how the force and its new aircraft would perform, but observers (including the Allies) soon realised that here was a new military force and potential adversary which was sorting out its teething problems in public. Its aircraft – especially the secretly built He 51s – were outclassed by the Russian-built Polikarpov machines flown by the Spanish government forces. The German bombers, too, proved generally inefficient at hitting targets – but this prompted the introduction of Junkers Ju 87 Sturzkampfflugzeug, better known as the Stuka – Germany's first dive bomber.

This aircraft was designed to cooperate with ground units in a close support role as a precision bomber, exactly following the lessons learned at Lipetsk. The main innovation was an autopilot that was fitted to control entry to and exit from bombing dives, ensuring maximum dive angle (pilots controlling their planes manually never dived steeply enough: the optimum angle was ninety degrees). Even the psychological effect of the Stukas on civilian populations had been evaluated at Lipetsk, and these experiments had led to the fitting of the notorious screaming siren, nicknamed 'the trumpet of Jericho', which whistled when speeds of 550 kph were reached in the dives.

So impressed was the Technical Bureau with the Stuka's performance that its then Chief of Staff, Ernst Udet, ordered that every subsequent bomber design should include a dive-bombing capacity on the grounds that such an accurate delivery of bombs was a more efficient use of precious manufacturing capacity than high-altitude attacks would ever be. Udet's comments were duly noted – he was a highly respected First World War ace and had taught Milch himself to fly – but his suggestions were scarcely acted on, as the next generation of bombers was already well into development and couldn't radically be altered on cost grounds.

Udet himself, as Student's successor at the Technical Bureau, became Head of Air Armament in 1939, with special responsibility for aircraft production. Unfortunately this highly talented man – he was a skilful political cartoonist – became addicted to both drugs and alcohol. Perhaps as a result, for there is no doubt that he was a man under increasingly extreme stress, he suffered from a persecution complex which was to lead to his apparent suicide, aged forty-five, in 1941. Göring ordered his death to be covered up. A communiqué was issued announcing that Udet had died testing a new weapons system, and he was granted a state funeral. However, Udet's criticism of the regime had become progressively more outspoken, and his friend, the play-wright Carl Zuckmayer, in exile in the USA during the war, wrote a play there in 1942 in which he suggests that Udet was in fact murdered by the Nazis.

The failure of the He 51 fighters prompted the firm of Messerschmitt to ship out prototypes of its new Bf 109 fighter to Spain. These performed successfully, and their pilots' experience in combat helped the manufacturer to improve the design. The lessons learned in combat, combined with the theories tried out at Lipetsk, helped perfect the attack system which depended on close cooperation between ground and air forces. Before Spain, for example, German planes still flew without an air–ground radio link, and therefore couldn't be directed by observers on the ground. Such shortcomings were soon to be rectified.

The slaughter of the First World War was still fresh in people's minds, and although Hitler's brinkmanship was apparent to all, a spirit of appeasement prevailed in Europe, while the USA for the time being stood aloof from the conflicts across the Atlantic. But his experiences in Spain – and perhaps particularly the success of the Condor Legion – encouraged Hitler to accelerate his plans. Göring had planned originally for the Luftwaffe to reach full strength by 1943, but it soon became apparent that the air force would have to be up and running well before that date. Hitler's confidence – especially after the bloodless coups in the Sudetenland and Austria, in the face of which the Allies did nothing – was forcing the pace, and Göring had to move with it.

Economic Realities

The Western Allies had done little to maintain their air forces in the years following the First World War. As we have seen, with dangerous complacency a few British voices even advocated disbanding the RAF altogether during the 1920s, arguing that since there would never be another war as great or intense as the last, there was no longer any need for a separate air force. Reintegrated into the army, it would serve as a bombing-only unit – following Trenchard's thinking. And as the Depression deepened around the world, defence cuts in all Allied forces became ever more stringent. By 1933 things were so bad in the RAF that it seemed as if the force were suffering itself from the restrictions of the Versailles Treaty, and its Chiefs of Staff were worried that the navy and the army might indeed succeed in having the force disbanded, dividing the resulting spoils between them. Aerial warfare was still a very new and relatively untried phenomenon: when Britain finally launched a rearmament programme from the mid-1930s onwards, it was thanks to media-fed hysteria over the threat of attack from the air, specifically by the Luftwaffe. It would be years before Britain caught up with Germany in terms of aircraft development, and not until the war was under way that a comprehensive plan like Milch's was introduced.

But Germany had its own problems over rearming at speed. The Air Ministry at first had been overly keen to put funds into aircraft projects and manufacturers, without considering the eventual drain this policy would have on the country's reserves of raw materials. A country like Germany has to import nearly all its raw materials – other than coal – and needs a stable economy and deep pockets to cover such purchases. It was the issue of financing the acquisition programme which was effectively to cap its speed and thoroughness. The worldwide economic recession that started in 1929 with the Wall Street Crash wasn't to improve until 1934, and was to inhibit German exports of finished goods as much as anyone else's; and the resulting loss of income naturally had a knock-on effect for spending. Given an unstoppable public demand for materials, coupled with the requirements of the military and of industry, one is left wondering what led Hitler to start the war at a time when things were so bad. We have mentioned his opportunism. Did he perhaps believe that by the 'peaceful' annexation of Austria and the resultant extra assets this gave him to draw on, the Third Reich would find the resources needed to embark on its programme of conquest? As early as 1923 Hitler had laid down in *Mein Kampf* his none-too-original plans for acquiring *Lebensraum* in the East – a subject that had preoccupied right-wing and military thinkers for at least two generations before Hitler, and which had been proposed again most recently by such figures as Hans von Seeckt and the English-born adoptive German, Houston Stewart Chamberlain, whose *Foundations of the Nineteenth Century*, published in 1899, had a profound effect on the Führer.

1937 saw Milch, Ernst Udet and Colonel Hans-Jürgen Stumpff (the Luftwaffe's Head of Personnel) invited to tour various RAF establishments (following an earlier British inspection of key Luftwaffe facilities). They visited airfields and some 'shadow' factories in Birmingham which could switch from car to aircraft production in short order. Later that same year, drawing on their impressive experiences (which were also surprising, given Britain's apparently relaxed attitude to rearmament hitherto), Udet gave a lecture in which he outlined a new primary consideration for aircraft-makers to take into account when submitting future tenders, namely cost. At first, he conceded, the Air Ministry had been only too willing to fund development, but now, with the other services suffering the effect of economic curbs, the time had come to rationalise the numerous projects in hand. There was to be a forty per cent cut in development personnel, the cost of aircraft had to be lowered, and components were to be standardised and simplified; production costs would thus decrease and as a result, it was hoped, profits on exports would increase.

Only through increasing exports would the long-standing balance-of-payments deficit improve and the acquisition programme get back on schedule. As an example of a project that had been developed diligently, Udet cited the Bf 109, and he urged other manufacturers to take a leaf out of Messerschmitt's book, for here was an excellent fighter that could easily be maintained in the field, which had been developed within a strict budget, and whose cost was favourably comparable with any current German rival then being produced.

It was clear that new projects such as jet fighters (then already on the drawing boards of companies like Messerschmitt's) wouldn't fare so well in such restrictive circumstances. The Air Ministry's unwillingness to back innovation and embrace change was partly due to conservatism, and partly due to belt-tightening. It was no mean feat that the visionary designs of the years that followed were realised at all. Had they been properly managed, who knows what the military implications might have been?

Opening the Catalogue of Errors

An industrialised culture needs innovation at its core if it is to be successful on the world stage, and during the 1930s the initiative formerly held by the aero industries of Britain, the USA and even Russia was gradually lost to Germany. German manufacturers were constantly innovating and refining their products, and overtook the competition in several key areas, spurred on by the urgency of their rearmament programme. One such area was the development of the jet engine.

The principles of the jet were patented by the young British inventor Frank Whittle, who ran his first engine in 1937 and saw it installed, finally, after many problems with the British authorities, in an operational aircraft, the Gloster E 28/39, in May 1941 – though it was not to be until the end of the war that British (and American) jet fighters flew in action. No one in Britain had the presence of mind to make Whittle's discovery classified information, and, following his 1937 lead, engineers around the world took up the new idea embodied in UK patents. It was in Germany that the greatest interest was aroused, and manufacturers such as BMW, Junkers and Heinkel all began their own jet-turbine programmes, encouraged by the prospect of an immediate global market in which to showcase their achievements, and supported by a powerful and indulgent Luftwaffe – though the Air Ministry remained sceptical.

The German aero industry at the time was, however, a house divided. At a secret conference at Göring's palatial country house, Karinhall, named after his late wife, in July 1938, the Reichsmarschall addressed an assembly of the country's plane-makers. He told them that the likelihood of war by 1940 was very high. The Third Reich would win it, he assured them, and Germany would become the greatest industrial power in the world. The markets of the world would, therefore, be at their disposal. But in order to reach this enviable position they would have to invest in the enterprise by producing aeroplanes at the cutting edge of technology, whether jet fighters or long-range bombers capable of carrying the war as far as the United States or well beyond the Urals to the east. He warned the industry to set its internal differences aside and encouraged them to explore the possibilities of cooperation and pooling equipment and parts, and in general to prepare for mobilisation.

Göring's call for new types of aircraft was in direct contradiction of Udet's instructions that models should be kept as simple as possible, and may have indicated the first signs of a strain between them in terms of policy. Three days after the conference, however, Hitler set in motion his plans for the annexation of the Sudetenland, which can have left the delegates in no doubt about his ultimate intentions.

November 1938 saw Milch and Göring announce a huge new acquisition programme which would form 100 Gruppen – 31,000 aircraft – by 1942. Given that the realisation of this project would have meant that Germany would import eighty-five per cent of the world's entire stock of aviation fuel, it's no surprise that the plan generated controversy. In December Milch pushed through a major reorganisation of the production system, both to cut back on its bottlenecks and to restrict the wastage of precious and expensive resources on too many new types of plane. From now on only 'superior' aircraft would get the nod for production: this was the reason for the drop in recorded aircraft production in 1939.

The new programme was supported by a vast, five-fold increase in funding, and when this is viewed in conjunction with the streamlining of both production and the bureaucratic process behind it, it is apparent that Germany was clearing the decks for action. History, however, was to show that optimism in the new plans was badly misplaced, as much of the project was given over to aircraft barely off the drawing board, such as the Heinkel He 177 heavy bomber. A production run of five hundred of these planes had been planned, but the He 177 never reached its potential owing to continuing design faults: either its engines kept overheating and breaking down or its landing gear failed. With black humour the Luftwaffe nicknamed it 'the flying cigarette lighter'. Putting too much faith in this and other unproven designs was a serious mistake and Germany was to fight the war with no serious equivalent to the large bombers favoured by the Allies.

Flickers of Common Sense

There were occasional flickers of common sense within the higher echelons of power. Perhaps sensing the future emergence of the jet engine as inevitable, early in 1939 Milch instructed the Air Ministry to set in train a research project to gain a better and more complete picture of how the new technology might work when actually installed in a fuselage. The Ministry in turn issued two development contracts. The first, to Junkers, required them to complete the new turbojet design which they had been developing since as early as 1936. This became the successful Jumo 004 series, of which more than 6,000 were eventually built. The second contract was issued jointly to Messerschmitt and BMW (who had been developing a separate turbojet of their own). Messerschmitt was heavily in demand for its new Bf 109 fighter, and the company's lean production methods and advanced designs were so admired that they were the natural choice for the job of producing a new jet fighter. The other firm which could have been approached was Heinkel, but as we shall see they were involved with their own semi-secret He 178 jet project at the time.

In June 1939 Göring organised a display of advanced aircraft and artillery for the benefit of the fascist regime in Italy under Benito Mussolini. Worried that the approaching war might be fought by Germany alone, Göring and Milch had already sought to encourage the Italians to join Germany in a military axis, persuading them that victory would be made possible by the use of the latest German technologies, for which manufacturing licences could be made available to Italy, and Mussolini, flush with his success in Abyssinia and the supine reaction of the League of Nations to it, concluded a Treaty of Alliance with Nazi Germany on 22 May.

In fact the Italians developed their own jet aircraft, and it is worth a short digression to describe it. In 1940 the Caproni Company of Varese was working in collaboration with an engine designer called Secondo Camprini who specialised in jet turbines, taking his lead from Whittle. The first product of this collaboration came with the CC1, a single-seat jet-powered monoplane that made successful flights at Talledo airfield near Milan in August 1940. A second, larger model, the CC2, was built and flown successfully from Milan to Rome on 1 December 1941, covering the 270 kilometres in 2 hours and 15 minutes. The CC2 was a low-wing monoplane with two enclosed seats and fully retractable landing gear. The nose section of the fuselage protruded quite a distance ahead of the cockpit and contained a long air inlet for the Camprini engine mounted directly beneath the cockpit, in an arrangement that German designers later came to realise only impeded the ultimate performance of the unit. The exhaust from the jet emanated from an adjustable nozzle in the base of the tail section, but was further augmented by adding extra thrust from air released from the compressor ahead of the jet. The reduced power from the long, slim intake required this compressor ahead of the actual jet in order to supply enough air under pressure to sustain the motor's operation.

While the Axis powers would certainly have been collaborating in sharing technical information, it isn't known whether or not this extended to jet research. In any case, with the international engineering community free to examine Whittle's patents before the war, there were sufficient resources in Italy to begin research independently of Germany. Not much was ever heard about Caproni's project, however, and it certainly didn't see further development.

Following his successful display to the Italians, Göring organised another presentation in July 1939, for Hitler's benefit, at the Technical Bureau's site at Rechlin, on Lake Müritz, about a hundred kilometres north-west of Berlin in Neubrandenburg. New anti-aircraft guns and piezoelectric engine-ignition systems were exhibited, Heinkel's new He 176 rocket research aircraft was flown, and the He 178 jet aircraft was unveiled. Although Hitler was told that all this new technology was still some way from production for operational purposes, he somehow persuaded himself that it was 'just around the corner'; such inflated optimism may have led him to make his move against Poland fewer than six weeks later.

The situation was made more confusing for the emerging innovators and designers within the aero industry when a month after the Rechlin display and shortly before the invasion of Poland, Göring, Milch, Udet and Luftwaffe Chief of the General Staff Hans Jeschonnek met and, in a surprising volte-face, especially in the light of the bullish impression they had given Hitler, abruptly announced a fresh restriction on aircraft research and development budgets. The emphasis now was to be placed on only a few designs then already undergoing trials – the Heinkel He 177 'Greif' heavy bomber, the Junkers Ju 88 medium bomber and the twin-engined Messerschmitt Me 210 heavy fighter. (As an aside, a manufacturer is always abbreviated within an aircraft's model name as an aid to identification: Junkers becomes Ju, Messerschmitt Me, etc.)

While this decision didn't completely shut the door on the next generation of aircraft, destined to follow in the wake of these types, it certainly put the dampers on their development. The effect would be profound, and by the time Germany had realised its mistake, in 1942, it was too late to rectify it. The Luftwaffe would have to fight its last battles of the war using more or less the same equipment with which it had attacked Poland in 1939.

The great missed opportunity – Germany's failure to capitalise on its lead in jet research – was due partly to misplaced nervousness about cost and partly to a lack of vision; familiar themes to those looking to draw comparisons with the treatment of Whittle at the hands of the RAF and the British government. Göring's personal vanities and whims got in the way of any leadership qualities he may have retained and, as the Luftwaffe was still a new service its officer corps was staffed largely by unquestioning young men, who had grown to adulthood under the Third Reich and were thoroughly indoctrinated in its tenets. In fact, Hitler had made sure that this crop of Aryan manhood also enjoyed rapid promotion in the army and, to a certain extent, the navy as well, in order to minimise any risk of independent thinking in the armed services.

There could be no political objection to the decisions handed down by the high command, especially when political considerations often took precedence over strategic ones. For these reasons above all, crucial development projects were held back. The joint Messerschmitt/BMW jet project (P. 1065), which eventually emerged as the Me 262, might arguably have entered service a full year before it eventually did so, and wonderfully innovative machines such as the Junkers Ju 287 jet bomber and the Focke-Achgelis Fa 223 helicopter would also have been developed further than they actually were. The political obstacles ahead of any inventive manufacturer were such that unless its Nazi Party credentials and/or contacts were copper-bottomed, it simply wouldn't get the largest and most prestigious contracts offered by the Air Ministry, irrespective of the quality of the tenders it might offer.

It wasn't to be until spring 1944, when Albert Speer's Reichsministerium für Rüstung und Kreigsproduktion – the Reich Ministry of Armament and War Production, usually abridged to RfRuK – grasped the nettle with the establishment of the Jägerstab (Fighter Staff) and began the active promotion of jets in place of conventional piston engines for planes, that the true potential of the jet plane – either fighter or bomber – could be realised. But by then it was a case of too little, too late to save the Third Reich.

Ahead of Its Time

Even though the introspective and timid system could work against a designer, it could never completely extinguish the flame of genuine creativity. An example of this is the story behind Heinkel's first efforts at developing a jet-powered fighter – an aeroplane that came close to beating Messerschmitt's Me 262 to production by a full two years.

Ernst Heinkel was born in 1888 and founded his eponymous aeronautical business in 1922. His interest in jet turbines stemmed from the early months of 1936, when Dr Hans-Joachim Pabst von Ohain, a student of Professor Pohl at the University of Göttingen, was brought to his attention. Heinkel became interested in developing Ohain's ideas for a centrifugal-flow turbine engine, which had surfaced when he'd applied for a patent the previous year for 'Method(s) and Apparatus for Producing Airflow for Aircraft Propulsion'. His ideas had been developed from early patents by Frank Whittle published in

1930, though they differed from Whittle's plans in envisaging the turbine to run on hydrogen, not aviation fuel as favoured by the Briton.

Ohain had been developing his project in relative obscurity but had reached the point where an industrial backer was essential if he were to go any further with it. Rather than take it to one of the engine manufacturers as might have been expected, however, Ohain approached Heinkel. His reason was that he believed Heinkel to be that rare plane-maker – a *visionary* still in business – who could not only further the design of the engine but build an aircraft around it in the process.

Heinkel, with a little urging from Professor Pohl, took Ohain on. Now with the funding he needed to proceed, Ohain worked quickly over the next two years, adapting his original engine design through two new variants, the transitional Heinkel HeS 2 and the new HeS 3A. Once again taking their lead from Whittle's own patents and descriptions of the turbine process, Ohain, with his assistant Max Hahn, designed their promising new HeS 3A engine first in a converted garage at the University of Göttingen's laboratory and later at Heinkel's own Rostock-Marienehe airfield. The engine, developed in 1938, ran on normal aviation fuel and was much more controllable, and safer in its operation, than its hydrogen-powered predecessors. (The loss of the *Hindenburg* airship in May 1937 perhaps contributed to the change of heart over fuel.) By the time they'd got around to secretly testing the sole 3A unit to destruction, mounted on the underside of a Heinkel He 118, the team was satisfied that its efforts were progressing in the right direction. Following this, it was decided to install the second example, the HeS 3B, in the airframe of a custom-built monoplane, which was designated He 178.

The He 178, which as we have seen was unveiled at Rechlin in July 1939, closely followed another (though entirely separate) Heinkel triumph, the He 176 rocket plane, which shocked the Luftwaffe high command and the Führer when it featured in the Rechlin display, with its not entirely unjustified impression of a manned firework.

The 178 itself flew for the first time on 27 August 1939, a full twenty months ahead of the British Gloster E.28, powered by a Whittle turbine. It was thus the first aircraft in the world to take off and fly on turbojet power alone; but the gathering of war clouds meant that its propaganda potential wasn't exploited to the full, as it might have been a few years earlier. With the outbreak of war at the beginning of September, the Air Ministry – the RLM – strengthened its resolve to prioritise regular aircraft production over research and development, and so the second flight of the He 178, for the benefit of RLM and Luftwaffe officials, was delayed until 1 November. The RLM had little to worry about in taking this stance, as Heinkel's project was riddled with problems and looked a long way from ever reaching production.

At its best, the crude, centrifugal-flow HeS 3B engine could bestow only a small power-to-weight ratio on the aircraft, endowing it with poor performance, high fuel consumption and unreliability. The bespoke airframe (the aircraft minus the engine) created difficulties of its own, the principal snags being directional instability above a certain speed, and landing gear which stubbornly refused to retract when the plane was airborne. Some observers simply believed that these and other problems originated from mounting the revolutionary engine *within* the fuselage, at a time when little was known of its likely operating characteristics. With hindsight, we might think of Heinkel as trying to build the then-equivalent of a space shuttle – teething troubles were to be expected, even inevitable.

These setbacks made an unfavourable impression on Air Ministry officials, who could see little point in meeting the development costs of new engines from a straight plane-builder, such as Heinkel; they preferred to see their money going into established engine-makers such as BMW. However, at the end of 1939 the new Head of the RLM's Technical Bureau, Helmut Schelp, a sympathetic and imaginative man, approved of Heinkel's turbojet development programme and managed to carry his sceptical Head of Power-Plant Development, Wolfram Eisenlohr, with him.

Now with renewed official interest, Heinkel ceased work on Ohain's original designs in favour of a new direction and moved the He 178, the only one of its kind, and its distant cousin, the He 176 rocket plane, to the Berlin Air Museum. In the end both were destroyed in an Allied air raid in 1943, leaving only photographs and film to record their achievements.

Encouraged by Schelp's support for his work in turbojets, Heinkel now invited a former Junkers engine designer, Max Mueller, to join the company. The new arrival was to recruit his own team of engineers to develop his designs for an entirely new axial-flow engine which had originally attracted Junkers' interest. Mueller's new engine became known as the HeS 30, and he was to lead his team in friendly rivalry with Ohain's group from then on. He had also brought from Junkers plans for experimental ducted-fan engines and these, too, were developed on a smaller scale, becoming the HeS 50 and the HeS 60, delivering 1,000 and 2,000 horsepower respectively.

For his part, Ohain was now engaged in creating the HeS 8 – a successor to the original HeS 3B unit, now mothballed in the Berlin museum within the He 178. Each new engine was matched fairly closely in terms of their projected power output (the HeS 30 planned to yield 800 kilogrammes of thrust; the HeS 8 to offer 700 kilogrammes), but in the end it was the question of reliability which was the deciding factor between the rivals, and the fact that the HeS 8 had an additional advantage in that while its diameter was only marginally larger than that of the He 30, it was less than half the weight.

By the spring of 1939, Heinkel also had a new Technical Director, Diplom-Ingenieur Robert Lüsser, who had arrived fresh from his previous post as head of the Messerschmitt design office. His first task was to design an all-new fighter airframe to accommodate Ohain's equally new HeS 8 engine, by then in the planning stage. Heinkel's own original project specification allowed for a single engine, so it's probable that either RLM pressure or Lüsser's time at Messerschmitt (and his knowledge of their top-secret P. 1065 project with BMW) influenced the switch to a twin-engined layout. Called the He 180, the all-metal aircraft had a long, slender fuselage which housed a brace of nose-mounted cannon (large-calibre machine-guns). Each wing was mounted midway up the side of the fuselage, with an under-slung engine, along with a then still rare retracting landing-wheel mounted slightly inboard of the engine. The high-mounted tailplane carried a finned rudder at each tip which set the design off and gave the aircraft a graceful yet purposeful look.

Although the design of the He 180 had been focused primarily on its being a fighter aircraft, Lüsser also managed to incorporate some revolutionary features. In addition to the fully retractable, tricycle undercarriage (a nosewheel and two main wing wheels), there was a compressed-air ejector seat and provision for eventual cabin pressurisation that would allow flights at high altitude. Heinkel built a number of full-sized wooden mock-ups in secret during 1939 to evaluate the best locations for small bomb loads, machine-guns and radio equipment, and used them to show senior officials such as Ernst Udet how the project was progressing. Udet was so impressed that he gave the He 180 his full backing, but he lived to regret his initial enthusiasm as the plane's two in-house power plants continually failed to live up to expectation; either running unreliably or with too high a fuel consumption.

But Udet apart, the RLM hadn't been fully informed about the He 180 project. Heinkel was developing the fighter entirely in-house and keeping officials in the dark, not wishing to hear their conservative and hesitant views too far ahead of production, and remembering the scorn Milch (and indeed Udet) had poured on the single He 178. It wasn't until Messerschmitt and BMW received contracts from the Air Ministry for their own jet-fighter project (the Me 262) that Heinkel finally received a measure of official support. In March 1940 the new aircraft from the Ernst Heinkel Flugzeugwerke received its official Ministry designation: the He 180 officially became the He 280, and work began in earnest to pit it against the RLM's favoured candidate from Messerschmitt/BMW.

At this point it is important to note that the German Air Ministry had a policy of giving all prototype aircraft a 'V' suffix ('V' for Versuchsmuster: 'prototype') so that the first prototype was designated V1, the second V2, and so on. These designations should not be confused with the much later flying bomb and rocket, the V-1 and the V-2. In this second case, the 'V' stood for Vergeltungswaffe: 'reprisal weapon'.

The first example nearing completion, in September 1940, was therefore designated He 280 V1. It was a year after the first flight of the He 178, but neither of Heinkel's two engine designs was yet sufficiently developed for flight-testing to start. Undeterred by the delay, Heinkel began constructing four more prototypes at his company's expense, so confident was he of their ultimate success.

The V1 began a series of manned gliding tests in which it was towed to altitude by an He 111 medium bomber and then released. The first of these tests, on 22 September 1940, was a success: the design threw up no major faults, and the pilot reported a 'neutral character', which was impressive, given the aircraft's advanced design and specification. Because the V1 still lacked its engines, the tests were conducted with weighted pods shaped like turbojets attached to the underside of the wings to stimulate the 'right' aerodynamics.

In March 1941, after forty-one flights, the V1 returned to the hangar to receive its first pair of engines. Although still not yet perfected, Heinkel felt that the competition (from BMW and Junkers) was catching up on him and also that the engines would be better tested in actual service than on static test-beds. And so, on 2 April 1941, with works test-pilot Fritz Schäfer at the controls, and powered by a pair of Ohain's HeS 8 engines, the V1 took off for a circuit round the Marienehe airfield, at a height of around 300 metres. For this trial the landing gear remained extended, and the engines were left exposed. They had a habit of leaking fuel when running, which could have been disastrous had it pooled within the outer streamlined cowlings that were normally fitted.

Everything went smoothly, although by the time Schäfer was landing the red low-fuel warning light had already been on for some time. The fuel tanks for this first flight were barely a quarter full, sufficient only for takeoff and a single circuit of the airfield, but he'd been flying with only a few instruments actually working, so the only way of regulating fuel consumption was to ease off the throttle. Test-pilots had to wait months before such rudimentary details were corrected, but such was the political pressure on Heinkel to start powered flights that they hadn't thought to wire up all the instruments beforehand.

So confident were the designers after this tentative foray, however, that an official presentation was arranged a few days later, on 5 April, again at Marienehe, in the presence of a number of highly placed RLM and Luftwaffe officials, including Udet, Schelp and Eisenlohr. The V1 wore its engine cowlings this time but the flight went well, and so impressed the previously sceptical Eisenlohr that from that moment on he became a passionate convert to promoting the cause of the turbojet, with an immediate rise in Heinkel's star as a result. Udet, however, despite his earlier enthusiasm for the He 180, could not be persuaded that jet power was necessary for a Luftwaffe engaged in a war dominated by conventional (and reliable) planes, and this pessimistic view was echoed by many others within the Air Ministry.

Despite support from the Technical Bureau, Heinkel's turbojet projects were now to be dogged by petty jealousies and professional apathy at the highest official level, and it was no consolation that other projects, such as Messerschmitt's Me 262, suffered in the same way. Had he lived, there is little doubt that Udet could have held back German research into turbojets indefinitely, and we might never have seen the plethora of designs that eventually emerged later in the war.

Notwithstanding Udet's reservations and realising it didn't pay to have all the R and D eggs in the baskets of Junkers and BMW, Schelp and Eisenlohr encouraged Heinkel to allow Ohain's team to begin work on their third-generation turbojet, the HeS 109–011. If anything, they probably thought that this would be the unit needed to turn the He 280 into a viable proposition. To enable the project to be set in motion, the Air Ministry arranged that same April for Heinkel to take over the firm of Hirth Motoren, a specialist manufacturer of aircraft piston engines and superchargers, with plants in Berlin and Stuttgart-Zuffenhausen. This move helped Heinkel overcome the acute skilled-labour shortage which military call-up was beginning to impose on industry as a whole. As a result, Mueller's HeS 30 project team (it was still going, despite being overshadowed somewhat by Ohain's team) was moved to Stuttgart to make space back at Marienehe for Ohain to wrap up development of the struggling HeS 8 and move on to his new HeS 109–011.

So Near . . .

Time passed. By the spring of 1942, despite the problems in his company's two ongoing turbojet projects, Ernst Heinkel was convinced that he had demonstrated enough of the He 280 for the officials of the Air Ministry to take it more seriously, the more so as the rival project from Messerschmitt was struggling. (They'd completed the airframe of their P. 1065 project, but the BMW engines were proving so unreliable that it could fly reliably only while fitted with a piston engine and propeller. Hardly the greatest advertisement for Messerschmitt, Heinkel's only serious rival in the rush to build the world's first operational jet fighter.)

In order to rouse the Air Ministry from its apparent torpor, Heinkel arranged a display for senior Ministry officials, in which a Focke-Wulf

190 (considered at the time a superior fighter even to the famous Messerschmitt Me 109) and an He 280 flew over an airfield at Warnemünde near Marienehe in mock combat. The jet ran rings round the Focke-Wulf and so impressed the RLM delegates that they quickly ordered no fewer than thirteen pre-production examples of the 280.

For Heinkel, though, the test merely highlighted some of the ongoing problems of the HeS 8 engines used to power the aircraft. But by this time Ohain and his small team had moved on to their new HeS 109–011 project full-time, all but forgetting the problematic HeS 8. With recurring issues such as excessive vibration in the HeS 8, simply because the design had been optimised for its small size and *not* smooth running, this display was the last nail in its coffin. It wasn't until a year later, in 1943, that the HeS 8 engine was to power another aircraft when the project was revisited, but even then the unit was still underpowered. This wasn't for want of trying. Units fitted to the third (V3) aircraft had been boosted to yield 600 kilogrammes of thrust (well short of the original aims), thus raising the plane's top speed to 800 kph, but during one of the early test-flights, again with Fritz Schäfer at the controls, the starboard engine shed a turbine blade. The result was a burst of intense and resonating vibration, and a sheet of flame that streamed from the back of the outlet. Luckily, Schäfer managed to land safely, and the V3, the fault rectified, was flying again within days. But one can imagine what he had to say about the HeS 8 units to the engineers when he climbed out of the cockpit.

During the early summer of 1942, however, with Ohain involved in the early stages of his new 109–011 engine and Mueller's project still continuing, the overall He 280 project emerged, if anything, bolstered from the successful display. So it was with great optimism that Heinkel ordered that the He 280 airframe programme be transferred to Schwechat, on the outskirts of Vienna, to prepare the ground for possible production beyond the reach of Allied intelligence and thus bombing. The two engine teams were left in Germany.

But the mood was soon shattered by a directive from Helmut Schelp at the RLM's Technical Bureau, in which he expressed his preference for the Junkers Jumo 109–004 engine to be specified with the production of the He 280. He had recognised the HeS 8 to be faring consistently worse in comparisons with the Jumo unit, developed by the outsiders in the race, Junkers, and was determined not to waste resources on no-hopers. Schelp also held the view that the HeS 8 would never be truly serviceable, that Ohain's new HeS 109–011 was too far off production, and that Mueller's HeS 30 was too radical to be reliable. He suggested that all of Heinkel's efforts be directed into the 109–011 at the expense of the other projects, even though the latest variant of the HeS 30 was now yielding 900 kilogrammes of thrust. Following an Allied bombing raid at Marienehe in the autumn of 1942, Heinkel took the opportunity to move Ohain's team south, to join Mueller's old team at Stuttgart, which led to cramped working conditions and competition for dwindling resources. Mueller himself had left Heinkel by this time, though, and, probably owing to a lack of technicians and resources, work on his HeS 50 and HeS 60 ducted-fan engines had long been abandoned. Both teams were now to almost merge together in developing the 109–011.

The (second) V2 example of the He 280 was duly fitted with these Jumo units and flew for the first time on 1 October 1942. However, the new engines were physically larger (and heavier) than the compact HeS 8 units and ended up closer to the ground, once mounted below the wings in the normal way. The problems this caused, such as their fouling the ground during takeoffs and landings, had to be solved before the V2 could fly safely. By reinforcing the landing gear, wings and fuselage, these components were better able to support the increased weight of their imported engines and keep them from contact with the ground. But despite the precautions, the V2 was written off in spring 1943 as a result of a landing accident in which its undercarriage finally collapsed under the weight of the engines. The sixth He 280 – V6 – appeared that October and was also fitted with Jumo engines, but was designed from the outset around their weight and performed well, even participating in armament tests with the Technical Bureau at Rechlin.

Now that Heinkel was beginning reluctantly to give way on the issue of accepting engines from other makers in the He 280 programme, another was tried out on the He 280 V4, which had been altered during its build specifically to accept it. Ironically, the new engine was BMW's own 109–003 unit, which had since been dropped from the joint project with Messerschmitt for being too unreliable (Messerschmitt now opting for the Jumo). The V4 flew for the first time on 15 August 1943 and was followed in October by the similarly configured He 280 V5.

In October Heinkel put forward a tender for a fighter-bomber variant of the 280 project, which would use two Jumo engines from the outset to give a top speed of 880 kph. For this He 280 'B' series, among a myriad of small improvements the proposed armament was doubled to six nose-mounted MG 151 cannon of twenty-millimetre calibre, and the twin tailfin assembly was replaced by a robust (and cheaper) conventional single tail and rudder. Compared with Messerschmitt's slow-to-arrive offering, the proposal was immaculately timed.

Three months earlier, both the Air Ministry and the office of the Generalluftzeugmeister had concluded that any production preparations for the Me 262 would be premature, and that Heinkel's proposal for production of the He 280 was unrealistic, given that the company's existing manufacturing capacity was running at full stretch in the wake of the on-going Allied bombing campaign and its war of attrition against German industry. Seeing the new variant, however, seemed to swing the RLM in Heinkel's favour, and the Ministry went so far as to begin negotiations with the company for a run of three hundred 'B' series fighter-bombers, to be produced under licence by the smaller plane-maker, Siebel. This was as close as the ill-starred He 280 was ever going to get to actual production.

... And Yet So Far

The Technical Bureau had been carrying out a running programme of direct comparisons between the two Heinkel and Messerschmitt projects. Both designs were competing for a promised production contract, but it was especially crucial to Heinkel that they win as a way of salvaging credibility for themselves as a plane-maker following the débâcle of the in-house engine. But just as they seemed to have succeeded, the fate of the He 280 was sealed.

Since the Me 262 had dropped the BMW units and had switched to using the same Jumo engines as some of the He 280's, the combination had proved irresistible. Compared with the similarly powered Heinkel, the 262 was proving more reliable, with a greater range, and the aircraft was somehow able to extract a better speed out of the Jumos. Realising what this could mean, Heinkel responded desperately by trying to stretch the 280's fuselage and enlarging the fuel tank to endow a greater range, but such amateurish attempts at rectification were frowned on by the Air Ministry. In the end the inevitable happened: Heinkel was ordered to stop all work on the 280 and merely to complete the last of the thirteen prototypes already ordered. Yet as far as Ohain's work was concerned, Heinkel was still behind his man, and work was continuing for some unknown point in the future when it might bear fruit.

Ironically, following a visit in April 1943 by Adolf Galland, Messerschmitt was also required to enlarge the Me 262's fuel tanks so as to increase the plane's range. Fuel consumption has such an impact on the viability of combat aircraft that one is forced to ask why such similar modifications weren't demanded sooner at Heinkel; especially for the 'B' series fighter-bomber, a decent operating range would have been essential. For his part, Messerschmitt made the changes fast, so that when Galland flew a 262 again a month later, on 22 May, he was able to report that his flight had felt 'like being pushed by angels'. After such praise from a senior figure and a major ace to boot, it was no surprise that the production contract fell into Messerschmitt's lap. What perhaps was even more galling for Heinkel was that, in a further ironic twist of fate, Messerschmitt himself had been holding out in the hope of actually manufacturing his Me 209, which was merely an improved variation of his original Me 109 piston-engined fighter. The Me 262 wasn't even his first priority.

With the benefit of hindsight it could be argued that Messerschmitt's superior contacts within the Nazi Party ensured that Heinkel would never have got the contract whatever he had tried and despite the fact that his company was still the largest producer of bombers in Germany at the time. There was another element to the equation, though: RLM officials wanted to force manufacturers to specialise within the areas they had already evolved in. Thus, Heinkel would produce their multi-engined though slow and lumbering bomber designs; Messerschmitt would produce their single-and dual-engined fighters, purposely designed for dogfighting styles of combat and other tasks, such as reconnaissance, where speed is an essential requirement. However, leaving to one side these considerations and the wrangling over dwindling budgets within the Air Ministry, as the war progressed it is also possible that the influential test-pilots of the Ministry's Evaluation Unit simply preferred the Me 262 to the He 280 for whatever reason and that in the end their opinions, like those of Adolf Galland, influenced the final decision. After all, for all its apparent remoteness, the RLM supplied the Luftwaffe with its aircraft and listened to what its pilots and crews wanted and needed from a new aircraft. If figures like Galland were supporting Messerschmitt, then there was little that could be said against their opinion.

So now, with the decision having gone against them, Heinkel's remaining He 280s faced a sad fate, although they weren't scrapped: the war effort required their involvement in aerodynamic research and as mules for the development of other engines. The original V1, for example, was moved to the Technical Office's centre at Rechlin to have its engines replaced by four Argus 014 pulsejets as part of the ongoing engine development of the V-1 flying bomb. These new, long and slim (and light) pulsejet engines lacked the power to get the 280 airborne, so its first flight thus equipped was taken courtesy of a tow from a pair of Me 110 heavy fighters acting as tugs. This occurred during heavy snow, however, and the pilot was unable either to retract the landing gear or to free the frozen rudder, leaving him little choice but to bale out of the uncontrollable plane. At around 2,400 metres, after a degree of struggling, he released the frozen tow-line and, after putting some distance between his stricken aircraft and the pair of tugs, used the ejector seat – the first such use in aviation history. He parachuted safely to the ground; the plane itself crashed and was destroyed.

The fate of the V4 is lost in the passage of time. Some commentators say that it was converted to use six Argus engines and was somewhat more successful than the V1 had been with its four; others say that plans were drawn up to use the six pulsejets but never implemented. From the sources examined for this book, the V4 is cited as a replacement for the wrecked V1, and ended up fitted with two BMW jets instead, with which its first flew in May 1943. This would have put it after the cancellation of the overall project and made it a part of the subsequent testing programme the remaining 280 prototypes were put through.

Mixed reports blur the histories of the other prototypes too. The V8 apparently made ten powered flights with an experimental *dihedral* butterfly tail on 19 July 1943 before its engines were removed; it apparently restarted its test programme in November 1944 as a glider. The plan was for this aircraft and the similarly unpowered V7 to be used in gliding trials prior to having Ohain's 109–011 turbojets (by now designated as HeS 11) fitted, for high-speed flight-testing. However, the persistent failure of the engines actually to materialise put an end to this project.

During 1944 the Jumo-powered V6 was further modified to use the single tailfin developed for the 'B' series. However, it wasn't flown until early in 1945, when it crashed during its first high-speed run over an airfield close to Berlin. What Heinkel or the RLM were thinking they could learn from such testing, so late in the day, remains unanswered; perhaps they were testing a new tweak to the Jumo units. Other sources state that the other aircraft were never flown: indeed, that in some cases they were never even finished, and a multitude of damaged components found by the Allies at Schwechat in April 1945 may bear out this theory. However, the general feeling must be that the 'fog of war' has created such confusion that the truth may never be known.

With all the problems Germany experienced in the latter years of the war, when fuel shortages even grounded tug aircraft for the glider versions of the He 280 as well as most other planes in the Luftwaffe, it can come as little surprise that despite its best efforts Heinkel was destined never to produce a jet aircraft that would fire a shot in anger. Their later He 162 Volksjäger was built in large numbers during the final months of the war, but as we shall later see in Chapter Six, it was accepted by the Luftwaffe too late to see action. To add insult to injury, this plane was powered by a BMW turbojet. After years of development, Ohain's HeS 011 was still far from being accepted into service by the end of the war. It had been the great white hope throughout for Heinkel and the RLM alike, yet it never reached an operational form and was probably the greatest disappointment the Heinkel company suffered during the war.

In the midst of the failure of the He 280, one mustn't lose sight of the fact that Heinkel played a pivotal role in stimulating official interest in the then exciting new technologies of jet turbines and planes. At a time when very few players in the world were dipping their toes into the water, Heinkel not only took up a revolutionary engine design from a maverick, though brilliant, university graduate, but also had the faith to build an entire aircraft to test it. There is no doubt that Ernst Heinkel saw and understood that the future of powered flight lay with the jet engine, at a time when the authorities and even fellow manufacturers on both sides of the firing line were either sceptical or dragging their feet. Whittle, as we have mentioned, had a frustrating time selling his idea to the British and found success only as a result of the pressures of war. If he had been given the early encouragement that Ohain and Mueller received from Heinkel, things might have been very different. For example, the Gloster Meteor – the RAF's first jet fighter, might very well have entered service at roughly the same time as the Messerschmitt Me 262, if not sooner, and not, as actually happened, at the very end of the war (by which time the German fuel situation had hamstrung the many Me 262s that had been built).

Chapter Two

HELICOPTERS

First Steps

Visitors to the 'variety' displays held during the 1938 Berlin Motor Show might have been forgiven for believing that the vision of the future glimpsed in the films *The Shape of Things to Come* and *Metropolis* had already arrived as they watched twenty-six-year-old Flugkapitän Hanna Reitsch flying the Focke-Wulf Fw 61 helicopter *inside* the Deutschlandhalle. Giving demonstrations each evening for the duration of the show, she whirled the machine around the vast space, making it dance and skip amid a blizzard of flashbulbs. Although both German and foreign spectators watched in bewilderment and wonder, the display was grist to the mill of Josef Goebbels' Propaganda Ministry.

Such a dramatic display of technological progress was unprecedented, and the Fw 61's appearance struck fear into the hearts of more than a few conventional plane-makers. Here at last was a true helicopter, of a simple and robust design, that really worked. Across the Atlantic, in the USA, Igor Sikorsky's experimental machine could still only hover for short periods of time while tethered, and was incapable of forward flight.

It was to be another six years before helicopters reached operational status with the Allied forces. Had luck been with their development in Germany, both the air force and the navy would have been using them widely from as early as 1940.

The story of early, rotary-wing research in Germany involves a number of key figures – luminaries who could foresee applications

45

beyond their own basic work in the field, and who knew the area was worth further investigation. We have to go back to pre-First World War Russia to find the very first true helicopter developments, aside from the fanciful work of da Vinci and Cayley. In 1904, Russian scientist Zhukovski published a study paper entitled *Lifting Payloads by Turning Wings*. His theory was that it might be possible for a series of rotating arms, each having the cross-section of a wing aerofoil, and spun at high speed, to power a vertical takeoff device. The basic principle of flight and the generation of lift requires that a wing be shaped with a slight curve in cross-section on its upper surface and a flat underneath. Air passes more quickly over the upper curve and is at a lower pressure than the air beneath. This differential creates lift, so either the aircraft – or the wings on helicopter rotors – must be moving fast to get enough lift to take off.

Zhukovski's theory inspired engineers of vision, such as Sikorsky and Yuryev, to begin tentative experiments. The Great War forced their deferral, but this was not before Yuryev had got his machine off the ground (in 1912) in a series of short hops. Yuryev's was a remarkable achievement, especially when one looks at pictures of his craft today, for it is possible to recognise elements of the modern helicopter within its Heath Robinson frame. It had a large rotor mounted above the fuselage, together with a smaller stabilising rotor on the end of a tail boom, and thus set the pattern for all that would follow.

After the war, and at the time that the Treaty of Versailles was still in force, German aircraft engineers began to investigate alternative forms of plane-building and propulsion in order to circumvent the restrictions they found themselves placed under by the treaty. It wasn't long before their efforts began to pay off, and one of the first to succeed, in 1927, was Anton Flettner. Flettner, a respected aero-dynamics expert in the field of conventional aircraft, now turned to studying the helicopter. His first design had one single large rotor with a small, twenty-horsepower petrol motor at the tip of each of its two blades. These little engines each powered a small airscrew that in turn kept the free-spinning rotor turning, giving lift as a result. At one stage this most ungainly craft actually got airborne, but it was wrecked when a sudden gust of wind destabilised it, causing it to crash and be written off in the process. Flettner was forced back to his drawing board, though the experience had provided valuable lessons that were to serve him well later.

Advent of the Autogyro

Meanwhile, the 1920s in Spain saw Juan de la Cierva quietly developing the concept of the autogyro, in which the main rotor is used not to propel the machine but solely to generate lift; a separate propeller, rear- or front-mounted, is used for forward motion. Such was Cierva's success with his idea that, following successful trials in Spain, he moved to Britain to continue his research. While there, he developed a definitive craft, the two-seater C-19 gyroplane. Its layout resembled a conventional low-winged monoplane, but with a shallow rear tail and shortened, stumpy wings with dihedral – upturned – tips. A four-bladed main rotor was driven by a conventional radial-piston aero engine which also powered a small, front-mounted propeller.

Though not a true helicopter, the gyroplane came close to having a helicopter's characteristic manoeuvrability. The fact that the design worked well and was fairly robust was a bonus, and was enough to attract many licensees. One of these was the German aero company Focke-Wulf, founded in Bremen in 1924 by the then thirty-four-year-old Heinrich Focke and his business partner, G. Wulf. The Focke-Wulf licence-built version of Cierva's gyroplane proved to be the starting-point for some of the later helicopter designs seen in Germany. German manufacturers were being actively encouraged to develop such unorthodox machines, and it therefore came as no surprise when Cierva was courted by them. Professor Focke held the post of Technical Director of his company, and as soon as they had acquired the licence to produce the C-19 in 1931 he set about improving the original design. To do this he had established within Focke-Wulf a rotor-wing research team, the core members of which were later to leave with him when he entered a new partnership and formed Focke-Achgelis.

The gyroplane Focke-Wulf produced, the Fw C-19, used a 150-horsepower Siebel Sh 14 engine, and was quickly nicknamed 'Don Quixote'. It was swiftly followed by the C-30, which appeared in 1933. This version retained the Siebel engine but dispensed with the vestigial wings, and for the first time the craft took on the appearance of helicopters familiar to us today.

Between 1937 and 1938, Focke developed the C-30 further and further away from its original Spanish design, finally creating the Fw 186 gyroplane. This was entered in a competition run by the Air Ministry to find a Short Take-Off and Landing (STOL) reconnaissance aircraft. Its rivals were the conventional Siebel Si 201 and the Fieseler Fi 156 'Storch' – 'Stork' – which eventually won. The design of the 186, however, while retaining the two open cockpits for the pilot and the observer, featured a much smoother and more streamlined fuselage, and the two front undercarriage wheels were mounted further outboard, on more substantial outriggers. The struts of the outriggers had curved profiles in order to minimise aerodynamic drag. Although it didn't win the competition, its development showed what might be possible in rotor craft of all types.

The Air Ministry wasn't the only military body interested in looking at helicopters more closely. In 1934 and 1935 the navy made known its requirement for a ship-based reconnaissance aircraft, the specification for which could be met only by a true Vertical Take-Off and Landing (VTOL) machine, since no aircraft carriers had been built in Germany. The navy's requirement aroused interest within the aero-engineering community, for Focke's Fw 186 fell into the STOL bracket and would thus be impracticable for ship use. Anton Flettner's response was to organise a plant in Berlin in 1935 which was eventually to produce true helicopters for the navy. He had produced his own first autogyro, the Fl 184, that same year, but had understood quickly that the machine couldn't fulfil the naval specification, any more than Focke could with his Fw 186. And Flettner's machine, even though it boasted a more comfortable enclosed two-seater cockpit, was inferior to the Focke-Wulf gyroplanes then flying.

Flettner therefore turned his attention to the principles of pure helicopter flight, and soon afterwards, in 1936, he unveiled an ungainly machine that provided a partial answer – the Fl 185. This used a twin-bladed rotor; at the end of each was a motor, with a small propeller half-way along its length. The 185 succeeded in making only a series of unsteady hops, but Flettner had intended it only as a test-bed for the 'real' prototype, which was already in development – the Fl 265.

Focke-Wulf were making real progress, meanwhile, on their own new helicopter project, and their Fw 61 would soon stun the world. Flettner was undeterred and carried on working steadily with his two colleagues, Sissingh and Hohenemser, in developing new approaches to helicopter control and design. He published numerous research papers from 1936 onwards, and these would, much later, help companies like Sikorsky to devise the sophisticated machines that were used later in the Korean War.

In essence, Flettner's Fl 265 involved the use of a pair of twin-bladed rotors, each counter-rotating against the other and using a shared hub. The machine seemed perfectly suited to naval requirements. The aerodynamic fuselage had fully enclosed seating for two; the now fully shrouded Siebel engine was mounted at the front, and used a similar cooling airscrew to that on the Focke-Wulf Fw 61. A complex, hand-built gearbox for the two rotors was mounted above the cabin and faired into the roof of the upper fuselage. A large tail section was considered essential for stability, and fixed outrigger-mounted landing gear completed the design. In all, five such machines were built, and they saw limited service and handling trials with the navy aboard cruisers between 1939 and 1940. In that time the record of the Fl 265 was excellent: there was only one serious accident, and the craft displayed a manoeuvrability that made the cream of conventional aeroplanes at the time look clumsy by comparison. One test involved a mock attack by Messerschmitt fighters. Not only could the Messerschmitts not find an advantageous position within the exercise but the Fl 265's nimble handling allowed it to gain the upper hand over them – which led some officials to consider using it as an alternative fighter and attack platform. Had such an idea been implemented, the Fl 265 would have become a formidable forerunner of the notorious helicopter gunships of the Vietnam War.

The navy was keen to develop the 265 further, but Flettner was already working on its successor, the Fl 282 'Kolibri' – 'Hummingbird'. Frustrated that the 265 wasn't to be taken further, the navy later worked with Focke-Achgelis. The new firm would become Flettner's main rival, in developing the Fa 330 'Bachstelze' – 'Water Wagtail' – for use in submarines as a spotter of Allied convoys.

Flight of the Dragon

Ever since Heinrich Focke had taken out his licence to produce Cierva's autogyro, he had been keen to move on to actual helicopters, and he had always seen the making, building and flying of the gyroplane as necessary steps towards achieving true helicopter flight. The closely knit team he had assembled for the purpose had not only worked on autogyros but from the outset had also secretly been engaged in developing helicopter designs. In June 1936 they reaped their first rewards with the maiden untethered flight of the Fw 61. This flight was the result of work begun in 1934. Then, using a standard Fw 44 trainer aircraft (used to familiarise new pilots to flight) as their starting point, Focke and his team first removed its wings, replacing them with strong triangular booms, made of tubular steel and aluminium spars, which extended either side of the fuselage. At the end of each boom was a three-bladed rotor and gearbox, each driven by a long propshaft which lay alongside the lowest spar. The diameter of each rotor was 7.5 metres, giving the aircraft an overall span of some 16 metres. A similar Siebel engine to those used in the autogyros powered the machine. In front of each engine a small airscrew was fitted, which served only to channel coolant air to the engine and not to provide forward motion.

The subsequent tests put the craft through a long series of tethered flights, culminating in the free flight of 1936 already mentioned; but it wasn't until 1937 that the first autorotative *landing* – i.e. using unpowered rotors – was practised. Focke-Wulf had succeeded in attracting several high-profile test-pilots to its new programme by then, to put the two prototypes of the Fw 61 – V1 and V2 – through further paces. Among the flyers were Karl Bode and Hanna Reitsch, who were joined later by Karl Franke of the Technical Bureau's test centre at Rechlin. Working on behalf of the Air Ministry, it was Reitsch and Franke who were to fly the most, creating and breaking several helicopter flight records in the process. Entered in the Fédération Aéronautique Internationale's 'G' class for rotor aircraft, these included an endurance time of 1 hour and 20 minutes, an altitude record of 2,439 metres, and an airspeed record of 122 kph.

The Fw 61 proved itself a worthy and versatile machine – so much so that its inclusion in the 1938 Berlin Motor Show was regarded as just one more phase of its testing period. However, Reitsch wouldn't agree to fly it in the Deutschlandhalle until Göring coerced her, since Franke, who had already done so, had snapped an outrigging hawser through flying too close to the roof. Following the accident, Göring lost faith in Franke and relied on Reitsch to fly all the shows thereafter.

Some time before 1938 the Air Ministry had shown itself so impressed by the Fw 61 that it issued Focke with a requirement to produce an improved design capable of carrying a 700-kilogramme payload. Sceptics declared that the requirement would be impossible to fulfil; but similar voices had earlier stated that the Fw 61 would never be capable of flight. Focke initiated development both in Bremen and in Delmenhorst. However, considered 'politically unreliable' by the regime, he had already been removed from the company he had co-founded.

This happened late in 1936 and may have been as much expedient as political from the point of view of the Party, though Focke was not a very convinced supporter of Nazism. The Air Ministry had decided to gear up production of the Messerschmitt Me 109 fighter and wanted to use Focke-Wulf's manufacturing capacity for the purpose. In consequence, the company was taken over by the electrical giant AEG. However, soon after this the Air Ministry took favourable notice of the Fw 61, and it was then that it encouraged Focke to establish a new firm that would be dedicated to the development of helicopters.

This Focke did, in partnership with the renowned pilot Gerd Achgelis, in 1937. The first task of the Focke-Achgelis company was to develop a helicopter to meet the Ministry's 700-kilogramme specification, and it set to work at Delmenhorst, a little to the south-west of Bremen, in 1938. At first they produced a scaled-up version of the Fw 61 capable of carrying up to six people, having a short-haul domestic airliner with Lufthansa in mind. The new machine was designated the Fa 266 'Hornisse' – 'Hornet' – and the development of the engine, transmission and rotor hub was contracted out to the BMW works in Berlin. Unsurprisingly, despite its theoretical civilian application, the Hornisse attracted the attention of the military and was reassigned the code number Fa 223 in mid-1939 by the Air Ministry (the RLM) prior to evaluation in various roles, including training, transport, rescue and anti-submarine patrols. The navy was also interested in the Hornisse, and early on in its career considered it as a possible replacement for the Eilboot torpedo boats (the infamous 'E-boats').

The real significance of the Hornisse, however, was that it was to be the world's first truly practical helicopter.

In September 1939, just after war had been declared, the first prototype of the Fa 223 – the V1 – left the Delmenhorst factory. Now nicknamed 'Drache' – 'Dragon' – it had a twin-rotor layout similar to that of the Fw 61, but there the similarities ended. The Drache was no toy but a purposeful and altogether superior machine, with a fully enclosed cabin and load bay. The single BMW engine was mounted amidships in a welded tubular-steel fuselage, complete with the familiar tailfin and rudder. The whole design looked superb for its time.

The first hovering tests showed up problems, however, and it wasn't to be until 1940 that it actually flew. No one had built a machine as ambitious as this before, so it was hardly surprising that problems large and small were cropping up nearly all the time. The first specified engine, a 620-horsepower BMW Bramo 323D, proved too fragile when running at high speed for any length of time, and it had to be replaced with a tougher 1,000-horsepower version in later prototypes in order to improve reliability and lifting capacity. Another problem, the biggest of all, was the severe vibration caused when the rotors moved out of phase. The reason for this was unbalanced driveshafts, manufactured to low tolerances: something that could be rectified only by greater attention to detail in the BMW engine plant.

Eventually, on 3 August 1940, with Karl Bode at the controls, the first untethered flight of the Drache VI was made. Over a hundred hours of ground testing had brought it to this point, and the sense of relief experienced by the team as they cleared this last hurdle must have been palpable. In fact, now that the niggles had been sorted out, the flight tests progressed so smoothly that in October Bode was able to fly to the Technical Bureau's test centre at Rechlin to demonstrate the craft there. At Rechlin the Drache broke some of the records established by its predecessor, and set new ones that were to stand for many years. A top speed of 182 kph was recorded, as well as a loaded weight of 3,705 kilogrammes, a climb rate of 528 metres per minute, and a ceiling of

7,100 metres. However, the Drache was still nowhere near capable of a role in the armed services, and Ministry officials told Focke-Achgelis to accelerate the development programme. The carrot was an initial production order for a hundred machines, the first thirty of which would be used for research and development purposes.

With the benefit of its hands-on experience at Rechlin, the Ministry was better able to focus on possible roles for such a machine, and it finally issued specifications for five variants. The first, the Fa 223A, was designed for anti-submarine work and carried either a pair of 250-kilogramme bombs or depth charges on external racks. The second, the Fa 223B, was to be used for reconnaissance duties and was fitted with a jettisonable external fuel tank of sixty-six-gallon capacity. Fa 223C was to be assigned to air–sea–land rescue duties and was fitted with a buoyant cradle at the end of the steel winch cable. This was to be lowered through a circular hatch in the floor of the cargo bay and could float on water, enabling a man to swim into it and secure himself, ready to be lifted safely back inside. The fourth variant, the Fa 223D freight transport, was designed to resupply mountain troops, using an electrically operated quick-release hook on the end of the winch cable and a steel cargo net. Lastly, there was the Fa 223E, to be designed as a dual-control trainer. But for now, the first few prototypes were all about getting airborne and less concerned with proving the worth of individual variants.

Unfortunately for Focke-Achgelis, the V1 was lost in February 1941, after 115 successful flights, as a result of sudden engine failure at a height too low for an autorotative landing. But it wasn't long before the V2 was ready to enter the test programme. It bore a close resemblance to the V1, though innovations included a fully glazed cockpit of a type not unlike that of the Heinkel He 111 bomber, familiar to pilots on both sides of the firing line. The laminated glass was later replaced by plexiglass, and it served a useful purpose in giving the pilot and the observer all-round visibility. The observer now also had a machine-gun that he could fire through a sealed weapons port mounted in the lower portion of the nose. In addition, numerous small improvements aided the aerodynamics of the craft, and subsequently these succeeded in raising the speed of later models to 220 kph.

The V2 did not last long: it was destroyed in an Allied air raid soon after it rolled out of the Delmenhorst factory, before serious trials had begun.

The V3 soon followed, and this prototype set the design features for all the models that were to follow. It featured a slightly deeper rear fuselage and open landing gear – the V2's wheels had been covered with streamlined spats. By the time of the V3's appearance, much to everyone's relief at the factory, the Air Ministry had dispensed with the notion of different variants and had settled on one multipurpose type that could combine all five roles. The V3 was the first craft to reflect this new thinking.

Hopes were high now; the project team was full of enthusiasm and optimistic about the future as the Delmenhorst factory began tooling up for production. The V3 had provision for all the specialist equipment previously specified: electric winch, dual controls, and so on. Its construction followed that of its predecessors in having a welded tubular-steel fuselage structure covered with treated fabric both to save weight and ease repairs. It was divided into four compartments: the cockpit was at the very front and accommodated the pilot and the observer/gunner; directly behind them was the load compartment, with its single entrance door on the starboard side. The fuel and oil tanks were located at its rear wall, and beyond them lay the engine compartment. Last of all came the separate tail section.

Access to the pilot's seat was through a single side door at the rear of the cockpit; the observer's seat could be tilted out of the way to allow entry. The engine was mounted, along with its complex and fragile gearbox, centrally in the fuselage and held in place with a series of tensioned steel hawsers. Much later, when a Drache ended up in the hands of the British, their failure to pay attention to advice relating to these hawsers was to lead to disaster, as we shall see.

The gearbox itself was mounted in front of the engine, and both received cooling air through an annular louvred gap in the fuselage between the cargo and the engine bays. Air would enter here, and after passing through a series of vanes it would be forced past the gearbox and the engine, cooling them in the process, before being exhausted through a similar annular gap between the rear of the engine compartment and a firewall divider in front of the tail section.

The large, 108-gallon, self-sealing fuel tank was mounted in a webbing harness hung from the roof of the fuselage on the rear wall of the cargo bay; the wall actually doubled up as the grille, forming the front of the air-intake opening ahead of the engine. It must have been incredibly noisy inside the Drache during flight, with the BMW motor thrumming away and no sound insulation between it and the cockpit. Air would have rushed around the load bay as well, and would have made life for the passengers there very uncomfortable and cold – especially when the Drache was operating, as it did, in mountain areas.

Sky Crane

Focke had wanted to move the concept of using a helicopter as a heavy transport further forward ever since the cargo variant of the Drache had been designed. His ideas were to lead to the development of the Fa 284 'Sky Crane' – a helicopter capable of lifting outsize and awkward loads, for civil and military use. It wasn't until Sikorsky built their own version of Focke's original specification in the 1950s that observers could appreciate just how far ahead of his time Focke had been with this concept. Here was a craft capable of carrying artillery pieces and tanks, as well as men and their equipment, directly to the battlefield, without the need of runways – even gliders needed a landing strip of some kind.

The initial design work was undertaken by one of Focke's contractors – Breguet, a French aircraft-maker working in Toulouse – based on a general scheme outlined by Focke-Achgelis. As it was originally envisaged, the Sky Crane retained the twin-rotor and outrigger system but employed a longer fuselage than the Drache's. Research for this book has thrown up two distinct designs within the project, but since each of them is referred to by the same Fa 284 designation, we will describe them as Project 1 and Project 2.

Project 1 first emerged from the Breguet design office some time in 1942 and closely resembled the established Focke-Achgelis format of having two contra-rotating rotors, one on either side of the fuselage. However, it appears that these tri-bladed rotors were of a new design, for their size bears no resemblance to those on the Fa 223 and appear indeed to be fifty per cent larger. Their construction was also new, being made out of wooden ribs around a central steel spar, covered with three-ply wood laminate, thus saving weight, costs and valuable materials. In plan form the fuselage had the shape of a large 'T', with the lower serif as the tail and rudder. The fuselage, therefore, had a broad, stubby nose, on either side of which were the massive tubular-steel outriggers, each with a rotor mounted at the end. At the base of each outrigger a single BMW 801 radial engine was mounted to power its adjacent rotor, and on the very underside of this was fitted a tele-scopically sprung wheel to cushion landings. To allow easy access to the engines and to save weight, no outer cladding was used on the fuselage except at the rear, where it shrouded the tail and the cockpit.

The plan was for each load to be carried and supported by an underslung steel net or cable, complete with an emergency quick release. The mounting for this was at the very front of the fuselage, exactly in between the outrigger spars. Towards the rear of the fuselage was the cockpit for two crew members, enclosed by a glazed canopy. A small castor wheel, allowing easier ground handling, was mounted in the base of the tail.

When interviewed after the war, the French design staff stated that the aircraft as originally envisaged would have lifted only two tonnes, but that with more powerful engines that figure could have risen to seven or eight tonnes. This estimate was based on experiences with the Drache when it was fitted with larger motors. Because of the problems likely to be encountered when driving the large, unproven rotors of the Sky Crane, and their bespoke mechanisms, a second project was initiated, employing standard Drache rotors.

Project 2 seems to have been more substantial than Project 1. For this project the fuselage had a figure-of-eight cross-section, almost as if two fuselages had been mounted one on top of the other and stuck together, blending aft with a conventional tailfin and stabiliser. The 'upper deck', of circular cross-section, provided space for the cabin, fuel tanks and additional storage. The larger, almost oval cross-sectioned 'lower deck' extended aft for some seven metres before gently curving upwards to blend with the underside of the longer upper deck and the tail. Its potential cargo capacity was getting on for double that of the upper deck, and the craft would have been capable of handling similar loads to the massive Messerschmitt Me 323 Gigant transporter, if not even greater. The nose section of each of the two fused decks was fully glazed, and, like the Drache, may have allowed

56

Taken in June 1938, Göring and Major General Ernst Udet attending Luftwaffe exercises on the Pomeranian coast. He later committed suicide in 1941 after reaching the rank of Colonel-General.

An intriguing picture, showing many of the luminaries featured in this book. Standing left to right, are Siegfried Günter, Dr Eugene Sänger and Dr Arthur Weiss. Seated left to right, are Professor George Madelung, Professor Ernst Heinkel and Professor Heinrich Focke. Notice that the document being studied by the group is a blueprint for the still-born 'Wespe' project.

Hanna Reitsch piloting the Fw 61 at the Berlin Sportslandhalle in 1938. Mounted as evening entertainment during the Berlin motor show running at the time, the audacious displays were the world's first glimpse at the possibilities offered by the helicopter.

The Fa 225 auto-rotating cargo glider. This is the model falsely accredited to have been involved in the successful German operation to rescue Mussolini from his imprisonment in September 1943 and the grafted-on Fa 223 rotor can be clearly seen.

Opposite An Fa 330 'Bachstelze' hovering close to its launching point and giving a good view of its simple landing skids and the tow hook arrangement. Note, too, how exposed the pilot is to the elements.

A seated American officer shows the short length of the 'Bachstelze' to full effect; and in particular, the central steel tube and its additional bracing for the seat and landing skids.

An Fa 223 at rest in an alpine setting; possibly V 11 or V 14. It was hoped the type's excellent performance in this theatre would confirm a regular production schedule, but luck and a disorganised Luftwaffe were not on its side.

A Messerschmitt Me 321 coming in to land.

The enormous Bv 238 V1 undergoing its trials on Lake Schaalsee, shortly prior to its discovery by USAF Mustangs and subsequent sinking.

A fine in-flight view of an Me 323; possibly a 323 E variant. The complex series of landing wheels – so essential in enabling the model to operate at forward grass landing strips – can be clearly seen.

A fascinating view of an Me 323 unloading its cargo of a light truck, under the guidance of Transport Staffel soldiers. The simple construction of the fuselage and its wide load bay proved the craft versatile and capable of absorbing a lot of punishment.

A unique air-to-air view of a pair of Bv 141 B-series models.

The Bv 141 V12; one of the B-series pre-production models. The offset tail section can be clearly seen in this view, with its benefits in visibility for the rear observer.

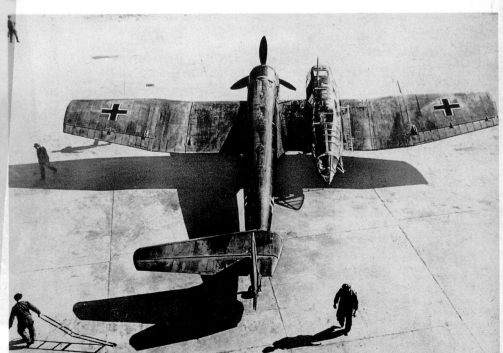

A rare picture of the Gotha Go 229 V2 (Horten Ho IX); the only example to fly under power. Its relatively compact size and revolutionary 'flying wing' profile can be clearly seen here.

A rare cutaway drawing of the Me 261, showing the spacious crew compartment to the rear. Note the large map table, with the rest bunks behind.

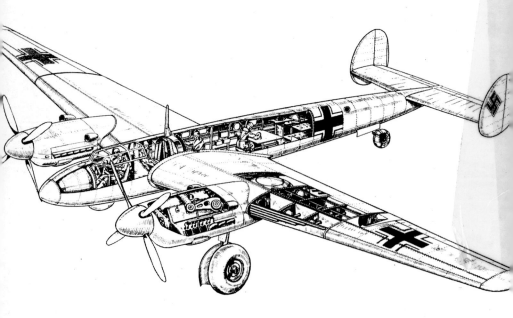

for the provision of a machine-gun position behind armoured glass.

Where the Sky Crane differed fundamentally from the Drache was in its engine mountings. Whereas the Drache made do with only a single BMW engine mounted within the fuselage to drive both rotors, the Sky Crane had, as mentioned, an engine for each rotor. The proposed specification for these engines remains a mystery, but it would certainly have had to be of a higher rating than that of the Drache. For Project 2 the rotors were again mounted on outriggers, but this time each main outrigger was almost commensurate with a full wing, the root of each blending with the upper fuselage. The engine on each was mounted two-thirds of the way along, towards the rotor. This shielded the driveshafts and minimised the number of gearbox components, which in turn saved weight and costs and increased reliability. At rest, the craft would have sat on the tail wheel and on two larger fixed forward wheels set on spars dropped from the outriggers directly below the engine mountings. The gentle upward curve to the rear of the lower deck was necessary in order to provide ground clearance for the landing-wheels and rear access for loading. At rest, the distinctive craft would have had its nose pointing skywards. Access to the cargo bay was by a single large door at the rear, the tailgate of which would, when open, be resting on the ground.

Because problems with the Drache had eaten up resources, Focke's plans for the Sky Crane were destined never to progress beyond a few plans and a handful of finished components. A semi-complete fuselage was rumoured to have been discovered in the ruins of Berlin in 1945, but the story has yet to be confirmed, and whether the fuselage, if it existed, belonged to Project 1 or 2 is not clear. Despite his disappointments, Focke didn't give up on the Sky Crane entirely, and at one time he proposed a hybrid version of the Fa 223 in which two fuselages would be joined in line, tandem-fashion, to form a long, four-rotor craft. The only additional work for such a project would be the designing of a new common central section, and a design was actually found by the Allies at Ochsenhausen, near Stuttgart. It was never implemented; the plan was almost certainly abandoned owing to a lack both of materials and time.

Series production of the Drache began at last in 1942, at the Focke-Achgelis factory in Delmenhorst; but it wasn't long before a British air raid flattened the site for good. The two surviving prototypes were both destroyed, as were the first seven pre-production machines then undergoing final assembly. The workers tried to restore the production line but found it slow and hard work, and in 1943, after turning out only another eight machines, they abandoned Delmenhorst to set up a new plant at Laupheim, near Stuttgart. The carefully planned Air Ministry test programme had, however, been given up for lack of helicopters, and service trials were postponed indefinitely. In the end, only seven machines were built at Laupheim before another air raid, in July 1944, halted production again. At the time of the raid, the V18 was ready for delivery, a further thirteen Drache machines were in assembly, and there were components for a further nineteen. But as the factory was virtually wiped out – only the wind-tunnel escaped serious damage – production and the long-awaited trials were halted once more.

Prior to the raid, things had been looking very optimistic for the Drache. The first to emerge from the Laupheim factory in 1943 had been the V11. This prototype was flown by Karl Bode for a series of information films made for the Air Ministry to demonstrate the amazing abilities of the helicopter. Loads such as a complete two-tonne Fieseler Storch aircraft, or the fuselage of a Messerschmitt Me 109 fighter, were shown being lowered precisely on to tank transporter trucks – Bode using the quick-release cable to great effect for a clean delivery.

However, the price to be paid for such revolutionary feats of daring is that sometimes they go wrong. A Dornier Do 217 bomber had crashed high up on the Vehner Moor, between Osnabruck and Oldenburg in Austria. Initially the V11 was sent to recover it, but the helicopter suffered a mishap of some sort – probably engine-related – and ended up crashing there itself before it could lift the aircraft.

It was decided to try to recover both, using the V14 Drache, as a dramatic demonstration of the helicopter's versatility. Crewed by Karl Bode and the most experienced helicopter pilot in the Luftwaffe, Leutnant Helmut Gerstenhauer, the craft began the recovery operation on 11 May 1944. Prior to its arrival, a small team of Focke-Achgelis engineers and a Luftwaffe recovery company had dismantled the V11 ready for lifting, and during the course of that day the V14 made ten flights, retrieving slung loads of components and leaving them on a track from where they could be loaded on to trucks. The operation continued into the next day and ended with the successful retrieval of all the major components of both the V11 and the Dornier.

Thus something positive was gleaned from the various setbacks that had beset the Drache, and many lessons had been learned in the course of this first operational experience. For example, it was found that the winch cable should be allowed to rotate, thus preventing the cable strands from twisting with the rotating movement of the load; and that an underslung load was better than overloading the small inboard bay.

Following this positive experience, the Air Ministry decided to begin evaluating the craft's potential as a mountain-region transport, and assigned the spare V16 Drache to the Mountain Warfare School at Mittenwald, near Innsbruck in Austria, with the V14 as backup. The main objective of the tests was to see how the Drache performed as a general-purpose all-weather transport, and how its VTOL ability could fit such a role operationally. As the Drache needed no runway and there was no airfield at Mittenwald anyway, the sports ground was pressed into service for the Drache to begin a series of trial landings at altitude. These trials were in anticipation of possible alpine warfare scenarios which might have developed had the war taken a different path in its latter stages. Numerous landings were made at heights of over 1,600 metres above sea-level on various peaks in the area and, because of the very small number of helicopters available, they were made with the greatest of care.

A typical flight consisted of transporting an artillery gun in the load net to a rendezvous with a unit of elite troops high up in the mountains. There, the men of the Alpine Corps would remove the gun from the net and attach it to the winch cable alone, the Drache then hoisting the gun to a higher point where it was impossible to land. The mountain troops would then detach the gun once more, before reattaching it using the special electric-release hook, when the gun would be flown back to Mittenwald. An outward-and-return flight from the base took some fifteen minutes. To have performed the same manoeuvre overland would have taken six hours or more. Thus it was clear to the Air Ministry and the Luftwaffe high command that here was a machine to invest in. Bode and Gerstenhauer, assisted by Unteroffizier Lex, made eighty-three flights over the trial period, with a total flight time of twenty hours. The V16 was still performing perfectly by the time the trials finished in October 1944.

Although the commander of the Mittenwald base, Oberst Kraitmeyer, was so delighted with the Drache that he applied for the helicopter to enter service with his mountain brigades as soon as possible, the Allied air raid on Laupheim in July had changed everything. Following the raid, the Air Ministry decided that it was fruitless to pursue the project any further and that the resources allocated to it should be redeployed in a more productive manner. Only days after the conclusion of the mountain tests, Focke was seconded to Messerschmitt's staff.

The demise of the Drache went hand in hand with Germany's deteriorating position. It was apparent to all but the most fanatical that the war was lost, and the situation throughout the high command was confused. The abortive coup and the failed assassination attempt on Hitler by officers of the Army General Staff on 20 July 1944 had led to a savage purge by the Gestapo. In addition to the internal strife, the Allies, swollen in numbers by fresh American troops, were winning the war in France to the west, while in the east Russia was now on the offensive. Erratic and erroneous decisions were inevitable as various departments vied with each other for precious fuel and materials available in ever smaller amounts. The Drache project was ditched so that resources could be diverted into more tried and tested means of keeping the Luftwaffe functioning.

In the midst of all the confusion, it was nevertheless surprising and even darkly amusing that only weeks after the Drache decision, Focke was given new orders again. He was not only to return to his company but to move his entire operation to Tempelhof Airport in Berlin, where he was to resume flight-testing, organise a third production line, and gear up to make four hundred helicopters a month! Clearly someone in the higher echelons of the Air Ministry had overruled someone else, but at that stage of the war any chance of fulfilling the new orders was scarcely feasible, especially as the new plant was to be established near such a prime Allied bomb target as Berlin. As if that were not enough, Focke's new orders came from the same administration that had dismissed him from Focke-Wulf eight years earlier, and which had since then constantly dithered about whether or not to put its weight behind his helicopter projects.

It seems extraordinary that the administration dwelt so long on development in this area, when, as we shall see, other projects, such as the Heinkel He 162 Volksjäger fighter, reached production only twelve weeks after leaving the drawing board. Surely the RLM could see the potential in the helicopters it had – so why did it not allocate the adequate resources that helicopter development was crying out for? The answer lies probably not only in the increasingly desperate shortages of materials and fuel but in RLM conservatism, lack of imagination and inability to conceive of uses to which helicopters could really be put, until the Mittenwald trials made them crystal clear. And by then it was too late.

The lion's share of available resources was by now in any case being channelled into the V-1 flying bomb and V-2 rocket, into the new jet fighters, and into U-boat production. Focke was faced with a totally unrealistic brief; he was still underfunded in any case, and only five Drache machines were still airworthy. The recovered V11 hadn't been rebuilt – instead, it had been pillaged for spares; and the V12 had been lost in the course of an ill-fated mountain rescue on Mont Blanc: while coming to the aid of a party of French climbers, one of the rotors disintegrated, causing the Drache to crash heavily on to its under-carriage. Its crew were killed.

A Water Wagtail

Autorotation is the name given to the effect of unpowered rotors biting into the air at speed to provide lift, and it is the main principle behind two other machines designed by Focke. The aerodynamic profile of the rotor blades – the 'pitch' – can be altered, either to act like a wing and create lift, or like an airbrake and slow the aircraft down for a controlled, safe emergency landing. The technique is known to every helicopter pilot, and it is a primary recovery procedure in the event of engine failure. However, it's necessary to have sufficient height and forward speed for the landing procedure to work: if the helicopter is too low or too slow, then either the rotors aren't turning fast enough to have any effect, or wind cannot be forced over the rotors fast enough to keep them spinning. Given the early problems he had experienced with the Drache gearboxes, Focke would have known all about the technique of autorotation and how to exploit it.

In 1942 the Air Ministry had begun to consider a possible requirement for a glider capable of steep landing approaches, which could deliver paratroopers or supplies within a smaller area than a conventional glider, and with greater accuracy and control. In the light of its proven Drache design, Focke-Achgelis was approached for help. Focke took to the project quickly and had soon sketched out the bones of a feasible machine. It would use the fuselage of a standard DFS 230 freight glider (of the type that was used during the paratroop invasion of Crete in 1941), and instead of wings it would have a single upper-mounted rotor from the Drache. Unpowered, the craft was designed to be towed to a release point before autorotating down to the landing zone and disgorging its cargo of troops and their equipment.

Once completed, the initial prototype was tested extensively. Towed behind a Heinkel He 45, its steep takeoffs and landings proved the validity of the concept. However, although it received an official designation – Fa 225 – it never saw service with the armed forces, and paratroops were deployed in other ways. Many reports after the war stated that Fa 225s had been used in the successful paratroop mission to free Mussolini from his imprisonment in a hotel at the top of Gran Sasso, the highest mountain in the Apennines, on 12 September 1943. The dictator had been dismissed from office on 25 July following a number of Fascist rebels voting for a restoration of the monarchy. King Victor Emmanuel III then instructed the new government to place Mussolini under arrest. But no concrete evidence appears to support the claim that Fa 225s were used in the mission, none has been uncovered in the research for this book and it seems that the paratroops involved used regular DFS 230 gliders. Other rumours circulating after the war claimed that Otto Skorzeny, the notorious SS-Standartenführer widely credited with running the mission, had considered using a Drache – the very same V12, in fact, that later crashed on Mont Blanc. Legend has the V12 becoming unserviceable at the last moment, forcing Skorzeny to use a Fieseler Storch as the actual 'getaway' aircraft instead. Once again, no evidence to support this view has been discovered. For the record, Skorzeny's role in the mission is actually quite minor as he commanded only the group of commandos who attacked the hotel; another group landed simultaneously at the lower cablecar station to prevent hostile Italian forces from reaching the hotel and foiling the plan. A Major Mors was in actual overall charge, but while Skorzeny, Colonel Student (in charge of the other group) and even Skorzeny's glider pilot, Meyer, all received decorations from Hitler, Mors received no credit. Hitler needed heroes at the time – figures the German public could admire – and so engineered the public news of the mission to throw a favourable light on its stars for the benefit of propaganda.

In looking at the Fa 225, the Air Ministry started to explore new possibilities, this time in developing a more narrowly focused, unpowered helicopter that could be *lifted* on the principles of auto-rotation easily and at low speed. The obvious application for such a craft was in spotting and reconnaissance duties for the navy, which duly began to look at the potential of the concept. The navy soon came up with a requirement for a small craft that could fly from, and be towed by, a U-boat. It followed that such a machine should be capable of being piloted by a naval rating.

Thus Focke-Achgelis was asked to develop what became known as the 'Bachstelze' – the 'Water Wagtail' (designated Fa 330). The Bachstelze was something of a sop thrown to the company to compensate it for the decision not to take the Fa 225 any further and was another proposition entirely: a tiny craft, it was designed to be assembled or dismantled easily and quickly within the confined space aboard a U-boat. It was built around a single steel tube which gave it its length. A basic tail-and-rudder unit was mounted at one end, and the totally exposed pilot sat on a thinly padded and uncomfortable-looking seat at the other. Mounted directly behind the pilot's back was a vertical tubular-steel pylon that fitted into a recessed notch in the main tube and was braced with additional steel outrigging at its base. The outrigging doubled as supports for the seat frame and also acted as landing skids. The vertical pylon was some 1.6 metres high, and at its top was mounted the single three-bladed rotor and its hub. The control mechanism for this was of a much simpler specification than the Drache's, but was still operated by the pilot in the usual fashion, via a series of linkages and rods, terminating in a joystick and rubber pedals in front of the seat.

To start the rotors spinning, a rope was wound round a grooved drum which formed part of the hub, the crew pulling out the rope as if it were a giant child's spinning-top. The tilting hub allowed the pilot to angle the pitch of the now-spinning rotors and thus achieve lift, and the surface speed of a cruising U-boat was sufficient to maintain continuous autorotation, given the efficiency of the rotor and the craft's minimal weight.

The rotor was of small diameter – 7.3 metres – and this made it possible to test the Bachstelze in the large wind-tunnel at Chalais-Meudon in France. The tests disclosed several problems relating to its stability in the air, and it was found that the rotor blades required additional wire bracing. For training pilots, a lower-mounted, tubular outrigger landing gear was mounted, allowing smooth and safe takeoffs and landing, after being towed above a runway from behind a speeding truck much like a modern-day parascending flight.

Operations

After the period of testing, everything went so well for the project that the navy commissioned full-scale production, which led to over 110 examples being built. Fa 330s were used successfully from February 1943 on the Type ix U-boats operating in the Far East. A telephone link, which ran down to the conning tower of the U-boat alongside the tow-cable, enabled the pilot to provide the captain with a running commentary on everything he could see. From the vantage point of his high-tech crow's nest, a pilot with binoculars could see for up to 40 kilometres when the Fa 330 was flying at its full height of 240 metres, whereas from the conning tower the view reached only 8 kilometers. And when the flight was over, the U-boat crew would simply wind in the tow-cable and pull the little craft down as if it were a kite – which effectively it was. The pilot, meanwhile, would operate a small drum brake fitted inside the hub which had the effect of slowing down the rotor and thus cutting lift, allowing a smooth landing back on the spray-lashed deck.

Stories of U-boats being forced to dive while their Fa 330s were still aloft have never been proved, though pilots wore lifejackets in case they had to bale out of their flimsy craft for any reason. If an emergency occurred, the pilot would detach the tow-cable and begin a gentle glide down. To avoid the potential danger of decapitation by the rotor blade on hitting the water, he would then pull a quick-release lever above his head which released the rotor assembly. This would shoot off skywards, dragging out a drogue parachute from within the vertical pylon as it did so, to which the pilot was strapped. The pilot then only had to unlatch his seatbelt before drifting down safely, unencumbered by the heavy frame of his craft, which would fall away into the sea.

Following the end of the war and the recall of all U-boats to their home ports, the little Water Wagtails became collectors' items within the memorabilia market, and examples could be found occasionally in junk shops, the vendors often unaware of the unique importance of these revolutionary yet innocent and fragile-looking machines.

Final Orders

After the flurry of confusion at the end of 1944, the third Focke-Achgelis plant was established at Tempelhof Airport at the beginning of 1945. The company had managed to retain two of the five surviving Drache helicopters on which to base new ones for their gigantic order, and by some miracle they managed to produce a new machine that same February. Almost immediately, it was commanded, on a 'special order from the Führer', to fly to Danzig (modern Gdansk) on the twenty-fifth of the month. Considering the conditions in which the flight had to be made, and the circumstances of the war at the time, that the journey was completed at all is a testimony to the ruggedness of this early helicopter.

Flown by Gerstenhauer and two colleagues, the brand-new Drache took off from Tempelhof on 26 February, after essential maintenance had delayed its departure by a day. It first headed south-west in the direction of Würzburg – actually *away* from Danzig. In any event, Gerstenhauer lost his bearings in a storm and had to land at Crailsheim to weather it. Once the worst of the storm had passed, they took off again and finally landed in Würzburg dangerously short of fuel – the weather had not lifted and they had been flying at a height of only a hundred metres, barely above the tree line.

Having refuelled, they flew north-east the following day and did not stop until they reached Werder, having travelled more than five hundred kilometres in just over six hours. The reason for the lengthy detour has never emerged, but since Werder is only a short drive from Berlin, it's not inconceivable that Gerstenhauer was acting as a courier – either smuggling people or papers out of, or back to, Berlin.

On the third day the team flew further north-east towards Stettin-Altdamm, but continuing bad weather forced them to land at Prenzlau – roughly fifty kilometres south-west of Stettin – for the night. The following day they tried to proceed, but the weather remained poor and they were forced to halt at Stolp-West for another night and take in more fuel – they had covered about four hundred kilometres in the proceding forty-eight hours.

By 5 March the war situation was becoming ever more dangerous, so Gerstenhauer decided to leave Stolp-West before the Russians captured both him and the Drache, and flew to Danzig directly – right over the heads of the advancing Soviet army; he was lucky not to have been shot down while performing this feat.

He reached Danzig only to find that the city was already falling, so he landed outside the city and awaited further orders. When these came, they commanded him to return to Werder. However, no extra fuel had been allocated to the Drache, so Gerstenhauer and his companions had to forage around the area in search of some, since without it the return journey was impossible. They were eventually able to fill their tanks and requisition a full forty-four gallon drum which they rigged up to the main tank after hauling it up inside the cargo bay: a handpump was used by a member of the crew to transfer its contents to the main tank while in flight.

After flying along the Baltic coast for some distance, they reached Garz on the Rügen peninsula, where bad weather once again delayed their progress. It was to be 11 March before they managed to get back to Werder. They had covered a record 1,500 kilometres in a total flight time of 16 hours and 25 minutes. Although they had not been able to fulfil their mission to Danzig, their epic flight bears testimony to the Drache's versatility, and it is worth remembering that even with such an early type of helicopter as this, impressive feats were possible.

In a belated attempt to add operational experience to the Drache programme, in January 1945 the Air Ministry assigned the other three surviving Drache machines to the Luftwaffe's only operational helicopter squadron, Transportstaffel 40 (TS/40), at Mühldorf in Bavaria, under the command of Hauptmann Josef Stangl, who also ran various Flettner machines. But it wasn't long before the unit temporarily had to relocate to Ainring, near Salzburg, and then again to Aigen, also in Austria. TS/40 was originally earmarked to take part in the so-called Alpenfüstung – the alpine 'fortress' intended by the Nazis to be their last redoubt and centre of resistance. (When the Allies overran the area a few months later, they found little evidence of its existence other than a few half-hearted roadblocks, one or two modest ammunition dumps and small numbers of SS troops posing as displaced civilians.)

On their arrival at Aigen, TS/40 found the airfield cluttered with various Messerschmitt Me 109s and other aircraft, so operations, even for helicopters, were all but impossible. As a result, the unit moved yet again, to a forest site deemed suitable at nearby Putterersee, where a group of abandoned lakeside chalets made a much more suitable billet for the crews.

Actual operations, once they got going, were restricted owing to lack of fuel, and when, at the beginning of May 1945, the US 80th Infantry Division advanced on Liezen, TS/40 withdrew first to Radstadt, at the foot of the Alps, and then back to Ainring. Of the three Drache machines, one was destroyed by its pilot to prevent it from falling into enemy hands, but the other two were seized by the Americans, who took Ainring soon afterwards. Stangl himself was captured as he tried to cross the border back into Germany.

Thus the Drache story comes to an end. The Tempelhof factory had been able to produce only four machines, though another fifteen were in production when the plant was overrun by Soviet forces. Of 37 machines, only 11 had ever flown, though between them they had accumulated some 400 hours of flying time and covered 9,000 kilometres, the V14 having logged the longest service at over 170 hours.

As the war ended, the USA was to use an entire aircraft carrier, the USS *Reaper*, to ferry examples of the Messerschmitt Me 262 and Me 163 fighters home, but they had room for only one Drache. The RAF objected to plans to destroy the other (the V14), so Gerstenhauer himself, along with two observers, flew it across the Channel from Cherbourg to RAF Beaulieu on 6 September 1945. RAF Beaulieu was home to the Central Landing Establishment, a cover name for the Airborne Forces Experimental Establishment, which had also received several Bachstelzes to test. Gerstenhauer's flight made history in itself, for it was the first Channel crossing by a helicopter, though any celebrations were to be short-lived.

The V14 made two successful test-flights at Beaulieu. Later reports about what happened on its doomed third flight in Britain have caused the truth to become blurred, but as far as research has been able to ascertain the problem was linked to the engine mountings. Every twenty-five flying hours the tensioned steel hawsers securing the engine had to be tightened using a special tool called a 'tensionmeter'. Such a tool wasn't aboard the V14 when it came over to Britain, so when Gerstenhauer warned the RAF technicians about the potential danger of ignoring this requirement, he was met with stony indifference, if not the suspicion that he was trying to hide something. As his advice was ignored, it came as no surprise to Gerstenhauer when, during a flight on 3 October, a driveshaft broke under the strain imposed by the swaying engine. It occurred as he was attempting a vertical ascent, but as he had reached only twenty metres he did not have enough height to make an autorotative landing. The Drache dropped like a stone and was wrecked. Fortunately, no serious injuries were sustained by the crew, but the crash ended British evaluation of the new machine for good, and valuable lessons were lost. Rumours that the remains were buried in a farmer's field remain unconfirmed.

The Humming Bird

Undeterred by the favour shown his rival, Anton Flettner had continued to work on his revolutionary helicopter designs following the success of his Fl 265. His dogged patience paid off when in July 1940 he unveiled his latest design: the Fl 282 'Kolibri' – 'Humming Bird' – and announced plans for production.

The layout of the Kolibri differed from previous Flettner models in that the engine was mounted directly behind the pilot, and behind the engine was a large conventional tail stabiliser that controlled the turbulence created by the wash from the rotors. Two contra-rotating rotors were used once again, each powered by their own driveshaft through a common gearbox. The tubular-steel fuselage was covered in fabric, with a sheet-metal cover over the hot engine, and it was equipped with a non-retractable undercarriage.

Of all the helicopters produced in Germany during the war, it was to be the Kolibri that saw the most service, flew the greatest number of hours, and pushed the technology furthest.

The Air Ministry and, in particular, the navy were so impressed by the prototype that fifteen were ordered, to be followed by thirty production-line models, all built to the original ship-borne reconnaissance specification. Following flight-testing throughout 1941 of the first two prototypes, all these machines were completed successfully at Flettner's factory at Bad Tolz, near Munich. The tests were designed to push the machines to the very limits of performance, and they did not stop with the first two prototypes. For example, the V5 was used repeatedly to practice takeoff and landing on a four-square-metre landing pad mounted on the cruiser *Köln*. Landings were easy, but takeoffs in rough seas turned out to be tricky for the pilots to master, and so the development of techniques was deferred until better handling methods had been developed.

As far as general reliability was concerned, the Kolibri made use of a robust engine of proven track record which required servicing only once every four hundred hours – as opposed to the Drache's twenty-five hours – and, although heavy for its size, its components were of such high quality that there was little need for servicing between general overhauls. One machine ran for 170 hours before needing attention of any kind.

The first two 'A' series prototypes had enclosed cockpits; all subsequent models had open cockpits and were designated 'B' series. By 1943 over twenty B-1 models were in service, seeing action in the Mediterranean, the Aegean and the Baltic. Their roles included ferrying items between ships and reconnaissance of Allied warships and submarines, but, as the war dragged on, Luftwaffe high command began to consider converting the Kolibri for use on the battlefield. Until this point, the helicopter had carried a single pilot, so a quick solution was to make room for an observer – believed essential for safe operations in a crowded combat zone. Thus the B-2 series was created, with what must be the most uncomfortable and dangerous dicky-seat ever devised:

an open, rear-facing seat directly behind the engine in a hollowed-out section of the aft fuselage. The unlucky soul who ended up here would have been even more deafened than the pilot; the pilot at least had forward airspeed to carry the engine fumes and noise backwards – precisely to where the observer sat. But despite the drawbacks, the B-2 turned out to be a useful spotter when used in conjunction with ground artillery batteries, and an observation unit was set up in 1944 comprising three Kolibri and three Drache helicopters.

Also in 1944, satisfied with the new craft, the Air Ministry issued a production contract to BMW to produce a thousand examples. But just as the Munich plant was gearing up, it was bombed and devastated by the Allies; the flattened site had had time to produce only twenty-four Kolibri machines. Although Flettner had planned a larger version, the Fl 339, it was never completed and what there was of it was lost in the confusion of the last days of the war.

At least the Kolibri helicopters went down fighting. They saw action on the Eastern Front, and in February 1945, when the Soviet advance had become uncheckable, the observation unit was able to spot the irresistible advance of the 1st and 2nd White Russian Armies – though such was the poor state of German forces at the time that they could only observe the advance – there were no ground elements to direct into a counter offensive. Towards the end, most of the surviving Kolibri machines were stationed at Berlin-Rangsdorf, still in use as artillery spotters, but falling victim one by one to Soviet fighters and flak batteries. The only one to survive fell into the hands of the Russians. Three of the aircraft had been assigned to Stangl's TS/40 helicopter squadron, and when the Americans captured the unit, they commandeered the two remaining machines they found. Thus ended another chapter in the German designs of military helicopters.

Other Designers

Other German engineers were engaged in helicopter development as well as Focke and Flettner. The Luftwaffe's conventional machines were slowly losing ground to the more sophisticated Allied aircraft, and the situation was partly redressed only by the emergence of jet fighters like Messerschmitt's Me 262. The Air Ministry looked kindly on the avant-garde ideas of all these engineers in the belief that at least in the field of helicopter flight some advantage might be gained, but it gave them little material encouragement. Smaller players, like Döbloff and the firm of Nagler and Rolz, developed ideas of their own, but lack of resources or Air Ministry dithering led to the closure of all the less important operations as time passed.

It was unfortunate that they were neglected, for some of the notions they had could have been of great value. Baron Friedrich von Döbloff, an Austrian, began building a small one-man helicopter in 1942; it bore a passing resemblance to the Bachstelze. Although it was incapable of independent forward flight and required a tow to get airborne, its unique propulsion system warrants a look. The pilot sat in front of the fuel tank, which fed a sixty-horsepower petrol engine mounted behind it. The engine in turn powered an Argus supercharger mounted within the rotor's hub above the fuselage. Here, air was drawn into a small scoop, then compressed and mixed with pre-heated petrol from the tank. The mixture was then channelled up into the rotor head itself, and from there into each of the three hollowed-out blades. At the tip of each blade was a small combustion chamber with a narrow outlet nozzle that directed the resulting exhaust-jet converting it into a rotating force capable of spinning the rotors without the torque problems experienced when driving rotors directly from an engine in the fuselage. In short, a jet-propelled helicopter.

Five prototypes of Döbloff's machine were built, all with semi-enclosed bodywork and successively more powerful engines than that of the original machine, but serious production was never considered. At the end of the war the surviving models fell into American hands and disappeared amid the military equipment and arms accumulated by the advancing Allies.

What were the Allies making of all this advanced technology? At the time of Hanna Reitsch's stunt-flying in the Deutschlandhalle in 1938, Sikorsky's own experimental model was capable only of non-directional tethered flight. Sikorsky's first operational model, the R4, didn't see service until 1944 in the Japanese theatre of war and was limited to basic reconnaissance owing to its small size and low range, although it did sterling service performing the first medevac – medical evacuation – in the Burmese jungle. During the war, the development of helicopters in Germany was far more advanced than it was among the Allies. Long after the war was over, one of the Drache pilots visited the USA and told USAF pilots exactly how his machine had ferried ammunition at Mittenwald. The pilots simply didn't believe him. As for the British, though usually great innovators, they failed completely to anticipate any need for the production of helicopters. When at last the country's first helicopter manufacturer – Westland – was established, it merely built Sikorsky machines under licence, having learned little from German technology and experience.

After the war, Döbloff moved to the USA and worked for McDonnell as their chief helicopter engineer. His innovative ideas included a project for a *disposable* one-man helicopter, the XH-20, which, although it didn't progress beyond an initial prototype owing to high fuel consumption and consequently limited range, is a measure of the originality of his thinking.

As for the Drache, though the British succeeded only in wrecking their example, its story didn't end with the war. Both the French and Czechoslovak aircraft industries began to build machines modelled on it from components salvaged from the Tempelhof factory. The Czechs built only two, losing both in crashes by 1949; but the French, who had secured the services of Heinrich Focke himself, assembled a new team for him under the auspices of the Société Nationale de Constructions Aéronautiques du Sud-Est (SNCASE).

The first task for Focke's new group was to rescue the blueprints for the Drache, which *French* troops had tried mistakenly to burn after capturing them. Two fuselages and a mass of components had been spirited out of Tempelhof, however, and the SNCASE factory at Argenteuil made additional parts as necessary. Designated SE 3000, the first Drache 'Mark II' flew in October 1948, drawing on SNCASE's previous experience in building Cierva autogyros under licence before the war – just as Focke himself had done.

The SE 3000 was, however, plagued with small problems, and it wasn't until 1950 that the test programme proper began, using underslung loads and so forth. A total of three examples were to have been built, but before that could happen SNCASE decided that twin rotors were a thing of the past and the project was shelved. Although it had made a large contribution to SNCASE's knowledge and experience, the SE 3000 turned out to be too unstable and unreliable for long-term peacetime applications. Although the problems it manifested might well have been easily curable with today's technology, and although helicopter development did continue, the question remains whether helicopters would ever have assumed such a prominent role in all our lives today without the initial impetus from Germany.

Chapter Three

GIANTS OF THE LUFTWAFFE

An Early Demand for Transports

The Luftwaffe high command had always viewed the wartime air force as much as a transport facility as a fighting service. At its height the Third Reich occupied most of mainland Europe and North Africa, and for its forces to have relied solely on land and sea lines for supplies would have been impractical. Aero manufacturers and designers therefore looked at how to construct large-capacity aircraft capable of resupplying the furthest-flung outposts of the Reich within a day, as well as having troop-carrying capability for large-scale assaults.

By contrast, Great Britain had little need for such planes: its empire was spread across the globe, and the distances between its colonies were so great that sea transport was the only viable option. As a result, the RAF had few air freighters at the start of the war, and these – all converted bombers or antiquated civilian airliners – turned out to be woefully inadequate during the years of conflict that followed. For this reason, along with the armaments supplied by the USA, the Douglas DC-3 Dakota transports were in great demand, and the Dakota, though also a converted civilian airliner, was to prove its worth as a military support aircraft. Without it, the Allied cause might very well have foundered, since there were few similar planes on the Allied side.

The Luftwaffe, however, had had its own transport aircraft even before the war, integrating them with the overall system and making full use of them in tactical situations. In 1919, days before the Treaty of Versailles was signed, Junkers flew the first prototype of their first transporter, the F 13. The F 13, an all-metal monoplane in the emerging

75

Junkers style, was to continue in production for 10 years, and over 320 were sold in more than 24 countries: a remarkable achievement, given the parlous state of the German aero industry at the time. And after the secret base at Lipetsk had been established, it was felt that a manufacturer should set up a plant in the USSR.

The reason for this was both to circumvent the Treaty of Versailles and to keep production costs down – they were lower in Russia than in Germany. Junkers duly set up a factory at Fili and set about designing a new transporter for it to build – fighters and bombers were not yet on the agenda at that time. Using the experience gained by producing a whole series of successive F 13 designs, Junkers came up with a simple, tough, three-motor model that employed a Junkers-built engine in the nose and two Mercedes-Benz motors on the wings. Although only nine aircraft were constructed, the layout and configuration worked well, and the G 23, as it was known, soon led to the G 24, which used all-Junkers engines. In 1926 the factory sought to replace the G 24, and after examining two different proposals settled on a model that continued the three-motor concept. Incidentally, a similar idea was being pursued by the Ford Motor Company in the USA. Called the 'Trimotor', it was Henry Ford's idea to build the rugged aircraft on similar mass-production principles to those he'd developed for building cars, and was a great success.

Iron Annie

The new design, called the Ju 52, first flew in 1932, and was sold extensively around the world as a civilian airliner. Various engines were used, depending on the export market, but both American Pratt and Whitneys and British Bristols were employed at one time or another. From late 1932 the first Ju 52s entered service with Lufthansa, to be used on the Berlin–London and Berlin–Rome routes. Capable of carrying up to 17 passengers, over 230 of these aircraft were to be delivered to Lufthansa alone, and they continued in service until almost the end of the war, flying regularly to Switzerland, Spain, Turkey, Portugal and Sweden.

The first military application of the plane took place during the Spanish Civil War when, nicknamed 'Iron Annie', it was used as a light bomber, though, as it quickly became clear that its usefulness as a bomber was eclipsed by specialised aircraft such as the Dornier Do 17, it soon began its 'proper' career as a transport. The first twenty aircraft supplied to Franco were used to ferry in 10,000 Moroccan troops – the first major military role the Ju 52 was to play.

Production was reorganised in the mid-1930s, and Iron Annie continued to be produced in ever-greater numbers. By the time the Luftwaffe established its Transport Command in 1937, more than five hundred of them were in service; and at the beginning of the war its supporting role in blitzkrieg offensives was crucial. Following the costly losses sustained during the invasion of Crete in 1941, however, the number of Iron Annies thereafter available was lower, and production finally ceased in 1943, after eleven years, as a result of the worsening situation on the ground and the need to divert precious matériel to fighter production. The following gradual attrition of the remaining Ju 52s made the army's situation worse, and for production to cease with no similar replacement was regarded in some quarters as sheer folly; but the decisions of Speer's Ministry of Armament and War Production were not to be questioned.

Versatile as it was, Iron Annie was noisy, narrow and cramped, and a devil to load and unload in a hurry since it had only one small side door. It desperately needed a larger door to provide rapid access, but the basic design was destined never to receive one. Two larger versions were built, however. The Ju 252 and 352 had larger side doors, but production was extremely limited and was cut off in 1943 along with that of the original 52. The Ju 352 also had another special feature which warrants a mention here. Its nickname was 'Herkules', and it was fitted with a hydraulically operated rear ramp as its main load bay door: identical in principle to a modern-day Lockheed C-130 'Hercules' as operated by air forces worldwide and many other subsequent transport designs. It ended its short production in 1944, a year after that of the 52 and 252.

It seems very odd that the Luftwaffe had to put up with such an old-fashioned design as that of Iron Annie in the first place. It may have been a reliable and rugged aeroplane, but as it had originally flown in 1932 it was practically obsolete by the time the war began. It was a slow flyer, and its labour-intensive construction methods were slow too

– and inefficient. The only obvious innovation that the machine could boast was its corrugated stressed duralumin skin, which could take a lot of abuse and gave the machine its necessary workhorse characteristics.

However, other designs were in the pipeline.

Sealion, 'Mammoth' and 'Giant'

Shortcomings in Iron Annie were revealed as plans took shape for Operation Sealion – Germany's invasion of Britain. From the moment that Transport Command started work with the Luftwaffe high command in planning its crucial role, the distances to be covered and the amount of equipment to be moved began to dwarf the capacity and capability of its existing freighters. An Iron Annie could carry only a few tonnes of small equipment up to about 1,100 kilometres, and this was considered inadequate, especially in view of the fact that vehicles and artillery pieces were going to have to be airlifted.

The ability to occupy large tracts of open country both quickly and with the element of surprise would pay off only if an army could establish an effective transport supply and therefore ensure ground superiority. This, however, would need transport aircraft superior to the Ju 52, and fast, if the Sealion timetable were to be met. Willy Messerschmitt realised that the invasion would require airfreighters capable of quickly getting to England adequate numbers of tanks and self-propelled artillery if the plan were to succeed. And since most of the British Expeditionary Force had escaped from Dunkirk there would now be an experienced army waiting for them.

Bearing all this in mind, Messerschmitt wrote to Ernst Udet in October 1940 proposing a plan whereby tanks be fitted with hard points (attachment points) capable of attaching to an overhead wing and rear tail section. Acting as gliders, they could then be towed over the Channel by up to four Ju 52s at a time, before landing on skids mounted over the caterpillar tracks of each tank. After shedding the glider components, they could advance on the enemy within minutes of landing and thus gain the element of surprise. Clearly Messerschmitt saw production possibilities here, but Udet remained unconvinced, especially when he calculated the likely cost of having four transport planes committed to each tank, the more so since while in flight both they and the gliding tank would be sitting ducks for any marauding Spitfire or Hurricane.

Planning for Sealion had begun in 1940, but the invasion plans were shelved in December following the Battle of Britain. Hitler now made the worst mistake of his career, turning his eyes towards Russia and his mind to a new invasion – Operation Barbarossa. Germany had always intended to move against its uneasy ally – the concept of *Lebensraum* in the east had always been central to Nazi thinking. It was just that having had to postpone the conquest of Britain, the conquest of the USSR was brought forward. Britain could wait until later, when Russia had been laid low and German air superiority over the Channel had been re-established. However, the war was now opened on two fronts; heavy transport would be required for both.

The Luftwaffe high command and Transport Command had to decide quickly what the best means of supplying that need would be. Should there be a new powered freighter to replace the Ju 52, or should they go for the cheaper and simpler option of a large glider, the potential of which had already been hinted at in Messerschmitt's tank-transporter proposal, and borne out by operations already undertaken using gliders that had been developed by the State Institute for Glider Research and the firm of Gothaer Waggonfabrik?

Given that the first mission of most transport aircraft into Russia – always, of course, depending on the ferocity of the reception they received from defending Soviet troops – was likely to be its last, clearly the most cost-effective solution was to use gliders. Having reached a decision, the Technical Bureau issued a tender for the rapid development of a so-called Grossraumlastensegler, a large-capacity transport glider, to the two manufacturers thought most likely to come up with viable proposals: Junkers, because of the Ju 52, and Messerschmitt, simply because the firm's star had risen with every project it had undertaken (with the possible exception of the Me 210 heavy fighter, which was proving unreliable in early trials). The basic specification called for the successful glider to be capable of carrying either an 88-millimetre gun with its towing vehicle or a medium tank. Under the cover name Projekt Warschau (Project Warsaw), Junkers were allocated the codename Warschau-Ost, and Messerschmitt Warschau-Sud.

The Junkers design didn't live up to expectations. Its Ju 322

'Mammut' – 'Mammoth' – had originally been conceived during the latter half of October 1940 for Sealion, but the company hadn't fully evaluated the project's given specification. The brief issued to Messerschmitt had allowed the use of steel in the construction, but that issued to Junkers had asked for an all-wooden airframe. Perhaps this was a blunder. Because the latter company was skilled precisely in metal constructions – witness Iron Annie – the project team immediately hit problems in finding enough wood of sufficient quality with which to make a start, and this situation led to a build-up of tension between the design and the construction departments. In the event, wood rot and weak glues were responsible for a number of failures in the prototype, which, when it eventually made its maiden flight, turned out to be dangerously unstable during the towed takeoff phase. The project was abandoned in 1941 on the orders of the Air Ministry, which could see no improvement for the design in sight, and today the Mammut is remembered only as having the largest wingspan of any aircraft developed by Germany during the war.

Messerschmitt's glider, the Me 263, on the other hand, presented the Ministry with no problems, and the contract was duly presented to them.

One is left wondering why Junkers were given unfamiliar material to work with. The Technical Bureau knew of the company's prowess in metal construction, so why force it to use wood? If the competition were to have had any meaning, a level playing field should have been provided; but with the hindsight of over half a century, it would appear that the dice were loaded in Messerschmitt's favour.

The Messerschmitt team, based in Leipheim and under the direction of Josef Fröhlich, had designed a deceptively simple machine, having paid attention to questions of cost from the first day. Rather than using a heavy steel monocoque – a self-supporting fuselage – in its construction, the team had opted to build a fuselage from interlaced tensile-steel tubing provided by the Mannesmann company, augmented with wooden spars and covered with doped fabric. This solution saved construction time and development costs, and also made for quick and simple repairs in the field if necessary. The weight saving by comparison with an all-metal construction was also significant, allowing for a greater payload. The Me 263 was redesignated the Me 321 and quickly earned the nickname 'Gigant' – 'Giant' – for the obvious reason of its vast size. The smoothly contoured nose stood over six metres high and opened out as two massive clamshell doors (which would rival those of a modern C-130 Hercules). The doors could be opened only from the inside, by Transport Command troops who would then lower ramps to the ground from the loading bay, allowing the tank or gun-carriage being transported to drive in or out. Smaller, passenger doors were located at the rear of the fuselage. The huge wing was all of one piece and was mounted on top of the fuselage; its construction was similar to that of the fuselage itself. The slim, tapered tail section extended aft behind the wing's trailing edge (the edge of the wing facing the rear; the edge of the wing that faces forwards, into the wind, is the leading edge).

A series of duckboards could be placed across the floor of the loading bay for reinforcement when carrying heavy loads such as tanks, or placed higher up in the fuselage to provide an upper deck for carrying troops. Over a hundred men and their personal equipment could be carried in this configuration. Compared with the Ju 52, the Gigant represented a tremendous advance, offering a loading bay some six times larger, at around a hundred square metres. Messerschmitt had also been clever enough to design the cargo bay, and its gross cargo weight of 23,000 kilogrammes, to replicate the permissible load-space of a train's 'flat car' – a low, flat wagon normally used to carry vehicles. If it could go by train, it could go into a Gigant.

It's not too difficult to imagine a likely scenario for the design. Trains laden with essential supplies and equipment would arrive at a specially prepared forward rail-head terminating at an airfield. Special cranes would be moved into position to transfer the cargo from the wagons to wheeled dollies. These would then be driven up to the fleet of waiting Gigant gliders and their tug aircraft, where more cranes would transfer the loads inboard, supervised by loadmasters from Transport Command who would ensure that the weight was distributed correctly – as is done today. Once they were happy, the loadmasters would signal the OK to the pilots. Then the clamshell doors would be closed and the Transport Command troops on board would take their seats for the flight.

Each Gigant would be towed by a five-engined Heinkel He 111Z tug. After revving up for what would have seemed an age, the ungainly formation would have begun trundling down the runway. An observer standing by the side of the runway would be deafened by the sharp roar of the five engines of the tug, and his nose would be stung by acrid exhaust fumes as the 111Z thundered past. Then he would hear the bass rumble of the glider's wheels as it lumbered past in a powerful rush before climbing into the air at a speed of only 80 kph, the Heinkel following it into the air a few seconds later.

With the Gigant, the restrictions placed by the relatively small Iron Annie on moving goods and equipment in volume would have been swept away, and the transporting of material could have been irrevocably revolutionised in Germany's favour. But in reality the system did not work as smoothly as in the scenario just given. In fact, difficulties were to lead to the development of a powered version of the freighter; but before looking at that story, it is worth taking a closer look at the history of the Me 321 Gigant and its career.

A glider requires no flight crew other than a pilot, and the first Me 321 Gigant was no exception to this commonly held rule. The single-seat cockpit was placed high up in the fuselage, just forward of the wing and above the nose doors. It was reached by a stepladder bolted to the inner wall of the fuselage. In order to keep costs under control and to speed up development, the Messerschmitt team opted for a simple undercarriage, mounting the aircraft on to four jettisonable wheels for takeoff, with a simple skid beneath the tailfin. The two Messerschmitt Me 109 nose-wheels at the front and the two Junkers Ju 90 main wheels at the rear were retrieved by ground staff and recycled. Landings were made on four extendable skids mounted in the underside of the fuselage.

The first prototype, Me 321 V1, lifted off from the Leipheim plant behind a Junkers Ju 90 on 25 February 1941 carrying three tonnes of ballast to aid weight distribution. Messerschmitt's test-pilot, Baur, reported heavy controls and sluggish responses during an otherwise uneventful twenty-two-minute flight. From then on it was decided to enlarge and armour the cockpit of future examples so that it could accommodate a co-pilot and a radio operator; and dual controls were installed to help handle the monster. Electric servo motors were also added, to power and move the huge wing flaps, and as a result of further tests provision was added later for a rear-mounted braking parachute twenty metres in diameter. Auxiliary rockets mounted on the wings were designed to assist in takeoff, as even the power provided by Messerschmitt Me 110 heavy fighters, also used as tugs, was insufficient to get a fully loaded Gigant airborne.

Takeoffs continued to be a major problem despite these improvements, and several accidents and near-misses were reported during the rest of the 1941 test programme. The single Ju 90 was not powerful enough to act as an adequate tug, and as an interim measure the Me 110s were brought in, a configuration of three, a so-called Troikaschlepp, hauling a single Gigant into the air. This was a difficult manoeuvre. The centre aircraft had a longer tow-line than the others in order to keep the three planes properly apart, but what with tow-cables snapping unexpectedly and auxiliary rockets firing erratically, the life expectancy of an Me 110 tug, and therefore its crew, could be short.

The whole programme might have come to an embarrassing end if Ernst Udet had not approached Heinkel and asked him to come up with a solution to the problem of the tug. Heinkel's response was the He 111Z. 'Z' stood for Zwilling – 'twins'. By taking two He 111 bombers and fusing them together with a shared central wing, the resultant five-engined hybrid was capable of towing a Gigant with ease with its single tow-cable and was soon adopted as the preferred tug. Despite this step forward, however, the Messerschmitt factories at Leipheim and Obertraubling in Regensburg were to produce only 150 Gigant gliders. The reason was that the aircraft was facing problems in Russia. Operation Barbarossa wasn't unfolding in anything like the way that had been envisaged, and the Gigant fell victim to the Russian climate, bad weather being only one such misfortune to befall the Gigant.

Although superior on the grounds of cost, the glider didn't have the ability to make successive approaches to crowded airfields, and once on the often muddy ground it was almost impossible to move without special vehicles which were in short supply on the Eastern Front. Transport Command troops were necessary on every flight, too, to repack the landing drogue parachutes and replace the takeoff rockets – if supplies of the latter were available. Added to these problems, and admittedly before the advent of the He 111Z, the Troikaschlepp arrangement provided only for a range of some four hundred kilometres in any one direction, which wasn't enough for a safe operating zone.

In early 1942 the remaining Me 321s were pulled out of frontline service in Russia, in anticipation of the forthcoming Operation Herkules, in which a fleet of the gliders, towed mainly by He 111Zs, were to have captured Malta. However, the plan was abandoned during the planning stage for want of sufficient tugs, so smaller raids were devised instead, involving assaults on targets such as the Romanian oilfields. After a year of inactivity, the Me 321s were sent back to Russia to be part of the relief operation for General Paulus's beleaguered 6th Army at Stalingrad; but by the time they reached the front line, no suitable airfields remained under German control in the Stalingrad area, and they were returned to Germany.

With the cancellation of the Stalingrad mission, the Gigant gliders were to see little further action, and they were either mothballed or broken up, though some were converted into powered Me 323s (of which more below). A planned operation for the summer of 1943, in which a fleet of the remaining 321s would have landed troops on Sicily, was abandoned owing to inadequate landing sites. Also, the distance to be covered was too great, even for the powerful He 111Z.

'Longer Legs' for the Giant

As a result of continuing feedback from Transport Command pilots and crews in Russia, the Leipheim team, this time under the leadership of Diplom Ingenieur Degel, had long since begun to look at ways of improving the operational capability of their design. They decided eventually on a powered version of the Gigant.

The new project, designated Me 323, could be developed rapidly, using engines easily adapted to the role. The French Gnome-Rhône company had continued to produce its own GR14N engine, as used in the Bloche 175 bomber. Borrowing this engine wouldn't place any extra burden on Germany's own overstrained and tightly controlled aero industry, so the GR14N was adopted. At first only four of them were fitted to a strengthened Me 321 wing: a pair were fixed to each leading edge, the starboard couple rotating in the opposite direction to that of the port couple to provide a balance of torque forces. The performance was modest: the top speed was only 210 kph – some 80 kph slower than the old Iron Annie – though this can be attributed both to its weight and aerodynamically inefficient large frontal area.

A fixed undercarriage had been installed on the 323: a bogie at the very front held four small wheels, while six larger ones were mounted in two tandem lines of three each alongside the outer wall of the cargo bay. All the side wheels were shrouded in an aerodynamic fairing and were attached to massive springs that would plant them evenly and surely on to the ground, no matter what the terrain. Each of the six rear wheels was fitted with servo-assisted pneumatic brakes, making the new Gigant capable of stopping within two hundred metres – a necessary precaution given the state of many of the forward position airstrips in Russia. This wheel arrangement still exists today, and the distributive approach to load-bearing pioneered on the Me 323 is evident on such modern aircraft as the US C-5 Galaxy transport.

The rear tail skid of the old 321 was retained, although it now touched the ground only when the plane was at rest if the finely judged centre of gravity (c.o.g.) had moved too far to the rear. If the front wheels remained off the ground after loading, the Gigant's cargo was judged to be too badly distributed for the plane to fly safely, and the weight had to be redistributed to balance the c.o.g. – a crude but effective control. Photographs show that a single man could pull the Gigant over on to its rear skid by himself if the aircraft were loaded correctly, so finely balanced could it be – though under battle conditions haste often prevented such accurate loading, and badly distributed cargoes often shifted about.

The four-engined Me 323 'C' series, the first produced, was considered a stepping-stone towards the six-engined 'D' series. It still required the aid of the Troikaschlepp or the He 111Z for fully laden takeoffs, but it could return to base under its own power when empty. This compromise clearly offered little advantage over the 321, so the V2 prototype became the first to feature six engines – the first six-engined aircraft in the Luftwaffe. It flew for the first time early in 1942 and effectively became the prototype for the 'D' series version.

The 'D' series had fewer side windows than the 321, which simplified it, reduced weight still further, and cut costs. There were, however, two extra crew members: a flight engineer was installed in his own small cockpit within each wing, between the inner and middle engines. Their job was to monitor the synchronisation of each of the three engines and the variable-pitch propellers on their wing, although the pilot could override their controls with his own if he so wished. In flight, the aircraft was considered harder to handle than its predecessor, and the presence of the engineers was intended to ensure that the pilot could concentrate on flying without worrying about the state of the motors. The jettisonable auxiliary rockets of the 321 were retained, with three types now listed for use: they could be specified in packs of eight, six or four, depending on their power, though they continued to be temperamental, and the flight crew had to wear protective clothing in case anything went wrong during their burn time of thirty seconds – which it frequently did.

By September 1942, with full certification approved by the Technical Bureau, both the Leipheim and the Obertraubling factories were delivering Gigant freighters for use in the Tunisian campaign. At first, two Gruppen were converted to the new 323s, having hitherto operated with Iron Annies. Using Sicily as their base, they ferried materials and troops across the southern Mediterranean to Rommel's Afrika Korps. In this theatre of war, with the risk of attack by Allied fighters increasing, some form of defensive armament was required – the original 321s had been unarmed. The Me 323 'D' carried a 7.9-millimetre MG 15 machine-gun in each of the nose doors, with two more on either side of the rear fuselage section. Extra Transport Command troops could be carried to man six heavier-calibre machine-guns from window ports along the length of the fuselage. However, experience in Africa necessitated the replacement of the nose guns with a pair of thirteen-millimetre MG 131 machine-guns and additional positions both in the nose and along the fuselage.

The 'Elastoplast Bomber'

Meanwhile, the original engines were earning a reputation for unreliability, the most common problems being excessive vibration and overheating. As the supply of engines from France was also subject to much disruption on account of the war, an alternative was sought in a unit based on the Gnome-Rhône design but built under licence; this was the 990-horsepower LeO 451. These were connected to twin-bladed, variable-pitch propellers, and the introduction of these alone brought a

30 kph increase in speed. However, there was an overall drop in power output, and this reduced the advisable maximum freightage to twelve tonnes. This payload, however, still far exceeded that of any other transport aircraft, anywhere in the world, in service at the time.

The beleaguered Afrika Korps, then struggling in Tunisia, came to respect the Gigant. The soldiers nicknamed it the Leukoplastbomber – the 'Elastoplast bomber' – although, in spite of rumours to the contrary, in service the Gigant was neither fragile nor prone to catch fire. In fact, it was capable of taking considerable punishment – more than any other aircraft. Allied fighters might exhaust their ammunition trying to shoot it down, but despite their efforts the Gigant would lumber on through it all to its destination. But it was not invincible, especially when carrying inflammable material: introduced as a replacement for the Ju 52 to ferry fuel out to the desert, forty-three out of forty-four planes were lost by the middle of May 1943, by which time Rommel's Afrika Korps had been defeated.

A drubbing such as the Gigant received in Tunisia let the aircraft in for some severe criticism. Although production had reached a level of almost one plane a day as early as January 1943, the losses it sustained in this role as fuel tanker couldn't be made up. However, now that its makers had gained vital experience, they were able to make additional modifications in a series of successive variants. One of the most important was an improved system for anchoring payloads and thus preserving the optimum centre of gravity. Another was to add a large broad-bladed anchor to the tail, which the crew could release during the landing approach to pull the aircraft up in a shorter distance, the anchor having gouged out reams of turf in the process. By April 1943 the basic production model – by now the 'E' series – boasted more powerful engines, larger fuel tanks, a strengthened fuselage and heavier armament than the 'D' series. The new armament included a rear-firing machine-gun for the radio operator and, behind each outer engine, an electrically operated turret fitted with twin twenty-millimetre machine-guns set in the wing and operated by remote control.

The 'Rhino' Version

The losses in North Africa had been so crushing that a new approach was needed if the Gigant were to stay in service. The problems caused by its slow speed couldn't be overcome, and its large bulk made it an obvious target for strafing by Allied fighters when it was on the ground. It was concluded that further improvements could be made to its defensive capability, and indeed that if enough weaponry were installed the plane could operate in an *offensive* role. Two or three prototypes were constructed with this in mind; they were given the name of Waffenträger – 'weapons carriers'. These WTs had no fewer than eleven twenty-millimetre machine-guns, and a further four of heavier calibre, while two extra (manned) turrets were mounted in the wings, the assembled armaments calling for a crew of twenty-one. More than one and a quarter tonnes of extra armour cladded the fuselage, and the clamshell doors at the front were replaced by a solid nose in which yet another gun-turret was installed. This distinctive feature earned the unlikely machine the nickname 'Rhino'. It was intended for use as an escort to convoys of regular Gigants, or (ultimately) as a launch platform for such weapons as the V-1 flying bomb; but its lack of manoeuvrability and speed were judged too much of a handicap, and convoys continued to be escorted by conventional fighters. There is, though, evidence that one of the Rhinos at least was used by the covert KG 200 Special Combat Group to escort the small number of B-17 bombers captured after their crews landed (or even crash-landed) by accident during their bombing missions to Germany and her satellites. B-17s were always being shot down, so spares were plentiful, and these aircraft were flown on missions over Allied lines to drop spies by parachute, to do the odd bit of bombing and just to confuse the enemy.

Production of the Gigant was wound down from late in 1943: confidence in the design had simply waned, and from May 1944 onwards most remaining Transport Command units still operating the planes were absorbed into the Luftflotte 4 Air Group and merged with sections operating the old Ju 52 and the Arado Ar 232. The Gigants continued in service on the Eastern Front, since in Russia the immense versatility of their design still proved highly useful – they could seat 120 fully equipped troops (200 standing), or they could carry 60 stretchers and medical attendants – a capacity unmatched by the Ju 52 or any other airfreighter. And although the Gigant's standard range of 745 kilometres wasn't great, additional fuel tanks could either increase this to 1,000 kilometres or enable the craft to push its payload up to a maximum capacity of just over 16 tonnes.

In the end, many of the Gigants were destroyed by their own crews to prevent them from falling into the hands of advancing Soviet troops, since the grass airstrips frequently became soft and boggy, making takeoff and therefore escape impossible. But even if they had been able to get airborne, overwhelming Russian air superiority would have ensured that few would have got back home.

Had production not been stopped, who knows what refinements might have been introduced. When production began, it took about 40,000 man-hours to build each Gigant; as the numbers increased and techniques were improved, the Leipheim factory managed to reduce this to 12,000 man-hours by the time production finally ended in April 1944. By then, a total of two hundred machines had been built by a largely semi-skilled workforce culled from the armed forces' own penal battalions (units of men sentenced by military courts for various offences). The Obertraubling factory had almost certainly been written off as a viable concern following intensive Allied bombing of the Regensburg area in August 1943, as the Allies targeted a ball-bearing factory in the region. Further planned variations included the fitting of other makes of engine; and the 'F' series was to have had a payload twenty-five per cent higher than that of the 'D' series. Perhaps the most striking of all the drawing-board 'specials' was a design for a 'Siamese' Gigant. Building the Me 323Z involved joining two fuselages together with a common wing section (as with the Heinkel He 111Z), and powering them with nine BMW 801 engines. The Weapons Research Station at Karlshagen was actively looking at a bomb weighing 17,700 kilogrames, and the Me 323Z was thought to be the only aircraft capable of carrying it. A single test-flight was apparently made by this leviathan in July 1944, but it had been strafed by Allied fighters before takeoff and hadn't been adequately repaired, as a result of which it broke up in midair with the loss of everyone on board, though it had managed to release a dummy bomb.

By the end of the war, no examples of the Gigant remained intact, and apart from the unlikely possibility of one turning up somewhere now, all we have left are images of this amazing aircraft.

Sea Monsters

Flying boats were the true monsters of the Second World War. Before the outbreak of war, many countries had been developing them as part of their national airlines. The British company Saunders and Roe, for example, had long been established in the field, producing aircraft used on long-distance routes to India and the further-flung colonies.

Germany, too, had its flying boat makers: Heinkel and Dornier both produced models, and the Hamburg company Blohm und Voss produced flying boats for Lufthansa which were later adapted for use by the Luftwaffe in anti-shipping and anti-submarine patrols.

During the spring of 1940 the Air Ministry placed a contract with Blohm und Voss for the company to develop a replacement for its Bv 138 flying boat, then about to enter service, which would be a larger craft than the company's other flying boat project, the Bv 222 'Wiking' – 'Viking'. Originally, the Wiking, powered by six BMW engines, was intended for Lufthansa, to go into service on routes to Germany's African colonies, for transatlantic crossings, and generally throughout Europe. By the time of its first flight in September 1940 it had become clear that this thirty-seven-metre-long flying boat had military potential in both anti-shipping and transport roles – which latter facility had already led to the installation of enlarged side doors on the first prototype. Fewer than twenty of these craft were eventually made, seeing service throughout the Mediterranean and in Scandinavia. The Wiking was the apogee of the Blohm und Voss production line in its day, though in turn, in the light of the contract, it was to lead to the more ambitious Bv 238.

The Blohm und Voss design team was led by Doktor Ingenieur Richard Vogt, who had worked for ten years designing flying boats in Japan before joining the Hamburg firm in 1933. In 1940 both Vogt and his Board thought that the war would last only a short time and would be succeeded by an economic boom that would stimulate a desire for foreign travel among the wealthy. With this in mind they had begun work on designs for a large airliner for Lufthansa. Project P. 200, as it was known, was to have been an immense flying boat, rivalling in size the 'Spruce Goose' designed by the American millionaire Howard Hughes. It was to have a wingspan of 85 metres, a loaded weight of over 220 tonnes and a range of 8,600 kilometres. It would have been capable of carrying 120 passengers in luxury.

Extensive experiments in the water tank showed that the keeled hull of a flying boat could be more slender than had previously been thought possible, which would lead to an improvement in hydrodynamic drag. In September 1940 an adapted Wiking was tested to put the new slender hull design through its paces, but in January 1941, as the war dragged on and hopes of an early victory faded, P. 200 was shelved.

The research done for the project, and the experience gained through it, were not wasted, as they were put to use in fulfilling the Air Ministry's contract. The new military-application flying boat was originally to have been powered by the new Junkers twenty-four-cylinder diesel engine, in which four six-cylinder engines were fused together around a common crankshaft. However, by July 1941 it had become obvious to everyone that the engine wouldn't be available in time for the plane, so the plans were altered to accommodate six engines from another maker; this meant increasing both the wingspan and the overall weight of the flying boat.

The Bv 238, as it was now designated, was to have a wingspan of some sixty metres. The forty-three-metre-long fuselage made the craft twenty-five per cent longer than the Wiking. It was to have an armament comprising twelve remote-controlled barbettes – heavily armoured fixed cupolas each having two or four cannon designed to fire either forwards or backwards depending on their location on the fuselage. Above each barbette, a glazed sighting station was mounted, looking rather like a goldfish bowl. The idea was that a crew member could stick his head into this acrylic blister and look out for enemy fighters. If any approached, he would then operate hand-control to fire the guns below him. In addition to the barbettes, the flying boat would carry either four wing-mounted torpedoes, over two tonnes apiece, or four anti-shipping glide-bombs as part of its marine warfare role.

The Air Ministry was duly impressed with the Bv 238 and presented Blohm and Voss with a contract for four prototypes. Three pre-production models were to be powered by Daimler-Benz engines, giving an estimated speed of about 370 kph, and a fourth was to receive BMW motors. The massive wing was fitted with self-sealing fuel tanks (designed to seal around any breach and prevent leakage) and other features such as electric servos to operate the wing flaps (as on the Me 323). A catwalk was even fitted to the wing's main spar to provide access to the engines in mid-flight. The keeled hull was clad in a rust-resistant alloy and featured powered bow doors above the waistline, permitting direct access to the lower cargo deck and preserving the integrity of the hull. The heavy flight controls were partly augmented by more servos, and the instrumentation was extensive, beginning to resemble what a modern pilot might expect to see today in terms of its sophisticated layout. A series of portholes provided adequate daylight the length of the cargo deck, and electric lighting was installed as required. A crew of ten was originally planned, to enable efficient docking and mooring.

As 1941 drew to a close, Blohm und Voss submitted another version of the aircraft to the Technical Bureau. This was the Bv 238-Land. The keeled lower hull was replaced by bomb bays and extensive landing gear. Three main roles were encapsulated within the design. As a heavy transport, the Land might have carried a cargo of 40,000 kilogrammes over 2,000 kilometres. As a heavy bomber, it might have carried a 20,000-kilogramme bomb load over 7,000 kilometres or 4,000 kilogrammes over 10,000 kilometres. As a long-range maritime reconnaissance craft, it might have covered a substantial part of the American eastern seaboard. So excited was the Air Ministry by the prospect of a transport with an even greater capacity and range than the Gigant that in February 1942 it issued an order for four Bv 250s (as the aircraft was now redesignated) in addition to the four 238s already commissioned. Blohm und Voss had meanwhile also considered a civilian version to replace their original P. 200 project, but their full attention was demanded by the work in hand, and the civilian airliner never left the drawing board.

Apart from the obvious differences in the hull, the Bv 238 and the Bv 250 shared the same armament specifications – except that the barbettes were replaced with more reliable and efficient manned positions. The maximum firepower now consisted of a forward dorsal turret with twin MG 151 machine-guns; nose and tail turrets with four

MG 131s in each; two pairs of machine-guns firing aft from beam positions and two quad-barrelled gun-turrets mounted in the trailing edge of each wing. Fitting these wing turrets required extensive re-engineering of the wing in order to share out the stresses in carrying the 3,600 rounds of ammunition allocated to each turret, so it was decided that only the fourth prototype be altered, as the main spars for the first three planes' wings were already finished and couldn't be altered without incurring huge costs.

Construction of a quarter-scale working model, called the FGP 227, was begun in 1942 to acquire data on the likely flight characteristics and production difficulties of the full-size version. It was fitted with six 21-horsepower twin-cylinder engines, three on each wing. Built by a team led by the German Diplom Ingenieur Ludwig Karch at university facilities in Prague, the project was scheduled originally to last a little over a year. Flight-testing was to take place at a small airfield close to the university workshops. For the tests, the model had a crew of two, each in his own cockpit arranged in tandem along the length of the fuselage. However, despite extensive ground handling and taxiing trials, it never came close to getting airborne. This resulted in a decision to take the 227 to the Evaluation Centre at the Travemünde proving ground, where new aircraft were tested prior to their acceptance into service. But as French POWs hoisted the model on to a flatbed railway wagon for its transfer to Travemünde, they deliberately allowed the hoist to slip – they were under the impression that they were handling a new secret weapon, and in any case it seems extraordinary that POWs were employed in looking after such an important piece of equipment. The 'accident' caused severe damage to the wing, and the 227 did not make its maiden flight until 1944. Even then its problems weren't over, for fuel-line blockages caused all six engines to seize, and the resultant forced landing caused further damage. It wasn't flown again until September 1944, but although it made a number of flights then, the flight trials of the Bv 238 itself were imminent by that time, so the 227's contribution to the overall project was, in the last analysis, minimal.

Although work on making the necessary components had started in 1942, the actual assembly of the finished aircraft wasn't begun until January 1944 at the Blohm und Voss flying-boat factory at

Finkenwerder. Some officials at the Air Ministry thought it highly unusual that such a large and expensive project should have been given the go-ahead at precisely the time that other large aeroplanes such as the Gigant and the Heinkel He 177 heavy bomber were being phased out in favour of smaller aircraft. However, the Bv 238 used few strategically critical components or materials, and the Finkenwerder plant, being laid out like a shipyard, was unsuitable for conversion to the production of smaller fighters in any case.

As a result, its development was considered a painless indulgence, and if and when it entered service it was anticipated that its role as a long-range maritime patrol craft would keep it out of harm's way. The first Bv 238 (the V1) started its flight trials in March 1945. It was unarmed, but, powered by its six Daimler-Benz engines, and with a fuel capacity of about 10,779 gallons, it was the heaviest aircraft, at over 120 tonnes, ever to have flown. It was not, however, the largest; that honour goes to the Soviet ANT-20 bomber.

By comparison with its smaller cousin, the Wiking, there were few similarities apart from the basic hull design. The wing of the Bv 238, for example, was much simplified in order to save weight, and its flaps remained uncovered by any outer sheathing. The outer wing floats were similar to those on the Bv 222 and could be fully retracted into the wing in much the same way as conventional landing gear, thus reducing aerodynamic drag and helping performance. Blohm und Voss's simple approach to its design ensured that the aircraft would need only a short build-time and that costs would be kept low – the latter consideration a high priority. But Blohm und Voss took a long time to build the V1 prototype because the company had decided to construct the production jigs at the same time – work which had cost over 600 000 man-hours. Their hope in doing so was that the project would make the grade to full-scale production whatever the outcome of the war – perhaps in Allied hands as a postwar project. However, with Germany's collapse imminent by the time of the first trials, the question of how many examples they could have produced when it took them eight weeks just to build a hull must remain unanswered. On the other hand, after just four experimental flights, the Bv 238 V1 was considered proficient by both its factory pilots and the Technical Bureau, and the go-ahead was given for further testing.

Initial flight trials were still going on when the craft was sunk at its moorings on the Schaalsee by marauding American Mustangs just four days before the final surrender in May 1945. The wreckage remained where it was and posed a hazard to local boats until it was finally dynamited at the end of 1948. The smaller fragments were removed for scrap. By the time of the surrender, the V2 prototype was eighty per cent completed and stored in a Bremen shipyard, and the hull of the V3 was well advanced at Finkenwerder. Both machines had been scheduled to receive 1,900-horsepower Daimler-Benz engines. Components for the V4 and V5 machines, which were regarded as pre-production aircraft, were also in hand, and work had begun on three of the Bv 250s.

Despite the hopes of Blohm und Voss, the end of the Bv 238 was also to be the end of the development of flying boats in Germany. In a dour, bleak and divided postwar Berlin, there was little enthusiasm for such activities, and the visions that lay behind the original P. 200 airliner project were now remote memories. Yet in looking at such aircraft now, are we to view them simply as follies – dinosaurs made extinct by the war and the 'brave new world' it paved the way for? In their time, the flying boats provided a luxurious and civilised mode of transport – and a means of crossing vast distances in greater safety than airships could offer. With the advent of the jet engine, the prospect of cheap air travel put an end to such a romantic way of flying, and its loss is lamented by the few who remember it.

A flying boat – even one powered by a jet engine – could take you directly to your holiday island, even to the beach in front of your hotel; but such simple efficiency and convenience have been lost sight of in the modern world. The Bv models have become outmoded only in their military applications. In peacetime, there is still a place for the glamour and romance offered by flying boats, and it is a great pity that the technology developed by gifted designers like Richard Vogt for Blohm und Voss has not been taken up since.

Chapter Four

THE HORTEN FLYING WINGS

A Silver Mirage

Picture this: July 1945 and the war is still on. The Allies are making slower progress into the heartland of Germany than they had once predicted, meeting resistance more fanatical and more stubborn than they'd expected.

The RAF Spitfire pilot has banked over to port to get a better glimpse of the strange shape ahead of him. At first he sees little. The powerful Merlin engine thrumming ahead of him, the pilot pulls out of his roll and straightens up, to find himself now right behind the most peculiar aircraft he has ever seen. It seems to have no tail or rudder, or any discernible fuselage, and for a moment he is taken aback. Although he has had no briefings about this kind of craft, the sight of its German insignia causes him to open fire on instinct. But even as he lines up the 'flying wing' in his sights, the damned thing is already pulling away from him. Cursing his slow reactions, he accelerates and climbs, but the Luftwaffe veteran flying the new Go 229 is already one step ahead and has used the power of his two Junkers jets to gain a higher altitude than his opponent. After throttling back a little, the German ace sees sunlight glinting on the Spitfire's canopy as it streaks past below him. This is his cue to attack, and after opening the throttles to both engines once again, he enters a shallow dive in the Spitfire's wake. Now within range, he fires off a rapid burst from his four 30-millimetre cannon at the Spitfire before turning away in readiness for a second pass. But he can see in his mirror that a second pass won't be needed, as the enemy plane begins a smoky spiral earthwards . . .

Lifting Bodies

Such a scenario never happened, but if fate had taken only a few different twists it might well have done. Even today, over half a century later, the Go 229 and its fellow craft look futuristic. Without doubt they were the most startling and original aeroplanes built during the war. They stemmed from the shared belief of three brothers that a flying wing was the most efficient design for an aircraft.

The Horten brothers, Walter, Wolfram and Reimar, who came from near Bonn, set out to prove their conviction by building scale-model gliders at the very beginning of the 1930s. At first, as others had done already, they had dismissed the concept of a flying wing as too outrageous to be practicable. Only after studying the work of such designers as the North American John Northrop, the founder of Northrop Aviation, and their fellow German Alexander Lippisch, did they find the courage to begin work on their gliders. Meeting with initial success, they went on to build their first full-size glider, the Ho I, in 1931. This set the naming pattern for all their future projects; from now on, only roman numerals were used.

Their many models had demonstrated the practical feasibility of the theories concerning the radical shape of the flying wing – a true 'lifting body'. The design for the Ho I, which was simply a scaled-up version of one of their models, provided a small bubble canopy on top of the wing's centre section, under which the pilot lay prone on a little padded bench within the wing itself. The all-wooden construction had a twelve-metre wingspan and was covered with doped fabric. Its undercarriage consisted of a single ventral skid mounted below the pilot's position. Following the pattern they had established with their models, and anticipating their later, even more ambitious projects, the Hortens built the Ho I with no tailfin or rudder. In flight, it was controlled by a series of elevons and flaps in the leading edge, near the wing tips. The flaps doubled as rudimentary air brakes and were used to slow the glider down and steady it for landings. Altogether, the Ho I logged around seven flying hours and won the Design Prize of 600 Reichsmarks at the 1934 Rhön-Wasserkuppe glider competition.

The competition had been held on a mountaintop, and although the Hortens had managed to get the glider there, they had no easy means of getting it home. They also had nowhere to store it long-term, so they decided to give it to their hero, Alexander Lippisch, to do with as he saw fit. But the fates were against Lippisch as he was equally unable to arrange for a tow plane to get it off the mountain and back to the Deutsche Forschungsinstitut für Segelflug (DFS, or German Glider Research Institute) at Darmstadt. Lippisch had to arrange for the glider to be broken up and burned on-site: an action that must have grated on the brothers, the more so since winning such a major prize with their invention.

The Hawk

However, the destruction of the Ho I had the effect of spurring the Hortens on to greater efforts on more than one front. Within a year they had completed their second glider, the Ho II. Of a similar arrowhead shape to its predecessor, the Ho II 'Habicht' – 'Hawk' – had a second set of elevons and a fixed tandem-wheel undercarriage instead of a skid.

The first test-flight took place in May 1935, only nine months after the loss of the Ho I, for the Hortens' work had been facilitated after a successful appeal for public donations. In August the brothers borrowed an eighty-horsepower Hirth Hm 60 petrol engine and connected it to a rear-mounted twin-bladed pusher propeller on their craft, to create the Ho IIm. The engine was mounted deep within the wing's central section, below and behind the pilot. The pilot himself, still in a prone position, now lay behind a fully glazed section of the wing, and the canopy covering his 'cockpit' was reduced to a discreet blister over the forward apex.

In 1936 all three brothers joined the Luftwaffe, but they were encouraged to continue work on their designs by both the DFS and the Technical Bureau. As a result, a year later they had altered the wing of the Ho II to provide even more stability and predictability in the already highly responsive controls. They had produced three unpowered examples of the new model by autumn 1937, which the Luftwaffe entered in that year's Rhön competition.

Meanwhile, Hirth had taken back the engine they'd lent the Hortens, and towards the end of the year the brothers started to think about relocating their operation to Berlin. At some point in 1938 Walter and Reimar both resigned from the Luftwaffe and began work on plans for a new glider, which they would develop and build on the improvements already made. The fruit of their labour, the Ho III, appeared later in the year and received an official designation, 8–250, from the Air Ministry, which had part-funded the project. The brothers were now making influential friends.

The Ho III was outwardly similar to the Ho II, but its wingspan had been increased to twenty metres, and it was to establish the pattern for its own successors in having a centre section of welded steel, with wooden single-spar outer sections for the wing. Two examples of the Ho III were entered in the 1938 Rhön meeting, and they met with success even though both aircraft were unfortunately lost when their pilots were obliged to bale out as a result of frozen controls.

A total of four Ho IIIs were built eventually, at sites in Berlin and Cologne. The third prototype was fitted early in 1942 with a 55-horsepower petrol engine and pusher propeller in a similar manner to that of the Ho IIm. After initial flight-testing it was moved to Göttingen, where it was demonstrated to the Aerodynamischen Versuchsanstalt (AVA, or Aerodynamic Trials Unit). The engine was found not to be powerful enough, and so in 1943 another Ho III was fitted successfully with an air-cooled VW-Beetle motor. The Ho IIIe, as it was known, was first flown in 1944, though what happened to it subsequently is a mystery.

An Early Albatross

The Ho IV project should have came next but it was shelved, to be followed by the Ho V. This was the first Horten design intended to be powered from day one, and it had a shorter wingspan than its fellows in consequence. To accommodate its two eighty-horsepower Hirth engines – the same type as was fitted to the Ho IIm the centre section of the wing had to be both wider and deeper – though in the event the engines were mounted just ahead of the centre section's straight trailing edge, and as the wing at this point was very narrow, the engines stood proud and couldn't be fully faired in. As a result, the engines sported their own aerodynamic fairings, and powered their

100

broad-bladed propellers without the need for a long driveshaft.

A specialist plastics manufacturer near Cologne began construction late in 1936. The Ho va was notable for the use of new materials for its outer skin and wing spars. It was completed in 1937, and the result was a source of amazement. Just as, many years later, the world would be impressed by the wispy and frail-looking 'Gossamer Albatross', which was the first plane to cross the Channel under human power alone, so it isn't hard to imagine the interest that the Ho va aroused in 1937: not only was it a flying wing – a radical design – but its outer skin was made of what we would call cellophane. Heady stuff.

A fixed tandem undercarriage was fitted, with a smaller, retractable nose-wheel upfront. The craft had positions for a crew of two, lying prone and side by side. Once again the cockpit was faired into the wing apex behind the leading edge, and such efficient aerodynamics gave a top speed of 280 kph, which, derived from such small engines, was impressive. The brothers also seriously considered using the various jet engines then in development, but the Technical Bureau at the time was sceptical and hesitant and put a stop to the idea by threatening to withdraw financial support if it were pursued.

Unfortunately, the first Ho va was to meet disaster on its maiden flight. Walter and Reimer were flying it and both were lucky to escape with their lives as the aircraft failed to respond to its controls during takeoff. A small hop was achieved, but the speed was too low to gain height and, following the inevitable stall, the plane crashed heavily and was written off as the brittle plastic components shattered. However, the brothers had guessed the cause immediately: the engines had been mounted too far back and thus displaced the centre of gravity. They salvaged the engines and set about building a second version.

Ernst Udet himself had instructed the Luftwaffe repair facility at Cologne, under a Major Dinort, to begin work on the Ho vb, and he promised the brothers that his department would pick up the bill. This provided a necessary confidence-booster to the pair, who were grateful for his intervention and the continued support of the Technical Bureau. The second Ho v was to return to more conventional methods of construction, using tensile-steel tubing, wooden spars and a fabric skin. Almost certainly as a result of their frightening crash, the cockpit was redesigned so that the pilots were no longer required to lie prone but now sat upright in regular seats, their heads and shoulders above the upper surface of the wing, and the seats enclosed by two glazed bubble canopies. The entire apex of the wing was also glazed, to give as much all-round visibility as possible. The mistake of placing the engines too far rearward was not repeated, and having mounted them further inboard the driveshafts were once again extended and shrouded. The maiden flight of the Ho vb, with Walter at the controls, passed off perfectly, but as other developments were claiming time, money and attention, it was impossible to continue testing the aircraft fully, and it was destined to stand in the open air at an airfield near Potsdam until 1941, its wooden components slowly rotting away.

Keeping It In the Family

By the beginning of 1938 the Horten brothers' work was attracting offers of employment and patronage from companies such as Heinkel and Messerschmitt. But as negotiations always broke down on issues like patent protection, Walter and Reimar rejoined the Luftwaffe in search of state support. The life of the third brother, Wolfram, took a different course: he became a torpedo bomber pilot and was killed during the Battle of France in 1940. But Walter and Reimar consolidated their positions, Walter through his already firm political connections and Reimar through his marriage to Udet's personal secretary. The Air Ministry was happy to fund their work and set up a new development unit for them, not least because German Intelligence reported that Jack Northrop's American-based company was working in a similar area of research as the Hortens were now entering: the use of jet engines in a flying wing craft.

The Hortens' new unit was designated Sonderkommando 9, and it was established in a disused transport repair depot in Göttingen, with access to a furniture factory in Minden for use as a construction facility. They were to enjoy more or less complete autonomy and would be virtually free of interference from the RLM's Technical Bureau – a unique position to be in.

By 1941 they were close to finishing another research glider, the formerly shelved Ho iv. This was developed to investigate the characteristics of the flying wing at high speeds, and it bore no resemblance to its predecessors. The wing was very thin and tapered and of an inordinately high aspect ratio – the ratio between the wingspan and its thickness. The aspect ratio was twice as high as formerly, militating against a fully faired-in cockpit, so that the pilot's canopy was more pronounced than before. In addition, the shallowness of the wing meant that the pilot was forced to adopt a strange kneeling posture during flight: there was simply not enough room for him to lie prone as before, and not enough depth for him to sit in a conventional seat.

The first Ho IV, the Ho IVa, was completed at a plant in Königsberg, and the second, the Ho IVb, which incorporated a plastic leading edge, was finished at a factory near Kassel. The Ho IVb was later to crash as a result of entering an irrecoverable spin at altitude. A later project, the Ho VI, followed up research into the high aspect wing, but the construction turned out to be too weak to fly safely, and it was scrapped.

Later in 1941 Walter became a member of the Air Staff at the Air Ministry, with special responsibility for single-engined fighters. In this new position of influence and authority, he revisited Potsdam to inspect his Ho vb, which was still sitting on the tarmac, mouldering away. At first, even Udet couldn't be persuaded to inject funds and resources into saving the aircraft and thereby enabling the brothers to return to work on it, but at last, in September 1941, a Luftwaffe detachment arrived in Minden whose task it was to restore the plane, which they did at the nearby Peschke aircraft repair facility. Reimar Horten was appointed unit commander, and his colleagues included three designers and an aerodynamicist with experience in flying wings, Heinz Scheidhauer.

The aircraft was in such a sorry state that the team quickly decided to convert it into a single-seater. Once this was done, it received the new designation Ho vc. It was painted in standard Luftwaffe camouflage colours and flew again in May 1942, piloted by Walter, before being returned to Göttingen, where it crashed heavily just over a year later during another test-flight. The wreckage was stored with the intention of reconstructing the plane after the war, but the plan was never realised. Allied troops found the badly damaged wreck themselves when they took the airfield, but it was decided not to waste time on restoration, and so the vc was burned. Before leaving it, it is worth pointing out that the Hortens intended to fit the vc with a single Argus pulse jet, which would have sat between the two propellers. The lack of a tailfin was expected to provide a clean airflow and thus minimise the horrendous vibrations experienced whenever the units were fitted to conventional aircraft.

On 4 April 1943 the two brothers presented a lengthy paper to the Flying Wing Seminar at Bonn. In it they stated that 'a swept-back wing without protrusions is suited to warding off cable barriers, barrage balloons, etc . . . the swept-back wing has advantages at high Mach numbers . . . sweepback becomes necessary for high-speed flight'. All these points could naturally have been interpreted as an indication of the brothers' intentions regarding the future use of a turbojet engine in one of their designs, but before their thoughts in that direction took more concrete shape, they produced the Ho VII. This was a two-seat 'trainer', powered by two 240-horsepower Argus AS10 air-cooled engines, once again driving a pusher propeller, and giving a speed of 340 kph. The Hortens had designed it nominally in order to familiarise pilots with flying such an unconventional machine. It was constructed on the familiar steel and wood frame, and built partly by Peschke – the brothers had obviously been pleased with the firm's work in restoring the Ho vb/vc.

The true reason for the Ho VII's existence was to test the flying wing concept for fighter purposes, though initially this was kept secret from officials. The new model was fitted with a fully retractable under-carriage, and was also the first to be tested in a wind-tunnel: hitherto the *modus operandi* had been to test scale models in the open air. The Ho VIIa was first flown at Minden during the summer of 1943, and after a year of trials an impressed Göring initiated an order for twenty examples, to be built by Peschke. At first the RLM wanted Argus pulse jets to be fitted, but after serious objections were raised by the Hortens the Ministry appeared to relent. Nevertheless the order was cancelled when only the second example was nearing completion. The Ho VIIa was eventually flown back to Göttingen in February 1945, but its undercarriage failed on landing and it belly-flopped badly. The damage was not repaired, and the aircraft finally suffered the same fate as the Ho vc.

The Hortens had been planning their first tailor-made combat aircraft since the autumn of 1942, and they wanted it to be their first jet-propelled plane. Given all the turmoil that had surrounded their other projects, it must come as no surprise to learn that the initial work was undertaken in secret by Sonderkommando 9 at Göttingen. In his influential new position at the Air Ministry, Walter Horten had access to much classified data regarding the new breed of German turbojet engines, notably the Junkers Jumo 004 and the BMW 003. If their new interceptor project were to stand any chance of success, the brothers reasoned, the Ho IX (8–229), as it was known, would have to use jet propulsion. Their view on this was later to save the project, at a time when the Air Ministry forbade any new piston-engined aircraft from entering service.

Their first attempts at a design resembled something by Alexander Lippisch, being more of a delta-winged glider than a true flying wing, and this was a design theme that would reappear later in another project of theirs. The first design was followed by two more – P. 52 and P. 53 – which both reverted to a pure flying wing format. A construction of tubular steel and wood was employed in the by now familiar design, but this time the single cockpit was placed as far forward of the centre section as possible, to give the pilot the best possible visibility when landing. The pilot was to sit upright in an ejector seat. There was to be a full undercarriage – fixed on the first prototype – and the two BMW 003 turbojets specified for the job were to be housed within the compact centre section, supplied with fuel from five self-sealing tanks in each wing. For additional braking power on landing, a parachute was to be used, stowed in the trailing edge of the wing at its centre.

Persuading Göring

The first prototype (V1) was designed as an unpowered glider, and it was to be used to test the aerodynamics of the design, since the Hortens were now being refused the use of wind-tunnels. The reason for this was that Allied bombers were wreaking havoc with German research centres, and what facilities remained had to be dedicated to major producers like Heinkel and Messerschmitt. A small unit, even with the status of Sonderkommando 9, couldn't hope even to join the queue.

In order to carry their project forward the Hortens had finally, in August 1943, to drop the secrecy with which they had surrounded it.

They gave a personal briefing to Göring, who gave them his immediate endorsement in return, insisting that the Ho ix fly under power as soon as possible. Hauptmann Walter Horten managed to secure a posting to Göttingen to supervise the project, while his brother, Oberleutnant Reimar Horten, became his Number Two. Now, with official backing, the project moved on apace. The V1 glider first flew in February 1944, though the Air Ministry wasn't officially informed of the work until later that spring, at about the time the construction started of the V2 example.

The first snag was that the BMW engines were found to be too big for their bays, and they had to be replaced with Junkers Jumo units. Then Erhard Milch gave the order that Sonderkommando 9 should be disbanded. Reasons for this decision are unknown, but Milch may have been responding to pressure from rival manufacturers, or from the Air Ministry and the Technical Bureau, either or both of which would have been furious at having been kept in the dark. As we saw earlier, relations between Göring and his deputy had become distinctly frosty by now. If Milch thought he'd seen an element of favouritism in Göring's treatment of the Hortens when other, more 'worthy' projects were being cancelled, then it is quite possible that he would have moved to shut the unit down.

The brothers' reaction was to form their own private company immediately, the Horten Flugzeugbau, to continue the project. However, that alone did not solve the problem, for as a result of a second, general order from the Air Ministry, technical teams had been dispersed throughout the country to prevent Allied Intelligence from learning the significance of certain sites, including Göttingen, and the Hortens' small, specialised group had been scattered.

This second general order did more harm than good, and not only to the Hortens' project. But as the progress of the war was affecting the bureaucracy of the Air Ministry adversely, Walter and Reimar were able to reconstruct their unit with little difficulty, though work was delayed by six months while they did so. The Air Ministry blocked any further supply of funds and resources to the project, as Milch had washed his hands of it, but alternative finance was arranged directly through Göring's office. It seems incredible that such an important project, at the cutting edge of aerospace research, not only had to be conducted in circumstances of the utmost difficulty, but also had to rely for its survival on what amounted to private funding.

Production at Last

While the V2 was being built, further testing of the V1 was undertaken at Oranienburg, near Berlin. The results were excellent, until an accident in March 1944 caused the project further delays as repairs were carried out: the fixed nose-wheel had partially collapsed on landing as a result of twitching from side to side. Once fixed, the V1 was moved to Brandis for further testing, where it remained until it was discovered by North American GIs after the war, in such a dismantled state that they decided not to restore it.

But at this point the Air Ministry performed another volte-face. Now impressed by the project, officials decided to take it out of the brothers' hands and began talks with the Gothaer Waggonfabrik company in late 1944. The Ministry wanted seven further prototypes, followed by twenty pre-production models, and they designated the Ho IX officially as Go 229. A two-seater, all-weather version, the Go 229B, was also designed, incorporating radar into a lengthened nose. The second and third prototypes served as models for this 'B' series type.

While initial construction began at the underused Gothaer plant at Friedrichsroda, work on the V2 continued at Göttingen, and, once completed, the V2 was moved to Oranienburg for testing in January 1945.

The V2 was designed for seven 'g' loadings – i.e. to bear a gravity-force seven times greater than that experienced at rest on the ground – a figure higher than for comparable 'normal' fighters – and was thus strong enough to outmanoeuvre virtually any other aircraft. The team at the Gothaer factory therefore wisely introduced only a few changes to the models it made. The cockpit was enlarged for greater pilot comfort, and an ejector seat was fitted. The turbojet housings and air-intakes were also made bigger, and the airframe and undercarriage were upgraded to cope with the greater carrying weights anticipated in use. The team also provided for four MK 103 or 108 cannon, two on each outer side of the engines, and hard points for two thousand-kilogram bombs, or two fuel tanks of about 275-gallon capacity each.

The centre section was a conventionally welded-steel tubing space frame with plywood skinning, apart from the exhaust outlets, and was therefore very cheap compared with the existing machines, which made intensive use of steel and other alloys. Apart from metal tips, the wing sections were made of wood and Formholz – moulded wood made up of wood-shavings mixed with resin. Such a construction would have provided an excellent response to Allied radar, since wood absorbs radar waves.

The wing structure itself comprised a single main spar, which held the two engines and an auxiliary spar to carry the trailing edge control surfaces. Two-thirds of each wing contained a flexible, self-sealing fuel tank with a total capacity of 660 gallons. The two Junkers jet engines passed through the main spar, their intakes merged with the wing roots and blended into the centre section, the only openings on the wing being the exhaust ducts and the low, contoured cockpit canopy. The plane had a tricycle retractable undercarriage – the single nose-wheel was actually the tail-wheel from a Heinkel He 177 bomber – and retained the drogue parachute to assist braking on landing.

For the first flight, on 2 February 1945, the V2's nose-wheel was locked down, yet the aircraft still registered a speed of 300 kph, and took off within 450 metres at only 150 kph. This flight, and a second on 3 February, presented no major problems, though on each occasion the pilot, Leutnant Erwin Ziller, released the drogue parachute too soon, which resulted in minor damage to the undercarriage. Repairs delayed a third flight until 18 February. By the following month they felt able to retract the nose-wheel, and the V2 attained speeds of up to 800 kph. Tragedy struck during one landing approach, however, when one of the engines cut out and caused the plane to crash, killing Ziller. The aircraft had completed only two hours' flying time when the accident occurred.

The V2 was written off in the incident, and immediately various questions were raised regarding procedures within the team. Why had the flight taken place at all, as neither Horten brother had been present? Why had previously expressed reservations about the engines not been acted on, and why had Ziller not ejected? Examination of the wreckage revealed an emptied compressed-air bottle, the function of which had been to activate the undercarriage in an emergency. The fact that Ziller had resorted to the emergency function lent weight to the theory that the pilot must have imagined that engine failure was total – in which case he would have assumed that hydraulic power to the landing gear would also have failed. After Ziller had released the compressed air to lower the undercarriage, the V2 would have become too slow to overcome the sudden aerodynamic drag of the extended wheels and their spats, and with no forward power it would have stalled. Admittedly one engine was still running down when the horrified onlookers rushed to the scene of the crash, and Ziller should have been able to use it to rectify the situation while still airborne, but he took the reason for his failure to do so to the grave.

Schräge Musik

Meanwhile, Gotha's Friedrichsroda plant had produced two night-fighter prototypes and continued work on the V3 and V6 pre-production prototypes and the two twin-seater prototypes intended as trainers and armament test-beds. As late as March 1945, Göring had confirmed the Go 229's place in the last-ditch Jägernotprogramm – emergency fighter production schedule. But within two months Friedrichsroda had been occupied by US troops; the development ended with the manufacture of components for the twenty pre-production units well under way, and the Americans discovered the complete centre section of the V3, which they took back to the US (where it is now stored at the National Air and Space Museum at Silver Hill, Maryland). Certain improvements in detail, added by Gotha, can be seen in the V3, and the later V4 Go 229B night-fighter prototype, which was seized when forty per cent complete, was designed almost entirely to a Gotha specification. It was also fitted with the so-called Schräge Musik – literally, 'slanted music' – weapon, an upward-firing array of rockets which was triggered by any aircraft overflying a photoelectric cell in the upper side of the aircraft. Had development continued, an armoured and pressurised cockpit would have been introduced, permitting flights at high altitudes. A cumbersome pressurised flight suit had already been tested, but it was uncomfortable and gave the wearer virtually no freedom of movement.

P. 60

The Go 229 never entered full production: although Göring included it in his Jägernotprogramm, only one version flew under power before US troops captured the Gotha factory. When Gothaer Waggonfabrik was originally appointed manufacturer for the Hortens' designs, the brief also extended to designing flying wings of their own, with little input from the brothers. The P. 60 was the first such breakaway design; it was envisaged as a heavy night-fighter to combat the British Mosquitoes and the American Northrop Black Widows. In service it would have complemented the Go 229, had production of both been able to continue, but these were times of the utmost difficulty for Germany, and one project tended to overtake another at desperate speed.

Indeed, from the very beginning of the Go 229 programme, Gothaer had been looking forward to its eventual replacement. The P. 60 exploited Gothaer's spare capacity and their long experience in building gliders, and its development ran alongside that of the Go 229. In the P. 60A, the pilot and navigator lay prone in a pressurised cockpit behind a glazed nose that blended into the overall arrowhead wing. As with the Hortens' designs, the conventional rudder and tailfin were dispensed with, replaced in this case with two small retractable aerofoils on each wing tip which could extend above and below each wing. When in level flight, these surfaces could be withdrawn to minimise drag, to be extended only when needed. The wings, swept at an angle of forty-five degrees, were fitted with long rear flaps to improve stalling characteristics, and the wings blended at their roots with the slightly bulbous fuselage. Mounted somewhat incongruously above and below the rear of the centre section were a pair of BMW 003 turbojets, with an additional Walter rocket motor sandwiched between them to assist in takeoffs and steep climbs. By comparison with the Go 229, the P. 60's armament seemed light, with only four MK 108 cannon; but this was thought to be adequate when the aircraft's high speed and extreme manoeuvrability were taken into account.

In February 1945 the Commander-in-Chief of German Fighter Command issued a revised directive to be met in future by all fighters with single and twin jet engines. These new and very high standards included improved equipment, an ability to take off within 1,000 metres, and greater flight endurance and range. As a result of this directive, the P. 60B was slightly larger than its predecessor, and it was proposed that the BMW jets be replaced with a pair of more powerful Heinkel HeS 011s, though the Walter rocket would be retained. Great things were expected of this new configuration, such as the ability of the plane to reach a height of 9,000 metres in *two and a half minutes*.

The third variant, the P. 60C, retained the basic layout of its predecessors and the more powerful engines of the 'B' version but reverted to a conventional cockpit and bubble canopy. Its extended nose was to house a 'Neptun' radar system. Envisaged as a sophisticated all-weather night-fighter, the original four cannon were supplemented by another pair, angled to fire upwards. When an upgraded specification was issued by the Air Ministry in March 1945, requiring provision for a third member of the crew, Gothaer had an ingenious solution ready: the navigator and the radar operator were placed in semi-reclining seats under glazed hatches set into the leading edge contours of the wing on either side of the cockpit. This permitted a reduction in the length of the cockpit itself – only the pilot occupied it now – and the insertion of a larger fuel tank, able to hold 4,000 kilogrammes of fuel and giving a range of about 2,400 kilometres with an endurance of nearly four hours.

Germany's defeat put an end to the P. 60 project, and it was never to resurface, even in the form of a working prototype for development within the victorious Allied air forces.

Although the Hortens' work on the Go 229 was to be their last in terms of partnership with Gothaer, they had continued to develop new projects of their own and were now working towards their next goal: supersonic flight. They had already decided to use the long-awaited Heinkel HeS 011 jet for this plan, and they opted for a small flying wing with a span of only seven metres, the pilot once again to be placed in a prone position within the centre section, looking out from behind an armoured plexiglass window. The design proposed a speed of about Mach 1.4, though how the brothers arrived at this figure is a mystery, given that they continued to be denied access to wind-tunnels and therefore had to rely on small-scale models for their calculations. They got as far as building a full-size glider, which was nearing completion when the

Allies entered Göttingen. The Allies, perhaps ignorant of its potential, destroyed it.

Another venture that the brothers developed away both from Gothaer and the Air Ministry was the Ho XIII. This was a private undertaking, and one they hoped would spawn a small interceptor project of their own. The first phase, the Ho XIIIA glider, was built at a glider research facility at Bad Hersfeld, about fifty kilometres south of Kassel, in Hessen, presumably to be well out of sight of curious officials. Its purpose was to explore the low-speed handling characteristics of a supersonic wing design. The prone pilot was housed in a kind of under-slung, though streamlined gondola, which appeared as a blister on the underside of the wing. The Ho XIIIA made a series of test-flights, starting at Göttingen in November 1944, before being transferred to Hornberg, where it was destroyed by POWs after they had been freed by advancing Allied troops. Unlike the projects of other aeronautical designers and engineers, notably those of the famous Wernher Freiherr von Braun, research for this book has revealed that the Horten brothers never employed forced or slave labour; but the mood of POWs after years of imprisonment was naturally angry, and almost any German target was valid. Had it been permitted further development, the jet-engined Ho XIII would have had a more acutely rear-swept wing than the glider prototype, and an elongated vertical stabiliser. Such a design would have resembled the Messerschmitt Me 163 'Komet', and especially the work of Alexander Lippisch for his LP. 13 ramjet interceptor. Even though the LP. 13 and the Ho XIII were unconnected, it is remarkable how close their basic concept is.

So convinced was Reimar Horten of the validity of the Ho XIII's design that after the war and intensive interrogation in London he moved to Argentina to carry out further work on supersonic aircraft. He died as recently as 1993, after a lifetime's work extending our knowledge of advanced aerodynamics and lifting wings. The British were to incor-porate some of his concepts into preliminary work on Concorde, via the Handley Page HP. 115, which was noted for its high tailfin and strongly tapered and contoured back-swept wings.

A CIA memorandum of 1948 confirms that the Gotha plant at Erfurt, East Germany, was in Soviet hands and that the Russians had found prototypes or plans there for the Go IX and the Go P. 60 night-fighter. It goes on to say that the Russians 'are now planning to build a fleet of 1,800 Horten viii-type flying wing aircraft. The wingspan is thirty-nine metres; the swept-back angle is thirty degrees. The Russian version is reported to be jet-propelled.'

This is an interesting comment, as the Ho viii was seldom mentioned during the war. It was primarily taken on by Sonderkommando 9 at Göttingen from mid-1943 onwards, and it was planned as a postwar commercial aircraft to carry sixty passengers within a gigantic wing spanning over seventy-nine metres. This is very much wider than the span mentioned in the somewhat paranoid CIA memo, but in fact the original seventy-nine metres was reduced to forty-seven, as anything larger wouldn't have fitted into any existing hangar on the base.

Once again making use of the wood and steel basic structure favoured by the Hortens, especially after their disastrous experience with the Ho va, the rear-swept wings blended with a straight trailing edge along which were six pusher propellers powered by six 600-horsepower BMW engines mounted within the centre section. After dismissing the airliner version in favour of a military transport, it was decided to carry the payload forward of the engines in an unpressurised bay. The Ho viii was designed to have a range of over 5,600 kilometres at a cruising speed of only 320 kph and at the relatively low altitude of around 1,500 metres, dictated by its unpressurised cabin. Although it was scheduled to make its maiden flight in November 1945, the end of the war put paid to that. There is no question that the Soviets indeed captured the Gotha plant at Erfurt, but why they didn't produce the 1,800 Ho viiis mentioned in the CIA report remains a mystery – if the memo's intelligence was accurate, that is.

In a separate development, the Horten Ho xviii was considered in late 1944 as their entry in a competition set up by Göring to find a new six-engined heavy jet bomber. Its chief rival was the Messerschmitt P. 1108, which in fact used only four engines. The xviii made use of a large delta-shaped fin and rudder above the flying wing. The crew were accommodated within the forward glazed base of this fin, again recalling Lippisch's LP. 13 fighter. This fin extended beyond the wing's leading edge and contained a remote-controlled machine-gun barbette. Six enhanced Junkers 004 turbojets were grouped under the centre section, each having a thrust of 1,052 kilogrammes. A bomb load of over 4,000 kilogrammes was to have been carried over 13,000 kilometres. Although no clear winner of the competition was ever announced, it seemed obvious to the Hortens that their design was the best and that the eventual contract would come their way.

In order to prepare for the likelihood of a production contract for the XVIII, they returned to the old Ho VIII project in January 1945 and began adapting it to serve as a prototype for the heavy bomber. The two models shared a similar size, and the complex centre section of the VIII could be adapted for the XVIII. In the adaptation, having no Junkers engines to hand, they replaced the VIII's BMW jets with six Argus AS 10s.

Göring did indeed award a production contract to the brothers verbally in March 1945, but work was destined to progress little further as Germany's collapse was by then imminent. Once again, US troops were to scrap this final Horten project, finding it only half-finished fewer than six weeks later.

Skeletons in the Cupboard?

It gives one pause when one considers that some of the Hortens' flying wing projects for the Luftwaffe are over sixty years old. For nearly sixty years the world's aviation industry has ignored the work of the Hortens. Was this because the GIs who discovered the surviving Horten machines destroyed them without stopping to consider what they might have learned from them?

Perhaps it isn't that simple. Only recently has the USAF revealed its B-2 Stealth Bomber. Based on the classic flying wing design, it needs dozens of computers to keep it flying, and it seems too complex, fragile and expensive to be a true combat aircraft. Half a century ago, the only computers around were machines that filled whole rooms. Half a century ago, the Horten flying wings were operating without any electronic aids, and yet they performed perfectly well. So where is the progress? Looking at the aerospace industry of today, there seems to be little evidence that any progress has really been made, apart from the addition of a range of electronic and avionic aids to aircraft whose design would still look familiar to Second World War pilots. Aviation design and technology have merely evolved, refining the basic details.

But just as a modern bicycle has all the basic features of the boneshaker, so a modern plane design shows no evidence of innovation, and certainly not on the scale practised by German designers like the Hortens in the 1930s and the 1940s.

One would have expected their ideas to be commonplace by now, but it seems that we still haven't assimilated them. Big business and political agendas have ensured that we may never get designs as radical again: if existing concepts from Boeing or Airbus serve their turn, why change them? Britain, for example, seems to have done little or nothing to capitalise on or develop the principles of the Harrier jump jet or Concorde.

As for the Stealth Bomber, if it has taken the USA fifty years to reveal an operational flying wing publicly, what, one wonders, remains concealed or suppressed? It is a pity that the pioneering vision of the wartime designers hasn't been allowed to flourish in our own age, for the benefit of all, in peacetime applications.

Chapter Five

MORE THAN THEIR SUM

Green Shoots of Innovation

Since the First World War, German aircraft-designers had been renowned as innovators, with such designs as the Fokker Triplane and the Zeppelin airships in the forefront of the new and dynamic industry. As we have seen, the Treaty of Versailles restricted their activity, and the edge of their invention was dulled temporarily as civil aviation took over from more stimulating military projects. With the seizure of power by the Nazis in 1933, however, designers who had been obliged to work on unsatisfying projects for fourteen years or so suddenly found themselves being given a free rein once more. The foundation of a new air force was linked in the national imagination with the re-establishment of German self-esteem, according to Goebbels's propaganda, and once the economic crises of the 1920s and early 1930s had been overcome the industry began to grow again. It found a new maturity and rediscovered its capacity for imaginative experiment. In the climate of the time, to experiment was to take a bold step, especially in view of the conventional aircraft then being produced, in Germany and in the rest of the world.

The Hortens were not the only real innovators in the German aircraft industry, although they were perhaps the most radical. This chapter discusses the work of some of their contemporaries.

(A)symmetry

In 1937 the Air Ministry invited plans for a tactical reconnaissance aircraft with all-round vision, which would carry a crew of three and

117

have a secondary role in supporting army ground units by laying smoke screens and directing artillery fire. The idea for this kind of aeroplane was new and stemmed from the experiences of the Condor Legion in Spain and tactical experiments at Lipetsk which, as we have seen, led to the development of the part the Luftwaffe was to play in the strategy of Blitzkrieg. The new philosophy held that a highly mobile army made up of tanks and motorised troops could make sweeping advances against a conventionally disposed opponent if the enemy were first softened up by strategic bombing. Spotter aircraft overflying the battle area could provide an ongoing reconnaissance picture and additional strike assistance. The Ju 87 Stuka was first developed in the primary role of strategic dive bomber, but the secondary role wasn't completely filled by the time of its introduction – hence this almost belated competition.

Aircraft designs entered for what was effectively a competition included conventional concepts from Arado – the Ar 198 – and Focke-Wulf – the Fw 189– and an unexpectedly wild card in the shape of the Blohm und Voss Bv 141.

The Bv 141 was probably the world's first asymmetrical aeroplane. It was designed by Richard Vogt for the Hamburg-based company, which had been in existence since only 1932 and was in fact a division of the shipbuilding firm of the same name. Vogt had returned from a ten-year stint in Japan, where he'd been designing flying boats, to succeed Blohm und Voss's former chief designer, Mewes, and his brief was primarily to work on steel flying-boat hulls, as well as new aircraft. Vogt saw the challenge presented to him as a chance to guide and influence an entirely new concern with no past history to live up to or be influenced by. Vogt decided to be brave.

His first major design, the Ha 137, was considered a rival to the Stuka, and although it was rejected by the Air Ministry it found itself in good company, as projects from Heinkel and Arado were also turned down. It was a sign of the growing fortunes of the Blohm und Voss aeronautical division, however, that from employing 1,500 people in 1935 it had over 5,200 on its books by 1938. This workforce would find itself heavily engaged in the flying-boat projects we have already described in the years to come; but for the moment, Vogt focused on the Bv 141.

The plane he put forward for Blohm und Voss's tender looked bizarre, though Vogt was confident of its performance. In developing his design he had looked at his rivals' work and become convinced that their symmetrical layouts compromised the reconnaissance work they were intended for. He wondered if an asymmetrical craft couldn't perform the designated tasks as well, if not better, and as a result he placed the crew in a split-level, streamlined pod which projected a short distance on either side of the wing, but well to the right of the centre line. Just to the left of the pod was a long fuselage that mounted a BMW radial engine at its front and blended into a conventional tail at the back. Vogt's design theory was vindicated in practice, because having the weight and drag of the cockpit adjacent to the fuselage countered the torque generated by the single propeller.

Unsurprisingly, the Air Ministry officials were sceptical and wary of such a radical design, but Ernst Udet, then the newly appointed head of the Technical Bureau, encouraged Vogt to persevere. This gave Vogt enough leverage to apply to Blohm und Voss's Board for funds to build a first prototype. As a result of this initiative, the Air Ministry felt obliged to take a closer look at the aircraft. Originally designated Ha 141 (the Bv designation wasn't introduced until 1939), the first proto-type flew for the first time on 25 February 1938, surprising sceptical onlookers, who believed that even if such an unorthodox craft could get airborne no one would ever be able to control it. But in the event the only problem encountered was caused by vibrations from the landing gear.

Udet was not among those surprised, as he had already flown the machine and come away impressed by its sweet handling. An order for three more prototypes duly came through. After a little badgering from Blohm und Voss, the Air Ministry agreed to accept the first prototype as part of this order, and as a result it was confusingly designated V2; the V1 and V3 prototypes followed. There was an evaluation by officials of the Technical Bureau, and as a result Blohm und Voss modified the crew compartments on the next two machines. The split-level was replaced with a single open-plan cockpit, which made for greater room and flexibility, and the use of a large number of plexiglass panels improved all-round vision, following the example of the Focke-Wulf 189 that was then undergoing similar evaluation trials and had already adopted a successful observation cockpit. The second prototype

119

appeared in September 1938 but almost immediately had an accident on landing and had to be withdrawn for repairs. The third followed a month later.

These two prototypes were then developed into a pre-production A-1 series, of which five were ordered, with further modifications. The first of the new group, the V4, joined the test programme early in 1939. Changes included alterations to the tail to make it symmetrical, increasing the wingspan, and a number of smaller adjustments. Setting the style for all future models, the pilot now sat on the left-hand side of the glazed nose. The observer/bombardier sat on his right, his seat sliding back and forth along a track. In the forward position he could use his bombsight to deliver the four fifty-kilogramme bombs slung under the centre section of the wing. He could also fulfil his primary role as observer in this position by operating a camera pointing straight down through an aperture in the floor of the cockpit. After sliding aft and locking his seat in the rear position, he could both use the radio and man a 7.9-millimetre MG 15 machine-gun placed in an upper cupola. The third crewman was the rear gunner, who lay prone in a conical glazed nacelle at the back. This rear position had an outstanding field of vision, and the mounting meant that the MG 15 could fire through 360 degrees – another Focke-Wulf design. In addition, the 'A' series carried two 7.9-millimetre MG 17 belt-fed guns that fired forward from the lower front of the cockpit, operated by the pilot.

When the V4 started its evaluation trials at Rechlin it soon suffered one of the model's intermittent hydraulic failures in the landing gear and had to be repaired following a one-wheel landing. Failure of the hydraulic system seems to have been the only major fault experienced in the A-1 series, but it plagued every example and was never resolved. Once in flight, though, pilots and officials were won over by the strange aircraft, and by January 1940, when the other prototypes had demonstrated the model's suitability for its role, the Air Ministry was making grandiose production plans.

But the Luftwaffe high command was not convinced. It thought the machine too avant-garde and too slow, and it blocked the plans in April. With hindsight, this can be regarded as a bad error of judgement, as the aircraft would almost certainly have performed well in the open terrains of Russia and North Africa, and it probably possessed sweeter

Fa 284 'Project 1' This illustration shows just how the Focke-Achgelis skycrane might have looked, had it become operational. The simple, tubular-steel construction of the fuselage would have provided for an immensely strong and light craft capable of lifting up to 8 tons, and would have given the Luftwaffe unmatched flexibility in supplying troops in difficult terrain – such as that found in Russia.

Lippisch DM 1 The sole DM 1 built was intended to prove the radical aerodynamics of the forthcoming LP 13a, although the war ended before it could be completed. In a highly secret operation after the war, it was finished under American supervision and then transported to the USA, where its design helped shape the experimental 'lifting body' aircraft developed by NASA during the 1950s and beyond.

Lippisch LP 13a With the distinction of being possibly the first and only aircraft to be powered by coal, had the LP 13a ever been produced there's every chance that far from being a laughable technological cul-de-sac, it could have outpaced and outmanoeuvred even the most agile fighters of the day.

Heinkel *Wespe* This proposal for a dual piston-engined VTOL interceptor employed a similar flight system to Focke-Wulf's *Triebflügel* project, yet seemed saddled with similar problems. How would its pilot or the closely mounted propeller blades have coped with a bird strike, for example?

Focke-Wulf *Triebflügel* As the war drew to its conclusion, Focke-Wulf, along with many other aero manufacturers, began looking at ever more radical schemes. The VTOL *Triebflügel* was one such proposal and employed three 'steerable' ramjets, each mounted at the tip of a wing blade. Set in a revolving collar which spun at high speed, these blades would have provided the lift to match the forward thrust offered by the ramjets.

Restored by the Dornier company in the 1970s, this fine example of a Do 335 A-0 preproduction aircraft remains one of the most purposeful and visually aggressive piston engine fighters ever built.

Another view of a Do 335, in this case the Do 335 V1, possibly taken during its initial flight on 26th October 1943. It differed from all subsequent examples built in having a separate intake for the oil cooler on the forward engine ahead of where the front nosewheel doors would be.

The Go 229 as it might have looked in Luftwaffe service livery. It illustrates well too how the Jumo turbojet is skilfully moulded into the short overall length of the aircraft. Notice how the rear exhaust outlet is uncowled to allow for adequate heat dissipation.

characteristics than its rivals as well. It would certainly have been faster than the Fw 189, and it would have had a higher operating ceiling. But, as far as decisions were concerned, Luftwaffe high command (as with the RLM) was not known for its consistency, and its officials continued to make erratic judgements throughout the war. In the case of the Bv 141 it is ironic that it was the generally conservative RLM that was blocked by the Luftwaffe, instead of the other way round.

Vogt had foreseen likely objections and, in an attempt to get round the problem of the 141's slow speed, he had already started work on the 'B' series early in 1939. In the 'B' series the original 865-horsepower BMW 132 9-cylinder radial motor was replaced with the 14-cylinder 1,560-horsepower BMW 801 unit. This brought with it such an increase in torque and power that the airframe had to be all but rebuilt to cope. The wingspan was increased to 17.5 metres from 15, and newly strengthened landing gear was added. The increased length of the fuselage obscured the view for the rear gunner, so a single aileron tail, offset to port, was adopted to rectify this.

The 'B' mockup was approved in February 1940, and the first of five development aircraft – the V9 – flew the following January. The Air Ministry still had great hopes for the model, as it was expected to combine the sweet handling of the 'A' series with a top speed of 500 kph. Unfortunately, the V9 performed badly. Instability and problems with vibration and hydraulics all conspired to whittle away the goodwill earned by its predecessors. The Technical Bureau even had to restrict its top speed to 450 kph – a source of embarrassment to Blohm und Voss – and not until May 1941 was the V9 finally delivered to Rechlin. Difficulties continued. There were complications with the supply of components. The V10 gathered dust for three months while the right propeller was sought. Vibration problems didn't go away, and, when the twin MG 17 guns were fired, choking cordite fumes invaded the cockpit, since the gun-ports were too short to fully vent the smoke. The V10 finally arrived at Grossenhain for tests in autumn 1941. It made a good impression there, and an order was placed for sufficient 141s to form a group ready for operation on the Eastern Front by the following summer. It was impossible to fulfil, since Blohm und Voss by then was involved in building the Fw 200 Condor maritime patrol aircraft under licence and couldn't gear up an extra production line for the 141.

The final aircraft in the series, the V13, was delivered in May 1943, but by then its fate was academic: the Fw 189 had overtaken the Bv 141 and was already in service.

Vogt's idea for an asymmetrical design did not quite die with the 141. In 1942 he was working on the Bv 237, a dual-purpose dive bomber and ground attack aircraft, designed originally around a single BMW 801 engine, to which a supplementary turbojet was later added in the design. The 237 was to give a maximum speed of about 575 kph and would have carried one or two crew. It would have had an all-wooden fuselage with tubular-steel spars running the length of the wings, and thus it would have been a tough aircraft in its intended role. However, like all Vogt's subsequent asymmetrical designs, it never developed beyond the drawing board.

Flight of Arrows

One might be forgiven for thinking that the Luftwaffe was interested in developing jet aircraft only as the war entered its final phase. Yet, despite its belief in the new engines as a potent answer to the continuous stream of Allied bombers then overflying the Reich daily, the aero industry still had a few other surprises up its sleeve.

The Dornier Do 335, which seemed at first to be a conventional aircraft, was in fact a brave attempt to provide the dying Luftwaffe with a powerful night fighter-bomber and reconnaissance aircraft; the Do 335 turned out to be one of the fastest piston-engined fighter planes ever built, owing to its unique design.

Dr Claudius Dornier, the founder of Dornier Werke, had spent most of the 1930s developing new bombers for the Luftwaffe; but ever since the First World War he had been fascinated by the principle of 'centre line thrust', whereby two engines shared the same line of thrust, one pulling and the other pushing. In other words, two engines would be placed back to back, each driving either a 'pusher' (rear-mounted) or 'tractor' (nose-mounted) propeller. The benefits were clear: in presenting only one engine to the air, the frontal area would be reduced and consequently there would be lower aerodynamic drag. In addition, the wing shapes would be cleaner, and if one engine failed there would be no adverse torque pull from the other.

The only problem was in coming up with a common driveshaft connection, and this was where Dornier's extensive experience with flying boats came in. He had already built examples using engines mounted in line and sharing a common driveshaft. What proved to be the turning-point, however, was his revolutionary concept of having the two engines at either end of the fuselage with the cockpit between them. By 1937 he had patented the idea, and, convinced that it would work in practice, he commissioned Ulrich Hütter of the glider firm Schempp-Hirth to design and build a small flying test-bed aircraft, using an extended rear driveshaft to work a pusher propeller.

The result was the all-wooden Göppingen Gö 9. It had a slim, graceful fuselage based on a scaled-down Do 17, and an eighty-horsepower Hirth engine mounted at the centre of gravity, beneath the shoulder-mounted wing. After flying successfully for the first time in 1940, and reaching a speed of more than two hundred kph, the Gö 9's achievement encouraged Dornier to design a fighter employing the same principle. Predictably, the RLM's conservative Technical Bureau decreed that he should stick to bombers. As we have seen, the officials there wanted manufacturers to specialise in fighters, bombers or transports, and felt that designers working in the various fields should stay with what they knew best and not branch out beyond their experience. Manufacturers and designers, of course, disagreed, feeling for their part that such a policy led only to stagnation and ran counter to encouraging innovation. It was for this reason that when the Air Ministry advertised its need for a high-speed intruder aircraft, Dornier responded with a private project he'd been working on: the P. 231. Using the in-line concept of his patent, his aeroplane claimed not only to meet the high performance specified, but also the capability of carrying a thousand-kilogramme bomb load.

The competition for the intruder project was cancelled later that year, owing to reverses in the war which led the Ministry to alter its policy in favour of defensive aircraft. Dornier, however, had all but completed his design for the P. 231. Rather than let all the hard work go to waste, he secured an interview with Milch and presented to him a fighter variant of the original concept, which his team had in fact been working on for some months. The Technical Bureau had already turned down the idea, but Dornier was so convinced of the validity of his project that he wasn't going to take the first 'no' for an answer. Milch, impressed by what he saw, approved the project and authorised an immediate order for twenty evaluation aircraft. Heinkel was commissioned to build them, and the P. 231 was redesignated Do 335.

As work got under way, the Air Ministry began changing its requirements, wanting variants of the 335, as multipurpose day-fighters, night-fighters, fighter-bombers, Zerstörers (destroyers) and reconnaissance planes. Dornier was used to this kind of official vacillation, however, and the first prototype proceeded fairly smoothly as the Ministry's requests were worked into the overall design. The first flight took place, after only a slight delay in the schedule, from Dornier's Oberpfaffenhofen airfield in October 1943.

The 335 took the form of a long and aggressive-looking low-wing monoplane with a cruciform tail section and a fully retractable undercarriage. A small bomb bay was fitted with an initial capacity of either one 500-kilogramme bomb or two 250-kilogramme bombs. The tail section, monocoque fuselage and wings were all metal, which was unusual at the time, as many of the new designs then appearing favoured cheaper and more widely available materials such as wood. An 1,800-horsepower Daimler-Benz DB 603 engine and propeller were mounted in the aircraft's nose, with a second motor placed in the aft fuselage, driving its pusher propeller through an extended driveshaft. A ventral scoop, mounted beneath the rear engine, fed air through to its radiator, while the front engine took air from an annular opening around its outer cowling. As the fear had been expressed that if the pilot had to bale out he would run the risk of being cut to pieces by the rear propeller, the designers fitted explosive bolts to the tailfin, which would take the propeller mounting with it as it detached, thus allowing a safe escape from the aircraft. An ejector seat was also fitted, although its operation became a pilot's nightmare. Reports exist of two 335s crashing during the test programme: their wreckage was found minus the bubble canopy over the cockpit, but the pilots were still there, dead, their arms torn out of their sockets. These were early days for ejector systems: the pilot had to release the canopy before triggering the ejector seat in a separate action. If he held on to the canopy for fractionally too long as the explosive bolts attached to it carried it off into the air, its weight and the forward speed of the plane would conspire to rip his arms off. If he was still conscious after that, he would face a horrific death, unable to eject or control the plane any more.

By November 1943 Hitler, now increasingly preoccupied with the development of jet aircraft, disagreed with Milch's repeated suggestion that the 335 be fast-tracked into production. The Führer, seduced by discussions with Willy Messerschmitt about the bombing potential of his new jet Me 262, even though the plane was still in development, ignored the possibilities that the slower but more reliable Do 335 offered, though the latter aircraft was virtually ready for service. When Messerschmitt boasted of the five-hundred-kilogramme bomb capacity of the 262, Milch had to remind Hitler that a version of the 335 had been produced which could carry a load of twice that. Although he had no objection to jet development, Milch understood the situation on the ground better than Hitler. He saw that jets alone couldn't save the day and that they would need a new generation of conventional aircraft to back them up.

Since Milch had stood up to him, and since he knew all about Göring's animosity towards his Number Two, it is perhaps remarkable that Hitler did agree finally to include the 335 project as a fallback. Evil as he was, and increasingly ill-advised, Hitler was not a fool and had probably taken Milch's arguments in, especially regarding what might happen if the jets didn't arrive on time and there were no backup. But the go-ahead wasn't given until May 1944, by which time, although a full programme was set in train, it came too late to be effective.

After the initial trials at Oberpfaffenhofen, the V1 prototype moved to Rechlin for evaluation. Reports from this phase of its testing were favourable. Only slight stability problems had been encountered, and the aircraft could fly on only one engine if need be. It could also take off on one engine alone – a formidable achievement.

More prototypes joined the trial programme and the test-pilots nicknamed the new machine 'Ameisenbär' – 'Anteater' – on account of its long nose, though the official codename for it was 'Pfeil' – 'Arrow' – since it had a cruciform tail not unlike the flights of an arrow. The pilots reported excellent handling characteristics, a tight turning circle, reassuring power from the two engines, and a remarkable feeling of strength and solidity from the overall design. The V4 was the first prototype of the Do *435* night-fighter version, designed to combat the sorties of the RAF de Havilland Mosquito. The 435 design placed a second crewman alongside the pilot, whose job was to operate radar and radio apparatus. The cabin itself was now pressurised. In the V5 prototype, armaments were installed: two fifteen-millimetre MG 151 machine-guns in the upper fuselage and one thirty-millimetre MK 103 cannon arranged to fire through the forward propeller hub. The V6, 7 and 8 were used to test other configurations of engines and weapons. The V9 was delivered to Rechlin as the final example on which the production model would be based. The first of ten pre-production aircraft followed in June 1944 with full armament, ready to begin trials with Erprobungskommando 335, an experimental unit established that September expressly to conduct tactical evaluation of the aeroplane.

By January 1945 the first true A-1 production model had arrived from Oberpfaffenhofen, complete with the definitive DB 603E engine and its larger supercharger. There were two new under-wing mountings capable of carrying either extra fuel tanks or a pair of 250-kilogramme bombs in addition to the 1,000-kilogramme load now available in the bomb bay. Similar to the A-1 was the A-4, an unarmed reconnaissance version, of which only one was ever completed by adapting a prototype model, fitting it with two cameras in the weapons bay and attaching extra fuel tanks to the wings. The DB 603G engines, which were to have been fitted together with larger superchargers and other refinements to give the A-4 a superior performance at altitude as a compensation for its lack of armament, never materialised.

Pfeil Themes and Variations: Nachtjägers and Zerstörers

Next in a long line of Pfeil variants was the A-6, adapted from the V10 prototype. This was an all-weather night-fighter, or Nachtjäger. The armament was the same as for the A-1, but three radar systems were planned, their aerials to be mounted ahead of the wings' leading edges. Another crewman was needed to operate the equipment, so a second cockpit was added above and behind the pilot, instead of the cramped side-by-side arrangement previously adopted. Apart from giving the aircraft a humpbacked look, the new seat ate into the space available for the main fuel tank, so the bomb bay was deleted and replaced with a redesigned tank. The negative effect of the extra weight and drag was a ten per cent drop in performance, though this was offset somewhat by fitting water-methanol-boosted DB 603E engines instead of the more usual DB 603As used by the first 335s.

The Nachtjäger was to have been produced by Heinkel at Heidfeld, near Vienna; but Heinkel was too busy producing their 'Volksjäger' – 'People's Fighter' – at the time and never got around to organising a production line. In the end, delivery delays on the radar systems – the consequence of Allied bombing of the Ruhr factories producing precision instruments – were to prevent the A-6 from ever being completed.

The final pair of 'A' series craft were the A-10 and the A-12 (developed from the V11 and the V12). These were trainers, which used the second cockpit developed for the Nachtjäger to house the instructor.

The 'Zerstörer' was the next in the Pfeil series to be developed. This took place during the winter of 1944–5 and the finished plane emerged from the Oberpfaffenhofen works as the Do 335 B-1. The role of the 'B' series in the Luftwaffe's plan was straightforward: the Zerstörer fighters were to take out the Allied fighters escorting the bombers as they flew in and then to harass the unprotected bombers themselves. The task required aircraft with considerable endurance and firepower. The single-seat V13 saw the replacement of the bomb bay with an enlarged fuel tank, and the two fifteen-millimetre MG 151s were replaced with two twenty-millimetre MG 151 machine-guns. The V14 which followed was even more heavily armed, retaining the twenty-millimetre guns and adding a thirty-millimetre MK 103 cannon to each wing. Both these Zerstörer prototypes were captured by French troops and removed to France in 1945, where they were tested at an airbase near Paris. In fact, they were the only two completed, although the V15–V20 group was in production as the war ended. This group included a pair of two-seater night-fighters with 'B' series heavy armament; another prototype was fitted with the DB 603LA engine, which had two-stage superchargers.

Other developments on the drawing board included three Pfeil machines that had a wingspan extended by 4.3 metres for greater performance at altitude, though their designs were never realised. There was also a Do 535 night-fighter in which the aft DB 603 engine would have been replaced with either a Junkers Jumo 004 or a Heinkel HeS 011 jet; the 535 was seen as a more effective 'fly swatter' for the RAF Mosquitoes than its predecessor, but it wasn't developed owing to the non-delivery of the Heinkel engine into service, the Jumo had always been there, but the 535 was geared around the HeS 011. Another non-starter was the Do 635 long-range reconnaissance aircraft, another 'twin' project, which aimed to join two machines together with a new central section. As the war situation worsened, so Dornier was obliged to pass work on this project on to Heinkel, who in turn passed it on to Junkers. Junkers started to develop the Ju 635 along similar lines, but again the adverse fortunes of war closed down the project.

The Do 256 was another variant which would have filled the role vacated by Messerschmitt's superseded Me 110 heavy fighter. The two in-line engines of the original Pfeil design were to have been replaced with a pair of wing-mounted HeS 011 jet engines. The nose would then have been free to accept the installation of four thirty-millimetre MK 108 cannon. The pilot's position was the same as previously, but his navigator was placed some distance aft, occupying the space formerly taken by the rear engine, in his own backward-facing cockpit. The 256 deviated too far from the original concept of the Pfeil, however, and in any case would never have reached production since Heinkel was having problems delivering the engines around which it was designed.

Germany's surrender put a final stop to production of the Pfeil. Thirty-seven had been completed, and a further seventy-odd were still awaiting final components and assembly. To have achieved even that much was notable, given the chaotic circumstances of the time. From 1944 onwards, no other new projects were considered for production unless they were either jet or rocket powered; that Dornier had managed to push the Pfeil through at all is a testament to his powers of persuasion, his connections in the corridors of power, the integrity of his design, and the standing of the Dornier Company, which by 1943 had produced over 1,800 Do 217 bombers alone.

As far as we can tell, the Pfeil never saw active service, although at a top speed of 760 kph it is still one of the fastest piston-engined fighters ever built; and the speed is all the more impressive when one considers that the Pfeil weighed three times more than the Messerschmitt Me 109, which it was aimed indirectly to replace. The

Oberpfaffenhofen plant was overrun by US forces in April 1945, and a handful of surviving examples of the Pfeil were taken to Britain and to the USA. All were eventually written off either in crashes or through general deterioration, except for one or two carefully preserved models. This was a sad end for an aircraft that ranks as the epitome of the piston-engined fighter. It was also one of the last of its kind. Following the war, designers and manufacturers of fighters worldwide turned almost exclusively to the jet. The Pfeil ended the era that had begun only thirty years earlier with the Sopwith Camels and Fokker triplanes of the First World War.

'Adolfine'

In the mid-1930s, when Germany's aero industry had emerged from the shadows and was designing striking new military aircraft, both the Air and Propaganda Ministries saw opportunities for generating positive publicity from its success. German manufacturers were encouraged to compete fiercely in breaking aerial records all over the world, using adapted production-line aircraft, rather than specially built models, as a means of increasing their cachet. The most successful of these was the Heinkel He 100 fighter, which raised the absolute world speed record to 745 kph in March 1939, and was originally suggested as a possible replacement for Messerschmitt's seminal Me 109.

A rare exception to this rule was the Messerschmitt Me 261. Messerschmitt's original Projekt P. 1064 was begun in 1937 as a general study for a long-range reconnaissance monoplane, and took the basic design and layout of the then new 110 heavy fighter as its starting-point. This meant a long, slim fuselage with two wing-mounted engines and a simple tail section incorporating two elevators on either side of the rear body, each capped with small endplate fins but with no main tailfin. The Air Ministry approved the project after becoming convinced that the plane was capable of taking the world long-distance flight record and gave it the designation 261. The plan was for a completed example to carry the Olympic flame from Berlin to Tokyo for the 1940 Games (which were aborted owing to the war) in a record-breaking nonstop flight. The undertaking captured Hitler's interest and hence the 261 got its unofficial name, 'Adolfine'. Willy Messerschmitt, who had founded his Bayerische Flugzeugwerke in Bamberg in 1923 at the age of twenty-five, found that his star was rising dramatically. On the urging of Dr Goebbels, the company was renamed Messerschmitt in 1938; it was from then on that Messerschmitt's aeroplanes took the prefix 'Me' in place of the earlier 'Bf'.

Although the 261's general configuration appeared orthodox, the design encompassed a number of highly unusual features for its day, setting many precedents. For example, the single-spar all-metal wing was sealed to serve as a fuel tank, and its depth at the root was only slightly less than the height of the fuselage it was joined to. The fuselage itself was of almost rectangular cross-section, providing space for five crewmen. The two pilots sat side by side, the radio operator in a compartment immediately aft of the flight deck, and at the back there were further compartments for the navigator and the flight engineer beneath a glazed section allowing natural light into the interior. Here, too, were bunks for rest periods. Because the wing was constructed in one piece, which passed straight through the fuselage, its main spar had to be bowed at that point to allow the crew freedom of movement. Power came from four Daimler-Benz DB 601 engines, a pair to each wing in a coupled arrangement known as the DB 606: each pair drove a variable-pitch, four-bladed propeller through a shared gearbox and generated a considerable 2,700 horsepower as a result. The extra weight of such a heavily fuelled and engined aircraft had to be allowed for in the design of the undercarriage; this comprised a nose-wheel and two large-diameter main wheels mounted in the undersides of the wings and retractable into wells behind the engines. The undercarriage's large wheels prevented the plane from getting bogged down on grass strips or tripping on obstacles.

The construction of three prototypes began in spring 1939 at Messerschmitt's Augsburg plant, but progress was slow since it seemed more and more likely that war would break out and that consequently the Tokyo Olympics would be cancelled. The 261's original design brief as a long-range reconnaissance craft appears to have been forgotten, and as the plane was therefore viewed as non-strategic it was in danger of being shelved altogether. But someone within the Air Ministry directed attention back to the project as a useful test-bed for evaluating long-range operations, and work resumed in summer 1940.

The first prototype flew on 23 December with Messerschmitt's test-pilot Karl Baur at the controls.

In the first week of 1941 Willy Messerschmitt wrote to Udet with the results of the maiden flight. Although his tone was optimistic in predicting an eventual range of over 20,000 kilometres for the type, he reminded Udet that the North Americans were already working on their B-17 'Flying Fortress', and that its arrival on the scene would establish their dominance in the field. His implication was that if the Air Ministry wanted to beat the B-17 to it, it would have to back him to accelerate development.

The second prototype flew during the spring of 1941. By now official thinking viewed the 261 as a long-range machine for maritime patrol. As a result, the glazing for the aft compartment was reduced and assumed a more aerodynamic 'blister' shape. Messerschmitt realised that armaments couldn't be fitted to fuel-carrying wings, and so both prototypes were tested for endurance right through until 1943. In March 1941 there was talk of sending one or both of them to drop propaganda leaflets on New York, but nothing came of the idea.

The V3 prototype arrived belatedly in spring 1943. It differed from its predecessors in having two 2,950-horsepower DB 610 engines (another paired design) and accommodation for two more crewmen. On 16 April, with Baur at the controls, the V3 flew over 4,500 kilometres in ten hours and unofficially claimed a new endurance record, which could not be confirmed as war conditions made it impossible for the flight to be adequately observed. Soon afterwards it was damaged when its hydraulics failed on landing, and was taken to Oranienburg for repairs. Thereafter it was used on *ad hoc* long-range missions for the Luftwaffe's reconnaissance division, though the 261 was never adopted officially, since not only could weaponry not be fitted easily into the wings and their integral fuel tanks but equipping it with radar and other equipment would have meant reducing the fuel load and consequently its range. The two earlier prototypes were damaged during an Allied raid on Lechfeld airbase in 1944 and subsequently scrapped.

Ahead of Their Time

When describing all the aircraft in this chapter, we have the impression of machines that were truly ahead of their time, and yet which paradoxically were outmoded by the time their development was complete. The Bv 141 lost ground to the less adventurous but more practical Fw 189; yet Blohm und Voss persisted. Perhaps the reason they did so was to try to recoup some of their production costs by seeing the type through to completion.

Dornier had persisted, too, with his Do 335, treating its development like a personal crusade, though it must have been obvious to him that it would have been superseded in any case, the moment jet designs were perfected. He himself abandoned his treasured in-line engine concept for his proposed Do 256 jet.

Messerschmitt's idea for the Me 261 was courageous, but why did it occur to no one from the outset that the fundamental difficulties of mounting guns to fuel-carrying wings would be insurmountable? Especially as the plane had been designed with a military application in mind? And yet had the 261 reached production in the form originally envisaged, its combination of range and speed would have made it a more-than-effective Atlantic patroller, reporting on the positions of Allied convoys and warships; and it would have been unassailable for quite some time. As it was, Britain was able to organise effective countermeasures against the spotter aircraft which eventually arrived, and the U-boats in the Atlantic were deprived of a useful eye in the sky during the early days of the war.

The real reason for the failure of these aeroplanes may lie in a mixture of wartime confusion and lack of vision from officials, coupled with a natural conservatism. It was only late in the war that the Nazi administration started to pay close attention to the real innovative potential of the designers it had working for it – but by then, of course, it was too late.

Chapter Six

THE VOLKSJÄGER COMPETITION

Origins

The story of the Volksjäger began early in 1944 when Air Ministry officials inspected a new jet-fighter project called P. 1073 'Spatz' – 'Sparrow' – which had been designed in semi-secret by a team within the Heinkel company led by Siegfried Günter. This project was to form the basis for Heinkel's own ambitious Volksjäger venture, and the story of the competition it was involved in serves as a good illustration of the extent to which political influence and self-interest within the Luftwaffe high command impeded progress in the German aeronautical industry as the country entered the closing phase of the war. When one examines the records now, one is amazed that anything was achieved at all, such was the disorder that existed before Speer took control of the new Ministry of Armament and War Production. Invested with sweeping powers to rally and direct what was left of Germany's industrial infrastructure, Speer was able to ensure the survival of the production of both aircraft and armament well into 1945. Given the dwindling state of resources and production capacity, his achievement, however regrettable historically, was remarkable.

Early in 1944, with an Allied landing in France on the cards which would impose fresh demands on the Luftwaffe, Heinkel's designers began to study the Messerschmitt Me 262 jet fighter. This was then on the brink of entering full service, but the Heinkel designers saw that its basic design was flawed in two principal areas. First, the Me 262 had been given fairly straight wings – the result of an imperfect understanding of high-speed aerodynamics at the time of

133

its design. By 1944, of course, it was understood that swept wings best served a jet engine. The second problem lay in the location of the engines themselves: they were mounted on the underside of the wings, and the extra drag this caused undermined the 262's overall performance.

German Intelligence would have passed on to them the information that both the British and the North Americans were developing jet fighters using engines based on Frank Whittle's original design. The Heinkel team feared that the Allied jets would have already overcome the problems inherent in the 262's design and would thus have immediate superiority over the Luftwaffe's new fighter. They therefore decided to work out a new concept for the jet fighter, with swept wings and a narrower fuselage, incorporating two of their own HeS 011 engines, one under the fuselage at the front, the other above the fuselage aft of the wings. The lower front jet solved airflow problems but created insurmountable new ones as far as ground clearance was concerned. The front engine was scrapped, the tail of the new fighter was adapted to a butterfly design, and the jet exhaust was directed between two anhedrally mounted fins. As the HeS 011 engine was still mired in development problems at the time, Heinkel used the same Junkers Jumo as the Me 262. The fact that they had plumped for an upper-mounted engine rather than one installed within the fuselage made adaptation to the Junkers motor all the easier.

The Allied landings began in June 1944, and these, coupled with the accelerating collapse of the Eastern Front, forced the Luftwaffe high command to identify the weaknesses in its fighter 'umbrella'. Göring had stated publicly long before that if ever Allied bombers flew over Germany, then people could call him 'Meyer' – a term of abuse. Now, the citizens of Berlin had started to nickname the air-raid sirens 'Meyer's hunting horns'. The Luftwaffe saw that the old warhorses like the Me 109 were losing ground to the new long-range Allied fighters such as the Mustang, used to escort the inexorable waves of US and British bombers. The bombers themselves were passing over Germany with little resistance, the Americans by day and the British by night, seemingly at will. Other Allied attack aircraft, like the Hawker Typhoon and the Lockheed Lightning, were targeting strategic sites with impunity, and the overstretched Luftwaffe could not do anything to stop them. It was time at last for the Air Ministry to get down to brass tacks.

Volksjäger

This led to one of the most inspired aeronautical projects of wartime Germany. The idea of the Volksjäger originally stemmed from the fertile mind of Karl Otto Saur, Chief of the Fighter Staff – Fighter Staff being an RLM department absorbed into Speer's new Ministry on 1 August 1944. Working to interest Göring, Saur took his inspiration from the Volkssturm, the German version of the British Home Guard, into which First World War veterans and boys too young for regular conscription (and those not already in the 'Hitler Youth') were drafted for duties ranging from tank-trap construction to actual combat.

He called for a simple, inexpensive jet fighter that could be mass-produced from available materials (stocks were dwindling rapidly) and which might replace the expensive, labour- and material-intensive Me 262. Saur's office liaised with the Air Ministry on the matter, and on 8 September a basic design specification was issued to all the major manufacturers.

The specification was indeed basic. Even so, in Germany's parlous circumstances, the manufacturer who won the contract would still have his work cut out to produce a single machine, let alone start production. The fighter was to be powered by a single BMW 003 turbojet and weigh no more than 2,000 kilogrammes fully loaded. It was to be armed with one or two thirty-millimetre cannon; its top speed was to be 750 kph with a maximum endurance of 30 minutes on its fuel load and the fighter had to be capable of taking off within 500 metres. The latter idea, for a short takeoff, no doubt stemmed from the damage sustained by German airfields through bombing. If the aircraft could fly from grass fields, so much the better – bomb damage to tarmac was expensive and time-consuming to repair.

The time limits set for fulfilment of these requirements were daunting: the submission date for proposals was 20 September, only twelve days after the notice had gone out, and the fighter was to be ready for mass production by 1 January.

The scheme had its objectors, among them Adolf Galland, the fighter ace, who believed in concentrating on the production of the already proven Me 262. The Messerschmitt company didn't submit designs for the new fighter, believing the time limits set to be unrealistic and impractical and pointing out that the specification for the project didn't even provide for access to essential components and spare parts: the suggestion was that any fighter that became unserviceable should be abandoned and replaced with another straight off the production line – a kind of *throwaway* plane. The only concession was that the engine of an otherwise airworthy fighter could be replaced in the field; and presumably all usable spare parts would have been stripped and recycled. BMW was working at full stretch just to produce engines, and there was little or no surplus production facility for spare parts in any case.

Undismayed by the dissenting voices, the Air Ministry, no doubt increasingly desperate, brought the deadline for tender submissions forward to 14 September – only six days after they had been invited – and on 15 September a hastily convened meeting was called in Berlin to consider the proposals received. The meeting was not to run smoothly owing to a fundamental bureaucratic error.

The submission from Focke-Wulf was thought unrealistic, even though its origins lay in a private project conceived by the company at about the same time that Heinkel was developing the Spatz.

Focke-Wulf's remaining factory capacity was by that time hard at work building Fw 190 fighters in the face of continuous Allied bombardment, and it is highly probable that the company would not have been capable of mounting a brand-new production line. The design it tendered consisted essentially of a cylindrical fuselage wrapped around the BMW engine, which was mounted aft, necessitating a long induction shaft from the air intake at the nose, which would have caused a reduction in power. The engine was mounted low down, which meant that there would be a significant danger of sucking in foreign bodies, such as grass or small stones, while taxiing, and given that alloy turbine blades were apt to shear off due to unknown and unmeasurable stresses, the planes would probably have required high maintenance – precisely what the Air Ministry wanted to avoid. The bubble canopy of the cockpit was mounted just forward of the wing roots, and the single main tailfin was surmounted with an arrowhead wing. The concept came in two variants, either with a swept or unswept shoulder-mounted wing.

Focke-Wulf's chief designer, Kurt Tank, was not convinced by the Volksjäger project, as he believed any new fighter built fast with limited resources would inevitably be outclassed by new Allied jets like the Lockheed P. 80 Shooting Star and the Gloster Meteor. His lack of conviction showed in the Fw proposal.

At the 15 September meeting the Air Ministry officials considered the P. 211 from Blohm und Voss to be the best proposal, although it, too, featured a low-mounted engine which would have had the same problems as the Fw design. Blohm und Voss had always been able to keep production costs down through a sparing use of costly materials in all its designs. In common with all the frontrunners in the competition, the company used a mixture of steel and wood in their plane's construction, keeping rubber and duralumin to a minimum. In the lead-up to the meeting, once they had realised that the rival Heinkel design was at least unofficially the favourite in the eyes of the Ministry, Blohm und Voss cut costs and development time for their own project still further by replacing the original swept wing with a straight one. The low-slung engine, again with a long induction shaft, still militated against it; but with its fuel tanks mounted in the wings, its overall range and performance were thought to be sufficient, and in terms of cost and quality of construction the P. 211 was a formidable contender.

The Arado company's design was similar to Heinkel's. Its E. 580 proposal mounted the engine above the fuselage and added a shroud to the front of the jet which reached down to the canopy of the cockpit. This would have had the effect of directing the air deflected off the canopy back into the engine, thereby improving operating efficiency. The disadvantage was that the arrangement restricted access to the cockpit and reduced the pilot's chances of baling out safely in an emergency.

Heinkel's representative at the meeting, Doktor Ingenieur Francke, was told that his company's proposal, P. 1073, failed to convince on the following five counts:

a) Endurance at sea level of only twenty minutes, not thirty, as specified.

b) The location of the engine above the fuselage could lead (as on the Arado design) to operational and maintenance difficulties.

c) Stipulated takeoff requirements were not met.

d) The time needed to dismantle the fighter for transport by rail was too long.

e) The fighter carried a single twenty-millimetre cannon (a thirty-millimetre cannon had been specified).

Francke immediately protested to the Ministry officials present that the rival submissions had had their weight and performance data calculated *differently* from those given to Heinkel and that the Heinkel proposal was therefore unfairly cast in an unfavourable light. The Air Ministry, wishing to appear as impartial as possible, accepted the objection, ordered the other teams to adjust their figures to fit the Heinkel model and to reconvene on 19 September. It is interesting that the others had to conform to Heinkel's specifications, not the other way round. Was Heinkel's design the one that best combined performance with cost-effectiveness, even if it weren't objectively the best overall? And were matters therefore being engineered to guarantee its success?

The 19 September meeting again confirmed the Bv P. 211 as the best candidate, though it broke up in a heated argument between the delegates from Heinkel, Blohm und Voss and the Ministry, and no firm decision was reached officially. The Bv fighter was good: its airframe met the weight criterion and was even somewhat lighter than Heinkel's model. It gave better all-round vision to the pilot, and because the engine was low slung and not mounted just behind the cockpit, not only was the pilot safer but access to the engine for maintenance was easier – the engine could be removed without the need of a crane. In addition, Blohm und Voss had come up with the fastest build time.

However, the meetings to decide on a winner were merely academic. Göring had already plumped for the Heinkel design, and if it fell a little short of its rival in meeting the prescribed specifications, what did it matter, since *he* considered it the better aircraft overall? No further investigation of the P. 211 was promised at the second meeting, and Francke even attacked it vigorously, pushing home the advantage he knew that Heinkel had in Göring's patronage and trying through attack to deflect attention from the Heinkel fighter's shortcomings.

In fact, as soon as the competition had been announced, the Heinkel team had worked night and day to develop the Spatz into the Volksjäger. Karl Otto Saur favoured their project from the start, and Saur was an avid Nazi who had the ear of Göring. It didn't matter that the Blohm und Voss machine was actually the better of the two. The only real advantage Heinkel had was spare manufacturing capacity.

On 24 September development of Projekt P. 1073 began. It isn't insignificant that when Hitler ordered the first Volkssturm units to be formed under Himmler's general command that same month, Göring, sensitive to any rivalry at the top of the Nazi tree, had wanted to set up complementary Volksjäger squadrons; Saur's inspiration was political as much as disinterested. Following a meeting with Artur Axmann, leader of the Hitler Youth, Göring arranged for an *entire year's* intake of teenagers to train on gliders – they were to be the first pilots of the new Heinkel Volksjäger fighters.

A final Air Ministry meeting on 30 September confirmed Heinkel's selection – to the fury of the other competitors. To legitimise the decision, scientists from the Aerodynamic Trials Unit were called on; they duly made a tentative suggestion that there was a faint possibility of unstable airflow into the Blohm und Voss fighter's engine intake – and therewith the matter was closed. An optimistic production rate of 1,000 fighters a months was projected, and the original He 500 designation (an old Messerschmitt project number) was changed, to confuse Allied Intelligence, to He 162 and condenamed 'Salamander' – the latter was never a nickname, as has often been thought. Final drawings were completed on 29 October, a day ahead of the schedule set by the Technical Bureau, and soon afterwards the first prototypes were nearing completion.

The method of production remains unprecedented even today: all the main phases of development proceeded simultaneously, and there were three final assembly plants. The first ten prototypes were built at Heinkel's own Schwechat factory near Vienna, but three manufacturing centres were established at other Heinkel plants. At Marienehe – 'Heinkel Nord'; at a former chalk-mine at Mödling, also near Vienna – 'Heinkel Sud'; and at a Junkers plant at Bernberg near Dessau. *Each* factory was expected to produce a thousand fighters a month. In addition, the Mittelwerke company was to be phased in over time, and it was to produce *two* thousand examples a month, as well as continuing its ongoing production of the V-2 rocket.

All three plants were to receive components from a huge network of over 150 sub-contractors specialising in different areas. For example, wooden components were to be produced by furniture-makers in Erfurt and Stuttgart and brought to the assembly plants by road and rail. The BMW 003 engines were to be produced in a former salt-mine (which provided protection from air raids) near Urseburg, to which both the Berlin-Spandau and Basdorf-Zülsdorf BMW engine plants had already been transferred. Unit production was scheduled at 6,000 a month. The steel fuselages were to be produced in old salt-mines at Egeln and Tarthun owned by Junkers, as well as in other plants dotted about Germany. The Tarthun plant was 300 metres under rolling farmland and held 2,000 workers capable of producing 500–700 fuselages a month. These were brought to the surface at night in massive lifts and moved by rail to the assembly plants, care being taken to avoid the attention of marauding Allied night-fighters. The entire programme was to be overseen by a specially formed construction group – Baugruppe Schlempp – under the direction of Heinrich Lübke. The schedule called for 1,000 completed aircraft by the end of April, and 2,000 a month thereafter.

The design of the aircraft was simple. It comprised a sheet-steel monocoque fuselage with a nosecap made of Formholz which as we have seen was effectively a forerunner of fibreglass. The single-piece wing was mostly made of wood, with detachable aluminium tips, and it was attached to the main fuselage at its shoulder with four bolts. The sharply anhedral tailplane was designed around the exhaust efflux of the jet: its elevators and rudder were of metal, with twin wooden fins inwardly canted at their extremities. The BMW turbojet was bolted directly to the upper fuselage, as in the original P. 1073 concept, and covered with three sheet-metal cowlings, giving all-round access. A small Riedel two-stroke starter motor was fitted within the cowling. Operated from within the cockpit, it would start the BMW jet without the need for additional ground crew and equipment. The standard 153-gallon fuel tank was mounted directly behind the cockpit and could be gravity fed by additional small tanks in the wing if required, the wood of the wing having been proofed to hold the fuel without leaking.

The cockpit was fairly spacious and, compared with the Me 109, was fitted with simple instrumentation. The traditional ability of German industry to produce precision instruments was by now adversely affected by the war, and as in many other areas at this time only essential instrumentation was installed. The cockpit was surmounted by a clear bubble canopy which gave good vision except to the rear where the engine was. It was equipped with a simple Heinkel ejector seat and parachute, a previous version of which had been seen in the He 280 and was now regarded as essential, since the fighter had a projected five- to ten-hour combat life only. In deference to the original Air Ministry specifications, twin thirty-millimetre MK 108 cannon were first fitted, but after severe vibration problems were encountered, and room for only fifty rounds per gun could be made, two twenty-millimetre cannon each with a hundred and twenty rounds were eventually substituted.

The first prototype, He 162 V1, flew from Schwechat for the first time on 6 December 1944, four days ahead of schedule, with Flugkapitän Diplomer Ingenieur Peter at the controls on behalf of the Technical Bureau. During this initial twenty-minute flight a speed of 840 kph was attained at an altitude of almost 6,100 metres, but it was brought to a sudden end as an indirect result of an Allied bombing raid. The only factory capable of producing the adhesives used in bonding the wooden fuselage together, the Goldmann plant in Wuppertal, had recently been destroyed. With production of the fighter running twenty-four hours a day and seven days a week, pressure to begin flight tests was enormous, and so unsuitable acidic glues had been used as substitutes on the V1. As a result, a weakly glued wooden undercarriage door was torn away in flight, unable to withstand the considerable loadings placed on it at high speed as the acid in the glue ate into the wood. Consequently, Peter had to abort the flight, but notwithstanding the mishap his report overall was favourable.

Four days later, on 10 December, there was a second flight at Schwechat in front of delegates from both the Luftwaffe and the Air Ministry, as well as Ernst Heinkel himself. Once again flying the V1, Peter tried an unscheduled low-level pass as part of his display. He shredded the leading edge and tip of the starboard wing as a result, going into an unavoidable barrel-roll which crashed the plane and killed him. Examination of the film shot at the time and of the wreckage confirmed that the faulty glue was to blame, but the decision was taken not to hold the project up. In order to quell the murmurs of dissent in some official quarters, Francke himself elected to fly the V2 prototype. Francke, a professor and a director of Heinkel, had once been a test-pilot for the Technical Bureau, so he was in an ideal position to allay any fears that might attach to the enterprise. The flight he made on 22 December was a success, as were subsequent test-flights in which he took the V2 to the limit, as well as putting the MK 108 cannon through their paces – thirty-millimetre cannon were retained up until the V6 prototype. The V3 and V4 were modified according to what Francke had learned: both received elongated tail booms, a more pronounced anhedral angle to the wingtips, and a dead weight over the nose-wheel to bring the centre of gravity forward. The V3 and V4 both took their first flights on 16 January 1945.

The initial ten prototypes were considered to be pre-production aircraft, constructed in parallel with the 'A-1' series then entering production proper. However, by 20 January 1945 it became apparent that all thirty-four aircraft partly completed by Heinkel at Marienehe would require additional strengthening, and so at its own expense the factory hired additional workmen to augment the line and rectify the first examples before they were shipped out. Prior to this, flight-testing had been restricted to under 800 kph as a safety measure. The V5 was used for static tests, and the V6, the last to be fitted with thirty-millimetre cannon, first flew on 23 January. The V7 was the first to be built to the new pre-production standard and was used for vibration testing. The V8, 9 and 10 all used the new twenty-millimetre cannon and were built to the same standard as the V7.

The first two 'A' series fighters proper flew on 24 and 28 January. They were allocated prototype numbers V18 and V19 and, fitted with the newly modified BMW 003E engines, they were used for endurance trials. Given the short lifespan of German jet engines at that time, maximum power could be sustained safely only for about thirty seconds, after which the engine would need a major overhaul (though in the case of the Volksjäger they were simply replaced). V11 and V12 were fitted with the Jumo 004 turbojet as tryouts for a later version. Prototype number V13 was omitted in deference to superstition. V14 and V15 were used as static test-beds. V16 and V17 were developed as prototypes for the He 162 S two-seat glider, which was to be used as a trainer for the recruited members of the Hitler Youth destined to be the pilots of the Volksjäger. They had larger wing and tail surfaces, a second cockpit replaced the engine, and they carried a simple fixed undercarriage. Speeds of up to 420 kph were recorded during dive tests. The V20 had a cheaper, simpler undercarriage than had been used hitherto. The V21 was used in armament trials. The V22 featured wing refinements; and the V24 and V25 were reserved for contingency testing. The other prototypes built up to number V36 were mainly used in attempts to refit the larger thirty-millimetre cannon.

The eventual 'A-2' production series was fitted with two twenty-millimetre MG 151 machine-guns which, as they weighed sixty per cent less than the MK 108s yet carried twice the number of rounds per gun, necessitated the introduction of an additional lead weight over the nose-wheel to maintain the correct centre of gravity. The possibility of engine shortage had been in the minds of the design team since the beginning, and provision had been made for fitting various alternatives to the BMW 003 unit. The Junkers 004 was one; another was Heinkel's own problematical HeS 011 – in fact, this engine was never to proceed beyond pre-production, and only nine finished examples are thought ever to have been built. The initial fighters to carry this engine were the He 162 'B-1' series, with a projected production schedule due to start in 1946, by which time the problems encountered during the engine's protracted development were expected to be solved. It is astonishing how late in the war Germany still thought it was in with a chance. Although structurally similar to the 'A' series, the 'B' series specification included a stretched fuselage and a larger fuel tank, twin MK 108 cannon (with a hundred rounds per gun), and a sustainable cruising speed of 880 kph at sea level.

Clutching at Straws

Project studies had also suggested fitting Argus pulsejets, though the unfavourable characteristics of those units were wholly unsuited to manned aircraft, as Messerschmitt's experience with its own Me 328 had shown. As a result, Heinkel designers didn't give them serious

143

consideration until, as German industry continued its dramatic decline, Fighter Command and Saur himself persuaded them to take another look. Göring viewed the idea with scepticism, and this attempt by Saur to curry favour with the Ministry merely reinforced his opinion. Göring was right: investigation into the possibility of using the Argus engines immediately threw up difficulties. There was insufficient takeoff power, even with two engines; fuel consumption was enormous; and as expected there was excessive vibration.

It was therefore decided that this particular variation should be adapted for use as an expendable manned missile. The longer 'B' series fuselages were used since the pulsejets could be mounted further aft, minimising the intrusive vibrations, and Heinkel put forward two proposals: one envisaged using a pair of Argus engines placed side by side, and the other suggested using a single powerful As 044 pulsejet in place of the existing turbojet. Given the weight of either configuration, performance estimates were very optimistic; and as the pulsejet performed badly at altitude, the craft would have been restricted to low-level strikes. In addition, it would have to be fitted with auxiliary rockets to get airborne. No one was fully convinced by the project, however, and it advanced no further than one prototype of the twin-engined version, which reputedly flew in March 1945 at Bad Gandersheim. The aircraft was entered in the later Miniaturjäger competition, but only half-heartedly, and subsequently it sank without trace.

The 'B' series continued in development, though, and soon led to the 'C' series, which matched the long fuselage with back-swept wings and the sharp anhedral 'butterfly' tail that had previously been seen on the He 280 V8. The 'D' series was essentially the same but featured a swept-*forward* wing similar to that of the Junkers Ju 287 jet bomber, which neatly removed a stalling tendency and permitted a higher taper of the wing's outline. Both 'C' and 'D' were supposed to carry a pair of thirty-millimetre cannon on special mountings that would enable them to fire slightly above the horizontal line. Neither type was built, but when the Allies seized the Schwechat factory they found a scale model with interchangeable wings.

The last He 162 the 'E' series, was developed separately and used BMW's experimental 003R engine – it was even flight-tested. The engine mixed a standard 804-kilogramme-thrust BMW 003A turbojet with an 11,227-kilogramme-thrust BMW 718 rocket, and although problems had been experienced with the rocket's fuel tank seals, it was hoped to have these ironed out in time to begin mass production by the summer of 1945. A spectacular performance was expected, including a maximum speed of over 1,000 kph at sea level (Mach 0.82), and an altitude of 1,000 metres was to be reached within twenty-four seconds of standing start, with 5,000 metres attainable inside two minutes. When using the rocket for climbing and the turbojet for level flight, endurances of up to forty-three minutes were expected. Only one 'E' series model was built, and whether or not it actually used the rocket is no longer certain, but it certainly flew with the BMW 003R.

Blind Faith

A large proportion of the new Hitler Youth intake seconded to train to fly He 162s were also members of the Fliegerkorps – the state-sponsored sporting flying club – which had supported the young pilot training programme as a means of maintaining its own *raison d'être*. High command expected that the bulk of the youthful trainees should therefore have little difficulty in training on the gliders before moving on to the powered jets that they were to fly in anger; though as the training period was to be between five and ten hours, the jump from novice to jet-fighter pilot seems a little optimistic. Nevertheless a training unit was established at Trebbin and took delivery of a number of He 162 S gliders in a single-seat version. The teenaged pilots were never to fly the real thing – luckily for them.

Before this ridiculous scheme could get under way the aircraft first had to be accepted by the Luftwaffe and proven to be practicable. In accordance with procedure, an evaluation unit was set up under the command of Oberstleutnant Heinz Bär. This unit was Volksjäger Erprobungskommando 162, operating under the aegis of the Technical Bureau first at Rechlin and later at Lechfeld. Ground crew training was, curiously, undertaken elsewhere. The test-pilots requested minor refinements as a result of the evaluation: the radio reception range needed to be increased and gun cameras needed to be installed; but these were details. Intermittent production, the result of delays in the delivery of supplies and components to the assembly plants, meant that actual operational duties for the Volksjäger could hardly be envisaged before May 1945.

No Straws to Clutch

The honour of commanding the first operational Staffeln was awarded to Oberst Herbert Ihlefeld's Jagdgeschwader 1 (JG 1) – fighter group – which had acquitted itself well in Operation Bodenplatte – Baseplate – of 1 January 1945 – an ambitious part of the Ardennes offensive in which the Luftwaffe had swooped on unprepared Allied airbases. On 6 February the unit handed over its Fw 190s and moved to Parchim, about sixty-five kilometres from the Heinkel factory at Marienehe, where they began conversion training alongside factory pilots.

A week after their arrival, JG 1 was reduced from its old strength of four squadrons to three, as IV/JG 1, owing to lack of staff and equipment, was dissolved and absorbed by the other three squadrons. I/JG 1 spent nine weeks at Parchim before transferring to Ludwigslust, about twenty kilometres to the south-west, on 8 April for final pre-operational trials. At the same time II/JG 1 was transferred to Marienehe, where it was equipped with fighters direct from the production line.

Only six days after arriving at Ludwigslust, I/JG 1 was again transferred, this time to its intended operational base at Leck, near the Danish border. Formerly a minor dispersal area, the base had become a major collecting point for surviving Luftwaffe units in North Germany, and its airfield was crowded with elements from several divisions, including Ar 234 jet bombers and Me 262s, as well as conventional fighters. Conditions were chaotic, supplies and maintenance facilities were hopelessly inadequate, and I/JG 1 was all but immobilised for lack of fuel. It wasn't unknown for one of the squadron's tankers to spend a week driving around the local area in search of enough fuel just to mount training flights, so bad had things become. And the general confusion was reflected at the highest level, as Hitler now placed the entire jet programme into the hands of the SS, under Obergruppenführer Kammler. Göring promptly responded by appointing his own 'Special Representative for Jet and Rocket Aircraft' – General Josef Kammhuber.

Meanwhile, ɪɪ/JG 1 continued its conversion to the He 162 at Marienehe; but its commander, Hauptmann Dähne, was killed over the Baltic on 24 April and by the end of the month Soviet forces had advanced so close to Marienehe that the base was abandoned; the squadron moved to Leck under its new commander, Major Zober. Soon afterwards, Zober merged his squadron with ɪ/JG 1, which became a group of three squadrons numbering more than fifty aircraft in all; and the group absorbed the remains of other units in the following days under the overall command of Ihlefeld. By this time, Bär's Erprobungskommando 162 had also been incorporated, into Adolf Galland's JV 44 elite fighter unit, and when Galland was wounded on 26 April, Bär assumed command. There wasn't much for him to preside over. After transferring the mixed unit of Me 262s and He 162s to Salzburg, he gave the order for them to be destroyed to prevent their falling into the hands of the Americans.

Snuffed Out

With the curious stickling for bureaucracy that typified much of the general staff, the Luftwaffe, even as the regime collapsed, strictly forbade the He 162s to go into action against the enemy because the acceptance certificate for the model had not yet been signed. Nevertheless, the fighters did engage – unofficially. The first operational flight was on 21 April, and a few days later, on the twenty-sixth, Unteroffizier Rechenbach made the first kill for the 162 in an engagement with two low-flying Allied aircraft. Rechenbach was posted missing the following day, but a second kill was registered by Leutnant Rudolf Schmitt of ɪ/ JG 1 on 4 May, who reported shooting down a Hawker Typhoon near Marienehe. (Both these kills are still officially unconfirmed.) That was the extent of the 162s' battle career.

Explosive charges had been laid in all the jets at Leck in order to destroy them if the Allies invaded the base, but the end of the war precluded such a drastic measure, and according to the terms of surrender the fighters were handed over to the victors intact. The Allied tanks that rolled into Leck on 6 May were followed two days later by British and American Intelligence teams ready to evaluate the captured technology. In total, about 120 162s had been completed and delivered to the Luftwaffe, and at least 50 more had been collected by their pilots direct from the various assembly lines. When hostilities ceased, another 100 were awaiting flight-testing and a further 800 were in various stages of construction.

Conclusions

The 162 was no aircraft for novices: its controls were quirky and even experienced pilots who were used to throwing their machines around the sky had to relearn basic techniques in order to get the most out of the model. The slim fuselage carried a narrow-tracked undercarriage similar to that of the Me 109, which meant that landings had to be made with caution as well.

As far as Göring's idea for an armada of Volksjäger units went, in the sense of a true aerial equivalent of the Volkssturm, the Luftwaffe records only one such group at Sagan-Kupper in 1945, though its activities aren't known; it was probably a basic trainer formation. The consequences of using Hitler Youth pilots in action would have been not only counterproductive but suicidal, and the story of the He 162 had for the Nazis the depressingly familiar moral of 'too little, too late'. Of the ten or so shipped to Britain at the end of the war, one was lost on its fifth flight at Farnborough in November 1945, when its tail section broke away during manoeuvres and it crashed into a barracks, killing the pilot. One fine example, originally with I/JG 1, can still be seen at the Imperial War Museum in London.

Despite all its shortcomings and vicissitudes, the Volksjäger programme as a whole still seems remarkable. To have got a jet fighter up and flying virtually from scratch within three months was very impressive; equally impressive was the organisation of so large a manufacturing base in the circumstances Germany faced late in the war. That Heinkel managed it, only to be thwarted in the end by an inefficient fuel supply, is to his credit, but it also points to the inefficiency of the administration. The Allies had been targeting German fuel dumps and German-controlled oilfields since 1943, and yet the Luftwaffe concentrated less on defending them with intense air cover than on sending increasingly ineffective fighter sorties out against Allied bombers as they flew over from Britain. Equally, high command must have known how little fuel was available by late 1944, and yet they happily set in train a huge fighter programme that would have needed millions of gallons if it were ever going to function. But by the end of 1944 most Nazis could not distinguish even the lies they told themselves from the truth, and squandered what few resources they had in the onward rush to their downfall.

Chapter Seven

LIGHTING THE BLUE TOUCHPAPER

Snakebite

Picture a forest clearing. The ground crew have been working there for a little over three hours, erecting a launch tower made up of what looks like a giant set of Meccano and organising the refuelling pumps. A lorry has just arrived with a precious cargo. The men unload what seems to be a rocket and manhandle it into position, slotting its wing tips into the two grooved rails running the length of the tower. The pilot arrives soon after the lorry, driving his own jeep. He's wearing a casual uniform: a black leather bomber jacket with a fleece collar over a standard-issue Luftwaffe *feldgrau* flight suit, and a flowing white silk scarf round his neck which just fails to conceal the Iron Cross First Class at his throat. He salutes the crew with a negligent *Hitlergruß* (Nazi salute) and walks towards his chariot. It sits on the launch platform some two metres above the ground, its nose pointed at the grey and wintry sky. The pilot climbs a ladder, and once he has reached the cockpit he swings round to climb in. This is an awkward manoeuvre, and he is helped by two ground crew already in position. Soon he is strapped in and ready to take off. The ground crew retire to a safe distance as the whine of the start-up generators begins to fill the air, soon followed by the muted rumbling of the rockets' fuel pumps. Their monotonous drone is swamped quickly by the roar of the five rocket motors themselves, so loud that they stun the senses. The air shimmers in the heat haze, and in a billow of smoke the chariot rushes up its launcher into the sky. The 'chariot' is a Bachem 'Natter' ('Viper'), charging to attack a fleet of B-17 bombers flying far overhead.

Once the launch area has been declared safe by a blaring klaxon and the smoke begins to clear, the team immediately begins the arduous task of packing all the gear away. They have just received orders to move the launch pad to another site where they must rendezvous with another Natter and its charioteer.

Such a thing never happened in fact. The war ended before the Natter had progressed beyond prototype testing, but the scenario illustrates what Allied bombers would have had to face if Germany had managed to hold on for a short while longer. In the existing histories of the development of rocket fighters towards the end of the Second World War, centre stage is usually given to Messerschmitt's Me 163 Komet, which was the pioneer craft of its kind. But there were others, like the Natter, to which less attention has been given in the past, and the aim of this chapter is to redress the balance. Before coming to them, however, it is worth considering German interest in rocketry as a whole, since here the seeds were sown which would grow not only into the terrifying military applications that we know today, but also into the rival programmes of space exploration in the USSR and the USA which started with Sputnik 1 in 1957 and led twelve years later to the first landing of a man on the moon.

The Deutsches Forschungsinstitut für Segelflug

We have already mentioned that the punitive (and deserved) restrictions placed on Germany by the Treaty of Versailles obliged Germans to find indirect ways of exploring their interest in flying. Gliding provided one permitted way forward, and in 1930 the eminent aerodynamicist Dr Alexander Lippisch built his highly original and successful delta-winged Delta I glider.

One gliding club in particular grew to prominence through the achievements of its members. This was the Rhön-Rossitten Gesellschaft, established in 1925 on Mount Wasserkuppe, near Fulda in Hessen. One early member was Willy Messerschmitt, who had been flying his own glider designs from the Wasserkuppe since 1921. In 1933 the club moved to Darmstadt-Griesheim aerodrome, where gliders could be towed into the air, rather than depend on air currents. Here, the club was taken over by the Nazis and converted into the Deutsches

Forschungsinstitut für Segelflug – the DFS, or German Research Institute for Gliding. Professor Walter Georgii was put in charge and extended its scope. He established a design department, directed by Ingenieur Hans Jacobs, which would be responsible for many future glider designs with military applications; and he recruited Hanna Reitsch as chief test-pilot in 1935. Among the models created and tested at the DFS was the robust transport glider DFS 230, of which over a thousand were built for use by the paratroop regiments, notably in the invasion of Crete in 1941, and the freeing of Mussolini from his mountain confinement in 1943.

As part of its study of gliding and soaring flight, in 1934 the DFS organised a private trip to Brazil for several eminent glider pilots, including Hanna Reitsch, who was not yet an employee of the Institute. The purpose of the trip was for them to experience the strikingly different conditions in that part of the world, and ride thermal currents ideally suited for soaring flight. Professor Georgii went with them and was gratified to see his pilots establish several new gliding endurance records. The Nazis were quick to make propaganda capital out of the event (such as newsreels and blatant press articles), and although not all members of the group were happy about this, because they felt their achievements were overshadowed by the propaganda itself, there was nothing they could do.

By the mid-1930s the DFS had been divided into several separate departments, each dealing with distinct lines of research. The Meteorological Section was led by Georgii, and Jacobs headed Design. Other departments looking into instrumentation and aerodynamics were established as time went on, especially after Lippisch had joined the DFS and began to evolve the idea for the Me 163 Komet out of models developed at the Institute. During the war, the DFS remained more or less independent of the military and was permitted to conduct research into areas unconnected with gliding, including its own range of advanced rocket-propelled aircraft, which culminated in the DFS 346 (described in Chapter Nine). Among other parallel projects closer to the original brief was the development of assault gliders.

A short description of German rocketry, discussed more fully below, is appropriate. Dr Hellmuth Walter's first rocket motor took to the air in February 1937 when one of his early prototypes was mounted on the underside of a Heinkel He 72 biplane trainer. At that time the rocket ran on hydrogen peroxide and a sticky-paste catalyst, and gave a thrust of 136 kilogrammes for 45 seconds. It was soon discovered that the catalyst paste could be replaced with a more efficient liquid catalyst, and two months later, in April, ground handling tests began with the new units. Two aircraft were now used to test the rockets for taxiing: an Fw 56 and a Ju A50 Junior. The new rocket performed well, doubling the thrust accomplishment of its predecessor, though only for thirty seconds. The reduced burn was acceptable because getting the power up was the most important first step. The success of this test generated so much optimism that a unit was retrofitted into the He 72 for in-flight testing. From these beginnings Walter went on to develop his pulsejet motor, which was used most notoriously in the V-1 flying bomb manufactured by Fieseler, as well as powering the Me 328. The use of pulsejets for manned aircraft, however, was to meet with little success.

Messerschmitt Loses His Touch

Throughout his years of success with piston-engined fighters, Willy Messerschmitt had remained interested in the idea of producing a cheap, simple and robust turbojet aeroplane. The Me 328, which was to fulfil this role, could trace its origins to work undertaken by the DFS in Augsburg in 1941 as they refined another Messerschmitt project, P. 1079. P. 1079 was a design for a small fighter in which various combinations of turbojet were installed. (The DFS research for the enterprise was later channelled into another Messerschmitt small fighter project, P. 1101, a prototype of which was captured by the Allies in 1945, leading to the development of the USAF Bell X-5 which made its maiden flight on 20 June 1951.)

In 1942, however, with the tide of war beginning to turn against Germany, Messerschmitt began to alter the role of the original P. 1079, and in due course the project led to the cheap jet fighter Me 328, four of which could be produced for the price of one Me 109. The Me 328 would be crude and slow, but Messerschmitt was concerned above all with saving crucial production costs at that point in the war. To do so he decided to use the Argus As 014 pulsejet, then in development for the V-1, in the Me 328.

As it was a bargain-basement aircraft, the Me 328 was mostly made of wood, with straight wings mounted low on the fuselage and an all-wood tail section of fairly conventional construction and appearance. The single-seat cockpit was high up in the fuselage, giving the pilot a good field of vision along an extended, tapering nose section. So far, so good. But the initial tests, using a full-sized mockup attached to the upper fuselage of a Do 217, went badly and were damaging to the project as a whole, owing largely to the variety and number of problems encountered by the use of the pulsejets. These jets functioned very simply: fuel was dribbled into the front of the air intake at short intervals. This mixed with the incoming rush of air, and the mixture was ignited under pressure within an internal-combustion chamber before exhausting through a rear vent, thus giving forward thrust. The main problem was that unlike a true jet engine, which produces continuous thrust and therefore little vibration, the pulsejet works in a series of short bursts or pulses – hence the name. As a result it produces vibration on a large scale, and when four such units are mounted on an aircraft, each operating on its own cycle, the aircraft becomes tough to handle. It's not hard to picture the difficulties encountered by the test-pilots who were brave enough to fly the early prototypes. The Argus was perfectly viable when used for the purpose for which it was designed; but when it was applied to manned flight it turned out to be not only a false economy but a disaster.

Messerschmitt's cost-cutting had resulted in an airframe of poor configuration and construction, and the pulsejets caused it to resonate horribly. At one stage, after a few tail sections had broken away under the forces imposed on them, the project's senior management realised that radical changes would have to be made to the design if it were to be rescued from complete failure. They had some success with the fitting of a 109 tailfin – large numbers were being produced as spares for the famous fighter, so they were readily available – but the central defect lay in the use of the Argus engines, which, it was also found, couldn't operate efficiently at what was held to be the 328's optimum altitude.

Plans were revised, drafted and redrafted. Perhaps the 328 could be used for operations in which speed and height weren't crucial? But there were still practical considerations which militated against the aircraft, and it is a wonder that Messerschmitt persisted with it. The fact that its construction was mainly wooden meant that no skilled metalworkers or frontline designers were delegated to the project – their talents were in greater demand elsewhere. The principal manufacturer was the Schweyer Glider Company in Mannheim, which had made gliders for Rhön-Wasserkuppe, but whose staff, depleted by the call-up, found the construction of a military aircraft almost beyond them. The only production team they could muster was small and inexperienced. However, ten prototypes were built; they were fitted with a variety of engines.

Two were tested as low-speed, low-altitude fighter escorts, possibly of Me 264 'Amerika' bombers (presumably the bomber would be towing the 328s as there was no way in which they could hope to reach the bombers', normal altitude). One had two and the other four Argus jets fitted. One of the test-pilots was Hanna Reitsch. It's not known what either she or her colleagues thought of the 328s, but the vibrations set up on the model with four Argus engines must have been unimaginable. To operate at all, either version would have had to be towed up to its best height by a Ju 88 or something similar, and in the end it was felt that the 328's low height capability meant that it simply wasn't worth using in this role.

Another variation was the 'B' series. This project involved mounting the plane on top of a medium bomber such as a Ju 288, a configuration that had already been tried and was known as '*Mistel*' – 'Mistletoe' – because the smaller craft would have been carried by the larger in the same way as mistletoe, a parasite, depends on its host. Carrying a 500-kilogramme bomb load, the 328 would be released at low altitude and used as a low-level ground-attack fighter. The 328 was fitted with a Walter-Schmidding takeoff rocket at each wing tip to enable it to accelerate away from the parent aircraft, and it had extendible skids on which to land. Only one version was ever built, as the usual problem of vibration hadn't been resolved.

The final version appeared in 1943. This was the Me 328 C. This time the fighter was fitted with a Jumo 004 turbojet, which solved the problem of vibration at a stroke but invalidated the whole project in terms of cost. In any case the 328's mediocre aerodynamics meant that an expensive turbojet would be wasted on it – though such thinking didn't hinder the development of the other cheap jet project the Air

Ministry went in for a year later – the Heinkel 162. Perhaps by then the war situation had become too desperate to allow either rational consideration or freedom of choice.

Some reports state that the Me 328 C was actually on the point of entering production in one of the many underground factories in Thuringia, but that the factory was destroyed in an Allied bombing raid before it could get going. There seems to be no hard evidence to support these reports, though, and it is unlikely that they are true. A version of the 'C' series was mooted at one point for use on U-boats from catapult launchers, but the expense of installing them, especially given the unreliability of the 328, quickly ruled this idea out too.

As the war drew towards its close, the 328 was considered as a possible suicide glider-bomb. In this role it would have flown with a large explosive charge in the nose section; but this extreme application was never taken up.

Von Braun Enters the Arena

Modern rocketry can trace its roots to the early 1920s when both scientists and enthusiastic amateurs were taken up with this futuristic field of research in the wake of the First World War. In the USA the pioneering work of Robert H. Goddard inspired people all over the world; but at the very beginning only a few people were aware of the potential rocketry had. One of these was a Transylvanian student called Hermann Oberth. During the early 1920s Oberth was in Munich studying medicine. It was there that he first developed an interest in rocket research, and by 1923 he had produced a book entitled *The Rocket Into Space (Die Rakete zu den Planetenräumen)*, in which he discussed the possible future construction of liquid-fuelled rockets and the problems their builders would face in getting them beyond Earth's gravity. Oberth's book was a milestone in the early days, collecting together as it did all the theories and technical descriptions that existed at that time. Its influence in Germany was so great that in 1927 an amateur Society for Space Travel was established – the Verein für Raumschiffahrt, or VfR. Its purpose was to explore the new science and pursue Oberth's thinking.

The members of the VfR flew their own experimental rockets from an abandoned ammunition depot in the suburbs of Berlin, which they renamed the Raketenflugplatz (Rocket Launch Site), and their activities attracted not only bystanders but many new members at every meeting. One of them was Wernher von Braun, the indisputable father of modern rocketry and an antihero if ever there was one – in terms of the weapons he developed for Germany, and the concentration-camp labour employed for the underground factories in which they were built. He was fifteen years old when the VfR was founded; he was soon to become one of its leading lights.

It was the realisation that rocket research could lead to advanced military aircraft and spacecraft which prompted discreet state support in 1930 of a proving ground at Kummersdorf, about thirty kilometres south of Berlin, under the aegis of the Army Ordnance Office. Kummersdorf's role was to investigate the use of simple rockets in the battlefield – perhaps as antitank weapons. But as work there got under way under the command of Hauptmann Walter Dornberger, so a new recession arrived which shook the country's delicate economic confidence. In 1932, the year in which von Braun became seriously involved in rocket research, the VfR had become so desperate for funds that it sought contract work from Kummersdorf, and this led to a small demonstration being put on for the benefit of the Ordnance Office. The military were sufficiently impressed to offer civil engineering posts in rocket development to leading VfR figures like von Braun and Klaus Riedel, but they didn't do this immediately. And the hoped-for contracts didn't materialise either. The VfR was forced to close its Rocket Launch Site, which reverted to being an ammunition depot two years later.

Perhaps the military had deliberately engineered the collapse of the VfR so that it could bring all rocketry work under its own wing. The Ornance Office took on only the cream of the VfR membership, and with people like von Braun working full-time in the field the army began to build ever-larger rockets, which it started to fly from a launch site on the small North Sea island of Borkum. Dornberger capitalised on his unit's success by approaching his superior, Generaloberst Werner Freiherr von Fritsch (who was later brought down as a result of his criticism of Hitler's war plans), and requesting greater resources and a larger operating area. Visiting Kummersdorf, von Fritsch was impressed. After careful consideration of security requirements, the small Baltic coastal village of Peenemünde was chosen as a suitable base, and the construction of a huge site began in the winter of 1936–7. Staff from Kummersdorf were transferred there slowly as buildings to house their departments were completed. The site was to see the development of the V-1 and the V-2 as well as numerous other special aerospace projects during the course of the war, until in 1943 the British launched the bomber raid codenamed Operation Hydra, which put an end to its effectiveness.

Before von Braun became wrapped up in planning for Peenemünde full-time, he made a series of proposals of his own. Among them was an idea for a vertical-takeoff, rocket-propelled interceptor which he submitted to the Weapons Office after joining its staff.

In spring 1937 von Braun had fitted several rockets of his own design in turn to the fuselages of a pair of Heinkel He 112 piston-engined fighters. These were used in ground handling tests and proved the reliability of his designs before he took one of the aircraft on to the next stage, which was flight-testing. Disaster struck in April when the He 112 crashed heavily – the selected rocket had failed and the pilot hadn't been able to regain control of the fighter – and it wasn't to be until the summer that another rocket successfully powered the second 112. The top speed of the fighter was found to have been increased by a third with the addition of the rocket – to more than 290 kph. At the time, however, rockets made by the Walter-Werke were thought to be the most reliable, so von Braun retrofitted these to his He 112 in 1938.

The entire experience led him to design his own interceptor, which was to have a rocket powered by nitric acid and visol (a fifty/fifty mixture of petrol and benzol). The unnamed craft was to be stored vertically in a hangar, supported on a trolley frame which engaged with and in turn supported two-thirds of each wing's trailing edge, so that the thing would have looked like a roosting metal bat. When the plane was due to fly, the trolley would have been wheeled outside and the interceptor would have taken off vertically directly from it. Once its mission was over and its rocket fuel expended, the craft would glide back to base and land on a ventral skid before being remounted on its frame and refuelled. But von Braun's concept was ahead of its time and he was unable to make much more progress with the idea, gaining greater success with the unmanned weapons he was later to develop. In fact, not until the advent of the Natter was the idea of a reusable vertical-takeoff interceptor explored again in any depth.

The 'Julia' Project

By spring 1944 it had become clear to Luftwaffe high command that serious measures would have to be taken if it were to counter the increasing waves of Allied bombers penetrating the Reich. The Me 163 Komet was turning out to be ineffective against the Allies' B-17 'combat box' formations, and the Me 262 was not yet being used in its true role as a fighter. As a result, several unusual schemes were now looked at for a new 'point-defence' plan which had been designed to stop the rot.

The basic thinking behind the point-defence idea was that Germany should be divided up into geographical boxes or parcels of land. Each area would contain its own specifically assigned fighters, and as the Allied bombers passed over so these interceptors would rise up like a swarm of wasps to attack them. As the bombers flew on, so they would meet one such attack after another, passing from box to box. The bombers' return home would meet equally stiff resistance as the fighters would have already refuelled and could be waiting for their return.

Essentially, the defence model needed a new kind of aircraft: one that would be cheap both to build and to operate; one that would be robust and reusable, and if possible have the speed to outmanoeuvre the Allied fighter escorts. If weight were to be kept low, then a short operating range and endurance would have to be accepted, but given the box system this wouldn't be a problem provided that the aircraft had a short turn-around time.

Various manufacturers were invited to put proposals forward later that year, and among them Diplomeur Ingenieur Erich Bachem made his first appearance with his submission of the BP 20 'Natter'. He was in competition with the Heinkel P. 1077 'Julia', the Junkers EF 127 'Walli' and Messerschmitt's Project P. 1104.

Heinkel won the contract. Bachem had submitted his proposal through influential but unofficial channels offered by his close associate Hans Jordanoff, and as Technical Director of the Fieseler-Werke, builders of the V-1 flying bomb, he also had close ties with Peenemünde. But his attempt to get in through the back door, as it were, cut no ice with the Air Ministry. There were other considerations. Heinkel was a preferred and established plane-maker and its Julia project had been in development since that August so it was actually granted the point-defence commission on 8 September. The company won because the Julia was easy and cheap to build and had low running costs. In addition, Heinkel already had its own dedicated woodworking shop in Vienna, which could be geared up to build the Julia very quickly. The Air Ministry could not really have hoped for a more suitable contender.

As for Messerschmitt's offering, it seems to have been an unusually half-hearted affair which never left the drawing board and was dropped as the company concentrated on the other pressures that the deteriorating situation in Germany was placing on all industry.

Like the Natter, which did in fact follow it into production later, the Julia used a Walter rocket enclosed in a fuselage of simple wooden construction. Armament was light – only a pair of twenty-millimetre MG 151 machine-guns – which suggests that the intention was that the fighter would dart through the combat boxes of B-17s, letting off opportunistic bursts of gunfire whenever a bomber crossed its sights. The Air Ministry ordered the construction of twenty pre-production models, and Heinkel duly placed the work with its woodworking plant at Vienna which, they felt, would be far enough away to be relatively safe from Allied raids. Because the Julia had been designed from the outset to a simple construction plan, it required only a fraction of the workforce later needed to build the Natter. Only twenty-five wood-workers were necessary in Vienna, joined by two specialists: a flight-control engineer and a foreman to interpret the plans. Overall leadership of the project was given to one of the two original designers, Walter Benz, who envisaged production lines based on woodworking benches – it was that simple. On 22 September the Air Ministry issued orders to proceed at a rate capable of delivering three hundred machines a month, which threw everyone into confusion, since they had barely begun to fit out the plant for making the first example.

Having secured the contract, Heinkel then appeared to prevaricate. It was as if they preferred to develop the project further rather than actually to make anything; although, of course, they may just have been preoccupied with other things – we just don't know. On 15 October the company submitted plans to the Air Ministry for further variations of the Julia. These involved a variety of different engines, armaments and cockpit configurations, and it wasn't until 26 October that Ernst Heinkel himself opted to develop one of them as the finished production design. The simple, cylindrical fuselage was unchanged and retained its wooden build, as did the rectangular-shaped wings, which were still mounted above the fuselage. The pilot, however, would now lie prone in a reduced cockpit, as this arrangement was believed to help offset the high 'g' force numbers expected – 'g' denoting the rate of acceleration due to gravity. During manoeuvres involving fast climbs, tight turns and dives, the pilot would be moving with or against the force of gravity at speed and subjected to a greatly magnified version of the effect one feels on a roller coaster.

The single Walter rocket motor within the fuselage was also retained, its two fuel tanks immediately aft of the pilot. On either side of the nose was now mounted a thirty-millimetre MK 108 cannon. The ammunition for each gun came from storage space adjacent to the fuel tanks. Instrumentation was minimal, including only the basics, such as an altimeter, an airspeed indicator and a fuel gauge.

The Julia was designed for vertical launch, and it was intended to land wholly intact on retractable skids which were mounted ventrally. Wind-tunnel tests began on a small-scale model; later manned gliding trials were carried out on a full-size version minus the engine. Unfortunately for the project, the fates were against the Julia, as the woodworking plant was unexpectedly bombed by the Allies later in the autumn. By now, Heinkel was already preoccupied with the Volksjäger project, and following the destruction of its works the Julia was sidelined, though the undertaking was moved twice – first to Krems and then on to Linz, to a sub-contractor's factory owned by the firm of Schäfer, who were asked to complete two powered models and two glider versions. Heinkel did continue to tinker with the design at their plant in Neuhaus on the River Triesting, but when the Red Army took the town all data on the Julia project there vanished. Maybe one day an archive in Russia will be opened that reveals them, but the likelihood is that they were mislaid amid the fog and confusion of war.

The Natter

Undeterred at having lost the competition to Heinkel, Erich Bachem used his contacts and credentials to secure an interview with Himmler, who showed an immediate interest in his project, seeing it as a point-scoring exercise for the SS over the Luftwaffe and the regular army. Within twenty-four hours the Natter proposal was referred back to the Air Ministry for re-evaluation.

Bachem had designed his fighter as a vertical-launch, rocket-propelled, semi-reusable interceptor. The idea was neither unique nor new, but where the Natter scored over its rivals was in its simple construction and its use of components that were not expensive or strategically important elsewhere. It was also versatile: its innovative launch rails could be fitted to a warship if necessary, endowing the remaining fleet with an aerial capability hitherto denied the ships, as the German navy had no aircraft carriers. Adopting a similar line of approach to that of Blohm und Voss, with their Bv 40 glider, Bachem had gone for a mainly wooden construction which could be built by unskilled and semi-skilled labour, with individual components assembled in any number of small carpentry shops dotted around the Black Forest region, and brought together as completed sub-assemblies at the Bachem finishing plant. This method of construction anticipated the system advocated as best practice by many manufacturers today.

The inventor had got hold of a modest undamaged factory at Waldsee, about forty kilometres from Lake Constance, which housed a small design office within its walls. He collected technicians from wherever he could find them, and a rocket expert from the Walter Werke, and began development in earnest in August 1944 through the newly formed Bachem Company, just in time for the competition already mentioned. By the autumn, having bounced back, Bachem had over 60 skilled staff on his payroll in addition to 250 largely female semi-skilled assembly workers who were farmed out to the various local sub-contractors working for the project. Because of Himmler's patronage, the enterprise was taken into the Emergency Fighter Programme from September 1944 and received the official designation Ba 349, along with an order for fifteen prototypes.

As originally envisaged, the Natter, which was not designed with a

163

landing capability, was to mount a two-stage attack. In phase one it would fire its assault rockets at enemy bombers within their tightly packed combat boxes before climbing to a higher level and then diving to ram another target for phase two, the pilot ejecting shortly before impact. But it was soon discovered that fitting an ejector seat was too costly and time-consuming, and that it wasn't worth sacrificing each aircraft after only one mission. Phase two was abandoned, and the plane was redesigned. Now, the rear fuselage, containing the valuable rocket engine, would break off and parachute to the ground for recovery and reuse. The pilot would parachute out at the same time, there having been no ramming manoeuvre. Other detailed design improvements continued with wind-tunnel testing, which revealed little to desire in the Natter's aerodynamics, until an overall final version was arrived at. In contrast to the Horten brothers, Bachem had access to every facility, even though the Hortens' Go 229 also fell within the Emergency Fighter Programme; the brothers were denied such basics as wind-tunnel time too.

The launch tower was first designed as a steel latticework structure like the big piece of Meccano described at the beginning of this chapter; it stood a little over twenty-three metres high. Towards the end of the war, as steel became ever scarcer, this was replaced with a simple nine-metre telegraph pole with a pair of shortened launch rails bolted to it. Common to both designs was the need for a solid concrete foundation into which the gantry could be secured, though the telegraph pole version could be quickly dismantled and removed from a mounting set into such a base. With dozens of these small foundations scattered around a launch area, ground crews could move their gantries from one to another fast, and Allied pilots would be lucky to trace them. We are familiar with the concept used by modern rockets such as the 'Ariane' series used by the European Space Agency. The rocket is free-standing on the nozzles of its boosters, needing an adjacent gantry only to top up fuel tanks and give service access. Any in-flight course corrections can be made by adjusting the angles of the nozzles to redirect the thrust. The Natter, however, had fixed nozzles; and as the 'g' force on takeoff could be so powerful that the pilot might momentarily lose consciousness, it needed a degree of built-in control as it left the gantry to avoid any erratic manoeuvres. As a result, the Natter was 'locked' into the launch tower, its ailerons fixed to direct it, once free of the tower, until its pilot was conscious again and could override the built-in autopilot. A steel winch mounted at the top of the tower was used to haul the Natter into the vertical-launch position. Running the length of the tower was a pair of slotted rails, some four metres apart, into which the Natter's reinforced wing tips were slid as it swayed on the winch cable. Once this was done, the lower sections of these launch rails were bolted into place, enclosing the wing tips securely. On launch, the fighter would run smoothly up these rails into the sky, by which time the pilot would have recovered and become acclimatised to the speed, ready to take the controls.

The chunky and inelegant airframe was made of wood, metal being used only for essential control linkages and so on. For its manned gliding tests only, a simple fixed tricycle undercarriage was fitted. The fuselage was a laminated monocoque with a single-spar wing that passed between two fuel tanks. The stubby wings had no aerodynamic control surfaces; it was left to the ailerons on the cruciform tail section to give the only control and generate most of the lift. The wing tips were sheathed in metal plating to reinforce them during liftoff. After giving consideration to several different armament types, Bachem opted for an arrangement of twenty-four hexagonal tubes in a honeycomb pattern, each holding a 73-millimetre Föhn assault rocket. There was also provision for thirty-three 55-millimetre R4M missiles, and both configurations were shrouded by a jettisonable plastic nose-cone. The look of the rockets gave rise to the nickname 'Raketenwabe' – 'Rocket Honeycomb'. As the pilot only had to aim for Allied combat box formations, it was hoped that semi-skilled pilots would be able to fly the Natters, thus saving training time and fuel on conventional fighters, and the resource of the fighters themselves, since their combat life expectancy was under ten hours.

Importance was placed on providing a suitably armoured bulkhead for the cockpit in case anything should go wrong during the launch or the firing of the weapons. Sandwich armour was placed around the monocoque sides and, as an aft bulkhead, an armoured plate was inserted between the pilot and the two fuel tanks behind him. Additional protection was provided by a sixty-millimetre-thick windscreen and ten-millimetre-thick side glazing. Instrumentation was, as usual, spartan, the weapons being aimed through a simple crosshair sight forward of the windscreen. The fuel tanks contained a 95-gallon supply of 'T-Stoff' fuel and a 45-gallon supply of 'C-Stoff' catalyst to power the Walter 509 rocket motor. The thrust-to-weight ratio was slightly less than that required for vertical takeoff, so four jettisonable 500-kilogramme-thrust Schmidding solid-fuel boosters were attached to the rear.

Initial acceleration wasn't calculated to exceed a 'g' force of more than 2.2, but as we have said an attempt was made to protect the pilot as far as possible by presetting the ailerons while on the ground (a practice established within the V weapons programme at Peenemünde) to give a consistent flight path so that the pilot could recover in time to complete his mission and release his rockets. The auxiliary boosters would be released at a height of between 170 and 190 metres via a radio link to an observer on the ground. At a range of around four kilometres from the Allied bombers, the recovered pilot would jettison the nose shrouding to expose the assault rockets before closing in for the attack. Once the attack was completed, the pilot would unbuckle his seat harness and uncouple the control column and the safety catches attaching the nose to the fuselage. The nose would then fall away from the airframe, taking with it the windscreen, forward bulkhead and instruments. Simultaneously, a parachute would open from the tail section, causing rapid deceleration. The pilot would then be thrown clear and return to the ground with his own parachute. This, at least, was the theory, though from the sound of things the shocks sustained by the pilot during all this buffeting might have proved fatal.

The precious rocket in the rear section would meanwhile also float to earth on the main parachute attached to the tail section.

By November 1944 the first aircraft from the initial batch had already been built, such was the boost the authorities had given the Natter programme. And in running the project the SS were keen to demonstrate their much-vaunted ruthless efficiency, forcing manufacturers of components to get the job done despite the general collapse of German industry. The first gliding trials also took place in November, with an unpowered Natter being towed up by an He 111, on loan from the DFS, to an altitude of 6,000 metres. The Natter was ballasted to simulate the weight of the finished aircraft, and the pilot, Unteroffizier Zübert, reported excellent stability and general characteristics. In addition, the Natter was attached to the tow-line by two mountings, one on each upper surface of the wings, and for the most part it flew below the He 111. This had two benefits: first, it minimised the problems involved in controlling the craft, as had the plane been attached by the nose the detachable shrouding there might have pulled away accidentally; secondly, because he wasn't flying in the slipstream of the tug, Zübert could assess aerodynamics and general handling more accurately.

The project was forced through at such a pace that the first test firing came only a month later, at Heuberg, on 18 December. This was a disaster: the auxiliary rockets burned through cables controlling their fire-extinguishers and as a consequence overheated and burned out, wrecking the Natter. Luckily, the test was unmanned. The second attempt four days later met with success: the Natter left the ramp and disappeared into cloud at 750 metres.

Towed gliding tests had continued meanwhile, and the first free flight was made on 28 February 1945, with Zübert at the controls. Prototypes were now being prefixed with the letter 'M' instead of 'V'; this first Natter prototype to fly free was the M8.

Ten further unmanned launches followed the first, though most were to crash and explode following hard parachute landings which mixed the unburned fuel residues with catastrophic effect. The launches also revealed the fact that even with the auxiliary boosters, the air speed wasn't high enough to give full control to the pilot. This led to a redesigning of the tail surfaces and the fitting of small control vanes in the rocket outlet, which had the effect of smoothing out the rocket thrust and gaining more lift and control. The improvements were introduced on the M16 and adopted for all subsequent models.

Progress was not without setbacks on the bureaucratic side. On 22 December, the same day as the first successful test launch had taken place, the project's controlling body, one of many special weapons development commissions then operating, decided that both the Natter and the Julia held little promise and should be terminated. The final recommendation was that all work on the Julia be suspended (its main manufacturing plant had already been destroyed by the Allies) but that the Natter be given a stay of execution in the light of its ongoing trials. Even so, all plans for mass production were suspended as the commission felt that the scarce supply of Walter rockets would be better diverted to develop rocket-assisted versions of the Me 262.

The Natter was actually saved because Himmler was still interested in the project and allowed development to continue under the auspices of the SS. But other factors militated against the smooth progress of Bachem's programme. The original brief had allowed only 250 man-hours of semi-skilled construction to complete one fighter; but problems with erratic autopilots and unpredictable Schmidding rocket boosters were causing that number to rise. The other main problem was that, probably as a result of the commission's cancellation order, supplies of the Walter rockets had slumped even further than anticipated. These obstacles conspired to delay a launching of the first definitive Natter until 25 February 1945.

The Natter was launched with a dummy in the cockpit, and the test was a success: both the rocket section and the mannequin parachuted down without mishap. The SS were sufficiently impressed to order that further trials now be undertaken with actual pilots at the controls and so, against the better judgement of the Bachem team, Oberleutnant Lothar Siebert took off in the M23 a few days later. What went wrong precisely is unknown, but Siebert was killed, probably because he was knocked unconscious when the cockpit canopy unexpectedly broke away during the launch. The Natter took off as planned from its gantry and disappeared from sight into the clouds, only to crash violently to earth some fifty seconds later in a tremendous explosion close to the launch site. The SS dismissed this as a 'technical hiccup' and saw no reason to interrupt test-flights, calling for other volunteer pilots.

Bachem's team had meanwhile decided to upgrade the rockets to more powerful Walter 509 C units. These featured an auxiliary cruising chamber similar in principle to those fitted by Junkers to the Me 263 project it had developed. The four unreliable boosters were replaced with a more powerful pair of Schmidding rockets, each giving about a thousand-kilogramme thrust. This new version of the Natter, designated Ba 349 B, was planned to come onstream after the first fifty 'A' series aircraft had been literally used up. It offered nearly double the endurance of the original Natter, at 4.36 minutes, though there was a small performance deficit due to a weight increase of about 57 kilogrammes. Overall, however, the Natter had an impressive performance record:

with forces of 2.2 'g' at launch, the climbing speed would have risen to over 1,000 kph as it neared its operating height of 12,000 metres. With its boosters set at a hundred per cent thrust, a range of over eighty kilometres would have been in reach.

In the event, despite the auspicious figures, only one 'B' series model was built and actually flown, and even then it had to make use of the original kind of booster, as the better Schmidding rockets weren't available. According to the author Renato Vesco, the only time a Natter flew in anger was on 29 March 1945, when Feldwebel Ernst Hemmer piloted one of the first pre-production models against a formation of B-24 Liberators and succeeded in downing two and damaging a third. Research for this book has, however, uncovered no hard evidence to support the assertion.

Two months before the final surrender, the team was moved for its own safety to a base at Waldhausen, further from the reach of the advancing Allies. The move was to signal the effective end of testing, as there were now not enough lorries, and not enough fuel for them, to provide transport for the Natters and their equipment; and even the SS was unable to procure any supplies, so dire had the general situation become. As for the production target, even though it was now reduced to twenty examples a month, it was still a pipe dream: there was no rocket fuel to power the Natter machines even if there had been the materials and means to make them. Dornberger, now a general, cancelled the programme on 20 March, and Bachem prepared to move the remains of his operation to Bad Wörrishofen in Schwabia, about ninety kilometres west of Munich.

On 24 April French troops entered Waldsee, but not before Bachem staff there had sunk the remaining rocket motors in the lake. As for Bad Wörrishofen, it was only a temporary refuge, for the team moved again to what was to be their final destination, an alpine valley near St Leonard in Austria. By now all that remained of the project were five Natter machines, a few auxiliary boosters, and the blueprints for the design. All these, together with the surviving team, US troops were to capture only a few days later.

Of the original fifty pre-production 'A'-series fighters, only about twenty-two had been completed, and only fifteen ever flew. As late as April 1945 a group of Natter machines was apparently set up at

Kirchheim near Stuttgart to attack bomber squadrons, but unconfirmed reports suggest that they were destroyed on their ramps to prevent them from falling into enemy hands as US forces advanced on the site. A footnote to the story concerns manufacturing blueprints and specifications for the fighter which were sold to the Imperial Japanese Army shortly before the end of the war, and smuggled out of Germany aboard one of the many cargo U-Boats maintaining contact between the two remaining Axis powers. Only one partially built example is thought to have been discovered by advancing US troops as they entered Japanese-held territory.

The Rest of the Field

The Natter wasn't the only point-defence fighter in development. One major rival was the Me 263, which, confusingly, was actually a Junkers project. In order to husband resources as Allied bombing raids made ever greater depredations on German industry, aeronautical manufacturers had begun to build each other's designs where they had the capacity, acting purely as sub-contractors. This system was facilitated by the fact that Speer and Milch had wisely reduced the number of types of aircraft in production, thereby freeing extra capacity and concentrating on production of planes for which there was an urgent demand. The Me 163 Komet, for example, was in production with a number of different makers from Messerschmitt themselves.

Junkers was one of these, and as they had ample experience of their own in design and construction, they decided to see what improvements they could make to the Komet. The Komet had three main drawbacks: limited range and low endurance, both overshadowed by its tendency to suffer accidents on takeoff and landing. Junkers, without reference to Messerschmitt or the RLM, set about redesigning the 163.

They took the standard production model as their starting-point and replaced the stubby fuselage with a longer, slimmer design. They then incorporated a pressurised cockpit and all-round armour plating, and – most important – a new undercarriage, which had a retractable nose-wheel and two inboard wheels set below the wing-roots, giving greater stability and reliability. The long fuselage incorporated larger fuel tanks, which increased range and endurance, and they were designed to empty at a set rate to obviate drastic variations in the centre of gravity. The Walter engine used on the 163 was unchanged, but an additional auxiliary combustion chamber was designed and added to permit more economical cruising and thus increase endurance further. Junkers stopped short of producing a new wing or tailfin, each of which was carried over more or less untouched from the Komet. A wing is one of the most expensive items to design, test and build at the best of times, and there was the luxury of neither time nor money in the closing months of the war. The resultant interceptor was designated Ju 248, and so impressed was the Air Ministry when presented with it out of the blue, as it were, that they immediately accepted it for testing. However, there was a sting in the tail for Junkers: the Ministry redesignated the aircraft Me 263, to give the impression of continuity in Messerschmitt's production, resulting perhaps from a wish to maintain the same administration.

The first unpowered glider prototype performed well, behaving more predictably than the Komet at low speeds, though it turned out to be somewhat unstable at higher velocities, once powered tests began. As a result, the 263 was pegged to a top speed of 950 kph. Preparations for mass production were well advanced by the end of the war, as it could have been constructed by any company already geared to build 163s, which was precisely Junkers' intention. It would have compared well with the Natter, too, as it was fully reusable and could have operated from conventional airfields without the need for an elaborate launching ramp. But the 263, like all these last-minute projects, came too late and never saw operational use.

If any of them had gone into action, how good would they have been? The Julia would have been a hard aircraft to shoot down from the point of view of a B-17 gunner. Its modest size and sharp handling would have made for a dancing target with a small silhouette and even smaller frontal profile. But how much damage could it have done to the heavily armoured Allied bombers? Its light machine-guns would have made little impression, though it might have served to draw fire away from heavier German fighters like 109s, and perhaps, with its great manoeuvrability, it could have distracted bomber pilots into making mistakes – one bomber could easily have been lured into crashing into another in the tight combat box formations.

171

The Natter was so specialised in its role that the degree of success would have depended on whether the pilot could have come within range of his targets in time to release his rockets. And even if he did, the question of his chances of survival once the plane broke into its component parts and he was supposed to parachute down is very open. Given time, the SS might have continued stubbornly with their pet project, but the Natter wasn't really living up to expectations and it is likely that even if the war had gone on, the project would have soon reached its shut-off point anyway.

As for the Me 263, this seems to have been the rocket interceptor with the greatest potential, and from a purely technical point of view it is regrettable that it wasn't developed as soon as the Komet's drawbacks became apparent. As it was, the Komet had a disastrous record: eighty per cent of all losses occurred during takeoff or landing, fifteen per cent through loss of control, and only five per cent as a result of enemy fire. Had it been possible to use the modified landing gear introduced by Junkers, the accident rate could have been reduced, if not arrested.

Finally, the various underground factories throughout Bavaria and Thuringia staffed by a mixture of slave, forced and military labour could not have continued to operate without fresh resources, even though they were relatively secure against Allied air attack. And even if the planes could have been built, there still remained the question of fuel.

As things turned out, of course, none of these projects produced an aircraft which was officially to claim any enemy aeroplane in combat, and they remain among the most intriguing technical follies perpetrated by Germany as defeat, except to the most fanatical, became undeniable.

Chapter Eight

THE TRULY BIZARRE

In 1926 Dr Alexander Lippisch built his first glider, which he named the 'Storch' – 'Stork'. By 1929 he had moved on to the Storch v, and with it believed that he had taken the conventional fuselage-to-wing relationship to its limit. He therefore turned his attention to delta-wing possibilities, made speedy progress, and by 1930 had built and flown his Delta 1 glider – which subsequently he fitted with a thirty-horsepower petrol engine. The major manufacturers had been keeping a close eye on Lippisch's work, and Focke-Wulf subsidised his Delta 3 project. Delta 3, which was powered by a pair of petrol engines, driving one pusher and one tractor propeller, was a great success, which led to Lippisch's being offered the post of Director of Engineering at the DFS.

Taking gliding aeronautics as its starting-point, and presumably its cover, the DFS began a top-secret rocketry research programme under the melodramatic title of 'Projekt X'. The idea was to combine the new delta-wing designs emerging from Lippisch's studio with Hellmuth Walter's rocket engines. Walter and Lippisch would later work together on the Komet, but their first collaboration resulted in the Delta 4, which received the official project designation DFS 339 in 1937. It differed from Delta 3 in that it had a single hundred-horsepower engine and a slight gull-wing dip in the profile of the delta-wing, with pronounced anhedral – that is, downturned – wing tips.

Walter's first rocket motor took to the air in February 1937 when one of his early prototypes was mounted on the underside of a Heinkel He

72 biplane trainer. At the time, it ran on hydrogen peroxide with a paste catalyst and gave only 160 kilogrammes of thrust for 45 seconds. As we have seen, it was soon discovered that a better result could be obtained if a liquid catalyst were substituted, and in April ground handling tests began with the new units. Two aircraft were used for the trials – an Fw 56 and a Ju A 50 Junior. The new rocket delivered about twice the thrust for thirty seconds, and, filled with optimism, the engineers retrofitted it on to the He 72 for in-flight testing.

The DFS then instructed Lippisch, under the auspices of Projekt X, to adapt his DFS 339 so that it could accept Walter's motor. Lippisch had anticipated such an order and had already designed two aircraft specially for the job. Neither used centrally placed rudders, and thus avoided any problems of turbulence on control surfaces which might have been caused by the efflux from the rocket's exhaust. These were the DFS 39 and 40, though only the 40 was to fly, its design immediately having superseded that of its sister. The first version to take to the air did so in 1938, powered for test purposes by a conventional piston engine. The rocket version was planned for later in the year, but Lippisch and Walter were overtaking the DFS schedule by already working on a more advanced type still: the DFS 194. This was due to receive a piston engine first as well, but in January 1939 the Air Ministry transferred the partnership to the control and direction of Messerschmitt, which ordered a rocket model immediately. Evidently the Air Ministry, gearing up for war, wanted to see a quicker return on its investment than a string of prototypes would provide, and hoped that the pragmatic Messerschmitt company would soon discover whether or not the experimental aircraft could be developed into an operational warplane.

Once the initial prototype had been completed in October 1939, ground tests of the Walter HWK R.I 203 motor began at Peenemünde-West. The first flight took place the following October, and in further tests the aircraft attained a top speed of 550 kph. A stubby, compact, delta-winged plane, the 194 closely resembled the earlier DFS 40, but lacked wing-tip fins. It retained a tailless design, though it had a tailfin immediately aft of the cockpit. So impressed was the Air Ministry at its aerodynamic performance and positive handling that it ordered a further three prototypes, which in turn led to the stubby, compact Me 163

Komet already described briefly and which, for all its faults, remains the only operational, reusable rocket-propelled warplane.

Even as the Komet awaited production clearance, the supply of Walter engines slowed down owing to lack of materials. Lippisch was consequently asked to modify the design to accept a conventional piston engine and propeller. The result, the Me 334, never got beyond the drawing board, but it did provide a hint of how the Komet might have evolved in another direction. Fitted with a retractable tricycle undercarriage, the 334 was to have a twelve-cylinder Daimler-Benz engine mounted forward of the cockpit, with a scooped-out intake replacing the aerodynamic nose of the rocket version. A long drive-shaft connected the engine to a pusher propeller mounted at the end of a slightly elongated rear fuselage. The tall, distinctive tailfin was discarded and replaced with a deep fin mounted ventrally – the relatively high undercarriage would have prevented this from striking the ground.

The design was never needed. Rocket production picked up once more, and the 163 went into service, to blaze its erratic and lonely trail in aircraft rocketry – a trail that over the following half-century has become ever more disused and overgrown.

Stratospheric Sänger

In 1933, especially in Germany, optimism for the future of rocketry was high. Eugene Sänger was one of the pioneers who worked outside the VfR. The publication of his *Rocket Flight Technique* in 1933 led to an invitation from the Technical Bureau three years later to set up a Rocket Flight Research Institute. Dr Sänger's work for it embraced many of the emerging ideas of the day, but his own particular project was the development of a stratospheric glider. He'd learned, both from the work of Robert H. Goddard and from rocket trials conducted by the VfR and his own Institute, that at extreme altitudes the thin air affects the behaviour of aircraft by reducing drag and consequently permitting greater speeds.

When an aircraft passes through the air at speed, the thrust energy produced by the engines has to accommodate three main forces if the machine is to fly at all: generation of lift (usually the function of a curved-surface aerofoil wing); gravity (lift and thrust must be sufficiently powerful to prevent the aircraft from crashing to earth); and friction (which, induced by the aerodynamic drag of the aircraft as it moves through the dense air at lower altitudes, slows the aircraft and can be reduced only by increased thrust; soaring flight as the advanced sporting gliders of the time developed, or improved aerodynamics – or a combination of these). The higher one flies the thinner the air becomes, and friction is reduced. The difficulty in thin air is maintaining lift.

The main problem facing Sänger before he could begin his experiments lay in actually getting an aircraft to reach stratospheric heights. The answer lay in rocketry. By June 1939 Sänger had constructed a one-twentieth-scale wind-tunnel model of just such a craft. But as soon as the war started the priorities of his Institute became more practical in application, and to satisfy the Air Ministry and keep hold of his funding Sänger turned his design for a stratospheric rocket-glider into one for a bomber.

This was to be a bomber such as no one had ever seen before – or would again. Flown by a single pilot whose cockpit was mounted in the forward section of the nose, the fuselage was of almost rectangular section, with chamfered edges. The slightly tapered tail section was made up of two horizontally mounted winglets capped with small endplate fins. These were used for control only at lower altitudes, since higher up the aircraft would have to rely on rocket thrust alone. The short, stubby wings blended with the flattened underside of the fuselage and turned the aircraft into a true lifting-body vehicle – indeed, the many NASA designs for such vehicles in the 1950s and 1960s stemmed directly from the principles applied by Sänger. These principles hold that when the underside of the fuselage is contoured correctly if only very slightly, it will generate lift in its own right in addition to the wings. Sänger fused the short wings of his bomber with the underside of the fuselage to form a seamless lift-generating area in his quest to maximise lift at the highest altitudes and in the thinnest air.

For takeoff from the ground, Sänger devised a system whereby the craft would be shot from a monorail track three kilometres long, resting on a freewheeling sled. The sled was to be fitted with a hugely powerful rocket by the standards of the day, generating over six hundred tonnes of thrust for eleven seconds. Sänger's ramp was the very stuff of later 1950s science fiction, and indeed was strongly reminiscent of the rocket sled and ramp which featured in the 1951 film *When Worlds Collide*.

The rocket on the sled would catapult Sänger's machine skywards to a height of about 1,200 metres and a speed of 1,850 kph, at which point the main engine would fire. This was also rocket-powered but would develop a relatively small (but of course still massive) thrust of over 100 tonnes, enough to take the aircraft to the outer reaches of the atmosphere, where it would have reached a height of 145 kilometres and a speed of 22,100 kph over a total flight duration of 8 minutes. Once the rocket had burned off its fuel, the craft would glide down towards lower altitudes, to about forty kilometres, skipping off the denser, thicker air it found there in much the same way as a flat pebble can skim across the water of a lake.

At 145 km the upper atmosphere is verging on actual space; had the craft ever actually flown, a later, larger and adapted version of it might – if one stretches the imagination – have been able to transport storm troopers or bomb loads into orbit around the globe and then drop them to land on any country within minutes of leaving Germany. However, as things stood Sänger's design, the very first of its type, was so compact that he had difficulty in fitting in a bomb bay; and it's unlikely, even if the project had progressed, that he would have ever been able to build a prototype large enough actually to function as a bomber. But, after all, he had proposed such a thing in order to cloak theory with practice and hang on to his grant.

Had a bomb been carried, it would probably have incorporated the same television guidance system as was proposed later in the war for some anti-shipping bombs such as the Henschel Hs 293. This system was also an innovation and it's worth a short digression to describe it, as it was an early ancestor of the cruise missiles and smart bombs with which we are familiar today.

The Hs 293 D variant took a standard Hs 293 wire-guided missile and substituted the wire-guidance system with a television system. In the past, a controller sitting in the carrier aircraft would have had to maintain its course, following the bomb down to its target and controlling its descent with a joystick while keeping it in view. His joystick control relayed signals down the wire to the bomb, the wire being played out at an enormous rate as the bomb sped to its target. These signals controlled servos acting on the missile's small winglets and could allow a degree of fine aiming to be achieved. In poor weather, or in the case of dropping a bomb from an immense height as would have been the case with the Sänger bomber, the system would be found wanting. The solution was to fit a television camera and an aerial transmitter to the fuselage of the bomb. The camera was fitted behind a nose-cone, which was double-glazed and heated to prevent condensation and was equipped with a battery. The axis of the camera's optics could be adjusted remotely by the aimer back in the carrier aircraft, giving him a variable view of the target. An aerial just like a modern TV aerial was fixed to the rear of the bomb's fuselage and transmitted pictures back to the aimer while he received his course adjustment signals simultaneously.

The system was developed by the German Television Company (Fernseh GmbH) in association with the Reich Post Office Research Unit – a body that was involved in a number of related experiments during the war. Given that ships were the main target, the best picture resolution needed to be horizontal. The picture was made up of 224 vertical lines transmitting 50 frames per second – the same as realtime video speed today. About seventy missiles were built and tested, though it isn't certain whether they were ever used in anger. One of the most notable human features of the concept was that the operator became agitated when the bomb hit the target, as he could see on the screen precisely what the consequences of his actions were. We are inured to such an experience through computer games and television, but sixty-odd years ago it must have come as a shock for someone to see the 300-kilogramme charge explode in front of him so to speak. Range was limited to only four kilometres, but plans were in hand to extend this and also to reduce the number of lines in the transmitted picture to fifty in order to counter Allied jamming measures. However, as with so many other technical innovations, adverse war conditions thwarted their introduction. Over 1,700 wire-guided systems were built and used in action right up until the end of the war – which begs the question: why wasn't the TV version more widely used? No one knows.

The putative bomb aimer on the Sänger bomber, then, might have used such a TV guidance system, well out of sight of ground observers and out of range of any Allied defence. And once the bomber had shed its load, it would have continued its skimming flight back to base, gliding home to a normal landing on its retractable undercarriage. Its range would have been 23,500 kilometres, with a flight time of about an hour. Luckily, such a machine never saw the light of day – but would it ever have done in that form? The design poses several questions which cannot easily be answered.

For example, did Sänger fully appreciate the 'g' forces likely to be met by pilots during the launch phase and the firing of the main inboard rocket engine? And what would have happened if the inboard engine had failed to fire? Would the pilot have been able to glide back to base anyway or would he have had to eject? Could he have ejected and lived at such an altitude? And even if he had been able to do so successfully, what about the danger of the massive crash and explosion when the aircraft fell to earth? And as far as the launch ramp was concerned, even if the Germans had used the prisoner labour available, how was the money and the steel to be got together to build a three-kilometre-long ramp? And in the unlikely event of one having been constructed, how could such a conspicuous thing be disguised and camouflaged? Given the success Allied fighter-pilots had with locating and destroying the relatively small ramps used in France and the Low Countries to launch V-1s, it seems that even if it had been implemented, the Sänger project would in the circumstances have been nothing more than a titanic waste of money and resources.

Back in June 1939, though, the future still looked rosy. Sänger had begun friction tests in the wind-tunnel and was beginning to realise how the performance of metals under extreme friction can degrade to the point of destruction. Not that long ago a promotional film was made by the consortium building the then-new Concorde airliner. In the supersonic wind-tunnel you could see scale models of the aircraft subjected to incredible stresses and temperatures, out of which came new lessons in aerodynamics and materials designed to withstand Mach 2. Yet thirty years before Concorde, Sänger and his team were trying to achieve *hypersonic* speeds of Mach 18. Without the technical knowledge available to teams such as those assembled to build Concorde, their job would have been all but impossible. Even today, the known speed record for a powered aircraft is around Mach 6.72 (7,277 kph) held by a NASA X-15 rocket plane. At these sorts of speeds, parts of the aircraft heat up to well over 3,000°C, which almost defeated the NASA specialists and would almost certainly have defeated Sänger's team. But undeterred, either protected by innocence or perhaps frustrated by the obstacles facing him which he was determined to overcome, Sänger continued to work on parts of his design, notably the rocket motor, until 1942, when he was ordered to report for work at the DFS.

Taking his assistant (and soon wife) Dr Irene Bredt with him, he spent the rest of the war at the DFS, involved with various ramjet projects.

Ramjets

The essence of a ramjet engine is a narrowing cone-shaped air intake which at high speeds mixes the inrush of air with either a solid or a liquid fuel. The mixture self-ignites under the intense pressure and provides massive amounts of controllable thrust energy. The difficulty arises in getting the ramjet to a comfortable operating speed. Below about 320 kph, the amount of air entering the chamber is insufficient to produce the sustained compression/ignition required for it to work. The ramjet-powered aircraft therefore needs a second, separate power plant to get it up to working altitude and speed. But it does have one great advantage over a conventional turbojet and that lies in the number of moving parts in its design. A turbojet engine, especially of 1940s vintage, is a complex beast requiring hours of servicing at frequent intervals. A ramjet needs little maintenance and attention, yet it is capable of developing the same, if not more, power with greater overall reliability. In recent times, projects such as the designer Alan Bond's 'Hotol' have sought to combine the properties of a ramjet and a conventional jet within one unit, but have met with only qualified success: business and investors are scared of radical technology. At the cusp of the second millennium, there is still no mass-produced ramjet in common use, and there seems to be no good reason for this. In the half-century that has elapsed since the end of the war, one would have thought that such a promising idea would have been exploited; but apart from several possible military applications that can only be guessed at, and the concept of the 'scramjet', which uses another engine to augment the ramjet's combustion process, there has been nothing.

Experiments with ramjets first began in Germany in 1937, but it wasn't until 1943 that the Air Ministry began to take a real interest in the subject, involving the DFS in ramjet development. During the war several manufacturers also took an independent interest in the concept, and their research came up with varying results. Heinkel's venture, the P. 1080, and a similar idea from the Prague-based Skoda-Kauba design office, the P. 14, represented attempts late in the day by the Air Ministry to marry Sänger's original design ideas to a usable fighter project – Sänger's hypersonic bomber plan having by then been shelved.

Heinkel's P. 1080 project kicked off in November 1944 – a busy time for the company – and given pressing deadline factors it incorporated a fuselage similar to the Volksjäger's in layout but with a larger tail unit and wings similar to those seen on its P. 1078 Miniaturjäger development. Two large ramjets were to be mounted on either side of the fuselage at the wing roots, with four jettisonable Walter rockets mounted beneath the fuselage to achieve takeoff and bring the plane to the ramjet's operational speed. The special Lippisch-developed fuel used in the ramjets – petroleum foam impregnated with coal dust – was held in a large pressurised tank to the rear of the fuselage. The design wasn't to progress far before the war ended, however, since Heinkel's other projects demanded more attention.

Skoda-Kauba's project was worked up in collaboration with the DFS from late 1944 on as well and was also to be powered by one of Sänger's ramjets. Compared with Heinkel's design, the P. 14 had a short, stubby fuselage and vestigial wings. Its armament consisted of a single thirty-millimetre cannon. As for fuel, it could have run on either liquid aviation spirit or coal nuggets in a similar manner to that proposed by Lippisch for his LP. 13a interceptor, mentioned in the next section of this chapter.

As with Heinkel's P. 1080 nothing came of the Skoda-Kauba enterprise. Soviet forces overran the Prague plant before any progress on the plane could be made.

The Future Starts Here

Following the successful DFS 'Projekt X' in 1942, Alexander Lippisch began another project in 1944 which was to lead to one of the most impressive and unusual designs of the war: a really practicable ramjet interceptor. Following the Komet, Lippisch had wanted to develop a true delta-winged tailless aircraft that would follow the lead Sänger had given in ramjet technology. After being appointed head of the Aviation Research Unit – the Luftfahrtforschungsanstalt, or LFA – in Vienna in August 1944, Lippisch placed a contract with an aeronautical engineering group from Darmstadt University to develop his ideas into a basic design. After only a few weeks, an air raid destroyed their research facilities and the team was obliged to move to Munich University to continue its work there in conjunction with fellow researchers from the Bavarian capital. The first fruit of the project, named the DM-1 after the two universities that had taken part in its design, was a glider. Three further variants were planned before work proceeded, via a route that was to prove tortuous, to the LP. 13a fighter – a destination that proved too far to reach.

The DM-1 had no discernible fuselage, being a pure delta wing, its leading edges swept back at an angle of sixty degrees. The rear fin and its rudder reflected the plan of the wing, rising vertically from the centre of the wing's trailing edge to some height before sweeping downwards and forwards at a severe angle, to finish a short distance from the nose. The cockpit was actually sited within this fin, at its base where it joined the wing section.

Originally it was planned to air-launch the DM-1 from a mounting on top of a Siebel Si 204 at a height of 8,000 metres. From this altitude it could dive at speeds approaching 560 kph, although later in the programme it was intended to fit the little craft with a rocket motor to boost its speed to 800 kph. Lippisch's original concept had comprised such a complete aerodynamic package that even at this early stage landing speeds were anticipated to be no more than about 70 kph – so low was the stall rate.

As for the other three planned prototypes, the DM-2 mounted a turbojet into a DM-1 airframe to test the delta wing at sustained high speeds. The DM-3 would have exceeded the 2's speed, as it was to have been fitted with two Walter 509 rocket engines (the Me 163 used just one). These would have given the 3 a speed in excess of 2,000 kph, at the high altitudes where the rockets could easily outperform normal jets. There was a plan for a DM-4, about which little is known, except that it was to be another delta wing, this time capable of supersonic speed. One interesting story about it concerns a report heard on Soviet radio which revealed that the plans for it had been 'acquired' by the USSR during the last days of the war. In fact the blueprints had been stolen by a Russian spy from a BMW roadster where they had been left by the project's leader, a Major Hazen. If the Soviets went on to build DM-4s, we haven't heard about it – yet.

Once Lippisch and his team were happy with the designs for these novel craft – even though they had actually built only the DM-1 – they began looking at the military applications for their research. But that would take time, and by autumn 1944 German high command wanted results wherever they could get them, at all costs, and fast. The Allies, mounting almost daily bombing raids, systematically were destroying key industrial capacity as well as causing 'collateral' – incidental – civilian damage – though the blanket bombing of such towns as Dresden on the orders of men such as the RAF's 'Bomber' Harris was yet to be perpetrated.

The German ability to wage war was being whittled away gradually, something which only Hitler himself appeared able to ignore, clinging as he did to the hope of an ultimate victory through the power of the new 'secret weapons', none of which would be ready in time to have any real impact – though Hitler wasn't the only one to delude himself in this respect.

Furthermore, the Führer, increasingly paranoid following the attempted coup by senior members of the general staff led by Oberst Claus Graf Schenk von Stauffenberg on 20 July 1944, had not only set in train a Gestapo purge that would see 5,000 Germans executed or jailed within four months but surrounded himself by even more toadying yes-men than before. All senior regular servicemen outside the Party and the SS knew that the war was as good as over, but as part of the madness of the time the Nazi machine went into overdrive and few dared disobey. Hundreds of thousands of Hungarian Jews, spared until now, were taken to Auschwitz and slaughtered. The

German people were exhorted to make greater and greater sacrifices for the burned-out cause. Aircraft were being built at an ever-increasing rate, but there was no fuel with which to fly them. And the Luftwaffe's reliance on older warplanes like the Me 109, which were by now outclassed by the Allied machines, meant that the death rate of fully trained and experienced fighter-pilots was spiralling. Yet, when an excellent machine like the Me 262 appeared in service, it was assigned as a fighter-bomber – a totally inappropriate role for a machine that was patently a pure fighter. Panic was spreading, and it showed in almost every decision made.

When the Air Ministry and the DFS approached Lippisch now, it came as no surprise to him that they were looking for immediate combat applications for his research. They took the line that, after all, they had been generous in their patronage since the Komet project, and that it was now time to call in favours once again. Lippisch took the hint and switched the focus of his work, upping the pace within his team at the same time. The first project to emerge after the change of tack was the GB-3 glider-bomb. It bore a marked resemblance to the DM-1 except that the former cockpit and nose sections were now occupied by a warhead. The GB-3 glider-bomb was designed to be dropped from a heavy bomber and then guided to its target electronically, but the project was abandoned before the year was out.

The first aircraft design came with the P. 11 late in 1944. For this, Lippisch designed a relatively straightforward delta-winged fighter which bore no resemblance to the advanced DM series. The P. 11 was really a flying wing fighter in the Horten style with wings swept back at an angle of forty-five degrees, a subtly protruding nose, and a forward cockpit with a bubble canopy. The trailing edge of the wing was straight, except for a small cutout section in the centre which shrouded the exhausts of the two Junkers Jumo 004 engines buried within the wing's centre section. On either side of the cutout there was a triangular tailfin which, however, no longer extended forward as had the tailfin of the DM series. An air intake was positioned in the leading edge of each wing close to the wing roots. Fuel was carried in large self-sealing tanks in each wing.

At a meeting at the Air Ministry in November it was suggested that the P. 11 be produced in tandem with the Horten brothers' Go 229,

Heinkel's doomed He 280 (the V1) on its first flight on April 2nd, 1941, with the works test pilot Fritz Schäfer at the controls.

Row upon row of unfinished He 162 'Volksjägers' await engines in the plant at Tarthun, near Magdeburg. Underground factories like this converted salt mine proved almost impossible for Allied bombers to identify and hit, but given the levels of corrosion suffered by the machine tools and infrastructure in such sites as a result of the salt, it's a marvel that anything got made there in the first place.

A captured Volksjäger wearing Soviet insignia. Proof – if any were needed – that the Red Army ended up with its own share of the spoils of war.

An He 162 in British hands, being readied for a post-war display of captured aircraft. This view clearly shows that whilst the engine had been blessed with good and open access for maintenance, it took mechanics with a head for heights to work on it.

The Bv 40 armoured glider. Its diminutive size can be seen to good effect here –
approaching a densely packed B-17 combat box formation a machine of this size would have
been all but invisible until it was too late.

The Ju 248 – better known as the Me 263. This evolution of the Me 163 'Komet' rocket
fighter came too late in the war to see active service with the Luftwaffe. Note the small
nose-mounted, wind-driven propeller used to power the electrical system.

A view of Oberleutnant Siebert preparing to take off in Ba 349 A M 23, on February 28th, 1945. The flight ended with Siebert's death – he may have been knocked unconscious by the unexpected release of the interlocks and sudden release of the canopy.

A retouched artist's impression of the Me 328; powered in this view by a pair of the Argus pulsejets.

An artist's impression of the DFS 346 in flight. Its streamlined cigar profile and rear-swept wings echo the shape of the American Bell X-1 machine of 1947, in which Chuck Yeager became, officially, the first pilot past the sound barrier.

The Ju 287 V1 was little more than a Ju 388 tail, cobbled to a He 177 fuselage and fitted with the bespoke experimental wing of the eventual '287. The auxiliary rocket pod, used to assist launching, can be seen mounted on the underside of the turbojet housed on the underside of the near wing. Note the cine camera mounted at the base of the tail fin – this recorded the in-flight behaviour of the many woollen tufts glued onto the outer skin as an aide to determining the aerodynamic characteristics of such an unusual configuration.

An air-to-air view of the Ju 287 V1. Its striking swept-forward wing configuration was a bold step in the history of aircraft design but has since influenced only a very few, subsequent types

The Ba 349 A 'Natter', as seen in a post-war exhibition. The twenty-four 73 mm Fohn rockets in the nose can be clearly seen, as can the rear-tilting canopy.

The He 178 was the first aircraft to take off and fly on turbojet power alone. This is the sole example, but it was lost (along with its rocket-powered cousin, the He 176) in an Allied bombing raid on Berlin's aircraft museum in 1943.

The only known photograph of the Henschel Hs 132 V1; the jet powered replacement for the Ju 87 Stuka dive bomber. Soon after this picture was taken, the Henschel plant was overrun by the advancing Soviet forces and nothing more was ever heard of the type.

A German artist's impression of the Fi 103 Reichenberg R-IV in flight. The proximity of the canopy to the intake for the Argus pulse jet is all too obvious here and would have made safe ejection by the pilot a risky proposition.

which at the time was undergoing its initial construction. However, even in those dark times, Lippisch held firmly to his interest in Sänger's work, and in the end the P. 11 was abandoned in favour of yet another proposal: the P. 12.

This was another flying wing design, which used a liquid fuel ramjet mounted within the central wing section. The flat delta wings had downturned, anhedral tips that reached to the ground, incorporating small, free-spinning wheels which were to act as stabilisers for a single retractable main landing-wheel beneath the cockpit.

It's possible that Lippisch abandoned this design because of the use of liquid fuel. But there may have been an additional reason. Not only was fuel in very short supply, as already stressed, but Lippisch had seen the terrible consequences for pilots unfortunate enough to have their Komet planes tip over on landing. Traces of the two volatile liquid fuels carried aboard in separate tanks to be mixed together in the combustion chamber could remain in the tanks at the end of a flight. If the Komet tipped over on landing – and its short length and the use of a single skid rail to land on made it prone to do so – the tanks often ruptured, and the resulting explosion usually proved fatal. As already mentioned, the vast majority of Komets lost went this way, and the plane was so dangerous that there was even a Luftwaffe joke in the best black humour tradition to the effect that, if you wanted to sacrifice yourself for the Führer flying a Komet, there was no need to bother to engage the enemy – all you had to do was take off, and if you survived that all you had to do was make a circuit of the airfield and 'land'.

Whatever the reasons for abandoning the P. 12, Lippisch was soon working on the P. 13, and this was perhaps the ultimate piece of 'Heath Robinson' technology of the entire war. Had it been built, however, Lippisch was in no doubt that it would have worked, and worked well.

Since the end of 1944 he had been working on a new kind of solid fuel which he thought might alleviate the shortages and be safer to use than a liquid. It involved suspending coal dust in a pressurised inflammable petroleum foam. The foam could burn quite happily in a rocket engine but was unsuitable for a ramjet, as experiments by Heinkel had already determined. But the principle behind burning coal in a ramjet was sound, and on that basis plans for the P. 13 went forward.

Lippisch had seen that the only fuel that was still cheap and plentiful in Germany was coal. The numerous mines were presently operated with slave labour to augment the normal, depleted local workforces, and produced coal for domestic use and a whole range of industrial purposes. Lippisch, following Sänger's lead again, understood that an efficient ramjet could burn any flammable material once working – it just needed to get up to operational speed. Using coal as the fuel would remove the deadly and swift consequences of crash-landings and would make ground handling easier and safer for ground crews and pilots alike. Not only that, but the economic advantages of using a ramjet rather than a turbojet, in terms both of fuel and simplified construction, were undeniable.

For his first attempt, Lippisch proposed to fill a wire-mesh basket with coal behind a nose-mounted air intake. It would protrude a little into the airflow and be ignited at the right moment by a gas burner. After a conventional rocket or a tow from another plane took the craft to operating speeds above 320 kph, the air passing through the ramjet would take the fumes from the burning coal rearwards, where, in a chamber under enormous pressure, they would mix with clean air taken from a separate intake within the main nose opening. The resulting mixture would be almost pure carbon dioxide, which would then be directed out through a rear nozzle to provide forward thrust.

Taking its lead from the DM-1 in terms of the new aircraft's design, the team elected to use a high and elongated tailfin, which again incorporated the cockpit at its base. This was mounted above a delta wing of only slightly greater thickness, the centre section of which carried the ramjet. There was to be a large oval intake in the nose. During wind-tunnel tests of the ramjet and the design of the coal basket, modifications were incorporated to improve efficiency of combustion. The coal used now took the form of small granules and not irregular lumps as previously, since granules produced a more controlled and even burn. In addition, the basket was changed to a rotating wire-mesh drum, which revolved on a vertical axis at a constant rate of only sixty rpm within the air intake. A jet flame from tanks of bottled gas would fire into the basket once the plane was up to speed, producing an even burn as it rotated. A burner and drum were actually built and tested successfully in Vienna by the team before the war came to an end.

A rocket would be needed to get the aircraft up to altitude and speed, but by specifying a common auxiliary unit used in assisting other aircraft, such as the Me 323, to get airborne, this could be achieved safely and cheaply, the rocket being jettisoned after use. The fuel load was calculated to weigh eight hundred kilogrammes, to give a forty-five-minute endurance. No information has come down to us regarding the armament, though it would probably have included one or two large-calibre machine-guns, the MK 103 cannon being too heavy and too large to be mounted on a plane this light and small.

So near and yet so far. Lippisch at this stage was ordered to leave his university team and return to contributing more variations for the original Komet project, incorporating turbojets and ramjets. None of these ever left the drawing board either.

Even the prototype DM-1 wasn't finished by the time US forces captured it in 1945. They were so stunned at what they found that they ordered its completion, by the student team that had built it and which they'd captured with it, in conditions of the greatest secrecy. Once this was done, the DM-1 was shipped to the USA under a tight security blanket and finally test-flown there. The results were, apparently, overwhelmingly positive, and the lessons learned from the DM-1 were incorporated into NASA research aircraft of the 1950s and beyond.

But if the ideas of Alexander Lippisch seem wild enough still today, we must also look at an equally intriguing proposal put forward by Heinz von Halem in September 1944 and taken up by Focke-Wulf as the 'Triebflügel', or 'Motorised Wing'. It was intended to be used as a point-defence interceptor in the same manner as the Natter.

Triebflügel *and* Wespe: *Further Horizons*

Designed to lift off from the smallest patch of level ground in the same way as a helicopter, the Triebflügel would have stood vertically when at rest, balanced on four swivel wheels, one in each of the four shrouded stabilising fins that projected from the tapering rear of the fuselage. A larger fifth wheel would have been mounted within the rear of the fuselage itself.

The proposed method of takeoff remains unique even today, although a recent American proposal for a cheap reusable craft to take satellites into low orbits looks remarkably similar to this 55-year-old idea. About a third of the way along the fuselage from the nose, three equidistant variable-pitch 'rotor blades' were mounted around a revolving collar set flush with the fuselage's outer skin. At the end of each of these blades was mounted a single Pabst-designed ramjet. To get up to the operating speed these units required, they each had a customised Walter rocket mounted within their housings. Before takeoff, the pilot would angle the blades to neutral pitch (a point where they created no lift), with the rockets firing straight down. Once the Walters were lit, the aircraft would shoot skywards, and once he had built up sufficient speed the pilot would then bring the blades simultaneously into a higher angle of incidence, having first started the ramjets. As the angle changed, the thrust and 'bite' of the blades into the air would set the collar spinning, thus creating a single, giant propeller, similar to the principles of the Döbloff helicopter described earlier.

Lift would then be generated in the same manner as with a helicopter's rotor blades, and be augmented by the thrust from the jets, the rockets by now having spent their fuel in getting the machine into the air and up to speed. On reaching the operating height of about 10,500 metres, the pilot would level out and increase the angle of the blades to bring their rotation speed, and that of the jets, into line with the forward speed of the aircraft. By rotating the collar at around 220 rpm, it would yield Mach 0.9 at the wing tips – more than enough for efficient ramjet operation. The arrangement ensured a minimum of interference from torque to the fuselage, and – at least in theory – provide a safe and dynamic aerial platform. But when one looks at the design today, it raises more questions than answers. How would the blades have withstood a bird strike? As the machine had no conventional wings to speak of, if any blade were to shatter, there would have been an immediate loss of thrust and lift. Not only that, but if a new and inexperienced pilot were to misjudge distances when engaging enemy fighters in close combat, there might have been a serious risk of collision between the blades and an enemy plane, with the same result.

However, while there may have been a few technical problems to overcome, such as accommodating centrifugal forces where the ramjets sat at the tips of the blades, or sealing the fuel pipes that led into the blades from the rotating collar, the overall concept seems sound in principle and offers as many pros as it does cons. The craft needed no runway; the ramjet power plant was simple to build at low cost and needed few moving parts; fuel oils of more or less any octane could be used, from diesel to aviation spirit; and the thing had a high-performance envelope and operational capacity. But once again time was not on the side of the development, and only a wind-tunnel version had been built and tested – to Mach 0.9 – before the war came to an end.

The thinking behind Focke-Wulf's project appealed to several other manufacturers and was later to appear again in a different guise with Heinkel's 'Wespe' – 'Wasp' – in 1945. It was to use a pair of HeS 021 turboprop engines and was intended to be a vertical takeoff fighter, though there is very little detail available about its precise specification. From rough plans published by HMSO in 1946, we can see that it, too, would have rested on swivel 'castors' in a vertical position, this time resting on six tailfins, and standing about nine metres high. The pilot – the only crewman – would have lain prone within the bullet-shaped nose-cone, his front-facing couch placed above a pair of heavy machine-guns, probably thirty-millimetre MK 108s. The two engines were placed inboard in tandem along the length of the fuselage aft of the cockpit, and they were separated from each other by a fixed annular collar. Unlike the Dornier Do 335, in which the tandem motors faced away from each other, in the Wespe the special propellers would have faced each other only six inches apart. Each of the twelve blades mounted to the propellers was attached to an arm that extended beyond the outer fuselage, permitting a degree of variable-pitch control to the blade. What the arrangement effectively provided was a set of contra-rotating rotor blades revolving beyond the outer circumference of the fuselage, which could be angled in pitch in the same manner as on a helicopter. To complete the design, Heinkel mounted an aerodynamic shroud around the reach of the extended blades to protect their tips from damage. The rather large and clumsy shroud incorporated small ailerons, too, and may have played a role in controlling the air efflux created by the whirling blades.

In effect, the Wespe was the piston-engined version of the Triebflügel and would have operated in a similar way. With the machine pointing skywards, the pilot would have run the engines up to speed, gradually pitching the blades to produce vertical lift, just as in a helicopter. Once an adequate height was reached, he would have decreased the angle of pitch on the blades to shift the direction of thrust from vertical to horizontal, the manoeuvre possibly augmented by flaps on the shroud and the tailfins, when forward motion would have been attained. When landing, the whole procedure would simply have been reversed. Like the Triebflügel, the Wespe's development was of course curtailed by the end of the war, and leaves us only able to guess at what have might have been. But there's also another device that must be spoken of – a device unlike any other which, if the rumours surrounding its existence are true, must rank as one of the most unusual machines the Germans ever got round to building.

More commonly known by the phrase 'Foo Fighters' (from the French word for fire – 'feu') or 'Feuerballs', these strange little remote-controlled craft were first alluded to in public in a small article in the *South Wales Argus* newspaper that appeared on 13 December 1944. The article opens by suggesting that the Germans had developed a novel new weapon in keeping with the Christmas season and goes on to describe the devices, as reported by an Allied air crew overflying a shattered Germany. Resembling 'silvery glass balls', the devices were appearing either singly or in clusters and were almost transparent, though probably metallic in their build. Why such an obscure newspaper should have run a story like this might seem to some to be an early exercise in news management – letting a small trickle of facts to escape perhaps in readiness for more information in the future.

The news of these strange and apparently inert floating bodies continued to circulate and even the *New York Herald Tribune* was moved to publish an article on 2 January 1945 shedding a little more light on the subject. It described how these Foo Fighters had been reported buzzing (flitting close to) RAF Beaufighters since November 1944 while they were over Germany – the Foo Fighters would merely fly alongside the aircraft at a set distance for a number of kilometres as if pacing or observing the aircraft's occupants. The author Renato Vesco reports in his book *Intercept UFO* that on 12 January 1945 – ten days after the *Herald Tribune* article – a series of reports on the mysterious phenomenon was made by several Allied bombing squadrons to their command unit in Dijon. Apparently, the number of reports warranted a full investigation, which was quickly shelved when it was realised that whatever was behind the strange craft posed no obvious warlike intent – after all, the craft seemed only to be passively observing the aircraft and not attacking them.

Following the war, reports surrounding the Foo Fighters and their supposedly German origin continued to surface, mostly as a result of investigative writers eager to look at hitherto concealed German (and in particular SS) activities that might have explained the phenomenon. What might the devices actually have been for, and could they have been man-made (and not, as has been suggested, extraterrestrial in origin)?

Their primary role seems to have been as a psychological experiment – a vain attempt by the SS to unnerve Allied bomber pilots sufficiently to force them into making errors. Combat-box formations were tightly packed: if a Foo Fighter appeared and caused an inexperienced pilot to swerve his bomber violently away, this could have untold knock-on effects if contact were made with other planes. The Foo Fighter could just carry on flying, but its mere presence would be enough to cause damage. A secondary role would probably have been to act as an ongoing proving ground – a flying test-bed for some of the more exotic materials and technologies the Nazis developed in the war. Right up until the very end of the war, the SS among other organisations was sponsoring a myriad of secret and semi-secret engineering and technological projects as a way of possibly staving off the inevitable; also, of possibly preserving a role for itself in business in a postwar Germany. If some of these inventions could be perfected and even patented while there was still time, the SS elite might have had a chance to set up businesses to exploit this work later. Certainly, as we've already seen, experiments had been undertaken into television-guided bombs, but many other experiments were connected with the aircraft industry. Electronic devices were developed to thwart and jam radar and sonar pulses, which could have rendered the remnants of the German Navy radar-invisible, as were infra-red tracking systems, which would have enabled the Luftwaffe's Nachtjägers – night-fighters – to track the exhausts of enemy planes. All that would be required to develop something like a small, unmanned craft such as the Foo Fighter would be a small, bespoke engine, an innovatory approach to aerodynamics and designing control systems.

If one looks at these innovations with an air of sobriety, it's quite possible to construct a case revolving around the miniaturisation of some of these technologies and their insertion within a small, self-propelled and automatically guided flying projectile – the Foo Fighter. The war would have been accelerating developments in all fields of research (remember that the Volksjäger flew just twelve weeks after the first drawing-board sketches), and it's therefore quite possible that the time-scale a company today might be used to would have been telescoped out of necessity.

People like the Horten brothers and projects such as the Triebflügel were pushing back the boundaries of knowledge, so such an explanation of the Foo Fighter is not improbable. Is it any surprise that such clandestine projects have yet to see the light of day?

What do we actually see when we look today at projects such as those described in this chapter? With the benefit of hindsight and in the light of subsequent research, we can perceive that the designs were doomed to failure. But that may be to miss the point. Why was the German imagination so fertile in this field? Was invention stimulated by desperation? Whatever the answer, at least designers like Sänger and Lippisch were trying to do something new and fresh; to make an original difference to their discipline. When one considers developments in other countries at the time, in the same field, one pretty much draws a blank. From the research conducted for this book, no project of a similar nature has emerged in either Britain or the USA – unless they existed but were nowhere near as widely documented.

The development of the ramjet was especially advanced for its time, and such jets might have been brought into successful operation, other things being equal, even in 1944. Nowadays, ramjet research is still dominated by the military, and one cannot help wondering how many secret aircraft are flying today using ramjet principles to achieve high speeds. At the time of writing, the USA is reputedly testing a classified spyplane, codenamed 'Aurora', which is capable of hypersonic speeds; and from the testimonies of eyewitnesses who have seen its distinctive smoke-ring trails, it appears to be powered by an exotic engine that burns fuel pellets in a rhythmic series of controlled explosions, directing the resultant thrust of energy for forward propulsion. Which all sounds very familiar.

It seems beyond question that the fifty-year-old visions of our aeronautical future described here, as well as many more unearthed by the Allies from the rubble of postwar Germany, are alive and well in some shape or form. Certainly they haven't all been forgotten. But where they are, and whether ordinary people will ever know about them, remains to be seen.

Chapter Nine

THE SOVIET ANGLE

The First Great Leap Forward

Germany's establishment of secret airbases in the USSR in the years following the First World War served to highlight how backward were the Russian air force and entire aeronautical industry. Letting in the Germans provided the young Soviet Union with an ideal opportunity of catching up with the world, and by the time the bases were abandoned in the mid-1930s the USSR no longer needed the alliance of convenience established in the corridors of Rapallo. Russia also learned lessons during the Spanish Civil War, and restructured its forces accordingly, moving them away from the purely strategic bombing model so favoured by Western tacticians towards the fluid manoeuvrability favoured by Germany.

The Second World War underscored the backwardness of Russian industry and the resultant handicap to the armed forces. Stalin knew – as Kutuzov had before him – that there was only one sure way to defeat an enemy invading from the west. Russia would have to take Operation Barbarossa on the chin and give way before it, regrouping its industries and armies further east, re-equipping the latter with Allied supplies and aircraft where possible, and new home-produced materials. The Germans had banked on a blitzkrieg in Russia and were not kitted out for a winter campaign. The Russians watched their enemy freeze through the winter of 1941–2 and began to look forward to an eventual victory in the Great Patriotic War. They also started to think about the world situation after the Germans had been defeated. As far as Stalin was concerned, the only superpower to rival the USA was the USSR;

195

and Communism should have as large a stake as possible in what would be a fractured Europe. Germany, which so narrowly slipped through Russia's fingers in 1918–19, was the great prize. But if such a goal were to be pursued at all seriously, the technologies and industrial sciences of the USSR would have to rival those of the West. Even so, as late as 1944 the Soviet Union was better at building basic tanks than developing any kind of ground-breaking aeroplanes.

But as 1944 passed and the Red Armies edged closer to Germany, major prizes were collected which could be analysed and used to stimulate home-grown projects which would catapult the USSR forward. Russian forces took Peenemünde and the underground research facilities at Nordhausen and Magdeburg. Unfortunately for the USSR, Stalin's hideous purges at home had so stripped his country of capable military scientists and staff officers that those who arrived at these vital scientific sites didn't appreciate their significance and tried to destroy them. However, some Intelligence reports did eventually reach Moscow which provided an indication of the importance of what had been taken, and responsible scientists were dispatched to evaluate the sites and assess what repairs would be needed to resurrect them.

This work was coordinated by a newly established committee that carried the laborious title of Special Main Directorate of the People's Commissariat of Aircraft Production (NKAP). Its remit was to examine the German aircraft industry and identify likely centres and technologies which could be removed to the USSR as part-payment of war reparations *vis-à-vis* its own aeronautical industry. The NKAP estimated total war damages to Soviet aeronautics at over US $870 million (unadjusted).

By the end of June 1945, and the settling of the zones of occupation of Germany as agreed at the Yalta Conference, the USSR in Germany had over two hundred principal aircraft production sites and a further four hundred or so plants involved with the production of engines and components. Most were in a poor state of repair, as a result of Allied bombing, and many had seen their technical workforces dispersed by the war. Nonetheless the NKAP, under General N. I. Petrov, saw these sites as prizes to be exploited to the fullest extent. To this end, four distinct teams – Special Technical Bureaux (OKBs) – were set up. Each group was detailed to continue the development work of various projects begun by their companies during the war. OKB-3, for example, was assigned the DFS 346 project, and OKB-4 was mainly concerned with the development of autopilot systems, based on the work of the captured Berlin Askania plant. OKB-1, led by the former Junkers designer Bruno Baade, continued with the Ju 287 project (see below). OKB-2 was run by Hans Rosing and his deputy, A. Bereznyak.

Aladdin's Caves

Thus, apart from Peenemünde, the Soviets seized many plants. Others included the Argus plant at Schosberg, the Arado plant at Warnemünde near Rostock on the north coast, and the important Zeiss optical works at Jena, which had been making bombsights and camera lenses throughout the war. Other factories untouched by the depredations of conflict were also taken, such as a converted paper-mill which was now a plant manufacturing BMW 003 turbojets. All of these places were ordered to continue production. By now Russian Intelligence was well aware of the extent of the bounty that had fallen into its lap, and how much it could be used to serve the USSR.

In addition to the four main aircraft types covered in this chapter, Soviet forces also managed to seize the BMW 718 rocket motor and the improved Walter 509 rocket, as fitted to the Me 263. An improved Me 262 was also found, as was a Volksjäger production line also at Warnemünde and run by Arado under licence to Heinkel. In the tunnels of Nordhausen they found copious stores of V-1 and V-2 weapons (though the Americans, who had first occupied the site, had already removed a hundred examples of the V-2), as well as missiles of other types, like the remote-controlled Henschel Hs 293 glider-bomb. They even found, and later copied, the world's largest die-forging press, which used its more than 33,000-tonne pressure to punch out complete, one-piece wing spars.

But aside from the actual hard material discovered, the Russians scooped their share of skilled technicians, engineers and scientists as well; and their 'bag' was as good as the West's. Among them were the engineer Rudolph Rental, who had been project manager on the Komet, and Doktor Ingenieur Adolph Betz, who was, among many other things, an authority on swept-wing aircraft.

One of the most striking of the aircraft the Russians captured was the Junkers Ju 287. This was the most important product of a programme of research conducted in 1943 by Junkers's chief designer, Professor Hertel, into the possibility of a future jet bomber that could outperform conventional fighters – the research coinciding with an Air Ministry directive that only jet power should be considered for warplanes from then on. The first jet bomber actually to appear following the directive was the Arado Ar 234 'Blitz', but it was built with straight wings, probably because the low-speed handling problems presented by swept wings hadn't yet been fully explored, and Arado needed to get on with construction to meet deadlines. As a result, the 234 neither performed at its optimum theoretical speed nor possessed the handling characteristics required of the type. In addition, it was barely bigger than an Me 262 – hardly the best starting-point for a new design for a bomber, especially when one compared it with the massive US B-17s which seemed permanently to darken Germany's skies during their remorseless daylight raids.

At Junkers, the designer Hans Wocke suggested that a forward-swept wing at an angle of about twenty-five degrees would solve most of the problems set by the Air Ministry's directive, and so radical was his idea that the company initiated a project to examine its possibilities.

Initial wind-tunnel tests proved the basic soundness of Wocke's concept although they did throw up questions regarding structural issues. The team believed these could be ironed out during testing. Junkers therefore saw real potential in the enterprise and presented it formally to the Air Ministry early in 1944, as well as to Göring during a visit he made to their Dessau plant. While there, he saw the initial model, and he was so impressed that the RLM very soon placed a development order with Junkers – in March – and designated the aeroplane Ju 287. War conditions ruled out building a full-size prototype of such a large and unusual machine, so they decided to construct and test a full-size set of wings only, mounting them on to an He 177 Fuselage donated by Heinkel. If the wing worked, the rest could follow.

The donated He 177, which was much modified for the job, received its new wings in April. The tailplane was cobbled together from Ju 388 medium bomber components, and since absolute structural integrity was required in order to test the wing, a massively beefed-up, fixed landing gear was adopted. The wing itself joined the fuselage at its base, was constructed completely out of metal, and built around two spars instead of the usual one to reduce the risk of warping. Power for this first prototype was supplied by four Jumo 004 B turbojets, of which two were attached to the sides of the forward fuselage and one slung beneath each wing.

Though the time for its development was short, the 287 still managed to spawn derivative models, though these were not destined to progress beyond wind-tunnel models. One of them, the EF. 122, resembled the 287 closely, with a single turbojet in the trailing edge of each wing and another pair on either side of the forward fuselage below the cockpit. This model was used as part of ongoing research into the idea for forward-swept wings and helped to determine the best locations for the engines of the 287. The EF. 125 was a real hybrid: its forward fuselage was similar to the Ju 388's, but the rest of the configuration was akin to the 287. In this version the wing-mounted jets were placed on the undersides and extended ahead of the leading edge. Another version, the EF. 131, would eventually appear, too, as we shall see.

Only the wing of the first prototype bore any resemblance to the eventual design, but it did fly from Brandis airfield on 16 August 1944, with Flugkapitän Siegfried Holzbaur at the controls. To provide additional thrust during takeoff, a jettisonable Walter 501 auxiliary rocket was fitted beneath each engine, with a parachute to permit intact recovery on the ground. Another parachute was mounted in the tail section of the plane to provide braking assistance on landing. Seventeen flights were made without serious incident – though the temperamental Jumo jets sometimes played up, and the rockets occasionally failed to fire. In all, though, the 287 made an almost surprisingly good impression. Little change to the trim of the aircraft was required when operating the flaps, and even high-speed landings at approaches of 280 kph passed off smoothly. Despite the intention to cover only low-speed handling with the first prototype, it was dived under full power at speeds approaching 660 kph; these experiments confirmed shortcomings such as the reduced effectiveness of the elevators both in tight turns and pullouts from shallow dives, which was attributed to lateral twisting of the wing. The first prototype also carried a cine camera mounted directly forward of the tailfin on a high tripod. Equipped with the camera, the aircraft was to fly with hundreds of woollen tufts glued all over it. The tufts moved in relation to airflow around the aircraft as it went through its paces. Using a method familiar to modern aerodynamicists, the filmed results were analysed and helped the designers interpret the forces they were up against in developing their idea, indicating what adaptations should be made, though it isn't known whether or not the results of the film really justified the effort.

Wind-tunnel tests of the models had revealed the benefit of mounting all the engines on the wings in order to reduce the severity of wing warping, and this change was incorporated into the second prototype. The number of engines was increased to six, and this time the then new BMW 003 turbojets were employed, a trio mounted in a cluster beneath each wing. The wings for the second prototype had been completed by July 1944, but all development on bombers was then suspended in favour of the various emergency fighter programmes being put in train. Junkers, however, from long experience of how wont the Air Ministry was to change its mind, continued work on the 287 – slowly, steadily and secretly, discreetly appropriating materials from other projects in expectation of the day when, the company believed, the Air Ministry would want to resurrect the project. Sure enough, in March 1945, for no obvious reason, the Ministry issued orders to recommence, together with instructions to prepare for mass production – of over a hundred examples a month – from December. Production models were scheduled to be fitted with four Heinkel HeS 011A turbojets, Heinkel's almost mythical new engine expected to be readily available by the end of 1945.

As a result of these new orders, the first prototype was transferred to the evaluation centre at Rechlin. It was destroyed there soon afterwards by an air raid before much work on it could be done, though work on the second and even a third pre-production prototype moved ahead at a Junkers plant near Leipzig. For the second prototype, the distinctive wing made the previous year was unchanged, though it was now fitted to a totally new fuselage, complete with retractable landing gear. As a result of work on the EF. 125 model, the forward fuselage was taken from the Ju 388 to save development time, and it incorporated a pressurised cabin for the four-man crew.

When Soviet forces overran the factory, they found the second prototype to be in the final stages of assembly. Assembly of the third prototype had just begun. The third was also to use the BMW units, though only four of them and in a configuration that returned to the same one of the first prototype. The third version was the most sophisticated, naturally. It was never built, but, had it been, it would have featured a pressurised cabin for a three-man crew, full operational equipment and a remote-controlled barrette in the tail housing two thirty-millimetre Mg 131 cannon directed by a periscope sight in the cockpit. One great advantage of the forward-swept wings was that a longer bomb bay was possible ahead of the rearward-mounted wing span. Equally important was an almost completely stable centre of gravity. The bomb load would have been 4,000 kilogrammes.

Another variant which was planned but never completed was the twinning of a 287 packed with explosives to an Me 262 carrier, forming the 'Mistel' bridge-buster. The idea was to crash the thing into any strategic bridges the army didn't have time to blow up in the wake of its retreat. Although Mistels in this combination were never built, the need to destroy bridges important to the Allied advance did arise, and to do the work the Luftwaffe was forced to use lighter variations of the Mistel, or suicide pilots from KG/200 squadron and survivors of the short-lived Sonderkommando Elbe as we shall see in the next chapter.

The Ju 287 was actually the starting-point for a wildly new project: the EF. 131. This was now developed more or less from scratch, though it took its lead from the Ju 287. The Ju 287 which we see in photographs today isn't representative of the finished plane at all, being mostly a cobbled-together amalgam of the He 177 bomber fuselage, fitted with a bespoke wing, simply to test its aerodynamic properties. What the Soviets were trying to do was go one stage further and build the real thing, designated EF. 131, using components for which there were no pre-existing blueprints or plans, but using the coerced labour of the original German technicians and engineers.

By July 1946 construction of the first of three planned examples was complete. Longer by 2.5 metres than the 287, it was fitted with six Jumo 004 engines (in clusters of three per wing) and had a design speed of 860 kph, with a range of 1,050 kilometres carrying a bomb load of 2,000 kilogrammes. But before any test-flight could take place, the project was swept up in a Security Police-led move to Podberezhye on Soviet soil. The move was probably occasioned by two main fears: that the Allies would find out that the Russians were flouting the Yalta Agreement – which, as we shall see, they were, and that from the German base a pilot could easily defect to a Western zone in the aircraft since its speed would outstrip any pursuing Soviet fighter.

Work on the EF. 131 continued alongside development of the second prototype Ju 287, which was completed, and flown by Flugkapitän Dulgen in 1947. In the course of trials lasting until 1948, it reached a reputed speed of 1,000 kph.

When the first EF. 131 began flight-testing in autumn 1946 at Podberezhye, its airframe was found to lack strength, and it needed extensive modifications which set the project back by two months. However, the lessons learned were incorporated successfully into the second prototype EF. 131, which first flew on 23 May 1947. The German test-pilot Paul Huelge made favourable comments on the first fifteen-minute flight, despite the failure on landing of the port undercarriage spar, causing the aircraft to list heavily to port and resulting in a damaged engine. Such a small mishap didn't put an end to the project – though later, greater complications would.

As test-flights continued, problems with undercarriage and tail section vibrations caused the aircraft to miss the Tushino air show in August 1947. The air show was a propaganda exercise at which the USSR was hoping to show off its captured German hardware to the world – in a bigger and better Soviet form. The EF. 126 Elli was on show here; but the failure of the 131 to make it was to seal its fate. Key personnel were removed from the development programme and the project seemed doomed to wither on the vine, even though it was obvious to all with any technical vision that here was a wholly new design that could meet higher and more ambitious targets easily, given a concentrated effort.

But the story didn't end there. Although the OKB-1 team had been more or less disbanded and were now working on less secretive projects, new Soviet turbojet designs were emerging which suddenly made the original 131 concept relevant once more. Under a new Soviet controller, S. M. Alexeyev, who was sympathetic to the requirements of his German 'guests', a new designation, EF. 140, was introduced within a reorganised OKB-1. The EF. 140 was a version of the EF. 131 with new Soviet engines and with both an armoured cockpit and a new defensive armament arrangement – there had been some rethinking concerning the EF. 131's reliance on speed as virtually its sole means of defence. The EF. 140 now had a pair of remote-controlled barbettes above and below the cockpit.

It made its first flight on 20 September 1948, and during a flight that lasted about twenty minutes the test-pilot reported everything as happening according to plan. However, after several short flights the fuel-metering systems to the engines began to give trouble: the engines were over-revving and getting damaged in the process, so that a decision was taken to halt the project while the fault was made good. On 24 May 1949 flights on a re-engined prototype resumed: tests culminated with a top speed of 904 kph and a range of 2,000 kilometres. But such promising developments were short lived. The Tupolev Tu-14 bomber was then about to enter service in the very role the 140 had aspired to. OKB-1 was then instructed to modify the design to perform as a high-altitude reconnaissance aircraft, redesignated 140-R. In order to give it the extended range of 3,400 kilometres required by the new specification, and the new operating altitude of over 14,000 metres, it was decided to fit newer, Soviet engines: the VK-1 design (copied from the Rolls-Royce Nene). Although test-flights continued into 1950, both the 140-R and a sister project – the 140-B/R high-speed bomber – were cancelled. They were the last forward-swept-wing aircraft in the USSR. The high command had concluded simply that there was no need to pursue this approach.

The DFS Legacy

The DFS 228 was the first of a three-phase DFS research project into high-altitude manned rocket flight. It was designed in 1941 to test the technologies of cabin pressurisation, an emergency pilot rescue system and a high-altitude rocket unit – all necessary for the overall enterprise to attain its aim of supersonic flight. Two examples were built and flown as gliders, though neither was ever equipped with a power unit. The first was captured by US forces towards the end of the war, though it isn't known whether or not they flew it themselves, and the second was destroyed by its technicians at Hörsching in May 1945 to prevent it from falling into Allied hands.

Phase two of the project was concerned with determining optimum wing forms for high-altitude work. For this phase the DFS acquired the Heinkel P. 1068. This had been a Heinkel design for a small jet-engined bomber capable of 870 kph. Using it as their starting-point, the DFS experimented with different wing configurations over five variants. Progress was slow. In April 1945 there was a fire at Wrede's, the sub-contractor. At the time one example of the phase-two version was nearly finished and another half-completed. The fire destroyed all material relating to the project, and operations were moved to Herzogenrath, only to be abandoned at Germany's defeat.

The third and final phase was supersonic flight itself and was to use the new DFS 346, which was based on what information had been culled from the two previous phases. Initial wind-tunnel tests were undertaken at the DFS installation at Darmstadt with a scale model, and the first results were encouraging. But by now it was the late summer of 1944, and both the Air Ministry and the DFS were keen to see quick progress. Therefore the Siebel factory at Halle was contracted to build a full-scale version, and started work after having received detailed plans completed in November. A DFS summary report for 1 August to 1 December 1944 mentions the 346 first: 'proceeding on the possibilities suggested by using rocket engines at high altitudes, it was investigated whether it was feasible to reach supersonic speed with a manned aircraft, and if possible break the sound barrier, or not. The investigations showed that by using present technical methods, such a thing must be possible at high altitudes. A proposal was submitted [to Halle] to develop an airframe as a research aircraft to clarify the aero mechanic difficulties that arise when breaking the sonic barrier, which cannot be tested in a wind-tunnel.'

The aircraft's streamlined fuselage had a cigar profile and was built throughout of duralumin alloy, with mid-mounted wings canted back forty-five degrees, and a short but broad fin and rudder supporting a swept, adjustable-swing tailplane near its top. Another unusual feature was that the ailerons and elevators were able to be used independently: the inner control surfaces with the largest area would have been effective at subsonic speeds; the smaller, outer surfaces, having no aerodynamic effect, would have simply 'stuck out' into the supersonic airflow, giving some control at supersonic speeds. Divided into three compartments, the 1.6-metre-diameter fuselage had a bubble-glazed cockpit section at the front, in which the pilot lay prone. The centre section housed the two 121-gallon tanks of C-Stoff and T-Stoff propellants for the two Walter 509 rockets, each giving over 2,000-kilogramme thrust, as well as a tank of kerosene. (Initially, incidentally, only one rocket had been proposed.) In the final versions, the rear section housed the rockets themselves.

The pressurised cabin contained full instrumentation, and in the event of an emergency the pilot could be saved by jettisoning the entire forward fuselage section using explosive bolts and deploying a parachute stowed in the rear of the fuselage. This would slow the aircraft sufficiently for a controlled descent. At 3,000 metres his couch would be pushed forwards automatically, out of the fuselage. He would then free-fall down to 1,500 metres, when he would detach himself from the couch and parachute down the rest of the way alone. The whole rescue system was designed to operate automatically in the event of the pilot's blacking out.

The 346 was designed to be launched from a piggy-back position atop a host aircraft at about 10,000 metres, starting off with initial gliding and dive tests at up to 900 kph to trim the aircraft before rocket power was applied, the speed then building up to Mach 2 at altitudes of 20,000 metres and more. The aircraft even had thrust enough to climb vertically, and the DFS expert Dr Felix Kracht believed that Mach 2.6 could thus be achieved at an altitude of 35,000 metres.

Unfortunately, though the Siebel factory had all the necessary materials, its time was increasingly taken up with conventional aircraft production, and the 346 was destined never to be produced there after all. A full-sized wooden mock-up was built to test component packaging, however, and when US troops seized the Halle factory in spring 1945 they found the first, unpowered 346 under construction. As the new zones of occupation were agreed, the Siebel factory was transferred to Soviet control. The USSR then took over the venture along with other projects, and the German technical crew carried on working on the 346 through to October 1946, when all the enterprises were moved in their entirety by train to the USSR. The work in Germany was in direct violation of the terms of the Yalta Conference, where the three major powers had agreed on the carving-up of Europe, but had specifically prohibited the development of new weaponry on German soil. But the Russians had been working in this field since soon after invading Germany in 1945, on the advice of NKAP reports that German scientists were leaving Russian-controlled areas in large numbers, and that their escape to the West was threatening to put the USSR behind in the postwar arms technology race. In the light of the escalating Cold War, the Soviet security police had decided that it was advisable to move all such undertakings into Russia, as far as possible from prying American and British eyes.

'Guests' of the Soviet Union

Although they were not strictly speaking prisoners, the 3,550 civilian engineers who were obliged to accompany the projects had no choice in becoming 'guests' of the Soviet Union. On arrival at their new home at Podberezhye, some 130 kilometres from Moscow, they were divided into groups under the authority of no fewer than nine Ministries. With the move, the OKB centres established in Germany were disbanded and on their arrival in the USSR the Germans were redeployed into wholly unsuitable fields of work: for example, aircraft designers were employed in planning prefabricated housing, aerodynamicists were used to design cars, and so on. Soviet initiative in spiriting these talented people into Russia was now being dissipated through political infighting and Kremlin bureaucracy. The famous Focke-Wulf designer Kurt Tank, responsible for the indomitable Fw 190 among many other projects, offered his services to the Russians; but they were so disorganised that they turned him away and he found employment finally in France.

Such a situation could not be allowed to continue. Soon enough, the teams sorted themselves out into two new groups. As we have seen, OKB-1, essentially the old Dessau group, was led by the former Junkers designer Bruno Baade and continued to work on the former Ju 287 and EF. 126. OKB-2 was headed by Hans Rosing and worked on the DFS 346. Each group was discouraged from communicating with the other and was kept in the dark about any other scientific advances made by other teams throughout Russia. Russia had suffered enormous losses during the war, and these 'guests' were still the enemy – necessary but not welcome, and certainly not trustworthy. The downside of this arrangement was that the teams underperformed as a result.

With the move to Podberezhye, the nature of the DFS project changed. Its aim was no longer specifically to produce a rocket reconnaissance aircraft but to do more pure research, investigating high Mach speeds of around 1.5 to 2.

The first DFS 346 glider was completed finally at Podberezhye, and in autumn 1946 it was transferred to the Soviet ZAGI research facility for wind-tunnel testing, while a second example began construction at the home site. Initial ZAGI tests showed that the wing shapes failed to come up to expectations. The wing tips were altered and small fins added to the upper surfaces, to improve aerodynamic stability. Later models had fins added to the undersides of the wings as well.

The revised 346 glider that had undergone tests at ZAGI was now designated 346-P (for 'Planer'). It was taken by barge to the nearby Tyoply Stan airfield, today an outlying suburb of Moscow, which was run by the Soviet Flight Testing Institute, and began trials in spring 1947 with the former Siebel test-pilot Flugkapitän Ziese at the controls. It made many flights, being carried up into the air by either an impounded B-29 bomber or a captured Ju 388, and then released, to make its own landing on special underwing skids.

Meanwhile, captured Junkers staff who had worked on the Me 263 and were now held at the Soviet base at Kuibyshev had begun to construct Walter rockets out of salvaged components.

Starting in spring 1948, further unpowered gliding flights were undertaken by the German pilots Rauschen and Motsch. Ziese trained on other German gliders in anticipation of making the first powered flight.

At first both the German pilots, and the Soviet test-pilots who joined the programme, complained of the restrictions imposed on them in lying in a prone position, claiming that it was unnatural and pointing out that in spite of all precautions it would be impossible to bale out in an emergency. The authorities' response was to say that the project would go ahead with the existing configuration and that the pilots' 'assistance' was therefore 'required'. The pilots had no choice; but their fears about the prone position were somewhat allayed when they saw the ejection tests. An American B-25 Liberator bomber, retained by the Russians as part of their 'lend-lease' arrangement with the USA, was used to test ejection procedures, having a mock-up of the front portion of the 346 fuselage in its open bomb bay. The procedures were tested successfully using mannequins; but whether anyone ever thought they would have to be used in a real situation is a moot point. In any case, as we have said, the pilots were given no option but to comply.

The second 346 was now complete. Designated 346-1, the design replaced the underwing skids with a single, retractable ventral skid. Walter rockets were not fitted and the 346-1 was used as a test glider. While Rauschen and Motsch continued tests on the 346-P, Ziese, also in spring 1948, now tested the 346-1 at Tyoply Stan. With a new Tupolev Tu-4 as carrier aircraft, he flew the 346-1 with a variety of ballast loads to simulate the number of rockets and fuel configurations the project was likely to require. During the test programme, some handling difficulties were reported, but they were regarded as being of no significance.

Work on the rocket had continued that year, and its first test-flight took place on 30 September 1949, when the aircraft was released at a height of 9,700 metres from beneath the starboard wing of the B-29 (incidentally one of three that the Russians had impounded). Ziese, at the controls again, reported via his radio the same handling difficulties that he had encountered before and was then forced to land at a high closing speed of 310 kph. The skid touched the ground and flexed, bouncing the aircraft up into the air again and making it hop another 700 metres before finally coming to rest on the belly of the fuselage, the skid having collapsed into its housing. Ziese's harness had also broken on impact and his body had been slammed against the instrument panel, knocking him out. An official report on the accident laid partial blame with the pilot for not having activated the locking mechanism for the skid quickly enough, but this seems a little unlikely in view of Ziese's long experience and his familiarity with the 346–1. It is more probable that a technical failure of some kind had occurred. The 346–1 was repaired and returned to testing, with the Soviet test-pilot, Kasmin, standing in for Ziese, who was recovering in hospital; but the same undercarriage fault occurred again, though this time, luckily for Kasmin, the 346–1 slid across snow which had fallen to obscure the runway and neither pilot nor aircraft sustained any serious injury. Tests were resumed once more, with the 346–1 now being released at heights of 2,000 metres; but the grass runway was now discovered to be too short for proper landings, and after a series of serious mishaps in which the aircraft came close to crashing, the programme was abandoned and attention was turned to the next model, the 346–3. This had a revised tailplane with greater sweepback, which allowed the maximum permitted speed under testing to rise to Mach 0.9.

The 346–3 appeared in May 1950 and was the only model to use both its rockets in flight. (The 346–2 appears merely to have been a static test airframe.) In the spring of 1951 it was carried up by an impounded USAF Boeing B-29 that had landed in Soviet territory during the war with engine trouble and released at altitude, with Ziese once more at the controls. After executing test manoeuvres, Ziese put his machine into a dive and activated one of the two rockets, accelerating to 1,100 kph, pushing the speed towards Mach 1, beyond which he would have broken the sound barrier. From what we can glean of the flight, Ziese had to back off before achieving his objective because of slight vibrations at his top speed, but he landed the machine safely on its skid, and the Russians awarded him 20,000 roubles in recognition of his courage.

Meanwhile, the first three prototypes were still in use, testing a new release system that was supposed to give a safer drop from the huge and stable B-29. However, the 346-P crashed immediately after its release, killing its Russian pilot. The 346–1 swept up into the wing of the B-29 following its release, before spiralling earthwards. Its pilot was luckier: he managed to bale out and parachute to safety. The machine itself crashed hard but wasn't destroyed; it was repaired and returned to use.

The 346–3 programme was still running. Beginning in August 1951 Ziese started a new series of tests designed to stretch the aircraft. The fifteenth of August saw the first of these new flights. He engaged the rocket, but during its burn of one minute and forty seconds he reported instability problems with the aircraft – not in themselves dangerous, but they were coupled to a failure in the cabin's ventilation system which caused the temperature to rise sufficiently to put Ziese at the point of fainting, although he managed to keep control and landed safely. A second flight passed off without incident. It was the third, on 14 September 1951, which sealed the aircraft's fate.

Ziese separated from his B-29 carrier at 9,000 metres and accelerated with both rockets for about two minutes. He was reported to have lost control of his machine during a high-speed run up to 20,000 metres, when one of the wings sheared off. Other reports merely state that he 'lost control'. Being a cool, professional test-pilot, Ziese remained within the pressurised cockpit of his plummeting aircraft until he was low enough to activate the escape system and he parachuted to earth safely. The plane crashed some distance away and was written off. An official crash report vindicated the basic design of the 346 and its rocket but rejected calls for the older 346–1 airframe to be uprated to take the place of the crashed 346–3. After spending 55 million roubles on the project, the USSR abandoned it. Ziese never flew anything like the 346 again, and he died of cancer in 1953.

Following this, the OKB-2 team was moved once again, to a site beyond the Urals – though it is hard to say for certain why. The move was due possibly to the development of the DFS 446 swept-wing interceptor, which reputedly used a multichamber liquid-fuel rocket and had a similar forty-five degree swept wing to the 346, as well as its retractable-skid undercarriage. If the 446 was indeed developed in the USSR, it would probably have contributed to later Soviet fighter designs, such as the MiG 15.

A New 'Stuka'

Much of Germany's military success early in the war came as a result of the dive-bombing tactics employed so skilfully by the Ju 87 Stuka. However, its slow speed and general vulnerability in the face of Allied fighter attack meant that it was soon outclassed in its original role.

With the advent of jets, the Air Ministry thought that a new dive bomber could be developed to repeat the Stuka's success. The only problem was that with the higher closing speeds now being reached, no suitable aircraft could be found which could withstand high-speed dives. The Henschel Hs 132 turbojet dive bomber was designed specifically to fill the gap, and was so well received by Air Ministry officials when presented with it in May 1944 that they ordered six examples – two 'A' series and four 'B' series.

For the 132 to work in its role, it needed to be able to withstand forces of up to twelve 'g' in a dive – the permissible norm being eight 'g' for piston aircraft. It therefore provided for its pilot to lie prone – which was thought to be the best position in which to withstand such pressures. It promised a small, fast and manoeuvrable aircraft – designed to be one step ahead of Allied gunners, whether airborne or ground-based. Given the state of German industry at the time, Henschel was obliged to use basic materials. The BMW 003 turbojet which powered it was mounted above the fuselage, as in the Heinkel He 162 Volksjäger. Although concerns had been raised about the efficiency of this layout, in the light of earlier research for the Volksjäger, the designers opted to go with the plan for the sake of expediency. Other corners were cut: the deletion of air brakes, for example, limited the diving angle and reduced speed but also accelerated development and saved money.

The 132 had the layout of a mid-wing monoplane, with twin fins and rudders and a retractable undercarriage. The wing, mostly of wood, tapered sharply, had trailing edge flaps, and housed the landing gear. The fuselage was mainly metal, to give the pilot protection from the small-arms fire of ground-based troops; and he lay with his face against a heavily glazed and fully faired nose-cone. The jet's air intake was immediately aft of the cockpit.

Three variants were proposed. The 132A would be powered by the BMW 003 and carry a single 500-kilogramme bomb; the 132B would have a Junkers 004 and carry a similar payload, but also have two nose-mounted MG 151 machine-guns. The 132C would have used Heinkel's long-awaited HeS 109–011 engine, whose greater power, had it ever appeared, would have permitted double the bomb load as well as the cannon. Construction of the first of three prototypes began in March 1945 at Henschel's Schönefeld works. Despite the threat from approaching Russian forces, by the end of the war the first prototype 'A' series model was close to being ready for flight trials. In fact it was scheduled to fly in June. One photograph exists of it (and is reproduced in this book), but then the Russians closed in and the craft was seized, together with the almost complete second and third prototypes. Nothing more was heard of them in the West, and research for this book has failed to throw any further light on the subject.

On a different tack altogether, November 1944 saw the Air Ministry issue a request for the simplest possible fighter, one that could be produced even more rapidly and more cheaply than the Volksjäger, by then in pre-production. This was not to be a semi-expendable aircraft like the Natter, but one capable of conventional operation. As much had already been done in the Volksjäger programme to simplify airframes, so now attention was turned to the simplification of engines, though power was not to be sacrificed. The power unit chosen, despite the experience with the Me 328, was the Argus pulsejet, because its use would cut 450 man-hours from the production time needed for a turbojet. (A ramjet would have been equally simple and cheap but needed a tow to get up to speed.) The idea was pie in the sky. There weren't enough pilots and there wasn't enough fuel to supply the Volksjäger programme as it was. In the end, only three makers submitted designs for the so-called Miniaturjäger – Blohm und Voss, Heinkel and Junkers. The Junkers entry joined the Ju 287, the DFS 346 and the Hs 132 in going to Russia.

The EF. 126 'Elli' was to have a metal fuselage and a wooden wing, with a simple Argus 500-kilogramme thrust engine mounted aft of the cockpit. Like so many planes that used pulsejets, jettisonable rockets were to be fitted to get it under way. Because it used a pulsejet, high-altitude work was out of the question, so the Elli was envisaged as a ground-attack fighter. In addition to two 180-round MG 151 cannon in the nose, it was designed to carry either a 400-kilogramme bomb load consisting of a total of 216 SD2 'Butterfly' anti-personnel bomblets under the wings, or a dozen air-to-ground missiles. The bomblets were designed to be scattered over an enemy troop formation. The air-pressure fuse on each would detonate it at just the right height to hurl shrapnel in all directions.

The Elli never flew during the war, but a detailed proposal was made in autumn 1945 by Bruno Baade to his new Soviet masters to further its development. By January 1946 a mock-up had been built at Dessau by the original OKB-1, and a further five craft were in the process of assembly. In May 1946 the first of the prototypes, the EF. 126, was ready for flight-testing. It used an Argus 014 pulsejet and had a loaded weight of 2,585 kilogrammes. Later examples used the better Jumo 226 engine.

The test programme was quickly to run into difficulties with the loss of the first prototype in a landing accident which killed the German test-pilot, Mathis. This occurred on 21 May 1946, and although attributed officially to pilot error (he had tried a steep landing approach and had bumped the aircraft back up into the air, causing it to break up on the final (probably stalled) landing), modifications were later made to the wings. Further tests that summer confirmed the essentially efficient handling of the aircraft, though the power remained a problem: the Argus units were hard to ignite and then didn't burn consistently; but the Jumos kept burning out both themselves and their cowlings. Furthermore, the supply of external rocket packs was dwindling – the Russians had neglected to restart their manufacture – so that takeoffs were becoming ever more restricted in number. In September 1946 the team was disbanded and the prototypes were dismantled, to be shipped back to the USSR.

Once in Russia, the re-formed OKB-1 took control of the project and restarted its development, working towards the goal of preparing three prototypes for the 1947 Tushino air show. They tested an unpowered glider example, towed up by and released from an old Ju 88 medium bomber, as well as making a series of static and in-flight rocket tests, again using the Ju 88 as their workhorse.

That is all that we know of the Elli. Junkers were working on a similar variant, the EF. 127 Walli, mentioned in an earlier chapter, which might have been more effective since it was designed to use an internally mounted Walter 509 rocket; but the Walli blueprints did not fall into Russian hands. Its role would have been the same as the Natter's, but the Walter 509 rocket was never adequately evolved, and the short development time set for the Miniaturjäger meant that the Walli enterprise was shelved, together with that of the Heinkel Julia, until operational lessons could be learned from the successful Me 262.

Apart from the aircraft themselves, the Soviet Union gained other benefits from its German booty. Lathes and machine tools in prewar Russian factories ran at only 600 rpm owing to bad electricity supplies and poor motors. British and American machine tools of the time ran at 3,000 rpm. But after the war, with the advent of many thousands of

German technicians and engineers as 'guests' of the USSR, things changed, benefiting both rates of production and quality of output. Furthermore, as the Cold War isolated Russia from the West, the new artificial country called the German Democratic Republic was to play a vital role in assisting the USSR's progress from backward agrarian to modern industrial state, though East Germany, as so many of the Soviet satellites, was virtually sucked dry by its master in the process. For example, it supplied Soviet ballistic missiles with their rocket fuel, delivered much of the electronics used in radar and control systems, and in the service of the USSR refined its existing tradition of precision engineering. If Russia hadn't realised how important it was to exploit German technical expertise at the outset, the chances are high that the Soviet bloc would have collapsed much sooner than it did. In fact, if Stalin hadn't had access to the captured military technologies and know-how, Russia might not have even become the superpower it remained until 1990.

There was great competition between East and West for German aeronautical experts. Within months of the final surrender, Wernher von Braun was comfortably established at Los Alamos, Texas. Willy Messerschmitt turned down British, French and US offers of work and spent a brief period in US captivity, but he attended the International Air Pioneers' Dinner in Washington DC in October 1953 and was received at the Pentagon on the fourteenth of that month. German scientists working on the Nazis' atom bomb programme were likewise spirited away to the USSR.

At the end of the war, Germany was a military and scientific Pandora's box which the former Allies, already squaring up for ideological confrontation, opened greedily.

Chapter Ten

THE LEGEND OF LEONIDAS

Sturmgruppe

By the winter of 1943 the Luftwaffe high command had realised that it was no longer possible to stop the increasing waves of Allied bombers with flak batteries or counter attack by conventional fighters. The USAAF B-17s flew in combat boxes – formations of fifteen aircraft, three abreast and five deep, facilitating all-round defensive fire power from about sixty heavy machine-guns. The average German fighter, presenting a large target area to the USAAF gunners, would be in trouble once it came within 800 metres of such a formation, and the range of its guns wouldn't be effective from much further away. At first, the Luftwaffe tried to get round the problem by fitting larger cannon with longer ranges to heavy fighters like the Me 110 or the Me 410, but this wasn't a satisfactory solution since even with the heavier armaments the fighters could do little more than harass the bombers from so far away.

With no new aircraft types coming into operation to attack the B-17s efficiently, the problem became very serious indeed, and it was compounded when the Allies introduced state-of-the-art escorts like Mustangs to their bombing fleets. Mustangs could run rings round most Luftwaffe aircraft, and they carried enough fuel to escort the bombers throughout a whole mission.

We have already discussed the aircraft being developed for point-defence work against the bombers. In the meantime, something had to be done. The possibility of using parachute bomblets against them was considered, the idea being to fire them from adapted rocket launchers into the air ahead of the bomber formation, which would then fly into the bomblets as they descended, exploding on contact, but the method, when tried, was far too subject to error to work. After this the Luftwaffe was reduced to exhorting pilots to take all 'necessary risks' to stop the bombers.

An experimental unit staffed by experienced but evidently fanatical volunteer pilots was set up as Sturmgruppe – Storm Group – IV/JG 3 in May 1944. It was equipped with 'old-fashioned' Focke-Wulf Fw 190s, which had been reinforced with special frontal armour. The entire group would go up and take on a combat box, in line abreast formation, presenting the enemy with such a wealth of targets deliberately to confuse them. In the attack, their orders were to hold off firing until as late as possible, and the pilots wore a 'whites-of-the-eyes' insignia on their jackets to show how close in to the enemy they were prepared to go. They had undertaken – no direct *order* had been given; rather *they* had given their word – that if they ran out of ammunition without 'downing' a bomber they would use their planes to ram one. The sorties flown by the Sturmgruppe were very successful: owing to the mad bravery of the pilots involved, on the first sortie on 7 July 1944 over twenty B-25 Liberators were brought down during the first two minutes. The Luftwaffe was so impressed that it set up a second group, II/JG 300. In fact the good 'kill' rate of the groups didn't come from ramming – the incidence of suicide tactics was small. The pilots simply flew right up to the bombers and shot them up at close range, like rats in a barrel, oblivious to the risks they were taking themselves.

Operating together, the two groups brought down about forty B-17s on 15 August. After that a third group, II/JG 4, was formed. All three units continued in operation, still using Fw 190s, until March 1945, by which time they had destroyed over five hundred Allied bombers – though only ten as a result of ramming. Only 150 Sturmgruppe pilots were killed – though of course far more fighters were lost – which is an extraordinarily low rate, considering their wildly risky tactics, and compared with the loss-rate of conventional groupings attacking the combat boxes.

Pro Patria Mori

One of the strangest designs to emerge in Germany during the last phase of the war was the Fieseler Fi 103, which was conceived with only one purpose in mind. Derived from the V-1 flying bomb, of which 32,000 were eventually made, the Fi 103 was a piloted version, intended for use against shipping or other heavily defended targets. In the original design for the V-1 developed by Fieseler, the possibility of converting it into a manned machine had been mooted, though the plan had been dropped since it was considered that such a proposal would do nothing for public morale, even if the public accepted the idea, which seemed unlikely. That it was considered in the first place is an indication of how little faith there was in the accuracy of the flying bomb; but in those early days of auto-navigation it was accepted that to get the thing to within fifteen kilometres of its target was the best that could be expected.

For real accuracy, a human controller would have to be used. As the war was about to open a new Western Front in France, and the Luftwaffe's conventional fighter forces were overstretched already, the original Fieseler proposal was considered again in more detail. Its main advocates were Flugkapitän Hanna Reitsch and Hauptmann Heinrich Lange. The pair led a group which argued the case for recruiting a select cadre of nothing less than suicide pilots – willing to sacrifice their lives for their Führer by deliberately crashing modified aircraft packed with explosives into otherwise unassailable targets. The plan was turned down flat by Milch and treated with stony silence in official quarters, but it had Hitler's tacit support and survived semi-clandestinely in a modified form. Himmler, in his mad way, also viewed it with approval, seeing it as a means of allowing officers and men in Luftwaffe jails to redeem the disgrace they had variously brought on their names. A Luftwaffe psychologist was asked to report on the likely mental effects on pilots who volunteered; his findings were positive, and the project now stepped up a gear.

217

The Leonidas Squadron

Reitsch and Lange were soon able to announce the formation of a new unit, and in doing so they stated its aims frankly. Quite unprecedented numbers of volunteers presented themselves as a result, the total growing to thousands. The director of the programme, General Günther Korten, who was Jeschonnek's successor as Chief of the Air Staff, instructed Oberst Heigl of the covert Kampfgeschwader 200 to set up a 'squadron' (in fact the unit was closer in size to a Geschwader, or group) and recruit volunteers from the list. Korten himself had not long to live: he died of wounds sustained when the bomb Stauffenberg set to kill Hitler exploded at a staff conference at the Wolf's Lair, Hitler's East Prussian headquarters that July.

Göring had bestirred himself enough to speak out against the suicide unit, but evidently was overruled by Hitler and Himmler, the latter having long since ousted Göring from his position close to the Führer.

The Luftwaffe's own 'special forces', KG 200, was divided into five groups. 'I' existed to deliver agents behind enemy lines; 'II' specialised in 'Mistel' combination-aircraft assaults; 'III' flew adapted Fw 190s equipped with torpedoes in an anti-shipping role; 'IV' was a training group; 'V' was now formed for the suicide missions. Unofficially, KG 200 'V' was also known as the Leonidas Staffel, taking its name from the king of Sparta who, preferring death to dishonour, led a force of three hundred Spartans against a vast Persian host at Thermopylae in 480 BC. Of the mass of volunteers for the squadron, only seventy were initially thought suitable. Each man selected was required to sign a declaration which ran: 'I hereby voluntarily apply to be enrolled in the suicide group as pilot of a human glider-bomb. I fully understand that employment in this capacity will entail my own death.'

It is interesting that the notion of suicide missions was accepted at all in a Western Christian country where there was no such tradition. Japan's kamikaze programme was one firmly rooted in tradition; but the Führer was the representative of a largely prefabricated mythology, based on cobbled-together 'Nordic' traditions, carrying a romantic nineteenth-century gloss and with little intellectual or symbolic content. The young men who volunteered to die for him offer a sad example of the power politicians can exert on simple souls, though in fairness to

218

them they may also have felt that by their deaths they might be able to save many hundreds if not thousands of their fellow citizens. The German public, by now demoralised and disaffected in any case, responded to the Leonidas Staffel with either disgust or indifference.

The Air Ministry was asked to investigate the technical aspects of the suicide missions and in turn appointed Heinz Kensche, himself a volunteer, to head the project's technical development along with Hanna Reitsch, in her capacity as test-pilot for the DFS glider training centre. At first the volunteers trained in regular gliders to give them the feeling for unpowered soaring flight, before they progressed to specially adapted models with cut-down wings. Using these, they were able to dive at speeds approaching 300 kph. Having completed this stage, the trainees graduated to the dual-controlled Fi 103.

Totaleinsatz

The German word 'Einsatz' has a wealth of meanings in English; in this context it is best understood by 'operation', 'mission' and 'commitment'.

Initially, both the Fi 103 and the Me 328 were considered as potential donor aircraft, but the Fi 103 was passed over in favour of a modified 328 carrying a 900-kilogramme bomb. When production problems and difficulties (yet again) with the Argus pulsejet caused this development to be delayed, one of the Leonidas sections suggested using a beefed-up Fw 190 carrying an extra-large bomb load in place of the fuel which would normally be carried for the return trip. Initial trials didn't go well, and in any case such a large and slow aircraft risked being shot down before it reached its target. Notwithstanding these reservations, thirty-nine volunteers were ready to undertake Totaleinsatz using modified Fw 190s by 9 June 1944. Himmler vetoed any operational action, however, and even the volunteers were worried about being shot down before they reached their target – which would have made a nonsense of their sacrifice.

Problems with adapting the Me 328 to glider-bomb use continued, and in the end Himmler, losing patience, moved to cancel the entire project. Fate, however, was to intervene in the shape of SS Standartenführer Otto Skorzeny. This unspeakably arrogant but brave officer had been looking into the possibilities of manned torpedoes for the navy as a way of resurrecting attacks on Allied shipping. Now he was briefed by Hitler to try to breathe new life into the aerial suicide bomber enterprise. He contacted Hanna Reitsch, who still had great faith in the project – not because she was a fanatical Nazi but because she genuinely seems to have believed in the idea of laying down one's life so that others might be saved.

The Reichenberg

With the next development, the absolute necessity of death was removed. Compared with the other options, the Fi 103, which was now reappraised, at least gave the pilot a slim chance of survival. It was quickly adopted, and in the summer of 1944 the DFS at Ainring took on the job of developing it. It was given the name 'Reichenberg'. In only a matter of days, a first version was ready for tests. Such was the impetus now behind the project – the Führer was evidently very keen – that within a fortnight four more examples were ready, and tests had been initiated with the volunteer pilots. At the same time a production line was set up at Dannenberg.

There were four basic variants: the R-I single-seat glider; the R-II, which had a second cockpit where the warhead would normally be; the R-III single seater, with the intake for a pulsejet fitted, to stimulate handling; and the R-IV, which was the standard operational model. Its conversion from the Fi 103 standard V-1 flying bomb was simplicity itself. The V-1 fuselage held the following items: a magnetic compass, an 850-kilogramme warhead; a fuel tank; two compressed-air bottles to power the control servos; the autopilot; and the servo controls. To transform the regular V-1 into a Reichenberg, a small cockpit was added in front of the air intake duct to the Argus pulsejet. The cockpit contained basic flight instrumentation and a plywood bucket seat with a padded headrest. The single-piece hood incorporated an armoured windscreen and could be tilted over to starboard to allow entry. The cockpit was in the compartment usually occupied by the two compressed-air bottles. Only one was used in the Reichenberg and it was fitted aft, in the space vacated by the autopilot. The wings had specially hardened blade edges to cut through barrage balloon cables.

The advantages of the Reichenberg were low cost, fast production time – only 550 man-hours – and the fact that its small size gave better protection than fighters would have had. It used no precious materials and it could be run on paraffin.

In operations, the planned idea was that an He 111 bomber could carry up to two Reichenbergs, one beneath each wing, before releasing them close to the target, the pilots maintaining contact with the bomber, when attached, via a telephone. In theory, the pilots would then steer their craft down towards the target, ignoring whatever defensive fire power there was, before jettisoning their cockpit canopy moments before impact and baling out. It was estimated that the pilots' chances of survival would be under one in a hundred owing to the high speed at which they would bale out and the proximity of the jet intake and exhaust just behind the cockpit. This would have been no secret to the pilots themselves, but at least they had a possibility of cheating death, and that might have had the effect of making everyone feel easier about the project too. Training started on the R-I and R-II, and, although landings on a ventral skid were tricky, they handled well, and it was anticipated that the Leonidas Squadron would soon be using the machines. Writing to Hitler on 28 July, Speer opposed wasting such brave men on Allied landings in France and suggested that, if they had to be used, it would be better to deploy them against Russian power-stations.

The first real flight was carried out in September at Larz, the Reichenberg being dropped as planned from the wing of an He 111. It crashed, however, when the pilot lost control after accidentally jettisoning his canopy – the result of which was that he was knocked out by the rushing wind. Miraculously, he survived. The second flight followed the next day but also ended in a crash. Subsequent test-flights were undertaken with greater success by the more experienced Kensche and Reitsch, Reitsch herself surviving several bad crashes almost unscathed during the trial programme.

But the Leonidas project was running into bureaucratic difficulties. No one seemed willing to take it on to an operational footing. It ended up on Göring's desk again, and he handed it to his Chief of Personnel, Bruno Loerzer, who successfully buried it. The project was finally shelved in October, though not before some 175 missiles had been converted. Apparently the official feeling was, after all, that public morale would be damaged if suicide missions were sanctioned. In the end the only formal suicide missions of the war undertaken in purpose-built flying bombs, were made within the Japanese Ohka project.

There may have been a simple, practical reason for scrapping the Reichenbergs. After the war, Skorzeny observed that the project had been dropped because of the perpetual fuel shortages. The Reichenberg might have been able to run on paraffin, but the He 111s certainly couldn't. On the other hand, Adolf Galland, who had always rejected the Reichenberg idea, argued that if a pilot's aim was to get as close to ground or airborne targets as possible in order to be sure of a 'hit', wouldn't it make more sense to do so and loosen off a fusillade of ammunition or rockets before beating a hasty retreat and returning to fight again another day? Such a proposal might have involved suicidal bravery, but not suicide as an absolute necessity. And it was thinking like this which led directly to such projects as the Blohm und Voss glider interceptor, where the pilots at least had an even chance of coming back alive.

A 'Medieval' Glider

Because one of the major difficulties in attacking Allied combat boxes at close range was their concentrated fire power, it seemed logical to present as small a front-on target to the enemy as possible, and which could be reduced to a minimum if there were no engine. Richard Vogt of Blohm und Voss therefore proposed to the Technical Bureau the idea of a glider fighter-interceptor, made from non-strategic materials in a project called the Bv 40. After being towed to its operational height by a conventional fighter such as an Me 109, it would glide into the combat boxes at a shallow angle of about twenty degrees, releasing its ammunition in a concentrated burst as it did so. The frontal area would be so small that no B-17 gunner would spot it until it was well within firing range for its own guns. Furthermore, if it still had sufficient lift after the first pass, it could swing round to make a second attack, this time deploying a towed aerial mine which it would swing against the fuselage of a bomber in the manner of a medieval knight using a ball and chain.

The key to the whole idea behind the Bv40, was simplicity, both in construction and use. Made from readily available and therefore cheap materials, the glider could be built by ordinary workers with basic skills. The cockpit was made from welded sheet metal twenty millimetres thick, in which the pilot lay prone on a padded couch, his chin supported by a cushioned pad. The side panels and roof hatch were eight millimetres thick, the floor a mere five millimetres. The windscreen was 120-millimetre-thick armoured glass, and two sliding armoured panels could seal off the side windows, thus giving the pilot's head greater protection. His legs were protected by eight-millimetre-thick plate metal. The central fuselage was made of riveted sheet metal bolted to the wooden aft section. The wings and tailplane were also of wood, and the wings were attached to the fuselage by means of four bolts. Landings would be made on a retractable ventral skid.

The armament originally envisaged was a single MK 108 seventy-round cannon; though, as it was thought that the closing speed of the glider as it approached the bomber would permit only one concentrated burst of fire, it was later decided that it would be better to divide the ammunition between two MK 108s. Attached to a jettisonable trolley, the Bv 40 would be towed up either by an Me 109 or an Fw 190 at the end of a thirty-metre cable.

In late May 1944 the first prototype was in fact towed up by an Me 110, its pilot reporting good handling. A second flight was undertaken on 2 June at Wenzendorf, following adjustments to the track of the trolley's wheels. The pilot cast off from the tug at 800 metres and 240 kph. He reduced speed to 150 kph and maintained good rudder control. However, at 140 kph the glider suddenly dropped from the sky and crashed through the airfield fence, seemingly having stopped generating lift. The pilot's fate is unknown.

The second prototype was tested on 5 and 8 June at a height of 2,200 metres and reached 330 kph. The third prototype was tested to destruction and the fourth was badly damaged, to be quickly replaced by the fifth. The sixth was towed from Stade to Wenzendorf on 27 July 1944 behind an Me 110. This was the Bv 40's first long flight, and the pilot complained of cramp owing to his prone flight posture. But the model had proved its overall worth, and nineteen further prototypes were ordered for completion by the following March, together with a batch of 200 Bv 40 'A' series.

But as usual the Technical Bureau of the RLM had begun to interfere, proposing changes to the original specification. It suggested that the Bv 40 be converted to carry a brace of rockets under each wing (the same R4M rockets seen in the later Natter project) in place of one of the MK 108s. The aerial mine was abandoned too, replaced with four fuselage-mounted containers carrying a supply of impact-fused charges. The idea was for the glider pilot simply to fly above the combat box and drop the charges on to the bombers below. Yet another proposal was for the Bv 40s to be carried up by and dropped from the wings of He 177 bombers, though it was found that the glider's weight made this approach impracticable. Then there was an idea that the Bv 40 could be adapted as a towed fuel tank for the Arado Ar 234 jet bomber.

Despite all these different ideas and plans, the Air Ministry still wouldn't commit itself absolutely to the Bv 40. In fact officials were not in agreement at all about the best way of attacking the combat boxes. Dithering and panic obfuscated their thinking, which didn't help. It's hard to see what made them hesitate. The Bv 40 was very cheap, even compared with converting the V-1 into the Reichenberg, and eminently practical. It used no materials that were crucially needed elsewhere or in short supply. Although the pilot would be placed at high risk, the Bv 40 wasn't a suicide aircraft, and the pilot's chances were probably better than those flying in a Sturmgruppe unit. It would be at its most vulnerable after it had made its attack, for its speed was relatively slow and it made an easy target, once identified, for the bombers' fighter escorts; but it could itself be escorted on its return flights by its Me 109 tugs, or defended from the ground by flak batteries.

The basic flight-testing programme had been completed by mid-July. Top speeds of 470 kph at 2,000 metres had been reached, and it was thought the Bv 40 could get up to 900 kph in a dive, but the Air Ministry finally pulled the plug on the project in the autumn, arguing that the Bv 40's lack of power would render it next to useless in real combat. Blohm und Voss refused to take no for an answer and suggested that the machine be fitted with a pair of pulsejets; but given the experience with the Me 328, this proposal foundered.

Zeppelin's Bullet

The Zeppelin Company put forward a project in November 1944 for a tiny 'rammer' aircraft, in which there was only just room for the pilot, which would be able to engage the enemy in two separate lightning attacks. It was so small that it could be towed up to height by an ordinary fighter, and after release it would fire its own single Schmidding solid-fuel rocket, which would take it up to a speed of 970 kph.

As it approached the combat boxes, it would fire a batch of fourteen unguided fifty-five-millimetre rockets mounted in its nose. Then the pilot would immediately select another target and literally ram it. This was no suicide mission. The pilot was to be encased in an armoured cockpit, and the little plane was to be equipped with razor-sharp wings to slice through the tail sections and wings of enemy aircraft, be they fighters or bombers. If it indeed survived the impact, it would then glide back to base to land on a single ventral skid.

This plan was not taken up. Perhaps someone realised that the pilot could suffer a momentary deceleration of up to 400 'g' in the process of hitting another aircraft at 970 kph. The most a human body can take is fifteen 'g'.

Messerschmitt were also interested in producing a ramming fighter, and during the autumn of 1944 they produced plans for two variants, the P. 1103 and the P. 1104. Scant details of either survive, but we do know that both had armoured cockpits and glazing and were powered by single-rocket motors of different makes. Following an attack, the pilot of the P. 1103 would detach his armoured cockpit from the fuselage (which would have been crippled in the ramming manoeuvre) and parachute to earth. The P. 1104 would return intact and land on skids. For secondary armament, both were fitted with MK 108 cannon which would have fired high-explosive thirty-millimetre shells. The design of the P. 1104 resembled the Me 328's profile but had fairly long and straight wings made of reinforced steel, designed to stand up to its ramming role. Messerschmitt's timing in the presentation of these ideas was poor, however, for both projects were turned down in favour of the Volksjäger programme, and the whole idea of ramming fighters was abandoned.

Send in the Clowns

In February 1945 the idea of suicide missions was resurrected in a proposal put forward to Göring by Major Hajo Herrmann. Herrmann's suggestion was that the virtually disused pilot training schools be reactivated. New pilots were getting virtually no training anyway, so wouldn't it be a good idea to give trainees the basics, allocate them a fighter – of which there were plenty still being made, and lying idle because of the fuel shortages – and send them into action in, say, slightly strengthened Me 109s, which they would smash into the sides of Flying Fortresses? The fuel used would be worth it because of the virtually guaranteed strike rate. Old Sturmgruppe hands could teach the basics of engaging the combat boxes and advise on the weak points of the American bombers.

Herrmann envisaged a group of two hundred volunteer pilots who would have ten days' training at Stendal airfield. Göring gave the scheme his reluctant approval. The Reichsmarschall was contemplating the inevitable surrender now and saw no political gain in opposing Herrmann's idea.

The new unit was called Sonderkommando Elbe, and under General Pelz, who would control it, Elbe made the first of only two missions on 7 April 1945 against a high formation of 1,300 B-17s and over 800 escorts. Over 180 members of the Sonderkommando took part in the battle, codenamed Operation Werewolf, using a mixture of Me 109s and Fw 190s culled from various training centres or dispersal fields, and they were escorted by over 40 Me 262 jets. The fuel for the mission had been specially requisitioned.

As they flew into action, Allied radio operators tuned in to monitor Luftwaffe frequencies were astonished to hear patriotic marches and the German national anthem being played to these desperadoes, between recordings of speeches exhorting them to die for Führer and Fatherland. Seventy-seven German aircraft were lost in the 'battle', the losses caused as much by sheer inexperience of flying as expert American gunnery. The young German fanatics, or dupes, depending on how you look at them, achieved precisely nothing, but it is a measure of the hysteria of the time that so many people were willing to sacrifice themselves for such a patently lost cause.

The second mass-suicide mission mounted from the air took place a few days later when on 16 April sixty pilots crashed their planes into the bridge over the Rhine at Remagen in a vain attempt to delay the Allied advance on the capital.

Thus the supreme sacrifice, as envisaged by Hanna Reitsch and her associates, was made in two actions – far too late, and to little effect. As to their other effect, on German morale, it would be hard to say whether anything could have sunk this any further. Most large German towns and cities had been the subject of Allied bombardment; some, like Hamburg, had been all but obliterated by it. The firestorms visited on Hamburg in 1944 swept through the city, engulfing every living thing. Given the destruction wrought on German cities by the Allies, it is surprising that there wasn't much more enthusiasm for the suicide squads, since a desire for revenge would arguably have been just as potent in summer 1944 as it was in February 1945, when the urge to hit back just once more in any way possible led to the desperate formation of Sonderkommando Elbe. The Sturmgruppen had shown that with sufficient daring the combat boxes could be opposed successfully, and yet the authorities hesitated fatally when presented with workable variations on the attack theme such as the Bv 40.

But whatever the Germans had done, it is unlikely that they would have been able to extend the war much longer; to have done so would only have prolonged the agony and drawn more death and destruction in its wake. Six months earlier, a concerted effort might have had some effect; but even that supposes a good supply of fuel and raw materials. The USSR and the USA had limitless resources. Once those countries were engaged against Germany, the war was as good as lost, and not all the visionary inventiveness of its aircraft designers could save it.

Chapter Eleven

GÖTTERDÄMMERUNG

The Price of Admission to the Top Table

With its massive rearmament programme in the 1930s, Germany under its Nazi government was going all out to secure a place at the international top table, defying most of the world powers in the process. By pretending to be more advanced than they were militarily, and pursuing an energetic and aggressive foreign policy *vis-à-vis* Austria and Czechoslovakia, where successful incursions were made with little bloodshed and no outright war, the Germans capitalised on British and American reluctance to commit themselves to another major conflict. In terms of aviation, as mentioned at the beginning of the book, aircraft merely in the prototype phase, or at best just into production, were presented as fully developed and/or being manufactured in numbers.

The major players in German industry – chemical plant owners, motor and aircraft manufacturers, shipbuilders, and so on – began murmuring to the government that, in order to avoid a shortage in raw materials brought on by Germany's dwindling gold reserves and a worsening balance-of-payments position, the country should start to invest in a programme of industrial-scale production of synthetic substitutes to reduce dependence on conventional supplies of oil, rubber and other essential material. The introduction of such substitutes would permit the rate of production to grow as desired, unhampered by restrictions caused by any failure in the supply of raw materials from abroad.

The German State had been aware for some time of the advantages of producing synthetic versions of the raw materials they could otherwise get only from outside and had encouraged synthetics producers with subsidies and tax concessions ever since the First World War. For such industrialists, and by extension potentially for most of German industry, the situation improved after the Nazis seized power, but the pace of production dictated by the new government, especially for the arms industry, was still too fast for the supply of raw materials to keep up with it. The Nazis therefore invested heavily in the synthetics producers.

One major beneficiary was the massive petrochemical conglomerate, Industriegesellschaft (IG) Farben – a name which later became notorious owing to its synthetic rubber factory and research station at Auschwitz-Monowice. One of the directors of IG Farben, Heinrich Gattineau, had long been an acquaintance of Hitler and had taken every opportunity to inform him of the progress his company was making to perfect the manufacturing process for synthetic petrol. Gattineau found the State willing to invest millions of Reichsmarks in his and other companies in the search for a solution to growing shortages of raw materials; and in September 1933, only a few months after the seizure of power, another IG Farben boss, Carl Krauch, told the Air Ministry that for an investment of RM 400 million they could raise production of synthetic petrol from 500,000 tonnes a year to over 1.8 million. A contract was signed that December; within a year similar contracts were agreed with companies making synthetic textiles. Göring had understood the vulnerable position of Germany's oil resources, with just under half of all the oil coming into the country deriving from only two sources – the USSR and Romania. If the international community decided to put pressure on these two to end their supply, Germany's ambitions, without the independence synthetic fuel would bring, would be at an end.

1935 was a difficult year for the still-fragile German economy. As the world emerged from its long recession, prices of raw materials began to rise. There wasn't enough money to buy in at the quantity still required to support the beefed-up armaments and other industries, and synthetic substitutes were never wholly to meet their needs anyway. Thus, the balance-of-payments position faltered. A financial downward spiral would have compromised the rearmament plan; and to make matters worse a poor harvest compounded the problem: money had to be spent buying food in from abroad to make up the domestic shortfall.

Hitler wanted his war, but he hadn't the materials or the economic base to sustain it.

An industrial survey for 1936 highlighted three main areas of concern: the increasing dependency of the Reich on imported raw materials (despite efforts to the contrary); low labour productivity and inefficiency of production; and an over-concentration of industry in the Berlin, Ruhr and Saxony areas. Industry would have to be relocated and spread out more thinly as a primary insurance measure in the event of war, and the immediate benefit of such reorganisation would be the bringing of employment to hitherto depressed areas. However, the problems identified in the first two areas of concern were not solved easily. The shortage of food and raw materials remained, the rearmament programme's demands were greater than its supply and there was a foreign exchange crisis.

The Four-Year Plan

Hitler had to put his house in economic order before he could proceed with his long-term plan of acquiring *Lebensraum* for Germany in the East, and the solution was a four-year plan, presented in October 1936. The plan was designed to make Germany as self-sufficient as possible, and it laid great stress on the fast development of the synthetics industries, though Hitler cannot have been the only one to think that within a very short time the problem caused by the lack of raw materials generally would be best solved by conquest.

In addition to more investment in synthetics, the country was to mine the low-grade iron reserves in the Salzgitter region, and firms such as Krupp were to form consortia to design and build blast furnaces that could extract as much as possible from such unpromising ore. Aluminium and magnesium were to be produced in greater amounts and used wherever possible to prevent the valuable stocks of ore from being depleted too quickly. The leadership of the Reich also organised extensive scrap-metal collections from the population, the donated pots and pans being melted down and recycled. Farmers were encouraged to become more productive and use chemical fertilisers to a larger extent, both to improve yields and the basic diet of the average German family.

Looking After the Luftwaffe

Despite every effort, the country couldn't avoid a shortage in the amounts of iron and steel being delivered to the aircraft industry, which was in competition with other areas, such as shipbuilding, for what little there was to go round. In October 1937 Erhard Milch was forced to concede that the level of Luftwaffe armament was falling far short of what had been expected as a result of the lack of construction materials. The shortages didn't only limit the number of actual aircraft made but also the number of gantries and cranes and machine tools installed in the factories: they affected the whole of the production line.

One hopeful sign was that Germany's production of aluminium was in much better health, and in 1937 the country produced over 100,000 tonnes – a quarter of the world's total. Raw bauxite came from Hungary and Yugoslavia, countries that accepted German goods and services in a barter system of payment which was convenient to arrange. Good as the production level was, though, the Air Ministry predicted that by 1940 this total would have to rise to over 288,000 tonnes if it were to meet the demands required by mobilisation. As a result, Germany looked to mine its own bauxite as well as increasing imports. At the same time it began to stockpile bauxite, which by the end of 1937 stood at reserves of more than 200,000 tonnes, and to husband the use of aluminium.

There remained the problem of fuel. Investment in IG Farben's programme was already bearing fruit, but the synthetic stuff produced so far was usable only in vehicles. Aircraft engines, especially the new breed fitted with superchargers, needed lighter fuels with a higher octane rating.

As a result, the Luftwaffe began stockpiling what reserves of aviation fuel it could, while it waited for a synthetic alternative. As early as the middle of 1935, the first of three huge underground tanks was opened in Derben. Others were to follow in Nienburg and Stassfurt. Well hidden and away from built-up areas, the tanks each held 75,000 cubic metres of fuel, and so successful was the project that by 1942 a further six had been established, giving a total capacity of 810,000 cubic metres. But it wasn't enough just to build the storage facilities, as the fuel itself needed special additives, such as lead derivatives, if the aero engines were to function properly; and the additives were corrosive and inflammable. Newly designed railway tanker wagons were required to transport the volatile mixture, and had to be used exclusively for the job. It was no good using old tanker wagons as traces of former fuel cargo, such as diesel, would mix with the new stuff and contaminate it. There was a crash building programme of new wagons and by 1941 over five thousand were available. Unfortunately for the Luftwaffe, many were commandeered by the other services later in the war, leaving the air force once more with too few for its needs.

In 1936 the synthetics industry came up with a fuel suitable for use in aircraft engines and production began. The cost was high – RM 185 a tonne, as opposed to Romanian oil at RM 124 a tonne.

Germany's need for oil in heating, lubrication and the increasing number of vehicles of all sorts, including ships and aeroplanes, was growing apace, and the government was worried. In 1936, of the 5 million tonnes consumed, only 1.8 million had been home-produced. The original four-year plan had required that the latter figure be 3.8 million by the end of 1937. The new synthetic plants would be capable of producing only 2.3 million by 1938, which meant that Germany would still have to import 60 per cent of its fuel by that time – an improvement, but far from great enough. Becoming self-sufficient in fuel was the goal Germany aimed for throughout the war – but it was one the country never reached.

If Germany had managed to hang on to the Russian and the Romanian oilfields the picture would have been different, of course. Capturing them did give the country a brief boost, but their loss after only a relatively short time simply accelerated the rate of decline.

When the war started, Germany was gambling hard. The country had only 355,000 tonnes of aviation fuel stockpiled, enough for only three months under mobilisation, and only a fraction of the amount needed for major sustained assault. Germany and the USSR were allied until mid-1941, and up until then Germany could rely on imports from there; but Operation Barbarossa opened the war on a massive new front at precisely the time when the country would have to fight for its fuel, not buy it any more. The mistake Germany made in opening up the war too widely and too fast, before it had adequate fuel resources to sustain it, would lead directly to the country's ultimate defeat. Pure luck, barefaced daring and the element of surprise had enabled the early blitzkrieg campaigns of 1939–40 to be successful; had any of the campaigns lingered on, the Luftwaffe would quite simply have run out of gas. And if Germany hadn't found fuel stocks to plunder in the countries it invaded early on, the Battle of Britain could still have been fought, certainly, but could barely have lasted a day longer than it did.

A War of Attrition

The terrible experience of Operation Barbarossa showed just how fragile even the Luftwaffe's fuel supply lines were. The enormous distances involved in carrying fuel to frontline airfields, and the paucity of remaining stocks left by the Soviets as part of their scorched-earth policy as they retreated, were grave problems throughout the campaign. By September 1942 the air force was down to its last fortnight's worth of fuel in reserves, and the war was being fought on two 'hot' fronts: Russia and the Mediterranean. Training missions were cut back to almost nothing, and the offensives on the Western Front were scaled down.

Training operations throughout the Reich began 1943 with stocks of fuel at two-thirds of the required level; this was before any of the concerted Allied raids to disrupt German supplies had even started. Although production of synthetic fuel was to rise dramatically from this point onwards, with total stocks in April 1944 reaching more than 574,000 tonnes, it had been achieved partly because of continuing restrictions on training use. Fuel rationing had a major impact across the board: on the quality and quantity of training given to new pilots, on military operations in general, and on the civilian infrastructure and population.

At first there had been little discernible impact on the German industrial war machine. The British had undertaken a few bombing raids on selected targets, but the Luftwaffe had retaliated, and although the damage to industrial and domestic property was great on both sides, it appeared to do little harm to either's ability to wage war. The German workforce was becoming used to having to move around and adapt, and large numbers of workers were moved from industry to industry as they were required – though many more went into the armed forces, their

234

places taken first by women and later by forced labour from the ranks of the conquered and the dispossessed.

But as the various industrial sectors jockeyed to increase production and competed for supplies, aircraft manufacture began to suffer, and the working day was reduced to eight hours, largely because there was a dearth of workers.

Because the workers they had were German citizens and civilians, and the most important of them were skilled and semi-skilled, coercion into longer hours would simply not have worked. During January 1943 the SS-Totenkopf Brigades decided to coopt large numbers of concentration-camp inmates as extra labour for the aircraft factories – a move welcomed by companies such as Messerschmitt, which were mass-producing aircraft, could use unskilled labour, and were keen to keep their production rate at least steady if not rising. Furthermore, prisoner labour represented a negligible extra cost. As a result of this initiative, over three thousand workers from the nearby camp at Dachau were trans-ferred to the Messerschmitt plant at Augsburg to work on the Me 109 production lines. The pattern was repeated across the country from then on. Slave labour was not ideal because it was neither committed nor trustworthy, but it was a means of filling the benches of workers who had been sent off to die for the Fatherland on the increasingly hopeless Eastern Front. For the prisoners themselves, factory work represented a better chance of survival than they had in the camps. Life expectancy in Auschwitz-Birkenau, for example, was three weeks.

It was the arrival of the United States Army Air Force (the USAAF), as it was then called, in the European theatre of war in large numbers during 1943 that turned the tide decisively against Germany. The Allies had long been developing four-engined heavy bombers, and now perfected examples were being brought into action and used with deadly effect on long-range missions into the heart of the Reich. As we have seen, the Luftwaffe was restricted to twin-engined medium bombers of the type it had used to attack Poland in 1939, because Göring had vetoed the widespread development of larger bombers. The Germans had no equivalent of the Stirling, the Lancaster or the Flying Fortress, and the nearest they had, the Heinkel He 177, was so prone to engine fires that its crews, as mentioned in Chapter One, nicknamed it the 'flying cigarette lighter'.

A Plague of Mosquitoes

With the advent of the RAF's superb, new, all-wooden de Havilland DH 98 Mosquito heavy fighter, the Allies became capable of flying audacious reconnaissance missions into Germany, and the Germans had no direct counter to these aircraft either. The Mosquitoes were at their most effective working in conjunction with the heavy bombers, and the Allies were quick to press home their advantage. It was clear to all that they had one. For example, a big raid of RAF bombers over Berlin in March 1943 destroyed over 20,000 homes, leaving 35,000 homeless and 7,000 dead. Even as officials began organising a clear-up operation a few days later, a lone Mosquito flew over the city on a new reconnaissance mission, unchallenged either by the Luftwaffe or even anti-aircraft guns. The event was embarrassing, but its message was telling: the Luftwaffe, once the pride of a rejuvenated Reich, was now ineffective against the growing threat to the civilian population. When considering Allied bombing of such targets, the German bombing of cities like London and Coventry should also be remembered. But there are strategic reasons for attacking civilians. If you can burden the enemy authorities with the problem of housing and feeding them, tending to the wounded and keeping them warm, you can divert attention from military and industrial production. Bombing civilians also has the useful effect of demoralising the enemy, and it is usually employed as a tactic when the enemy can't hit back, demonstrating the aggressor's superiority. Analysis of the ethical issues comes later, in peacetime. In wartime, from a purely tactical point of view, the policy is not without its advantages.

As a result of the humiliation of the March 1943 air raid, Milch suggested to Hitler that development of four-engined bombers should begin immediately, and that production of existing fighters be increased to meet the waves of Allied bombers expected to come in force at any time. Milch also told the Führer that the Allied production figures he had intelligence of were probably not exaggerated and shouldn't be ignored; this was met with stony silence.

Attacks by the RAF continued throughout March, hitting Nuremberg, Stuttgart and many other targets both in Germany and France. Hitler ordered Göring back from one of his frequent holidays in Rome to direct counterattacks on Britain. But when the Reichsmarschall did come back to a shell-shocked Berlin, all he could say was that his bomber fleet had been squandered in supplying the beleaguered army at Stalingrad.

Plodding Crates

Göring then launched himself into a tirade against his generals and civilian manufacturers, berating them for not having produced a suitably reliable four-engined bomber capable of mounting attacks on Britain. Obviously he had forgotten, or chose to forget, who had vetoed such a project in the first place. He also wanted to know why they had not learned from the wooden construction of the few Mosquitoes that had been shot down how to build something similar. When his cowed listeners sought to justify themselves (no one dared to criticise him – another weakness of the Nazis which was to lead to their downfall) by mocking the Allies' 'plodding, four-engined crates', Göring retorted that at least they could *plod* on to their targets and then *plod* back to base without catching fire or breaking down, as German bombers – presumably he had the He 177 uppermost in his mind – were wont to do.

Milch then suggested that in order to increase production the country should follow the British example and recruit more women into the factories, to offset the increasing labour shortages. To this, Göring replied that 'perhaps the women could work from home', thereby exposing his astonishingly poor grasp of the situation and adding to Milch's frustration. Göring's decision to increase the production of existing aircraft at the expense of the development of heavy bombers meant that by the time Britain was well into reorganising and modernising the RAF, and by the time the USAAF was ready to throw its might into the European fray, it was too late for Germany to meet the demands that the changed circumstances of the war were making.

Meanwhile, the Allies were keeping up the pressure, with attacks almost every night, and not only were the raids continuing but their size was increasing, not only in numbers of bombers but in the sizes of the individual bomb loads. The versatile and fast Mosquito was now being produced in a light bomber version too. German high command

and the RLM were in disarray. Milch's contempt for Göring was apparent to everyone; Göring himself was slipping back into his drug addiction, and Hitler was growing impatient. Something had to be done.

'V' for Follies

In May 1943 Milch arrived at Peenemünde for a demonstration of the two new Vergeltungswaffen – reprisal weapons – with which Germany hoped to strike fear back into Britain: the army's V-2 rocket and the air force's V-1 flying bomb.

After each system had been launched twice, only one of the V-2s had performed well; but given that a V-2 cost almost a hundred times more than the far simpler V-1, and that Milch was an air-force man, his decision to authorise continued development of the V-1 rather than the V-2 at this stage cannot come as a surprise. Yet each project eventually would absorb many hundreds of thousands of skilled and forced-labour workers, tie up much industrial capacity and consume vast amounts of rocket fuel and expensive raw materials. For what? Neither the V-1 nor the V-2 project ever won territory for Germany, neither arrived in time to prevent the Allied landings in Normandy the following year, and neither lived up to the promise of ultimate victory that Hitler naively or wilfully believed they held. Arguably, thousands more conventional aircraft – even jets – could have been built for the same money; though if they had been, given the fuel shortages, they might have simply joined the numbers already sitting idle on the tarmac. The V-1 flying bomb, and the V-2, the world's first ballistic missile, did some damage to London in the months they were used between summer 1944 and spring 1945, bringing misery and death to civilians in the closing months of the war; but few of those launched found their targets, and many of the V-1s were deflected by Spitfires that intercepted them and tipped them off course. They were an expensive folly, more interesting as prototypes for what was to follow them than as weapons relevant to the Second World War.

Milch's tour of the Peenemünde site was followed by an exhibition organised by Göring at Insterburg airfield for the benefit of Hitler and other senior Party and military personnel, including Reichsführer SS

Heinrich Himmler. It was during this morale-boosting display of Luftwaffe prowess that Willy Messerschmitt took it on himself to suggest to the Führer that a small series of adaptations were all that would be needed to convert his new Me 262, being shown off at Insterburg, into a high-speed bomber. Messerschmitt knew that the Arado Ar 234 jet reconnaissance bomber then in development was running behind schedule and he thought he could steal a march on it. The consequence was that the 262's entry into service as a fighter – the role for which it was designed and to which it was ideally suited – was delayed by months as bomber adaptations were tried and tested. Milch was incensed, but at the same time expended a lot of energy trying to convince his colleagues of the capabilities of his own pet project, the Dornier Do 335.

Wild Boars

The Allied raids continued unabated. June 1943 saw over 2,000 tonnes of bombs dropped on Düsseldorf, 1,500 on Bochum and on the steel-making town of Oberhausen; the same month saw many more attacks on many other towns the length and breadth of the country. Milch's prediction that 1943 would be the year when German cities began their suffering was turning out to be true.

But it was also in June that the Luftwaffe appeared to have come up with an answer to the RAF's night raids. It came to be known as the 'Wilde Sau' – 'Wild Boar' – system.

The essence of the plan was very simple, and involved small numbers of radar-equipped night-fighters gathered above German targets which had already been lit up by Allied Pathfinder bombers in advance of the main bombing formation to follow. As the main wave of bombers arrived at the target, they themselves would be illuminated as silhouettes by the flares parachute-dropped by the Pathfinders. Moonlight would be of additional help to the Wild Boars, as were the bright flames that occasionally leaped from the engine exhausts of the RAF planes, but radar was the most important – indeed essential – element.

The Wild Boars would now come, firing their planes' machine-guns from out of the darkness. The strategy required a lot of courage from the night-fighter pilots, but their depredations were so successful, at

239

least to begin with, that Allied top brass in Whitehall even considered suspending raids for a time.

But the Allies had another card to play, and they did so now.

Called 'Window', this supremely simple method of jamming and fooling German radar systems was first used in July in a notorious raid on Hamburg. It involved the release by other Pathfinders of millions of tinfoil strips into the night sky over the target. These played havoc with the radar systems on the ground, so that by the time the bombers arrived, not one ground observer was sure whether or not he could believe the information on his screen. The Wild Boars, similarly blinded, were able to shoot down only twelve of the seven hundred bombers over the city. This represented a drastic drop in their strike rate and barely had any effect on the damage done by the raid. With no quick means of countering 'Window', the Germans could do nothing but submit to the relentless pressure kept up by the RAF by night and the USAAF by day. As the summer passed, more and more cracks began to show.

Hemmed In

Such was the devastation that at a private meeting on 1 August Albert Speer told Hitler that if just six more cities were hit with such deadly effect as Hamburg had been, then the war would be over. Quite apart from the domestic death and destruction, every branch of the military was feeling the effects of the crippling blows being dealt to industry.

As far as the aeronautical industry was concerned, Göring was effectively no longer capable of fulfilling his office, and it was left to an exhausted Milch to sort out production problems. To compound them, his Chief of the Air Staff, Hans Jeschonnek, a brave but inflexible man who had become increasingly depressed at Germany's inability to hit back at the blows raining down on it, committed suicide at the age of forty-four.

Milch decided to transfer idle fighter units in the far corners of the crumbling Reich back to Germany itself. He also began to organise the dispersal of the remaining aircraft manufacturing plants into secluded or underground sites before they, too, fell victim to the inexorable raids.

He had his work cut out for him. As the war progressed, so Göring's influence and that of the service he'd helped create had waned, and the Luftwaffe, which in mid-1943 ought to have been given top priority, now ranked only sixth in line for industrial relocation. It ranked even below the Reich Railway Service, which, under Speer, was commandeering vital wagons and tankers from the Luftwaffe before allocating them elsewhere. Even so, in the middle of what was a logistical nightmare, Milch was able to secure thirty million square feet of factory space in which to relocate his manufacturers: a remarkable achievement, but no more remarkable than the fact that some of Germany's planemakers were still exporting. During the most difficult years of the war, when senior Luftwaffe staff were clamouring for as many fighters as possible, companies like Messerschmitt were still trading on the international market as a means of maintaining some form of currency exchange as well as diplomatic relations and foreign contacts. Apart from delivering many aircraft to Germany's allies and satellites such as Croatia, Finland and Italy, precious Me 109s were being delivered to the air forces of neutrals like Spain and Switzerland.

Milch the Seer

During August 1943 the fortunes of the Wild Boars began to rise again, as a result of changed tactics: the planes now relied less on radar and more on visual contact established by searchlights on the ground and star shells fired from flak units. During the RAF's next raid over Berlin – the city's civilian population had been largely evacuated by this time – they sustained the loss of about fifty-six bombers, and a jubilant Milch took great pains to tell everyone that as long as such dents could continue to be made in the enemy, the RAF's nerve would be broken and it wouldn't be able to keep up the pressure. He further believed that as the rate of German fighter production was now averaging two thousand a month, a turning-point might soon be reached.

Milch also took the opportunity to remind anyone who would listen that if the powers that be had listened some months earlier to his call for a stouter defence of the German core territory – the Heimat – then the country wouldn't now be in such dire straits. His standing was buttressed by the fact that the RAF did indeed suspend bombing raids in early September 1943, having lost too many aircraft in relation to

241

successful bomb hits over Berlin and other targets since the Wild Boars' tactics had changed. The main bombing effort would be carried by the USAAF's daytime raids from now on, though German night-flying superiority was destined to last only another month. And with the collapse of Italy, and the consequent opening of a new confrontation to the south, any small respite would be short lived.

Germany still controlled northern Italy. Throughout the early years of the war, the Nazis had supplied their Fascist ally with millions of tonnes of raw materials and oil. Now Germany was at least able to take back such supplies for itself, while at the same time stripping Italy's industrial north of anything it needed. Germany also found that Mussolini had not been altogether candid about how much of the material supplied he had actually used: Italy had in fact been stockpiling to such an extent that even Göring was moved to remark, 'They have more copper than we have! . . . The most amazing is the fuel oil: in two tunnels, we have found enough fuel oil to have kept their entire navy operational for a year!' Over 65,000 tonnes of very welcome aviation fuel were also discovered by the German defence force which had now been deployed in the north of the country.

Allied armies, however, swept through southern Italy, and by September 1943 they had captured intact the town of Foggia and the fifteen airfields surrounding it. Milch knew that the flight time from any of them to Vienna was shorter than the flight time that separated London and Berlin. The Americans soon found this out too, and on 1 October they began using the Italian bases to mount air raids on northern Italy, southern Germany and Austria.

'Bomber' Harris

Sir Arthur Harris, Chief of RAF Bomber Command, of whom the unattributed remark was made, 'thank God he's not a German', had always wanted to get back into attacking German cities, believing this to be the only really effective way of bringing the enemy to its knees. As a result of persuading Churchill to accept losses of around 400 to 450 aircraft as the price that would have to be paid for Germany's surrender, Harris ordered the RAF to resume its raids early in October 1943, striking at Berlin again within six weeks. The German defenders had been expecting them, however, and during the lull they had been preparing extensive anti-radar countermeasures.

But the RAF had changed their tactics as well, and successfully wrong-footed the Luftwaffe, forcing it to split up its forces to attack several small formations of bombers rather than one large one. In addition, the USAAF bombers now had the latest RAF radar, and were using it with great accuracy during their daylight raids. On 9 October they attacked the Focke-Wulf plants at Marienberg and Anklam in East Prussia, devastating ninety per cent of the facilities.

Göring and Milch were able to patch up their differences sufficiently that October for a tour of aircraft manufacturers. Their first port of call was the Messerschmitt factory at Neuberg, where Willy Messerschmitt himself implored Göring to supply more labour for the Me 262 project, telling the Reichsmarschall that if he didn't there would be further delays of up to six months. Göring's hands were tied. Speer, the new favourite, had been authorised by Hitler himself to second workers away from the aero industry to areas of greater perceived need, such as – of all things, at this stage of the war – tank production. (But when Göring later caught the Führer's ear for long enough to remind him of this, Hitler exploded with rage and ordered that Messerschmitt get his workers at all costs.)

Their tour took them next to the main Junkers turbojet plant, which was about to be transferred to a former army barracks at Zittau, with production due to resume the following January. Göring urged them to start looking for somewhere else instead, if possible an underground site – which was, apparently, the first time that the Reichsmarschall had shown any awareness of such possibilities. Having seen the large Messerschmitt and Junkers plants – and he was about to see the Arado factory – Göring was at last beginning to realise how vulnerable the industry was to destruction by the Allies. Did he also, finally, realise how crucial the Luftwaffe was at this stage of the war? Air domination was going to be the key to any future victories, but Germany's air force had the most played-out leader of any of the services. Göring did at this stage energise himself enough to organise, via his numerous officials, a plan to get as much as possible of the German air industry into underground or 'hardened' sites – reinforced against air attack – and at a meeting on 8 November with the Gauleiters of Germany's shattered regions, he urged their cooperation.

But mid-November was going to bring difficulties from something quite different from the Allies: there had been no rain for some time, and Germany now experienced its worst drought for ninety years. There was little water in the rivers to provide hydroelectric power, and that meant a fall in the amount of aluminium produced, as well as synthetics, since all depended on water and electricity as part of the production process. Although there was still plenty of oil available from Romania, there weren't enough shallow-draught barges to bring it up the depleted waterways. Existing barges were forced to carry lighter loads if they were to avoid grounding.

This was a serious setback, and it was compounded by the resumption of air raids on Berlin by 'Bomber' Harris on 18 November. The raids lasted until the following March, when they ceased after a night of particularly heavy RAF losses. By then, however, many of the newly completed Ministry buildings had been destroyed, and Berlin as a functioning administrative centre had been crippled.

Escape from the Hydra

There was no comfort to be drawn from the V-weapon programme at Peenemünde. With the precision-instrument factories of the Ruhr and in other regions lying in ruins, the necessary testing programme for both the V-1 and the V-2 had been seriously delayed. And what little V-1 testing had taken place had revealed faults with the compass and gyroscope controls. The autopilot was fond of throwing the weapon far off course – a large percentage were simply to fly into the blue beyond – and some of the missiles were even breaking up in midair as a result of faulty welding of the steel plates of the fuselage. The RAF attack on Peenemünde – Operation Hydra – had caused delays of weeks. These technical faults and the lack of replacement instruments caused delays of months. Then the Fieseler V-1 factory at Kassel was destroyed, in yet another air raid, and production was further delayed while a new site for the plant was found. In November 1943, already 150 test-flights behind schedule, the Fieseler branch of the V-1 business was relocated in the massive Volkswagen factory at Wolfsburg.

Luckily for the whole project, Milch had cultivated a good relationship with Himmler, who was able to allocate the use of a single 'tunnel' in a huge underground factory at Nordhausen which was under construction for the SS. This allowed a secret and protected base for the manufacture of the weapon, and a backup facility should Wolfsburg be flattened in an air raid. The only problem was that the mechanics of setting up a duplicate operation were huge in terms of cost, disruption/ and time. The investment paid off, though: at the end of November every single V-1 of the two thousand manufactured at Wolfsburg had to be scrapped owing to continuing faults in construction.

Milch's 'Big Week'

The problems of allocating sufficient resources to any or all of the competing services and categories within the services – were they, for example, tanks, submarines or aircraft – bit more and more deeply from the midpoint of the war onwards. Albert Speer and his deputy, Karl-Otto Saur, tended to favour the army and continued to channel resources and personnel into the V-2 project at the expense of the V-1. But the position of the navy and the air force was weakened across the board, and Milch became concerned at the second-rate treatment workers in the aero industry were receiving. Workers in the support services for the army got extra rations and supplies: no such concessions were made to anyone else.

Milch argued – and it is very hard to see why it was necessary for him to – that without the protection given by air defence, the factories that made tanks and field guns and armoured cars for the army would be wide open to attack by Allied bombers. But he came to understand that unless someone in the Ministry of Armament and War Production took a personal and direct interest in the Luftwaffe, the service would continue to be treated like a poor relation. He resolved to resign and pass his mantle on to Speer and Saur. Hitler would not get rid of his old comrade-in-arms, Göring; but Göring did nothing to fight for the Luftwaffe's interests any more, and the Führer clearly regarded him as a broken reed. Milch, however, could not approach Hitler over Göring's head or behind his back. What Milch needed was something that would give him a demonstrable reason for the course of action he had decided on.

He didn't have to wait long. On 20 February 1944, in an operation codenamed Big Week, the USAAF began a huge series of raids against aero manufacturing plants, designed to bring the industry to its knees before the Germans had time to disperse it to more secure locations. The operation marked a relaunching of the daylight air raids, this time with the support of recently introduced long-range fighter escorts – the P-51 Mustang and the P-47 Thunderbolt. At the same time the RAF planned to attack the same targets by night – and although the RAF couldn't match the size of the USAAF attack, the combined effect was prodigious. By the time the assault was brought to a close – after only five days, because of bad weather – dozens of Allied bombers had been lost, but the havoc wrought more than justified the cost. More than 75 per cent of the targeted buildings had been destroyed, together with over seven hundred Me 109s, and production facilities for twin-engined heavy fighters like the Me 110 and the Ju 88 had been all but wiped out. Such utter devastation threatened the very survival of the industry.

Disastrous as the raid was, it provided Milch with his opportunity. He pointed out that he had been in favour of wide dispersal of facilities as long ago as 1941. Now, if it were still possible to coax a phoenix from the ashes, it would be up to Speer, with all the executive power of his huge Ministry, to do it.

Milch himself was not simply going to bow out. He designed a new administrative apparatus for the Luftwaffe, which he called the Jägerstab – literally, the 'fighter staff' – working within Speer's Ministry and chaired jointly by Speer and Milch. Its primary objective was to ensure the smooth continued production of warplanes, and, perhaps even more important, their precision components and spare parts through a network of about seven hundred widely dispersed factories.

In the light of attacks on such crucial plants as the ball-bearing factory at Schweinfurt, which had now been bombed twice, Milch's plan made absolute sense to all concerned and was quickly adopted. Factories were to be relocated in underground sites or spread over a wide area, but with reasonable access, for obvious reasons, to railways. Speer himself designed two fortified factories; they were never in fact built, though their concept is worth describing: a huge concrete dome was to be constructed, large enough to cover an area of about 300,000 square metres, and covered with turf to make it look like a low hillock

246

to enemy spotter planes. Naturally enough, there was neither the manpower nor the resources to undertake such a project, and one can't help wondering if the work in progress wouldn't have been noticed by one of the many Allied reconnaissance aircraft prowling the German skies at that time. Underground sites actually used included natural cave systems and converted or disused mines. Some were actually hollowed out of mountainsides by slave labour.

The Jägerstab

Göring was away on holiday again, but Hitler was ready to jump at any plan that would stave off the Allies and so gave the Jägerstab his blessing. The most urgent task it faced was the relocation under ground of the production facilities for the Me 262 jet fighter, miraculously untouched by Operation Big Week. They were duly transferred to the vast underground plant at Nordhausen.

Milch's idea of obtaining better treatment for the Luftwaffe by getting Speer personally involved had paid off, and funds and resources which previously he had had to fight for were now readily available – though of course Big Week had so frightened the high command that they saw at last how necessary adequate air defence was. The other surviving production plants were geared up for a seventy-two-hour week, and their German civilian workers were encouraged by extra food and clothing rations. Where targets had been hit but not hopelessly destroyed, rubble was cleared and production resumed as soon as possible, even if that meant working within the roofless shells of factories. Uncomfortable as this was, at least the ruinous state of the buildings provided a sort of incidental camouflage: if Allied planes were reported in the vicinity, machines could be covered with tarpaulins and the workers could hide, and all the Allied airmen would see was the shell of a ruined factory.

There was some respite from bombing attacks in spring 1944 as the Allies turned their attention to making air raids on the rail and road networks in France in order to disrupt German lines of communication there as much as possible in anticipation of the projected invasion from Britain later in the year. During the breathing space, previous levels of fighter production were largely restored, and it will be remembered that the plan was to increase output in this area while scaling down the building of bombers. Milch and other senior staff were pleased at the speed with which the holes made by Big Week had been plugged but remained worried that a return of Allied air raids would see attacks on Germany's synthetic oil plants. Without fuel for the fighters, Germany would be defenceless.

The Umbrella's Not Working

The Allies were well aware of the need to bomb the refineries but had decided to concentrate their first efforts on the aircraft manufacturing centres. Believing that damage to have been done satisfactorily, later in the spring, on 12 May, the USAAF began a series of attacks on the synthetic oil refineries at Leuna and Pölitz; this was done, of course, to make sure that what German warplanes survived wouldn't have sufficient fuel to support their troops in the coming battle for France. Unfortunately for Germany, these devastating raids confirmed Milch's worst fears. In May 1944 over 195,000 tonnes of aviation fuel had been produced, to supplement the large stocks already mentioned. However, following the raids on Leuna and Pölitz, production fell to about 52,000 tonnes in June and kept falling during the months that followed, from 35,000 to 16,000, and finally, in September, to 7,000 tonnes. This was compounded by the loss of the Romanian oilfields to Russia in the same month.

In May fuel stocks had been sufficient for only three months. When D-Day came, the Germans could put up only 319 sorties, against over 14,700 from the Allies. Not only had the Germans expected the landings to be in the Pas-de-Calais rather than Normandy, but so many of their fighter squadrons had been recalled to Germany that the Luftwaffe presence in France had become far too weak to be effective. The Allied air forces met virtually no resistance. Even the V-1s that had been deployed in France were for the most part destroyed on their ramps. Only those sited in the Low Countries in well-camouflaged locations would be used to any effect – and even that was of no military value – as the war entered its final, tormented phase.

As for Milch, he finally resigned from the Jägerstab. He had been continually frustrated by the insistence of his colleagues that the Me

262 should be used as a fighter-bomber rather than as a pure fighter, and following a particularly stormy meeting with Göring, Hitler and Speer at Hitler's Berghof residence he took markedly less interest in the department he had been instrumental in establishing. On 20 June, as the Allies dug into their five beachheads, Speer's Ministry assumed full responsibility for all aircraft production. This effectively forced Milch to relinquish his posts as Director of Air Armament and as State Air Secretary, although he returned to office as a deputy minister within Speer's newly expanded Armament Department, RfRuK.

Slipping Through the Fingers like Sand

Following D-Day, German industry continued its downward plunge, hastened by the dire shortages of fuel. As the German Army retreated from France into the Low Countries, Allied Intelligence intercepted and decoded almost pathetic orders to Luftwaffe units, directing them to have aircraft pulled by *oxen* when taxiing rather than to waste fuel doing it under their own power – so bad was the situation. Luftwaffe reconnaissance flights over Egypt and Cyprus were cut down to one a month, and internal courier flights within Germany were banned during the mornings for fear of attack by Allied fighters. In August the order that signalled to many the beginning of the end went out to all operational Luftwaffe units then engaging the Allies in the west. It came as a direct result of the Allied attacks on the synthetic oil plants and was in three parts. First, fighters could make unrestricted flights only if attacking bombers; secondly, reconnaissance flights could be carried out only in support of actual fighting on the ground, and not as a matter of routine intelligence-gathering; finally, all ground-attack and bomber aircraft were to be grounded, unless the results of an operation could be more or less guaranteed to be successful. In fact the German fighter forces suffered great losses as they sat on the tarmac through strafing raids by Allied warplanes; and by the time the Luftwaffe fell back to Paris in mid-August its remaining ground-attack forces were all but non-existent. Four well-equipped fighter squadrons were sent from Germany as reinforcements, but the pilots were newly qualified after skimped training and their losses in action were horrendous.

By September the Luftwaffe had to retreat to bases in Belgium. It held on for a month before retreating again back into Germany. Both retreats were conducted in a confused and unplanned manner, leaving ground crews unable to prepare for the reception of aircraft at the new bases. The situation for pilots returning to bases in north and west Germany was chaotic. They had had to abandon equipment and even aircraft in retreat, and at home there was such a lack of fuel and spares that they were virtually unable to do their job any more. Morale could hardly have been at a lower ebb, and as the Mediterranean Front collapsed, senior figures in the administration began to consider the possibility of a negotiated peace before it was too late. Unfortunately, the abortive coup of 20 July 1944 caused Hitler to tighten his grip on power, and although even Himmler was secretly putting out peace feelers, the SS rank and file and the Gestapo remained fiercely loyal to the Nazi regime, knowing that they had no future without it.

The defensive dispersal of German industry had continued meanwhile. New facilities for Messerschmitt were being built under the fir trees in the forest of Horgau, about twelve kilometres outside Augsburg, with their own water supply and ideally placed close to road and rail connections. The evergreens would eventually shelter a large camp of twenty-one wooden barracks and hangars: construction started in September and was due to last six months. The site was destined to produce wings for the Me 262. The largely civilian workforce of 850 was expected to turn out 250 wings a month: hard work, but at least they were in the open and had fresh air. Thousands of others, working in underground sites like Nordhausen, or in the Volksjäger plant in a converted salt-mine at Tarthun, near Magdeburg, suffered constantly from bronchial complaints and headaches. In the salt-mines particularly equipment tended to deteriorate quickly too.

The Horgau site was completed, but operated for only six or seven weeks before it was captured by the Allies.

By Christmas 1944, following another lull in Allied bombing in the late autumn, production slowly crept back up again, providing enough fuel and resources for the Ardennes counteroffensive, Operation Bodenplatte – Baseplate – on New Year's Day. However, Bodenplatte was really no more than a last brightness before the flame died. A new Allied offensive over four months between December and March hammered all but the very last nails into the German coffin. As for the Luftwaffe, a few elite or extreme units continued to fly, but even they were forced to send oiltankers out on week-long foraging expeditions to rustle up fuel. Any German resistance to the Allied onslaught by now was academic: it was just a matter of time, and everyone, except the most self-deluded fanatics, knew it. People went on fighting none the less.

Allied Intelligence was taking no chances, however, and in fact overestimated Germany's remaining strength. On 5 January 1945, USAAF generals Doolittle and Spatz warned Eisenhower that they would have to make pre-emptive strikes against Germany's jet-fighter production plants if the war were not to drag on into the summer. The generals estimated that 10,000 tonnes of well-aimed bombs would set Me 262 production back three months. Eisenhower agreed to their proposal, and on 12 January Spatz issued a new directive identifying the new jet factories as the 'principal objective for attack'. If Hitler could prolong the war beyond the summer, he warned, he would have 'jets of such superior performance and in such numbers as to challenge our aerial supremacy over not only Germany but all of Western Europe'.

But it was far too late for that. Even if the Allies had called off the attack, Germany wouldn't have been able to put a single extra Me 109 into the air.

In April 1945, as the Sherman tanks of the US Third Armoured Division rolled through the small town of Nordhausen on their way to their historic meeting with the Soviet forces on the banks of the River Elbe, they were to stumble on a massive secret arms cache. The commanding officer, Colonel Welborn, had noticed among the streaming columns of refugees a number of men wearing the striped garb of the concentration camps. He questioned some of them, and they led him to the nearby village of Niedersachswerfen, where they found a great artificial cave which had been cut out of the rock by the prisoners. Inside was an intact V-2 production line, together with many as yet unarmed missiles. There was also a V-1 production line, and an assembly line for Junkers jet and piston engines. The US soldiers were overwhelmed at the size of the place. There were ten kilometres of tunnels, making up just under half a million square metres of floor space. All of it had been excavated by slave labour. Originally a secret fuel dump, it had been taken over and enlarged by the 'Todt' Labour Organisation and the SS, before Speer's Armament Department took control of the Mittelwerke company which had operated the plant. The underground factory was in the Russian zone, so technically its contents would have to be handed over to the USSR; but, as mentioned, the Americans managed to smuggle out a hundred V-2s before doing so and shipped them to the USA to reunite them ultimately with their designer, Wernher von Braun.

The Russians were unaware of the subterfuge, but the British had cottoned on and sent a Royal Navy cruiser in pursuit of the USN ship carrying the V-2s across the Atlantic. Britain wanted a share, and after a hurried and possibly heated diplomatic exchange some of the missiles were handed over. The V-2's influence is clear in American and British missiles of the 1950s and 1960s, such as the Hughes GAR-1 Falcon and Blue Streak.

The Luftwaffe of the Third Reich, with all its aspirations, was finished. Its fortunes had followed those of the Reich itself: initial and spectacular success followed by complacency and an overstretching of resources which proved fatal. Without the means to keep ahead of the game, the Luftwaffe, despite the originality and inventiveness of the designers working for it, was finally overtaken by the British and especially the US air forces, which had ample funds and unlimited resources. In the end it was the Allies that benefited from the work of Messerschmitt, Heinkel, Dornier, Lippisch, Sänger, von Braun and the rest. Germany, for the second time in less than half a century, had to pay the price for its own vainglory.

APPENDIX

Specifications

Bachem Ba 349
Type   Single-seat, semi-expendable interceptor fighter
Power plant   One Walter HWK 509A-1 Bi-fuel rocket motor rated at 1,704 kg thrust for takeoff, plus four jettisonable solid-fuel boosters
Performance   Maximum speed: 800 kph (496 mph); service ceiling: 14,000 m (45,920 ft); initial climb rate: 10,881 m/min (35,689 ft/min); Endurance: 2 minutes
Weight   Fully equipped: 2,200 kg (4,850 lb).
Dimensions   Wingspan: 3.6 m (11 ft, 8 in); length: 6.1 m (20 ft); height: 1.3 m (4 ft, 3 in)
Armament   Twenty-four 73-mm HS 217 Fohn *or* thirty-three 55-mm R4M unguided rockets

Bachem Ba 349 B
Type   Single-seat, semi-expendable interceptor fighter
Power plant   One Walter HWK 509C-1 Bi-fuel rocket motor rated at 2,004 kg thrust for takeoff, plus two 1,002 kg-thrust solid-fuel boosters
Performance   Maximum speed: 800 kph (496 mph); service ceiling: 14,000 m (45,920 ft); initial climb rate: 11,368 m/min (37,287 ft/min); endurance: 2 minutes
Weight   Fully equipped: 2,200 kg (4,850 lb)
Dimensions   Wingspan: 3.6 m (11 ft, 8 in); length: 6.1 m (20 ft); height: 1.3 m (4 ft, 3 in)

Armament: Twenty-four 73-mm HS 217 Fohn *or* thirty-three 55-mm R4M unguided rockets

Blohm und Voss Bv 40
Type Single-seat interceptor glider.
Power plant None
Performance Maximum speed in 20-degree dive: 470 kph (292 mph); service ceiling: 7,000 m (22,960 ft)
Weight Empty equipped: 838 kg (1,843 lb); fully equipped: 951 kg (2,092 lb)
Dimensions Wingspan: 7.9 m (25 ft, 9 in); length: 5.7 m (18 ft, 7 in); height: 1.6 m (5 ft, 3 in).
Armament Two 30-mm MK 108 cannon with 35 rpg

Blohm und Voss Bv 141 B-0
Type Army cooperation and tactical reconnaissance aircraft
Power plant One BMW 801A-0 fourteen-cylinder, two-row axial engine rated at 1,560 hp for takeoff.
Performance Maximum speed: 370 kph (229 mph) at sea-level, 438 kph (272 mph) at 5,000 m (16,400 ft); service ceiling: 10,000 m (32,800 ft); maximum range: 1,545 km (1,180 miles)
Weight Empty equipped: 4,700 kg (10,340 lb); fully equipped: 6,100 kg (13,420 lb)
Dimensions Wingspan: 17.5 m (57 ft, 4 in); length: 14 m (45 ft, 9 in); height: 3.6 m (11 ft, 8 in)
Armament Two 7.9-mm MG 17 machine-guns firing forwards, two rear-facing 7.9-mm MG 15 machine-guns, firing from flexible mountings. Underwing racks for four SC 50 kg bombs

Blohm und Voss Bv P. 211
Type Single-seat jet fighter
Power plant One BMW 109–003A turbojet rated at 802 kg thrust for takeoff
Performance Estimated maximum speed: 750 kph (465 mph) at sea-level, 860 kph (534 mph) at 8,000 m (26,240 ft); estimated service ceiling: unknown; maximum range: 720 km (447 miles)
Weight Fully equipped: 2,475 kg (5,445 lb)

Dimensions Wingspan: 8.4 m (27 ft, 6 in); length: 8.7 m (28 ft, 6 in)
Armament Two nose-mounted 30-mm MK 108 cannon.

Blohm und Voss Bv 238 V1
Type Long-range transport, maritime patrol and bomber flying boat.
Power plant Six DB 603G 12-cylinder, liquid-cooled engines, each rated at 1,900 hp for takeoff.
Performance Maximum speed: 425 kph (264 mph) at 6,000 m (19,686 ft); service ceiling: 6,300 m (20,664 ft); maximum range: 7,853 km (4,878 miles)
Weight Empty equipped: 50,800 kg (112,014 lb); fully equipped: 70,000 kg (154,350 lb); overload permissible to 100,000 kg (220,000 lb)
Dimensions Wingspan: 60.2 m (197 ft, 5 in); length: 43.4 m (142 ft, 4 in); height: 12.8 m (41 ft, 10 in)
Envisaged armament Four MG 131 in each nose and tail turret and in turrets behind each wing; pairs of MG 131 in fuselage beam stations and two MG 151 cannon in a dorsal turret; wing bays for twenty 250-kg bombs and external racks for either four LD 1200 torpedoes; four 1,000-kg bombs; four Hs 293 missiles or, finally, four BV 143 glider-bombs

DFS 346-3
Type Single-seat, rocket-powered research aircraft
Power plant Two Walter 109–409B rocket motors, each rated at 2,004 kg thrust for takeoff
Performance 1,100 kph (683 mph) at 10,000 m (32,800 ft) in Soviet tests; German estimates of 2,125 kph (1,320 mph) at 20,000 m (65,600 ft); Mach 2.6 at service ceiling of 35,000 m (114,800 ft)
Weight Fully equipped: 5,300 kg (11,660 lb)
Dimensions Wingspan: 8.9 m (29 ft, 1 in); length: 11.7 m (38 ft, 4 in); height: 3.5 m (11 ft, 5 in)
Armament None

Dornier Do 335 A-0 Pfeil
Type Single-seat fighter-bomber aircraft
Power plant Two DB 603E-1 12-cylinder, liquid-cooled engines, each rated at 1,800 hp for takeoff
Performance Maximum speed: 763 kph (474 mph) at 6,500 m

(21,320 ft); service ceiling: 7,196 m (23,602 ft); maximum range: 1,395 km (867 miles) at full power
Weight Empty equipped: 7,260 kg (15,972 lb); fully equipped: 10,000 kg (22,000 lb)
Dimensions Wingspan: 13.8 m (45 ft, 2 in); length: 13.9 m (45 ft, 6 in); height: 5 m (16 ft, 4 in)
Armament One engine-mounted 30-mm MK 103 cannon with 70 rounds, firing through propeller hub, and two 20-mm MG 151 cannon with 200 rpg, in upper fuselage. Either one 500-kg or two 250-kg bombs in the bomb bay, plus two 250-kg bombs externally

Fieseler Fi 103 iv Reichenberg
Type Single-seat, expendable ground-attack aircraft
Power plant One Argus As 109–014 pulsejet engine rated at 350 kg thrust at sea-level
Performance Maximum speed: 650 kph (404 mph) at 2,500 m (8,200 ft); maximum range: 330 km (205 miles) from launch – 32-minute flight
Weight Fully equipped: 2,170 kg (4,774 lb)
Dimensions Wing span: 5.7 m (18 ft, 7 in); length: 8 m (26 ft, 3 in); height: 1.4 m (4 ft, 6 in)
Armament One 850-kg high-explosive warhead fitted with an impact fuse

Flettner Fl 282 B-1 Kolibri
Type Tactical reconnaissance helicopter
Power plant One Siebel Sh 14A engine rated at 165 hp for takeoff
Performance Maximum speed: 150 kph (93 mph) at sea-level; service ceiling: 3,292 m (10,797 ft); maximum range: 300 km (186 miles) with auxiliary fuel tank
Weight Empty equipped: 735 kg (1,617 lb); fully equipped: 975 kg (2,145 lb)
Dimensions Rotor diameter: two 12.3 m (40 ft, 4 in); length: 6.6 m (21 ft, 7 in); height: 2.2 m (7 ft, 2 in).
Armament None

Focke-Achgelis Fa 223 Drache
Type General-purpose helicopter
Power plant One BMW-Bramo 323 Q3 supercharged nine-cylinder engine rated at 1,000 hp for takeoff
Performance Maximum speed: 175 kph (109 mph) at sea-level; service ceiling: 2,010 m (6,592 ft) vertical climb, 4,880 m (16,006 ft) forward speed; maximum range: 700 km (435 miles) with auxiliary fuel tank
Weight Empty equipped: 3,180 kg (6,996 lb); fully equipped: 4,315 kg (9,493 lb)
Dimensions Diameter of each rotor: 12 m (39 ft, 4 in); overall width: 24.5 m (80 ft, 4 in); length: 12.3 m (40 ft, 4 in); height: 4.4 m (14 ft, 5 in)
Armament One 7.9-mm MG 15 machine-gun; two 250-kg bombs or two depth charges (optional)

Focke-Achgelis Fa 225
Type General-purpose glider helicopter
Power plant None
Performance Maximum towed speed: 190 kph (118 mph)
Weight Fully equipped: 2,000 kg (4,400 lb)
Dimensions Rotor diameter: 12 m (39 ft, 4 in); length: 11.2 m (36 ft, 8 in); height: 4.4 m (14 ft, 4 in)
Armament None

Focke-Achgelis Fa 284 Sky Crane Project 1
Type Heavy-lift cargo helicopter
Power plant Two BMW 801 radials, each rated at 1600 hp for takeoff
Performance (Estimated) maximum speed: 208 kph (129 mph); service ceiling: 6,000 m (19,680 ft); maximum range: 400 km (248 miles)
Weight Empty equipped: 8,100 kg (17,820 lb); fully equipped: 12,000 kg (26,400 lb)
Dimensions Diameter of each rotor: 17.8 m (58 ft, 4 in); overall width 37.3 m (122 ft, 4 in); length: 13.72 m (45 ft); height: unknown
Armament None

Focke-Achgelis Fa 330 Bachstelze
Type Tactical reconnaissance glider helicopter
Power plant None

Performance Maximum towed speed: 40 kph (25 mph); minimum (stall) speed: 27 kph (17 mph); maximum range: dependent on tow; maximum length of cable – service ceiling: 150 m (492 ft)
Weight Empty equipped: 70 kg (154 lb); fully equipped: 170 kg (374 lb)
Dimensions Rotor diameter: 7.3 m (23 ft, 9 in); length: 4.3 m (14 ft, 1 in); height: 1.7 m (5 ft, 6 in).
Armament None

Focke-Wulf Fw 61
Type Experimental helicopter
Power plant One Siebel Sh 14B unit rated at 165 hp for takeoff
Performance Maximum speed: 122 kph (75 mph); service ceiling: 2,410 m (7,904 ft, 8 in); maximum range: 230 km (143 miles)
Weight Empty equipped: 800 kg (1,760 lb); fully equipped: 950 kg (2,100 lb)
Dimensions Diameter of each rotor: 7.5 m (24 ft, 6 in); overall width: 15.5 m (50 ft, 8 in); length: 7 m (22 ft, 10 in); height: 3.4 m (11 ft, 2 in)
Armament None

Focke-Wulf Triebflügel
Type VTOL rotary-wing point-defence interceptor
Power plant Three Pabst/Focke-Wulf ramjets, each rated at 836 kg thrust, *and* three Walter auxiliary rockets, each rated at 660 kg thrust, for takeoff
Performance (Estimated) maximum speed: 1,000 kph (621 mph) at sea-level, 840 kph (521 mph) at 11,000 m (36,080 ft); service ceiling: 14,000 m (45,920 ft); maximum range: 2,410 km (1,496 miles); climb rate: 8.2 seconds to 1,000 m (3,280 ft), 11.5 minutes to 15,000 m (49,200 ft)
Weight Empty equipped: 3,200 kg (7,040 lb); fully equipped: 5,175 kg (11,385 lb)
Dimensions Overall diameter of spinning wing: 10.8 m (35 ft, 4 in); length: 9.1 m (29 ft, 9 in); height: unknown
Armament Two 30-mm MK 108 cannon, plus two 20-mm MG 151 cannon

Gotha Go 229 A-0
Type Flying wing, fighter-bomber aircraft

Power plant Two Junkers Jumo 004B-1 axial-flow turbojets, each rated at 892 kg thrust for takeoff
Performance Maximum speed: 977 kph (607 mph); service ceiling: 16,000 m (52,480 ft); maximum range: 1,899 km (1,180 miles)
Weight Empty equipped: 4,600 kg (10,120 lb); fully equipped: 9,000 kg (19,800 lb)
Dimensions Wingspan: 16.7 m (54 ft, 8 in); length: 7.5 m (24 ft, 6 in); height: 2.8 m (9 ft, 2 in)
Armament Four MK 103 or MK 108 cannon and two 1,000-kg bombs in an internal bomb bay

Gotha P. 60 Nachtjäger
Type Flying wing, night-fighter aircraft
Power plant Two Heinkel HeS 011A turbojets, each rated at 1,303 kg thrust for takeoff
Performance (Estimated) maximum speed: 980 kph (607 mph) at 5,000 m (16,400 ft), service ceiling: 14,000 m (45,920 ft); maximum range: 2,650 km (1,646 miles) at 12,000 m (39,480 ft)
Weight (Estimated) empty equipped: 6,000 kg (13,200 lb); fully equipped: 9,980 kg (21,956 lb)
Dimensions Wingspan: 12.4 m (40 ft, 7 in); length: 10.7 m (35 ft); height: unknown
Armament Four 30-mm MK 108 cannon

Heinkel He 162 A-2 Salamander
Type Interceptor aircraft to Volksjäger specification
Power plant One BMW 003E-1 turbojet rated at 801 kg thrust for takeoff
Performance Cruise speed: 790 kph (490 mph) at sea-level; maximum speed in 30-second burst: 837 kph (520 mph) at 6,000 m (19,680 ft); service ceiling: 12,010 m (39,392 ft); maximum range: 620 km (385 miles)
Weight Empty equipped: 1,758 kg (3,867 lb); fully equipped: 2,695 kg (5,929 lb)
Dimensions Wingspan: 7.2 m (23 ft, 6 in); length: 9 m (29 ft, 5 in); height: 2.6 m (8 ft, 5 in)
Armament Two 20-mm MG 151 cannon in forward fuselage with 120 rpg

Heinkel He 178

Type   Experimental jet-powered aircraft
Power plant   One Heinkel HeS 3B turbojet rated at 500 kg thrust for takeoff
Performance   Maximum speed: 600 kph (373 mph); service ceiling: unknown; maximum range: unknown
Weight   Empty equipped: 1,620 kg (3,564 lb); fully equipped: 1,998 kg (4,395 lb)
Dimensions   Wingspan: 7.2 m (23 ft, 6 in); length: 7.5 m (24 ft, 6 in); height: 2.1 m (6 ft, 8 in)
Armament   None

Heinkel He 280 V5

Type   Experimental jet interceptor aircraft
Power plant   Two Heinkel HeS 8A turbojets, each rated at 750 kg thrust for takeoff
Performance   Maximum speed: 900 kph (559 mph); service ceiling: 11,500 m (37,720 ft); maximum range: 650 km (404 miles)
Weight   Empty equipped: 3,215 kg (7,073 lb); fully equipped: 4,310 kg (9,482 lb)
Dimensions   Wingspan: 12.2 m (40 ft); length: 10.4 m (34 ft, 1 in); height: 3 m (9 ft, 9 in)
Armament   Three 20-mm MG 151 nose cannon

Heinkel P. 1080

Type   Ramjet-powered interceptor aircraft
Power plant   Two Sänger ramjets, each rated at up to 1564 kg thrust for takeoff, *plus* four jettisonable Schmidding auxiliary rockets, each rated at 1,002 kg thrust
Performance   (Estimated) 1,000 kph (621 mph) at sea-level; service ceiling: unknown
Weight   Fully equipped: 4,300 kg (9,460 lb)
Dimensions   Wingspan: 8.9 m (29 ft, 2 in); length: 7.4 m (24 ft, 3 in); height: 2.5 m (8 ft, 2 in)
Armament   Two 30-mm MK 108 cannon

Henschel Hs 132A
Type Jet-powered dive bomber
Power plant One BMW 003A-1 14 turbojet rated at 800 kg thrust for takeoff
Performance (Estimated) maximum speed: 780 kph (485 mph) at 6,000 m (19,680 ft); 700 kph (435 mph) laden; service ceiling: 10,500 m (34,440 ft); maximum range: 1,120 km (696 miles)
Weight Fully equipped: 3,400 kg (7,480 lb)
Dimensions Wingspan: 7.2 m (23 ft, 6 in); length: 8.9 m (29 ft, 2 in); height: 2.1 m (6 ft, 9 in)
Armament One 500-kg bomb

Junkers EF. 126 Elli
Type Point-defence fighter
Power plant One Argus 109-044 pulsejet engine rated at 500 kg thrust for takeoff
Performance Maximum speed: 780 kph (485 mph) at sea-level: service ceiling: unknown; maximum range: 350 km (218 miles)
Weight Empty equipped: 1,100 kg (2,420 lb); fully equipped: 2,800 kg (6,160 lb)
Dimensions Wingspan: 6 m (19 ft, 7 in); length: 7.6 m (24 ft, 9 in); height: 1.4 m (4 ft, 6 in)
Armament Two 20-mm MG 151 cannon; optional auxiliary bomb load of 440 kg (968 lb) or 12 Panzer Blitz ground-attack rockets

Junkers Ju 287 V1
Type Heavy jet bomber
Power plant Four Junkers Jumo 004B turbojets, each rated at 902 kg thrust for takeoff
Performance (Estimated) maximum speed: 1,000 kph (621 mph); service ceiling: 10,800 m (35,424 ft); maximum range: 1,500 km (931 miles)
Weight Empty equipped: 10,230 kg (22,506 lb); fully equipped: 20,000 kg (44,100 lb)
Dimensions Wingspan: 20.1 m (65 ft, 9 in); length: 18.6 m (61 ft); height: 5.5 m (18 ft)
Armament None

Lippisch DM-1
Type   High-speed research glider
Power plant   One auxiliary rocket (never fitted)
Performance   Maximum speed: in dive 560 kph (348 mph); estimated 800 kph (497 mph) with rocket
Weight   Empty equipped: 297 kg (653 lb); fully equipped: 460 kg (1,012 lb)
Dimensions   Wingspan: 5.9 m (19 ft, 4 in); length: 6.3 m (20 ft, 8 in); height: 3.2 m (10 ft, 5 in)
Armament   None

Lippisch P-13a
Type   Ramjet-powered interceptor
Power plant   One solid-fuel ramjet plus auxillary rocket
Performance   Maximum speed: 1,650 kph (1,025 mph), ramjet requiring 800 kg (1,760 lb) fuel for 45 minutes
Weight   (Estimated) empty equipped: 1,100 kg (2,420 lb); fully equipped: 2,300 kg (5,060 lb)
Dimensions   Wingspan: 5.9 m (19 ft, 4 in); length: 6.7 m (21 ft, 10 in); height: 3.2 m (10 ft, 4 in)
Armament   Two 30-mm MK 108 cannon

Messerschmitt Me 261 V3
Type   Long-range monoplane
Power plant   Two DB 610A 24-cylinder, liquid-cooled engines, each rated at 3,100 hp for takeoff
Performance   Maximum speed: 619 kph (385 mph); service ceiling: 8,260 m (27,092 ft); maximum range: 11,028 km (6,850 miles)
Weight   Unknown
Dimensions   Wingspan: 26.9 m (88 ft, 2 in); length: 16.7 m (54 ft, 8 in); height: 4.7 m (15 ft, 4 in)
Armament   None

Messerschmitt Me 263
Type   Rocket-powered point-defence interceptor
Power plant   One Walter 109–509C rocket rated at 2,004 kg thrust for takeoff

Performance Maximum speed: 1,000 kph (621 mph); service ceiling: 16,000 m (52,480 ft); maximum range: 160 km (100 miles) from launch – 15 minutes
Weight Empty equipped: 2,105 kg (4,631 lb); fully equipped: 5,305 kg (11,671 lb)
Dimensions Wingspan: 9.5 m (31 ft, 1 in); length: 8 m (26 ft, 2 in); height: 2.5 m (8 ft, 2 in)
Armament Two 30-mm MK 108 cannon

Messerschmitt Me 323 D Gigant
Type Heavy transport aircraft
Power plant Six Gnome-Rhône 14R radial engines, each rated at 1,140 hp for takeoff
Performance Maximum speed: 285 kph (177 mph); service ceiling: 3,100 m (10,168 ft)
Weight Empty equipped: 27,330 kg (60,260 lb); fully equipped: 43,000 kg (94,600 lb)
Dimensions Wingspan: 55 m (180 ft, 4 in); length: 28.1 m (92 ft, 2 in); height: 9.6 m (31 ft, 5 in)
Armament Five 13-mm MG 131 machine-guns

Messerschmitt Me 328 A
Type Pulsejet-powered escort fighter
Power plant Two Argus As 109–014 pulsejet engines, each rated at 300 kg thrust for takeoff
Performance Maximum speed: 755 kph (472 mph) at sea-level; service ceiling: 6,800 m (22,304 ft); maximum range: 805 km (500 miles)
Weight Empty equipped: 1,545 kg (3,400 lb); fully equipped: 3,238 kg (7,125 lb)
Dimensions Wingspan: 6.4 m (21 ft); length: 6.8 m (22 ft, 3 in); height: 2.1 m (6 ft, 9 in).
Armament Two 20-mm MG 151 cannon

Sänger-Bredt Stratospheric Bomber
Type Hypersonic research aircraft/bomber
Power plant One Sänger rocket rated at over 100 tonnes thrust; duration 11 minutes; maximum range: 23,500 km (14,600 miles)

Performance Mach 18 at altitudes of 145 km (90 miles)
Weight Unknown
Dimensions Wingspan: 3.6 m (11 ft, 9 in); length: 28 m (91 ft, 8 in)
Armament One free-falling glider-bomb

GLOSSARY

AVA (Aerodynamische Versuchsanstalt) See next entry
AVG (Aerodynamische Versuchsanstalt Göttingen) The University
of Götingen Aerodynamic Trials Unit
A-Stoff Type of rocket fuel: LOX – liquid oxygen
Anhedral A negatively angled (turned-down) surface of a wing on
an aircraft relative to the horizontal
Bf Messerschmitt aircraft prefix 1934–8; replaced by 'Me'
BMW (Bayerische Motorenwerke (München) Bavarian Motor
Works, Munich
BRAMO (Brandenburgische Motorenwerke) Brandenburg Motor
Works, Berlin
B-Stoff Petrol
C-Stoff A rocket fuel catalyst (30 per cent hydrazine hydrate, 57 per
cent methanol and 13 per cent water) used by the Walter rocket motor
c.o.g. Centre of gravity
DB Daimler-Benz
DFS (Deutsche Forschungsinstitut für Segelflug) A German
Research Institute for Gliding
Dihedral A positively angled (upturned) surface of a wing of an
aircraft relative to the horizontal
Diplom Ingenieur Licensed/certified engineer
DLH (Deutsches Lufthansa) German Airways
DLV (Deutsche Luftsport Verband eV) The first DLV (1902–33)

was the original, apolitical Federation of German Flying Clubs. It was superseded by the organisation of the same name, which is the one this book is concerned with, the German Air Sport Union (1933–7). This in turn gave way to the overtly military Fliegerkorps (NSFK) in 1937

Dr Ing (Doktor der Ingenieurwissenschaft) Doctor of Engineering
Erprobungsstelle Proving ground or test centre
eV (eingetragener Verein) Club or registered association
Flak (Fliegerabwehrkanone) Anti-aircraft gun(s)
Flugkapitän Flight Captain (civilian aviation rank)
Flugzeugbau Aircraft manufactory
Forschungsanstalt Research establishment
Gauleiter Administrator of a Gau, the main territorial unit of the Nazi Party. Germany had 42 such Gaue
General der Jagdflieger General of Fighters
General der Kampfflieger General of Bombers
Generalfeldmarschall The highest field rank below the (Nazi) rank of Reichsmarschall. RAF: Marshal of the RAF; USAAF (USAF): Five-Star General
Generalleutnant Air Vice-Marshal/Two-Star Major-General
Generalmajor Air Commodore/One-Star Brigadier General
Generaloberst Air Chief Marshal/Four-Star General
General der Flieger Air Marshal/Three-Star Lieutenant-General
Geschwader The Luftwaffe's largest aircraft grouping. Usually operating aircraft confined to a single role and made up of three Gruppen, plus one Stab operating four planes, making a total of ninety-four planes. Towards the end of the war a fourth Gruppe was added to many Geschwader to absorb the losses. In a bomber Geschwader, this fourth Gruppe was another combat unit, but in all others served as an operational and holding unit for its three companion Gruppen. The commander of a Geschwader held the title of Kommodore and was usually a Major, an Oberstleutnant or an Oberst
GmbH (Gesellschaft mit beschränkter Haftung) Limited company
Gruppe Air-force wing: the basic operational block, comprising three Staffeln each with nine planes, plus a Stab, *usually* with three aircraft, making a total of thirty. Combat attrition would eventually come to deplete this size, though Gruppen could be merged where necessary.

The Gruppe commander held the rank of Kommandeur and was usually either a hauptmann or a major.

Hauptmann   Literally 'captain'; RAF: Flight-Lieutenant; USAAF: Captain

HVP (Heeres Versuchsanstalt Peenemünde)   Army Research Unit, Peenemünde

HWA (Heereswaffenamt)   Army Ordnance Office (Berlin)

HWK (Hellmuth-Walter-Werke)   Hellmuth Walter Works – rocket engine model, manufactured by Krupp at Kiel

JABO (Jagdbomber)   A fighter-bomber

Jagdflugzeug   A fighter

JG (Jagdgeschwader)   A fighter group

JGr (Jagdgruppe)   A fighter wing

Jäger   Literally 'hunter': a fighter or fighter pilot

Jägerstab   The cross-ministries Fighter Staff for fighter production

Jumo (Junkers Motorenbau)   Junkers Motor Company

JV (Jagdverband)   Fighter formation

KG (Kampfgeschwader)   Bomber group

Kommandeur   Commander of a Gruppe

Kommodore   Commander of a Geschwader

Kommando   Special fighting or working unit. A Sonderkommando is a unit with very specific duties

Kriegsmarine   Navy (military)

Leutnant   Lieutenant

LFA (Luftfahrtforschungsanstalt)   Aviation Research Institute. It had offices in Munich and Vienna and was headed by Dr Alexander Lippisch from 1944

LTS (Lufttransportstaffel)   Air transport squadron

Luftflotte   Air fleet, air force (civil or military)

Luftwaffe   Air force (military)

Major   RAF: Squadron Leader; USAAF: Major

Me   Messerschmitt prefix from 1938

MG (Maschinengewehr)   Machine-gun

MK (Maschinenkanone)   Machine-cannon

M-Stoff   Methanol (rocket fuel)

NSDAP (Nationalsozialistische Deutsche Arbeiterpartei) National Socialist German Workers' Party

Oberleutnant   Luftwaffe: Chief Lieutenant; RAF: Flying Officer; USAAF: First Lieutenant
Oberst   Group Captain/Colonel
OKH (Oberkommando des Heeres)   Army high command
OKL (Oberkommando der Luftwaffe)   Air-force high command
OKW (Oberkommando des Wehrmachtsgeneralstabs) General staff, high command
PaK (Panzerabwehrkanone)   Anti-tank cannon
Panzerstaffel   Anti-tank squadron, (probably using *Zerstörer* aircraft)
Projektbüro   Project design department
RAF   Royal Air Force (GB)
Reich   The German State; the Nazis called theirs the Third Reich after the two previous historical periods of rule – the ancient First Reich and the Second under the Prussian, von Bismark, which ran from 1871 until the 1918 armistice, when the emperor Kaiser Wilhelm II abdicated
Reichsleiter   State administrator
Reichsmarschall   Nazi-invented top rank used by Göring as commander-in-chief of the Luftwaffe
Reichspost   State post. Throughout the war, the Post Office's own research institute carried out investigations into nuclear energy, with a long-term aim of making an atom bomb, and getting into rocketry
Reichswehr   National army of Germany formed after the Treaty of Versailles
RfRuK (Reichsministerium für Rüstung und Kriegsproduktion)   State Ministry for Armament and War Production
Ritterkreuz   Knight's Cross, an order of the Iron Cross and the first level of the five highest decorations for valour. To the Knight's Cross can be added, in ascending order; oak leaves; oak leaves and swords; diamonds, oak leaves and swords; diamonds, golden oak leaves and swords
RLM: (Reichsluftfahrtministerium)   State Air Ministry (1933–45)
rpg   Rounds per gun
R-Stoff   Zyladene tryethalmine (Tonka 250) – rocket fuel
Sicherheitspolizei   Security police force formed in the immediate aftermath of the Treaty of Versailles and permitted for a time to operate aircraft that had been used by the air force of the First World War

Stab Staff
Staffel Squadron
Staffelkapitän Staffel commander, usually a Leutnant, Oberleutnant or Hauptmann
Stuka (Sturzkampfflugzeug) A dive bomber, though used specifically of one type of aircraft – the Junkers Ju 87
Sturmgruppe Assault wing
SV-Stoff Rocket fuel: 88 per cent nitric acid and 12 per cent sulphuric acid
T-Stoff Rocket fuel: 80 per cent hydrogen peroxide, plus oxyquinoline or phosphate as a stabiliser
Technisches Amt Technical Bureau of the Air Ministry
Transportverband Transport Command (Luftwaffe)
USAAF United States Army Air Force (USAF from 1947)
'V' (Versuchsmuster) Prototype
V-1 (Vergeltungswaffe 1) Reprisal weapon 1 (Fi 103 flying bomb)
V-2 (Vergeltungswaffe 2) Reprisal weapon 2 (A-4 ballistic missile)
VfR (Verein für Raumschiffahrt) The Society for Space Travel
Viermots Luftwaffe slang for Viermotorige – 'four-engined' – bombers
ZG (Zerstörergeschwader) Destroyer group – the name applied to units of heavy fighters such as Me 110s. Later used for ground-attack units and strategic defence aircraft
Z-Stoff Calcium permanganate (rocket fuel)

INDEX

Index

German bases in, 12–14, 17, 76, 195; Flight Testing Institute, 207; NKAP, 196, 206; OKBs, 196–7, 202–3, 206, 213; ZAGI research facility, 207

V-1 flying bomb, 35, 42, 61, 88, 154, 159, 179, 197, 217, 220, 238, 244–5, 248
V-2 rocket, 35, 61, 159, 197, 238, 244, 245, 251, 252
Verein für Raumschiffahrt (VfR), 157–8, 175
Vesco, Renato, 169, 190
vibration problems, 52, 86, 104, 119, 121, 141, 144, 155, 156, 202, 209
Victor Emmanuel III, 62
Vogt, Richard, 90, 95, 118–22 passim, 222
Volksjäger see He fighters
Volkssturm, 135, 139
VTOL reconnaissance aircraft, 48, 59

Waffenträger, 88
Walter, Hellmuth, 153–4, 173, 174
Walter rocket engines, HWK R.I 203: 173–5; 501: 110, 111, 153–4, 156, 159, 161, 162, 171, 181, 188, 199, 207; 509: 166, 168, 183, 197, 205, 213
Walter Werke 157, 163
War, First World, 7, 8, 10, 19, 23, 46

water supplies, 244
Weapons Research Station, Karlshagen, 89
Welborn, Colonel 251
'Wespe' fighter, 189–90
Westland, 72
Wever, Air Chief of Staff, 8
When Worlds Collide, 177
Where Eagles Dare, 1
Whittle, Frank, 26, 29–32 passim, 44, 134
Wilberg, Kapitän Helmut, 9
'Wilde Sau' system, 239–42 passim
'Window', 240
Wocke, Hans, 198
Wrede, 204
Wulf, G., 47

X-15 rocket plane, 180
XH-20 helicopter, 72

Yalta agreement, 196, 202, 206
Yugoslavia, 232
Yuryev, 46

Zeiss, 197
Zeppelin, 10, 225; airships, 117
Zerstörer fighters, 124, 127
Zhukowski, 46
Ziese, Flugkapitän, 207–10 passim
Ziller, Erwin, 108–9
Zober, Major, 147
Zübert, Unteroffizier, 166–7
Zuckmayer, Carl, 23